TH_
DAUG

An addictive crime thriller with a fiendish twist

D. E. WHITE

Detective Dove Milson Book 2

First published 2020
Joffe Books, London
www.joffebooks.com

ISBN: 978-1-83526-245-0

AUTHOR'S NOTE

All the characters in this book are fictional, except where historical fact dictates. I would like to thank the following people for their sharing their expert professional knowledge/family history/opinions and views during the course of my research: Rose Von Bertele, Steve Topley, Eric and Dee Storey, Sarah Ablewhite, Andrea Larnmouth, Susie Carpenter and Hayley November.

The horrific Nazi hypothermia experiments conducted at Dachau in 1943 are well documented. It was while I was watching a documentary that the women connected with the experiments were briefly mentioned. The name 'the Ice Daughters' is a fictional creation, as is Helena herself, but her story I have pieced together through my own research in the course of this book and even though it must be stressed that this novel is a work of fiction, it has its roots in historical fact.

D. E. White

'*Three little girls went out to play,
but only two came home that day . . .*'

PROLOGUE

I know I could have saved a life that day.

I see his face beneath the ice, the elation turning to panic, fingers scrabbling frantically beneath the surface.

The voice returns in my nightmares, and sometimes when I stretch out my hand he takes it, clasping my fingers with icy digits. I know then he is safe and it was all in my mind. It never happened. The relief makes me dizzy, and the heavy burden of guilt is gone.

But the stark reality always takes over, and the voice in my head whispers, as cold and harsh as the winter snow, "Leave him!"

So I do nothing, obeying the voice. For a while, I was thrilled by the magic we created, dazzled by my own sense of self-importance and our childish dreams. Now I see how naive I was, and wonder at how long it took for the spell to shatter, for me to see the thin line between true evil and sanity.

It's happening again, and I can do nothing to stop it.

CHAPTER ONE

The man was curled in a foetal position, as though he had died trying frantically to warm himself. His naked body was frosted with ice crystals, his hair spiked white in the harsh floodlights.

"Shit," DC Dove Milson said quietly, as she and her partner, DS Steve Parker, signed the duty log and booted up before ducking under the tape to get closer to the victim.

In the near distance, the blackened side of an outbuilding showed where the fire had been, stark and raw against the winter night sky.

DI Jon Blackman was already on scene, talking to the incident commander from the fire service, and he lifted a hand in greeting to Steve and Dove. The uniformed Duty Officer was talking to some first responders, who were helping to set up cordons.

The Crime Scene Manager, a petite blonde woman in a white suit, was moving carefully around the body, taking notes, directing two men who were taking photographs and measurements. A large area around the body was sealed off with yellow tape, which hung limp and still in the darkness beyond the floodlights. The remains of the fire sent a rank, sour smell of smoke across the icy air.

"Any thoughts, Jess?" Dove asked the blonde woman. She couldn't take her eyes off the victim. "He looks like he just came out of a freezer."

Jess and Dove had been friends for years, going way back. They worked well together, and Dove's inclusion in the Major Crimes Team had strengthened their bond. Jess straightened from her initial inspections, and pursed her lips, sending a long breath dancing into the coldness of the night. "That's pretty much how it appears. But it's been cold enough these last few weeks that he could have simply been outside. The temperature is going to bugger up any completely accurate time of death. No obvious signs of injury."

"And the woman who's missing?" Dove tore her gaze from the dead man, and instead glanced at the activity around the remains of the fire. The fire officers were still busy, calling information to each other, working steadily and methodically. They would not release this particular area to police until their own work was concluded, by which point it would be heavily contaminated by water.

The small farmhouse stood overshadowed by trees, their winter-bare branches stretching like skeletal hands across the roof, clawing at the windows. A square, frost-covered garden surrounded the building, and a wooden gate led out onto the slightly tumbledown farm buildings. The body lay directly opposite the garden gate, on the concrete of the yard. It was a clear, icy night with glittering stars and a crescent moon, now faded into the background as the artificial light washed blue-white across the crime scene. Anyone coming out the front door of the farmhouse would have seen the dead man instantly.

"Haven't heard anything yet," Jess said, making another note, and turning to confer with one of her colleagues. She paused and her expression softened slightly, "I do know her kids are okay though. The DI's gone straight up to the house."

After a quick preliminary look at the immediate scene around the body, Dove and Steve headed towards the small square farmhouse for further instructions. Carefully following the identified route, using the stepping plates someone had already efficiently laid out, they also signed in with the officer at the cordon around the house.

DI Jon Blackman was standing in the garden, talking quickly into his mobile phone. He held up two fingers to the newcomers, and they waited impatiently as he wrapped up his conversation.

DI Blackman didn't waste time with preliminaries, but was unfailingly polite to all his team. He was a tall, lean man, with a shaved head and quick grey eyes. "The 999 call came into the fire service at 3.20 and they responded with two appliances. According to the caller, the barn was well alight and she was worried about her livestock."

"The caller was Tessa Jackson, I presume?" Dove stamped her feet to keep them warm.

"Yes. She stated she was alone in the house with her two daughters, and she woke to see flames outside her bedroom window. No mention of the body."

Dove swung her gaze to the top floor of the farmhouse, imagining the woman opening the window, leaning out in horror at what she saw. If the body had been there when she called, it was possible she could have missed it. The barns formed a U-shape slightly to the west of the property, so if all her attention had been on the flickering flames . . .

The DI continued, "Her two daughters are fine, and a relative, the sister, is coming over to be with them. They slept through the whole thing and only woke when the first responders arrived. The Duty Officer has got hold of a map of the area and is currently checking council CCTV in our nearest villages. He's also started fast-time enquiries on the possible routes our offender might have taken."

"So we don't know if Tessa was snatched from the house, or if she went out to the fire?" Dove queried.

"We don't. There are no signs of forced entry, and the kids didn't hear a thing. I never thought I'd wish for a fall of snow this winter, but it would've been very useful last night.

4

As it is, you can see the mess of grit and ice we'll have to pick through for prints . . ." He waved a hand in a disgusted gesture. "I've got Lindsey establishing an early relationship as Family Liaison Officer. There are no close neighbours, as I'm sure you have noticed, and we have no ID on the frozen victim yet. It's possible he is known to the family, so I'm hoping the sister will be able to shed some light on his identity, poor bastard."

The DI paused, running a gloved hand over his bare head in a familiar gesture of impatience. "Before you go, check out this little set-up in the porch . . ."

Steve and Dove moved up the garden path, pausing in front of the taped-off area. Just outside the door, on the first step, was a peculiar arrangement. Carved from ice, no more than six inches high, a king and queen like those from a chess set stood proudly, surrounded by a pile of scattered ice cubes. The snow was brushed clean around the artwork, and to the left of the porch a crooked snowman, with twig arms and wonky button eyes, surveyed the scene.

The chess pieces looked like perfect replicas, and glittered menacingly, faceless and angular against the backdrop of the red front door.

CHAPTER TWO

"That's bloody weird," Steve said.

"And it doesn't look like it's been disturbed, so Tessa must have come out of another door." Dove looked across the frosted garden.

"The back door was open when the first responders arrived," the DI told them. "It's on the west side of the house. Have a look around the perimeter now and liaise back here with Lindsey. I'll be back at the station by 7 a.m. for a team briefing. Oh, I had an initial chat with Fire Investigation and she has confirmed it looks like a can of diesel from the shed next to the barn was used as an accelerant. It was concentrated in one particular area, so probably either never intended to cause major damage, or our perpetrator was spooked and just managed half a job."

"Maybe he was behind schedule?" Dove suggested. "Even with help, there is a hell of a lot going on here. Setting up the little scene on the porch would have taken a while, not to mention body placement, abducting Tessa . . ."

The DI agreed, "We could easily be looking for multiple offenders."

She and Steve turned away from the brightly lit house, their footsteps crunching on the frosty grass of the garden, the scattered patches of snow left from the previous week. It was a clear night, with stars still high in the sky. Dove tried to picture Tessa's movements. "So she made the call from her mobile phone, got assurance that the fire service were on the way. Then she came outside?"

"If she came out the back door, she might not have seen the ice sculptures *or* the body," the ever-observant Steve pointed out. "Perhaps she pulled a coat and boots on and ran out to see if she could tackle the fire herself, missing the gifts from our perpetrator completely. After all, she said in the call she was worried about her livestock."

"It would have taken the fire engines a while to get here," Dove said thoughtfully, looking back at the rutted driveway winding through the woodland. It had taken around ten minutes to get from the end of the drive to the main road. "Perhaps it was all placed after she was taken?"

"Like you said, though, not much time in between her call and the fire response. If our perpetrator had to unload a dead body, arrange a weird chess set, abduct Tessa and escape down the very same drive the first responders used," Steve pondered.

"I wonder if she ever reached the yard at all?" Dove's eyes were on the yellow glow of her torch. The glare of the floodlights was centred around the body and the house, but soon the search area would be widened to include the whole property. She and Steve always liked to throw ideas back and forth at the beginning of a case. First impressions were often the most important.

"Well, she wouldn't have been able to work the hose because the outside water pipes must be frozen," Steve said, running his eyes over the yard as they approached the buildings, all the time treading carefully, eyes searching the ground. "So no chance of her trying to put out the fire. I'm guessing those troughs have automatic water and food and the system must be lagged so it doesn't freeze."

They glanced at the wide metal troughs set alongside the barn. There was some kind of mechanism in each, but they were empty now.

The barn door was flung wide and the cows were in the yard, shifting restlessly, their big dark eyes darting between the intruders. The warm, pungent smell of farm animals and straw permeated the night air.

"She might have been going to shift them into the fields, but they only got as far as this yard," Dove suggested.

The metal gates to the other barns were shut and locked, so they continued on a semi-circular route, careful not to interfere with the crime scene techs and first responders. There were no signs of an intruder, despite two quad bikes left in an open shelter, and an array of farm machinery in another. The yard was neat and tidy, with no signs of a struggle. No blood spattered the moon-washed concrete, swept clean of snow and dirt. Apart from the burnt wall of the barn, which showed black and stark, it was all eerily clean and tidy.

The Fire Investigation Team were assessing the damage and making sure there was no chance of reigniting from the smouldering remains. Dove and her partner exchanged greetings with the incident commander, but kept a careful distance from the area the team were working on.

Evidence was vital and detailed reports would come in from all the emergency services involved, but the first impressions, and the information gleaned from them, could mean life or death for Tessa Jackson. Later, when this part of the scene was released, SOCO would move in to gather anything they could, creating search continuity between the various areas.

"You would have had to bring a vehicle right up to the house to drop the victim next to that wall. He's practically at the garden gate," Dove pointed out to Steve, as they returned to their starting point, walking quickly to warm themselves. She swung round to gauge the distance between the barns and the victim. "With this big freeze, it will be pretty impossible to get any tyre tracks or footprints, and like Jon said, we could really have done with some nice fresh snow, instead of these patches of ice crystals."

"Perpetrator's good luck, but crap for us," Steve agreed. "Do you think this was a warning? If Tessa knows the victim . . . Perhaps whoever left the body didn't reckon on her coming outside and when she did, they panicked?"

"Or the fire was set to draw her out, and the body to freak her out? Maybe she knows who the dead man is? I don't see the point of burning down the barn wall unless it was to get her out of the house," Dove said thoughtfully, scuffing a pile of ice with the toe of her boot as she talked.

Steve agreed, "If I wanted to cause damage, I would have gone for the silage barn, or the machinery. The tractor and quad bikes must have tanks of diesel that would have gone up just like that. This is careful and deliberate."

They began to walk back to the house, stepping carefully around the yellow crime scene tape in the garden. "Let's have a quick look inside, and grab a word with Lindsey before we head off," Dove said, even though she could already see a couple of her colleagues through the lighted downstairs windows.

DS Lindsey Allerton was an experienced FLO, and would as usual slip straight into her role of providing a vital link between the family and the investigation. Not only could she feed back any information for the case, but she would also give the family the comfort and reassurance of having a constant source of police information.

The farmhouse, a smart-looking building with a white-painted front door and red-brick exterior, had granite work-tops in the kitchen and top-of-the-range appliances. Clearly money had been spent on it, and it didn't quite match the tumbledown farm buildings. Dove and Steve blinked in the sudden warmth and light, and unzipped their thick jackets. Dove unwound her scarf, and brushed strands of hair from her face.

The children were in the kitchen, bundled up in jumpers and dressing gowns, hair tousled and eyes red from crying. They both looked up as the strangers entered.

Lindsey, curly-haired and athletic, with one blue eye and one hazel-coloured, a rarity Dove considered quite stunning but which Lindsey often dismissed as weird, was making hot drinks.

She paused for a quick greeting as her colleagues came into the room. "We're just waiting for their aunt, Callie Jackson, to arrive. She's going to look after the girls. Social services will drop in tomorrow for a check as well. The family have a case-worker apparently, but she hasn't been in touch for a while."

The children regarded Dove and Steve with wary expressions. They were similar in appearance, with long, straight brown hair and pale, watchful blue eyes.

"Mum's going to be home by morning, though, isn't she?" one of them asked.

Lindsey knew she couldn't promise that. However much she wanted to. "We are trying hard to find your mum, Allison, and as soon as we hear anything you will know."

The smaller child was biting her nails. She was kneeling up on the kitchen stool. Her small feet stuck out behind and Dove could see she was wearing one woolly blue sock, and one thin cotton pink one, decorated with unicorns. Her wide gaze met Dove's. "Mum said he might come one day. That's why we live here, away from other people."

"Cerys!" The elder snapped at her sibling. "You shouldn't say things like that."

"But Mum said . . ." Cerys blinked hard, eyes shining with tears again. "She said if anything ever happened to her, it would be him coming back."

Lindsey popped two steaming mugs in front of the girls and slid into the seat opposite. "It's quite okay to tell us things like that. Who was your Mum worried about?" Her voice was smooth and even.

The little girl was still addressing Dove. "You look a bit like Mum, but your hair is wavier and her eyes are green. Yours are sort of brown and gold, like stones, aren't they?" She dipped a finger into her drink and sucked it thoughtfully, reflectively, still watching Dove. "She said that Dad might come for us one day and we should be ready."

The elder child sat and scowled, lips pressed firmly together, brows drawn, but she made no further attempt to hush her sister.

"Do you know where your dad lives?" Dove asked, with a quick look at Lindsey. Her colleague gave a barely discernible nod.

Cerys considered, took a sip of her drink now, grasping the mug with both hands as though to warm them, and then answered with a milky moustache coating her top lip. "He lives in Manchester. I don't know where, but I heard Mum talking on the phone last week and she said she was glad we had come down here, even though she still loves Manchester . . . Then she said she could never go back, because that's where HE was."

"Shut up, Cerys!" Allison burst out suddenly. "Dad didn't mean to do those things, and Mum never said she we couldn't go back home one day . . . she wouldn't say that!"

The younger sister turned to her sibling with saucer eyes. "You shut up yourself, and how do you know what Dad thinks?" She slid off her chair and started to hit Allison with both fists, crying, "You shut up!"

The DI appeared in the doorway and beckoned as Lindsey, with outward calm, separated the two flailing children, and pulled out a box of books from under the table.

From the porch, Dove could see Jess and her team working a methodical grid system which would hopefully snag even the tiniest piece of evidence. Each person involved was walking carefully, slowly, occasionally pausing to bend down and add to evidence bags, or snap a photograph.

She zipped her jacket back up with a snap, pulling on her gloves, addressing the DI. "The kids gave us the impression their dad might be something to look at. They said their mum was hiding from him."

"I already checked and he has a whole load of previous," Jon Blackman said, looking up from his iPad. "A domestic violence case that ran on and on. It ended two years ago when Tessa left her home in Manchester and took her kids to a women's refuge."

"So this could even be an open-and-shut case?" Steve suggested hopefully.

The DI laughed. "Since when do we ever have neat little cases which wrap up on scene?"

"True. Can't hurt to be optimistic, though." Steve was grinning.

"Right, now if you've had a look round, go down to the station and warm up." He studied the sky in disgust. "This bloody Arctic weather! I'll see you there, when Jess has given me all the preliminaries she can and I'm done with the scene." His expression returned to its usual sombre greyness, and he added, "If the ex-husband has taken her, we'll make damn sure we're on his tail as soon as possible."

"And the body?" Dove queried.

"Nothing yet." The DI's voice was still grim as he regarded the white tent now hiding the dead man. "Get back to the station and start collating the statements as they come in. You can also get the ball rolling on our victim's ID."

Dove was walking back to her car when she spotted it. There was an old shed on the corner of the property. The door was wide open, and the corrugated iron roof had fallen in.

She blinked, focusing on something at the edge of her torchlight, next to the end of the building and as Steve came over, she pointed to an object on the ground. It was stiff with frost, but still instantly recognizable to Dove.

A child's sock, pink and decorated with unicorns.

CHAPTER THREE

"What's that? You still got gloves in your pocket? Bag it and hand it over to Jess," Steve said, adding his torchlight to the area, hovering over the item of clothing.

"The youngest girl, Cerys, was wearing the other unicorn sock when we saw her in the kitchen," Dove said, a niggle of fear for the young girls rising in her stomach. She pulled off her outdoor gloves, dumped them on the ground and pulled on a pair of thin latex ones. "She had odd socks on, so I noticed. But she can't possibly have been out here, can she?"

"Both children were in the house when the fire service got here," Steve murmured, sweeping his torch in wide slow arcs across the immediate area.

The woods were closer to the house this side, closely packed trees barely allowing the rutted driveway to pass out into the yard. In the summer months, the dense woodland might feel claustrophobic, but now the harsh winter had stripped away leaves and undergrowth, leaving nothing but drifted snow and darkness.

Dove thought of the child, her wide blue-eyed gaze and her frank innocence, and her racing heart rate dropped a little. "You're right. I think she would have told us if she had been. It's more likely it was dropped out here during the daytime for some reason. My niece used to wear her socks like gloves when she was little!"

"The older girl, Allison, seemed very defensive when it came to her dad," said Steve thoughtfully. "It would be a sure way to get Tessa out the house if her child was used as bait."

"But then left behind? Put them back to bed with a fire started in the yard?" Dove said doubtfully.

"If it was the dad, Allison might have trusted him. We need to find out if she's in contact with him, and if Tessa knew," he added.

* * *

Dove followed Steve back to the station, where they joined the queue for coffee. Typically, both machines in the corridor were out of action, which meant far too many bodies trying to hit the kitchen area for their early-morning caffeine fix.

As usual when a case was just starting, there was the heightened sense of urgency, of adrenalin shooting from person to person. There was an awareness of not wanting to waste any of the evidence collated during the Golden Hour. In an ideal case, the missing person would have been found during that precious hour, or at least an excellent lead extracted, but Tessa seemed to have vanished into the crisp, cold night air.

The core MCT night shift, who had formed the initial response to the call, were now joined by extra officers. Search and Rescue teams were already spread across the area around the farm, combing the woods and fields, checking outbuildings and the nearby derelict quarry.

In this case, of course, they would be running a parallel investigation into the frozen corpse discovered at the scene. The fire, the body and the missing woman made a complex and challenging start point.

Dove and Steve went straight to work, collating their reports with the others from their colleagues in the emergency services as they were sent through. Lindsey emailed through a statement from Tessa's sister, Callie, who was currently the last person to see her, and therefore now a significant witness in the case.

"The sister says she seemed a little jumpy the last few weeks, but wouldn't tell her why. Tessa finally admitted she thought someone was following her, but she hadn't actually seen anyone," Dove said, speed-reading the report.

"Was it called in to the station? I suppose her nearest would be Abberley of Eversham . . . Or her social worker. Anything official?" Steve asked, pausing behind her, a sheaf of paperwork in one hand, phone in the other.

"No. She had no evidence and given her history — her sister says she is prone to anxiety attacks — Tessa felt she wouldn't be taken seriously," Dove said, scrolling quickly down the page. "Tessa's parents live in Lymington-on-Sea . . . The family is from Spinningfields, in Manchester, originally . . ."

"Anything else come in on the body?"

"Nope, but the initial fire report confirms a small can of diesel was used as an accelerant. The proper report won't be in until tomorrow when they've run some more tests. I spoke to the incident commander just now, and he is also working two other cases. He says this fire was fairly well contained, and it was unlikely to have spread much further given the weather conditions." Dove showed Steve the photographs which had just popped up on her screen. "There were other cans stored in the open shed next to the vehicles, but not used. We saw those at the scene."

"Maybe there's a connection for Tessa or our perpetrator between the fire and ice aspect? The iced body, chess pieces, the fire . . ." Steve mused, pulling his jumper over his head. "Bloody hot in here now. Which muppet messed with the heating?" He scowled across at the next desk, but the occupants had their heads down, tapping at their keyboards.

Dove was also down to shirtsleeves, but she looked at his sweaty face with concern. "Probably broken again. At least we've got too much heat and not the other way around. I'm going to ring Lindsey and see if she's coming back for the briefing." She picked up her phone and scrolled through for the number.

"Hi, Dove. Did you get the statement from Callie Jackson?" Lindsey asked briskly.

"Yes, I just wanted to see if the kids had mentioned anything about the sock I found in the yard?" She had texted Lindsey and sent a quick snap before she bagged up possible evidence.

"No. It matches the one Cerys is wearing today, though. I did bring it up, but Allison just said her sister was always losing her clothes. She is being very cagey about the dad, but I'm pretty sure Cerys would have told me if she was outside earlier."

"Thanks Lindsey, it was just a thought."

"No worries. Both she and Cerys are behaving as I would expect, though, torn up with worry about their mum, so there doesn't seem to be any friction between mother and daughters. The same reaction from the sister, Callie. She's very anxious to help, and in tears most of the time. I checked, and Allison does have her own phone. As it wasn't locked, Callie and I had a quick look through her messages," Lindsey said.

Dove noted the change in her voice, and felt her own heartbeat quicken in response. "And?"

"I'll send over a screenshot, but she has been in contact with an unknown number, and the last message they sent to her was: *Are you sure you still want me to do it?*

"And her reply was: *Yes.*"

CHAPTER FOUR

I'm glad I didn't know what was going to happen. My sister used to say she wished she could travel into the future for just one day, to see what it was like. The thought used to scare me. Not because I ever imagined my future would be like this, but simply because I didn't want to know. I was content with my quiet life, and my dreams.

But now, in these strange times, as soon as I heard the news, I knew I would be next. My childlike delight at the fresh fall of snow was lost in the rotten stench of fear.

I can't explain how I knew. It wasn't a premonition as such, but more a certainty, knowledge of a trial I would have to endure. When it happened, I realized it was something nobody should ever have to face.

It was night when I was taken, in the snow. I was watching from the window when he came. The ice crystals lined up, perfectly uniform along my window ledge. I stared into the darkness and brushed the glass with my fingertips, protected from the bitter cold outside, yet still shivering.

I wasn't thinking of the beauty of the night as I left the house, because my vision was blurred with tears. I could smell fear and anger, and it seemed to lie thick in the air, as tangible and real as his smoky breath dancing next to my own. My shoes filled with the icy crust that transformed the world into a sugar-coated wonderland.

It seems like mere minutes since he was killed, but of course it has been much longer. I know I screamed, shoving my hand over my mouth, shaking and shaking like I would never stop.

There was blood on the snow. I could see it as I twisted and fought in vain. It was a spreading dark stain marring the winter perfection, framing his body. My cheeks were wet with tears, breath coming in painful gasps.

Terror sped my heartbeat and made my limbs tremble so I could hardly stand. The bruises on my face and bare arms stung as I was dragged away. A hand over my mouth prevented me from screaming again, but the threats whispered in my ear would have done that anyway. For everyone, there is at some point in your life, a person or people you would die for, and it was no different for me.

When we arrived, the smell of pine and wildness softened the air for a brief moment, but the poignant sweetness was soon overwhelmed by the stench of death.

Bad things happen in the snow.

CHAPTER FIVE

By 6.30 a.m., the tiny office kitchen area was overflowing with wrappers and cups, and the scent of burnt toast floated across the open-plan office space. Glimmers of light had started to seep into the darkness outside, heralding another freezing morning. Ski jackets had become the new normal attire for any police officers assigned duties outside the station.

Weather forecasters predicted the unusual metrological phenomenon, which the media had dubbed the 'Big Freeze', would continue, possibly even until Christmas. In town, emergency provisions were being made for the elderly, the vulnerable and the homeless who congregated underneath the pier and around the ancient churches. Dove's elderly neighbour had told her the last time it had been so cold in this area had been way back in the winter of 1963, when 'the milk froze in bottles on the doorsteps, and the waves washed up great splinters of ice.'

Dove had dug out her ski socks, thermal under-layers and woolly hats. She normally enjoyed the winter weather, but this was bone-chilling, icy and dangerous. The skies were too often filled with ominous snow-laden storm clouds. As it thawed the thin crusts of ice which sometimes formed at night, the sea washed sparkling crystals across the frozen beaches. Normally she spent her spare time surfing or swimming. It took a lot to drive her away from the water, but the 'Big Freeze' had done just that.

The police station was a fairly new building, with far more space than the old one. The main briefing room could comfortably hold the fifty or so officers who had now gathered, balancing coffee cups, iPads, notebooks, and toast wrapped in paper napkins.

The team, now fuelled by caffeine, were eager to crack on with the case at a time when optimism was high, and early success possible.

Shock and distaste were always expressed over the murder victim, but as always Dove loved the sense of working as a cohesive unit to find the killer, the way everyone contributed, the ideas chucked around, argued over, discarded. Having previously worked on her own, she was often surprised how much she enjoyed being part of the team.

Other officers, needed to answer the phones, start door-to-door and rake through CCTV, and the specialist media team were trickling through into the outer workspace. Forensic Technical Experts would dredge through any computers, phones or electronics discovered in the course of the investigation. Jess, as Crime Scene Manager, would be present at the post-mortem, ensuring everything was correct and all evidence from the scene was processed as quickly and efficiently as possible.

DCI Franklin, a grey-haired, broad-shouldered giant with a deceptively shambling appearance but a razor-sharp brain, was talking to the DI in the corridor as Dove passed. She caught a few phrases, enough to know that Tessa was still missing, and her heart beat a little faster in frustration. Already, more than three hours had passed since the woman made the 999 call.

She took her seat next to Steve and took a pull on her third coffee of the morning.

Finishing his conversation, DCI Franklin kicked off the briefing, mug of tea in hand. "Right, ladies and gents, here are the facts as we know them so far. Tessa Jackson, thirty-three, put through a 999 call at 3.20 this morning stating one of her outbuildings was on fire. First responders alerted us to the discovery of a body. We don't have an ID yet, but it looks to be a male in his late teens or early twenties. He was left naked, and according to early information from our CSM, cause of death is unknown. We'll know more after the post-mortem, which has been scheduled in for nine a.m. Tessa was missing by the time the first responders arrived, at 3.40. They saw no trace of any other vehicles or movements around the area."

There were a few murmurs, and nods from those who had been at the crime scene.

"Tessa Jackson is a single mum and her two daughters, aged six and ten, were in the house when first responders arrived. Both are unharmed and now in the care of a relative. DS Lindsey Allerton is acting as FLO for the family. She should be back in soon, and will be talking to the family's social worker as soon as possible. Naturally, there will also be a Group meeting . . ." he glanced at his watch, ". . . at twelve, so we can liaise with our local divisions and community groups."

"Any truth in the rumours this is a domestic abuse case?" DC Josh Conrad asked, scanning the photographs on the screen, which showed the farmhouse, the victim Tessa Jackson, and her daughters. Tessa, with her long dark curly hair and intense dark green eyes, stared back at them. Her daughters beamed for the camera, but their mother was barely smiling.

The DCI nodded slowly. "Kevin Hibbs is Tessa's ex-husband and father of the two girls. They divorced two years ago. As I said, we are currently liaising with social services, but his previous convictions and information from a family member suggest Tessa was afraid he would come after her. She lived in a remote location. The house is practically off the grid, and impossible to see from the road." He nodded at his colleague and made a few notes on his pad.

DI Blackman put in, "The last person to see Tessa Jackson was her sister, Callie, who was at the farm last night. She said they put the kids to bed at 8.30 p.m. and watched a film together before she went home at 11 p.m. She lives alone, but the CCTV on her road confirms her car returned to its permit parking space at 11.30 p.m. Ms Jackson has no idea as to the identity of the victim. We are keeping an open mind regarding Kevin Hibbs. It is possible his eldest daughter has been in contact with him recently." He proceeded to assign jobs, pairing officers off in his usual efficient manner. He and the DCI worked well together, and the team was solid, with everyone having their own speciality.

Dove and Steve were given the task of continuing to look for an ID on the body, and they went straight back to their computers as soon as the briefing broke up.

The board was up on the clear glass screen which separated the main briefing room from the open-plan office space, and Tessa's timeline was already filling up nicely as they pieced together her movements before the 999 call. But the frozen victim's remained blank both before and after the time of discovery. Photographs from the scene were pinned neatly underneath the times and dates.

It was imperative they discovered the man's identity as soon as possible, because his presence was clearly a link to Tessa's disappearance. Where the hell had he come from, and why had nobody missed him?

An hour later, as Dove took a quick break to snag another coffee, she checked her phone. A text from her fiancé, Quinn, made her smile, and she took five precious seconds to tap out a reply. They had only been engaged for seven months, and moved into Dove's house following a previous split.

Quinn was a paramedic for the local ambulance service, and their shifts meant they often had to snatch a few moments together when time allowed. Since they had become engaged, Dove felt the bond between them, that had always been evident, become stronger. She felt safer, more confident, now she had let Quinn back into her life. Finally, she had pushed her past away and started to heal. Her relationship was precious to her, and she was determined not to repeat past mistakes.

At half past eleven, the DI walked behind their desks, heading for the door and the Group meeting, talking quickly into his mobile phone. He broke off as he passed, putting a hand over the phone. "I'll be tied up for a while on this call. Can one of you ring Jess for an update?"

"Do you want to call Jess or shall I?" Steve asked Dove, frowning at his screen. "We need something more to identify this victim, so we don't have to trawl through every single missing person in the country. And before you say anything, there are none in this area in the last three months that fit the description."

"I'll ring Jess," Dove said, and punched out her best friend's mobile number.

"Hi, Dove, how's it going?" Jess's sharp Northern accent sliced through Dove's jumbled thoughts.

"Chaos, aka the usual. No word on Tessa Jackson, and we could do with anything you've got to help identify the victim. I know it's early, but—"

Jess cut in, "But you want information like yesterday. Always, love. Okay . . . bloods have gone to the lab, but we're queued as usual. Budget cuts are a bitch, aren't they?" There was a pause and a rustle of paperwork. "You're lucky I managed to book him in so early, the pathologist owes me a favour and this is looking like a big case. So . . . Caucasian male, looks to be early twenties, weighs around eleven stone. Time of death is within the last seventy-two hours, but we will know more after the lab tests. In the absence of any other obvious cause of death, it's possible he suffered primary hypothermia — that is, hypothermia due to environmental exposure. Hypothermia, unchecked, can cause cardiac arrest and organ failure, and can be fatal. He was discovered frozen in the foetal position, which suggests he was transported to the spot where he was found in a small temperature-controlled space. Best guess, he was still alive when he was placed in some kind of freezer, and assumed the position to retain warmth."

Jess paused, and Dove could hear the quick tap of a keyboard. "The core temperature and the physiology suggest the victim had been frozen for at least forty-eight hours."

Dove considered. "Maybe he was kept somewhere for a long time before he was killed, and again for a while afterwards. We could be looking for someone who went missing *years* ago."

"You're the detective, I just pass on the facts," Jess told her. "But his frozen position means his body could have been transported more easily, perhaps."

"Like in a car boot?"

"Unlikely. Unless that particular car boot had a freezer inside. Once he was frozen, to keep him like that, the temperature would have had to have been maintained. No evidence of injury, nothing to suggest he tried to escape from wherever he was. Poor bloke was literally frozen solid, which made post-mortem very difficult, as you can imagine. I may never be able to defrost a chicken dinner again after watching that," Jess added. "No signs of sexual abuse. He does have a small wound on each wrist which could be from some kind of restraint, like ties. Hard to be sure, and it could even be a small cut from a knife on each wrist or even a needle mark. The frozen state makes it hard to tell, and it appears the hypothermia has slowed the body's natural response to injury."

"Interesting. Any distinguishing marks, tattoos, piercings?"

"No. I did find one anomaly which might help, and I'll send some pictures over. He had the number two drawn on his torso in permanent marker. Apart from that, nothing at all. This particular John Doe is clean as a whistle. We'll try for DNA and fingerprints, of course. Sorry, Dove."

"Thanks anyway. Crap there's no ID, though . . . This is going to be a tough one, I can feel it," Dove said. "He hardly popped himself into a chest freezer and went to sleep, did he?"

"Might have done, but again, unlikely. Although I'm never surprised by anything people do now. You always say it'll be tough, anyway. It's those old bones of yours. That's what happens when you hit thirty-five, love," Jess told her sympathetically. "I'll send the blood results and tox screen straight over when I get them. But don't hold out too much hope, will you? Whoever froze this guy will probably have realized how much evidence they were destroying."

"Thanks for that, Jess. You are a little ray of sunshine as always." Despite the seriousness of the investigation, Dove was smiling as she ended the call. Jess could always make her laugh, and she valued their banter, and just as much, she admired her friend's ability to juggle two small children and a demanding job.

Steve raised an eyebrow, and she shook her head. "Nothing we didn't already know, apart from the fact the number two was written on our victim's torso in black marker pen," Dove continued thoughtfully. "Someone likes playing games, don't they? It's like a treasure hunt . . . A fire, a frozen body, a missing woman, and a chess set made of ice. Now we find the perpetrator has been drawing on his victim."

"Not to mention," Steve added, "it makes for a bit of a twisted treasure hunt — if this is number two, where the hell is body number one?"

CHAPTER SIX

"Why would you freeze a body?" Dove asked, pushing stray strands of her hair from her face and ticking the possible answers off on her fingers. "To destroy evidence, to freak out Tessa, to leave a message for us? Because I'm pretty sure our victim didn't shut himself in a freezer on purpose."

"Perhaps the death was accidental and the killer felt remorse, especially if the victim was known to them," Steve suggested, pulling an energy bar from his back pocket and unwrapping it with enthusiasm. "I'm knackered already. And the caffeine isn't working, so I'm going to try these instead."

"Aren't you meant to have those after a workout?" Dove queried, amused.

"Probably, but I need to stay awake. Anyway, you're one to talk, with your addiction to jelly sweets," Steve retorted, taking a bite and turning back to his screen and picking up his glasses again.

Dove stuck her middle finger up in retaliation and attacked her keyboard with vigour as he laughed.

"Guys, I got something from CCTV from one of the farms near the next village," called DC Josh Conrad. "We spoke to the owner earlier, and he just sent the file through . . ."

Several of the team, including Dove and Steve, crowded around the blurred pictures. At 1.30 a.m., a white van drove slowly along the narrow road, and paused right next to the farm driveway before continuing. Unfortunately, the angle of the van and the camera made it impossible to see the registration plates.

"Is that some kind of signage on the driver's door?" Steve said, peering over Josh's wide shoulders. "Why don't people bother with better quality CCTV?"

"Too expensive — and it's not like this is a high-crime area. It's the back of beyond," Josh said. A fairly new recruit to the MCT, he was well over six foot five with curly black hair and dimples. He often told Dove how annoying it was that everyone assumed he must play basketball when sailing was more his thing.

"He said it's set up so he gets anyone who comes through the gates, but as the van didn't swing in . . . The timing is right, and it looks like whoever was driving wasn't sure where they were going. Maybe they paused by the drive to check their sat nav, or even thought this farm was the one they wanted." Josh clicked his mouse, and the van drove back past the farm entrance in the opposite direction. Again the plates were obscured, but the clock in the corner recorded 3.34.

"Looks like only the driver in the van." Dove was squinting at the pixelated photos. "And Jess thought the victim had been frozen into the shape he was by being kept and transported in a small freezer."

"Plenty of space for a commercial freezer in the back of one of those." Jon had finished his call and joined the group. "I had a mate who delivered meat in that exact make and model, and he had it all configured with cold storage racks and freezing equipment."

After the initial interest, the group dispersed, and Dove went back to her screen. By lunchtime, she and Steve had trawled through all of the potential matches, including both local and national searches via HOLMES, and had a shortlist of five men. The victim had been well nourished, with no obvious signs of drug abuse, according to Jess's report, which narrowed the search slightly.

The trouble was, if the man had only been missing a short time, it was unlikely to have been reported. It was only when an employee failed to show up for work, mail piled up by apartment doors, or even a nosy neighbour noticed a lack of comings and goings, that many people were discovered to have completely vanished.

Dove took a quick break to grab a sandwich from the food van in the car park. She stretched her arms and rolled her stiff shoulders gratefully, zipping her thick padded jacket right up to her chin, pulling her knitted hat down over her cold ears.

The media were going to love this case. She could already see a couple of reporters lurking by the main gates. The strangeness of the crime — a frozen man found during the Big Freeze — jolted her, made her uneasy. Had his death been an accident someone had tried to cover up? She disregarded this now.

If you wanted to hide a body, you wouldn't deliver it right to someone's door. The scene had been so carefully arranged it was almost like artwork, and each part must have meaning, for Tessa or for the perpetrator. It tied in with the fact that the fire had been so small and contained it almost seemed to have been part of the set dressing.

She checked her phone as she walked towards the queue for the van, dragging her thoughts away from the case and concentrating on not losing her footing on the treacherous ground. The sky was a deep brilliant blue now, yet the air was freezing, nipping at cheeks and noses, making eyes smart.

No messages from Quinn, Dove noted with a twinge of disappointment as she checked her phone, but that wasn't unusual if he had a busy shift. They would catch up later and hopefully, if he wasn't too exhausted, share a bottle of wine, a curry and their latest Netflix binge series. She smiled to herself at this thought, aware it wouldn't be every couple's idea of domestic bliss.

Sand and grit had been spread across the car park and last week's snow still lay in dirty drifts around the perimeter fence line. Dove sighed at the length of the queue, joined the end, and was about to put in a catch-up call to her sister, Ren, when her phone rang.

She normally ignored withheld numbers, which usually meant unsolicited sales calls about insurance, but this time she answered it without thinking, her mind on the case.

"Is that still the number for Dove Milson?"

"Yes, who the . . . Shit! Rose?" Dove recognized the distinctive smooth, slightly hoarse voice within seconds, her brain clicking sharply from her current case to her recent past.

"Yeah. Sorry it's been ages, I only just found your number and you know how it is with work."

"It's fine, Rose, I remember." She ran her free hand nervously over the top of her hair, smoothing it down. With Rose's voice came other thoughts of her time on the Unit.

"How the MCT treating you? Bet the coffee at the new place is better than ours." She sounded amused. Rose's low voice might be sexy, inviting illicit secrets, but in real life she was shorter than Jess and so slender her wrists were half the size of Dove's. She looked the most unlikely person to be a CHIS handler, which was probably one of the reasons she had been so successful.

It was an old joke between them, about broken coffee machines and reused granules. Not even really funny now, but it tugged harder on her memories. Rose. Dove inhaled deeply to calm her racing thoughts, which skittered straight back to her past career an elite informant handler. If she had once been one of the best — and according to Chris, her old boss, who was always nagging her to come back, she had been — Rose was right up there with her.

"So what can I do for you? Or is it just catch-up time?" Dove asked lightly. "Don't worry, you're not interrupting anything vital, apart from my third caffeine-and-carb fix of the morning. I'm just queuing for the food van and I might be here a while."

"Right. I just . . . Look, Dove, I've got myself into a bit of a situation and I need help. I'd like to get your take on it." Suddenly the voice didn't sound so confident.

"Okaaaay. What kind of situation?" Dove said warily, feeling her stomach clench. Her relationship with Rose had been slightly toxic at times, and despite the banter, she wasn't sure she wanted to get dragged into any high drama. She glanced round at the queue, but nobody was listening. Other phones were out, cigarette smoke curled into the air and the buzz of chatter drowned her conversation.

If Dove had trodden a thin line between light and darkness, good and bad, Rose had always dived right in. Far more so than Dove, nothing had mattered to her but the result. Unlike Dove, ironically, she had so far been unscathed.

"I've got this informant. Let's call him AJ . . . and let's say he's part of a fairly big and prominent gang. He's been giving me good stuff for six months now, but in the last couple of weeks he's been calling a lot to talk but not giving anything out. Said he thinks they know he's a grass, and that he's being watched and all that crap . . ." She hesitated.

"Why don't you cut him loose?" Dove suggested. "If he's lost confidence, and if he thinks he is in trouble, he probably is — they usually know — and you need to cut ties before the trail leads right to you. You don't need me to say this, Rose."

"I want to get rid, but the thing is there's something planned for next weekend. Something big. He's trying to get the details, but he says he needs to stay off the phone as much as possible, so if he calls, it'll be just to set up a meet in the car."

Dove bit her thumbnail, shivering as the wind whipped across the car park. The stench of the diesel generator behind the food van was making her stomach turn. She stepped away slightly to avoid the fumes. "Sounds dodgy. What does Chris think?"

"He said the same as you, but then he said if it got a result it would be a big step up for the Unit, and for me. This is major turf and I could save lives."

"Not if you're dead," Dove pointed out bluntly. "Look, Rose, I keep up with what's going on, and I can guess who AJ might be affiliated with, or a similar gang anyway, and you need to pull the plug if there is any hint, any gut feeling something is wrong. For his sake and yours."

"I'm sorry to dump this on you, but you know what it's like because you've been through it. If I go to one of the guys, they'll see it as a weakness," Rose said, her voice sharp. "You know what most of them are like down here. They still think my success rate is down to me spending all my time with my legs apart. Stupid fuckers."

Dove stamped her feet to warm them, flexed her fingers in her gloves, deciding to ignore the bait dangled in front of her nose. It wouldn't help getting into a row with her former frenemy. "I get it, honestly I do, but if I could do it again I wouldn't have turned up to that last meeting. I had all the feels you're getting now, I knew something was wrong, but I did it anyway and it cost me . . ." Dove paused and swallowed hard as old emotions flickered back. But it wasn't the tidal wave of pain that had crushed her before. Therapy, time and Quinn had brought acceptance and a sense of calm to her life. The darkness would never fully go away, but she could see her way out of it now.

"I just wanted to talk to someone who knows how it works, and kind of weigh up the options," the other woman said carefully. "Is it worth taking the chance to save those lives, maybe prevent another turf war?"

Dove considered. Had she really rung for help, or was she just spreading her drama around? But why would she call Dove? There were others still on the Unit who would be far more receptive to the story, who would give her the validation she wanted, be willing to pick through the bones of the operation.

"Dove? What are you thinking?" Rose's voice was softer, but Dove still hesitated. Rose was also a great actress, able to charm anyone, and switch personalities in an instant, depending on who she was talking to. Depending on what she wanted . . .

She spoke carefully, deliberately. "Look, you know what happened to me. It nearly cost me everything — my life, my boyfriend, my career. Thanks to one decision, and my resulting injuries, I can never have kids, Rose. Think about it and think hard. Any doubts, and you see if there's another way around it. Ask Chris to spread the word something's going down. It might discourage whatever is planned, or at least postpone it until more information leaks through."

"I'm sorry," Rose told her, "I knew it was bad, but I didn't realize you couldn't have kids now. Fuck, that's worse than you ever made out. Why didn't you tell me?"

"I couldn't. The more people I told the more it made it real," Dove told her, "I'm okay. I'm in a good place now." She could hear Rose breathing into the silence that followed; pictured her sharp-faced, narrow-eyed, her long hair hanging over one skinny shoulder as she weighed up her options.

"Shit, I've got to go — my other phone's ringing," Rose said suddenly, blood-pumping alertness instantly replacing her casual tones. "Thank you, Dove, and speak soon."

"Stay safe, Rose," Dove said quickly, on impulse. She ended the call and stood for a moment in the patchy sunlight, remembering the burst of adrenalin when the 'other phone' rang, the challenges to be faced, the persona to be changed. Her own heart was racing in sympathy. You never really left the Unit, and the nightmares were still there. Receding, but still lurking like faded ghosts in the deepest recesses of her mind. The CHIS got into your blood, into your brain, until you lost sight of the real world. It was a deadly game, and whatever her circumstances, she hoped Rose was going to make the right choice.

CHAPTER SEVEN

I stared into the darkness, trying to block out the horrors. Forcing my mind away from the present, I came to rest on childhood memories. I always wanted to be a doctor.

My parents owned a butcher's shop, and that's where I gained my knowledge of anatomy. But animals didn't interest me, because I wanted to know how the human body worked. How it could run, swim; how my brain could process so much and yet was so small? Childish thoughts and curiosity, I suppose, but always following a similar path.

Later, my parents watched in awe as I sliced off the limbs of my dolls, and carefully stitched them back together. Sometimes I would experiment and stitch an arm to the place where a leg should be, or add an extra limb to another unfortunate doll.

Blinking as dust hit my face, I broke the spell and I was back in the darkness. The sweet and sour smell of blood made bile rise in my throat. This was my new reality. Terror gripped me again, shaking me violently between razor-sharp teeth, and I realized tears were running down my cheeks.

This wouldn't do. I couldn't show weakness this early on.

I squared my shoulders, stuck my chin up and felt a tiny fire still warming my body, deep inside. I wouldn't show them I was afraid. Not ever and no matter what happened to me.

CHAPTER EIGHT

Finally reaching the top of the queue for the food van, calm now and back in the present, Dove inhaled the luscious smells of burgers, chips, onions and fried bacon, and placed her order.

A huge bacon sandwich and brown sauce gave her an energy hit and she was soon back at the computer, attacking the keyboard with renewed enthusiasm. She stared hard at the face on the screen, flicking back and forth between the post-mortem photographs from Jess. More than once she was convinced she had a hit, but time and time again, it wasn't quite a match.

The victim's fingerprints had been taken, but if he had never been printed, he wouldn't be on file. The same went for a DNA match with the bloods. If it wasn't on file, for whatever reason, they wouldn't get an ID.

The man had a strong jawbone and broad bone struc-ture. He looked muscular, and as Jess had said, in the peak of health. Maybe an athlete? She rubbed her forehead in frus-tration, and without thinking, downed the last of her cold coffee, wincing at the bitter dregs.

Steve was just finishing up on the phone as he walked back into the office, his mobile between ear and shoulder, hands laden.

He was talking quickly, urgently, and she waited hopefully. "You got anything?" she asked, as he finished the call.

"Call apparently came into Eversham this morning. Bloke who claimed his brother went missing last week, and the description fitted our frozen body. He seemed like a possible until he started jumping back and forth between now and last year," Steve said, polishing his glasses on his shirt sleeve and yawning.

"What do you mean?" Dove tapped the pencil against her teeth as she pulled up another missing persons report which had been emailed over from another division.

"Stop doing that — it's really annoying!" Steve removed the pencil from her fingers, and she glared at him. "I mean, he was one of those people who starts off well, and ends by saying his brother was abducted by the government, who have been after him for years because of his work for the secret service."

She stared at him. "Really? That's a good one, if a bit common."

Steve shrugged, taking a huge bite out of his BLT and slumping into his chair, tapping on the keyboard. When he could talk again, he continued. "His brother died in 1997."

"Perhaps the aliens brought him back," Dove suggested, yawning.

"Maybe. I don't think our victim is a mispo. At least, not yet. Which suggests he hasn't been missed and therefore was killed recently, which fits with what Jess just sent over about decomp," Steve said, ripping open another protein bar. "Before you say a single word, a protein bar is better than a chocolate bar, isn't it?"

"Mmmm . . . I guess. Jess did say it was hard to tell due to the frozen state." Dove suddenly swung her chair round and studied the photographs from the post-mortem. "It is definitely a number two, isn't it? Not a Z?" She rotated the picture to look from another angle.

"Nah . . ." Steve peered at the victim. "It's a number. I wondered earlier if it was an initial or something, but I don't think so. It does raise the question of where the first body might be, or if there is a number one? Maybe two is significant for him, and this isn't about running a sequence . . ."

They had worked well together from the start, chucking ideas back and forth, personalities gelling. Dove hoped they would get to stay as a partnership if she eventually got promoted to DS. Jon had told her he was pleased with the way she had settled into the MCT, and they had discussed this as a highly probable career path in her dreaded six-month review.

At the very back of her mind was always the possibility of returning to work as an informant handler. Her old boss had received funding for a new unit, and in the spring, had offered her a job overseeing four handlers. It would have meant promotion, but also a partial return to the claustrophobic darkness of the Unit. Her history as a brilliant handler had been tarnished when she was abducted and tortured by a gang. One tiny slip-up generally meant death when you were dealing with organized crime, and, as she had told Rose, she had been literally scarred for life.

With the MCT, she was never totally alone in the darkness. There was always her partner, other members of the close-knit team, and the wider ring of other specialist officers to confer with. Very rarely she missed the independence, and never at the beginning of a case. Mostly, she just reminded herself how lucky she was to have a career at all.

"The other option regarding the number two on his chest is simply that our victim is second on our perpetrator's hit list . . ." Steve answered, yawning.

Dove knew he was struggling with work and baby duties, and slapped him sympathetically on the back. "I bloody hope not. I'll get you another coffee to keep you awake. I need to print out another ton of paperwork too. Nothing from the door-to-door yet, mainly because nobody lives down that way . . ." She stood up, fishing in her pocket for loose change. "Want anything else from the machine?"

"No thanks, I'm good." He waved an energy drink in her direction.

She shook her head, "Good for you. Hope it tastes better than it looks."

"You'll be jealous when I start sporting an eight-pack," Steve told her optimistically. His new health and fitness drive seemed to be in response to his status as a new dad. One-month-old Grace was absolutely gorgeous, but was also causing both new parents many sleepless nights. As a result, Steve had decided to get fit. He was even working out at the local gym on the rare evenings off.

Dove suddenly leaned over and stared again at the number on the man's chest, biting her thumbnail. Something was stirring at the back of her mind, and she tapped in a Google search, peering at photographs. "Look! This is what the number just reminded me of," she said.

Steve leaned over and peered at the website. "Triathletes?" His voice was doubtful.

"Not necessarily triathletes," Dove said impatiently. "It could be any sporting event, a swimming race, or a bike race, I don't know, but look, the numbers are drawn on foreheads or chests, depending on who's wearing what gear. I was just thinking about what Jess said. He was very muscular and at peak fitness . . ."

She shrugged, turning back to her gallery of athletes, "If he was doing an endurance race and got caught out by the weather . . . but everything round here has been cancelled and someone would have noticed, called for medical backup, if it was an official event."

"He also wouldn't have been a human ice lolly if he'd been simply exposed to the elements for long enough to get hypothermic," Steve pointed out, "It's bloody cold, but we aren't in the Arctic Circle yet."

"I'm going to ring round the local sports clubs, just to see if they have any information," Dove said. "It would explain why we don't have a number-one body. If there were a few people involved in a race and one was singled out, that might work?"

"Let Jon know," her partner said, after he had flicked through the gallery. "I agree the image is similar, but what race could possibly be going on in this weather? Everything local would have been cancelled. Even you admitted the sea is too bloody cold to swim in!"

Dove pulled a face. "It is. Our victim was naked too, which means he was either stripped because his clothing might have made him identifiable, or perhaps he was naked when he died?"

CHAPTER NINE

Two hours later, with no progress apart from dead-end leads, and a huge amount of information to process, Dove stepped outside to clear her head. She hated being in the office, but in this weather it made sense to work inside as much as possible. Remembering she had forgotten to call her sister earlier, she scrolled through her numbers with icy fingers.

"Hi, Dove, how's work? I saw the news about that missing woman and a frozen body. Sounds like the stuff of nightmares, especially in this weather," Ren said.

"It's pretty full on, and I reckon we'll be in till late tonight," Dove replied. "I know we were meant to meet up tomorrow, but can you do Thursday instead? Sorry, Ren, but you know what it's like . . ."

Ren ran a busy café in town, occasionally helped out by her two daughters, and her spare time was limited, which made Dove feel doubly guilty about cancelling their longstanding arrangement. "No worries, I kind of thought you might be tied up after I saw the news story. Um . . . okay, Thursday . . . I've got someone doing the lock-up at the coffee shop, so I'll be home from about six. I presume you want food?"

There were four part-time staff members at the coffee shop, and they often filled in when Ren was tied up with her family.

Dove tried hard to catch up with both her sisters on a regular basis, and invariably they would all congregate at Ren's cosy home, along with her two daughters and grandson. This meant they didn't disturb Quinn if he was working the next day. Her other sister, Gaia, had a flat above the strip club, although more of a luxury apartment, all glass and marble, it wasn't an ideal place to hang out, especially with a toddler.

"Only if you have something in the oven," Dove said, "I'll grab a bag of goodies and come straight over for about nine thirty, shall I?"

"That's fine, I'm used to yours and Gaia's random hours," Ren said, amusement in her voice. "Can you let me know as soon as possible if you need to rearrange, though, otherwise I end up with a mountain of food to eat myself, and I've put on enough weight this winter as it is!"

"Don't be silly, you look gorgeous, and of course I will let you know, but fingers crossed. See you Thursday," Dove told her, and killed the call. She and Gaia were tall and rangy, taking after their father in stature, but Ren had hourglass curves and a low husky voice. Gaia used to say she would be a star turn in the club, but she quit talking like that after her niece went missing. Even now Eden was home, that kind of banter seemed inappropriate.

It would be good to see her sisters, to be all together catching up on each other's busy lives. Occasionally Dove and Ren grabbed a quick coffee, or the girls, Delta and Eden, dropped by on days off or weekends. Gaia, a whip-smart businesswoman who had recently added another strip club to her growing property portfolio, was harder to pin down.

Plus, their relationship had always been spiky, with Dove very much on the side of law enforcement, and her sister more than occasionally crossing the line into illegal enterprises. However, events of the last six months had driven the three sisters closer. A new and unexpected grandson for Ren had smoothed the path further, as had the news of Dove's recent engagement.

* * *

Back inside, her mind returning to Tessa Jackson's children, Dove stopped by Josh's desk on her way to the printer, and he glanced up and winked. "Have you finally come over to ask me out?"

Dove grinned at him. It was a joke between them, which had begun on his first case with the MCT. "You're too tall for me and that's getting a bit old now. You need to find some new material." She returned to the subject in hand. "We've drawn a blank on mispos so far. How are you getting on with the ex-husband Hibbs?"

"Loads. The worst news, or best for him, is that he has an alibi. Sort of."

"Shit."

"He was a work until 3 p.m. yesterday, which is confirmed by CCTV and his boss. Greater Manchester sent a couple of uniform round to break the news of his ex-wife's disappearance, and he gave a statement. Apparently, he was really panicking about being blamed for her disappearance and the murder."

"Okay, but you don't look disappointed enough . . ." Dove said, watching his face as the dimples appeared again.

"Right. He left work at three, so it's highly unlikely, given the timings and weather, that he then jumped in a van and drove six hours down to Tessa Jackson's place, but it is possible. Just."

"Which would have brought him down here by around nine?" she said, swiftly calculating a rough journey time.

"Yeah, but the weather would have slowed him down, and would he have risked it if he is the perpetrator? We thought from the scene the offender had a tight time schedule. Any hold-up on the motorways would have screwed it for him, if it was Hibbs." Josh leaned back in his chair and ran both hands through his hair, linking them behind his neck. "He works at a place called Ski and Sky. Manages a team that maintains the dry ski slopes, the indoor sky diving funnel, and the ice rink. Ski and Sky is located on the Manton Leisure Park, right next to the motorway, so an easy place to start a journey down south."

"I've heard of them. There's a Ski and Sky down here too, I think?" Dove said, her mind ticking off the possible scenarios. "You're right, it would have been tight timing to get down here . . . In fact, pretty near impossible unless he drove like a speed demon. Did the traffic cameras pick him up?"

"Nope. He does own a company van, but his is blue and a different make to the one on our CCTV footage. It also has a colourful logo across the side and rear doors."

"And then there's our body . . . It would have taken time to get it in the vehicle, and he would have been heavy, too . . . Unless he and the freezer were already loaded into the van by then?" Dove suggested, aware she needed to get back to her own assignment, but unable to resist a snippet of information. After all, she reasoned with herself, it was all connected.

"He categorically denies any contact with his ex-wife and daughters since the divorce, two years ago," Josh said, rolling his shoulders. "God, I hate sitting at a desk. I'll need a massage to sort my back out after this."

"Good luck with finding someone to do that."

Dove grabbed her paperwork from the printer and went back to her desk. Why would Hibbs lie about contact with his daughter? Surely if he had managed to make contact, it would be better to admit it than become a suspect in a murder case.

She dumped her pile of reports as her phone pinged with an email from one of the local police divisions. She read it quickly, heart racing, and put through a call, crossing her fingers aliens and government conspiracy were not mentioned.

"Hi, it's DC Dove Milson on the MCT. Just following up on a missing person report you had three days ago. Charles Richardson?"

"Looks like his flatmate reported him missing. I'll send it over now."

She bit her nails in anticipation, waiting for the potential match, desperate now to make a tiny bit of headway after half a day of dead ends. The full report hit her inbox minutes later.

"Got something! Steve, look at this," she called to her partner. "Charles Richardson, twenty-two, was reported missing by his flatmate three days ago, so the day before we found the body. Looks like it was filed in the wrong place, because it didn't come up on HOLMES. Bloody hell."

Steve studied her screen, eyes bloodshot behind his thick glasses. "A strong possible. Looks like our guy too, although it's kind of hard to compare a living face with a frozen one."

Dove was still reading, taking quick notes on her pad. "He works at Richardson Autos, and told his flatmate, Tony Garner, he would be away for a while, but back on the four-teenth. Tony says he does go away for extended periods for work, but always comes back on time and has never been out of contact for this long."

"Parents?" Steve queried.

"Yes, they own Richardson Autos by the looks of it, but they haven't filed a mispo report. Odd, you'd think if he didn't show up for work, they would have been more worried than his flatmate," Dove said. "Let's get this over to the DI, and then he can get the ID process started." She looked over at the board and mentally added the details to the timeline, even before they were confirmed. It felt like progress, a step closer to finding the killer and a step closer to finding the missing mother.

CHAPTER TEN

Steve was digging unenthusiastically into a tomato salad, and Dove was on her fifth coffee, as DI Jon Blackman called across the room. "So a quick update for all of you, before we crack on. We now have a positive ID for our victim. Charles Richardson. He was twenty-two, and worked in the family business, Richardson Autos. His flatmate reported him missing. Dove and Steve, I want you to get statements from the flatmate and parents ASAP. I want to know where the hell he's been and what he's been doing. Josh, any word back on the tech from Tessa Jackson's place?"

Josh shook his head. "Nothing that jumps out right away. She used a couple of dating apps, was on a few parent forums, and social media, but she seems to have been super careful about what she posted. We are still recovering all the deleted emails and searches. Oh, she had two mobile phones, one of which has been recovered from the house. The other is still missing. The recovered phone looks like an old one she hasn't used in a while, but it still has a SIM card."

The DI made a few notes before he continued, his eyes now on the timelines. "We did a fast-time check on her number at scene, because she used her mobile to call 999. Nothing popped up, and from the cell site enquiries, it was switched off just before she left the farm, so no joy yet. Okay, Lindsey, anything from the family?" The DI turned towards the FLO.

Lindsey nodded, and said briskly, "We chased up the text messages on Allison's phone and the number was registered to Kevin Hibbs. She admitted she has been in contact with her dad for the last couple of months. She says he was actually down here two weeks ago, and they met while she was walking to a friend's house after a school club, but swears he wasn't down here last night. Allison also says she has no idea how he originally found them or got her phone number."

"Bloody hell," Steve muttered. "That's a bit odd. Especially as the dad said in his statement he'd had no contact with his family."

"Exactly. I should add she seemed pleased he had come to find her, and not afraid of him at all." Lindsey glanced at her notes and added, "You're right, Steve, Kevin Hibbs gave a statement to our colleagues, which has been added to the file, stating categorically he hasn't seen Tessa or the girls since they left. If he's lying, that's going to come back and bite him."

"Let's get moving then, people," Jon said. "Steve and Dove, get over to Richardson Autos and follow up on the flatmate."

* * *

The Richardsons lived on the far side of Abberley, but the main roads had been gritted, so it took barely twenty minutes to get through the traffic and out onto the industrialized area to the north of the town.

"If Kevin Hibbs has lied in his statement, he could be involved after all," Steve suggested.

"I can't see him making that journey down here, unless he has help already in the area, and maybe he's just terrified this is going to be . . ." Dove broke off to the answer the phone, hitting the hands-free button. "Hi, boss?"

Jon's call was short and to the point. "Duncan has had to go sick, so as you're headed that way, can you drop into Ski and Sky and see if they have a record of Kevin Hibbs's recent visits, and any CCTV?"

"No worries, we're really close to Richardson Autos now," Dove told him.

Steve looked at the luminous digits of the clock on the dashboard. "It's going to be a late one if we do Ski and Sky as well. What are your thoughts on Hibbs anyway? You almost seem more interested in him than our victim. Is it one of your 'feelings'?"

"I'm a detective, idiot, not a psychic! It's all connected, and as usual, it's driving me nuts I can't fit everything together all at once," she retorted, turning into the car yard. A rusting sign sagging on rotten poles, and the lines of bottom-of-the-range cars with faded prices propped in the windscreens, didn't appear to proclaim prosperity.

"That's good, you work better when you're in that kind of mood," he said, laughing at her expression.

"Whatever." Dove edged the car across the tight-packed ice and gravel into a vacant space. She couldn't explain it, but finding Cerys's sock, coupled with Allison's defiant defence of Hibbs, had rattled her. Maybe she was still thinking of another father who had betrayed his girls?

The car yard office was a large Portakabin and both parents were huddled inside on a torn orange sofa, waiting for the police officers. The cabin was muggy and claustrophobic, smelling strongly of car oil and faintly of electrical burning. It was warmed by four storage heaters.

Jacky, Charles's mother, small, with tiny bird-like features and a cigarette hanging from her yellow fingers, was understandably still distraught at the news of her son's death, but couldn't shed any light on his recent movements. "I would have said come up to the bungalow, but your colleagues are still in there searching for . . . things."

Dove and Steve reassured her that this was perfectly normal during the initial investigation, but she just nodded, staring into the distance, tearing a tissue to shreds. Her husband slumped silently next to her.

Her eyes were swollen and bloodshot, her brown hair falling over her forehead in lank, greasy strands. Despite the warmth of the Portakabin, she was wearing a thick, darned woollen jacket with leather-patched sleeves. "Charles said as business was slack he was going to stay with a friend up north for six weeks. We last saw him on the seventh of October. He had dinner with us and went back to the flat."

Dove frowned. "That's quite precise. Why six weeks?"

"I don't know. He was right, business isn't good. In fact, we . . ." She glanced nervously at her husband, but he just shrugged his massive shoulders and continued gazing into space, unfocused, grief clear in his eyes. His tall body seemed almost shrunken, hunched over his knees like an animal in pain. "Don hates to hear me say it, but we're going under. The yard and house will have to be sold. We've tried our best, but the new dealership up the road sucked the life out of our business. Bankrupt. Such a horrible word . . ."

"Charles left college and came straight out to work here. It was supposed to be his and the other lads' when we retired. Now we've got nothing, and Charles is dead," Don said, focusing suddenly on Dove's face, bringing the subject back to point. He was now nervously rubbing big oil-stained hands across his ruddy face. "I had a go at him for taking off and leaving us, but then he said he might be able to get a few business contacts from this mate he was staying with, so I let it be."

"But you don't know the name of the friend he was staying with?" Dove queried.

Don fidgeted in his grease-stained plastic chair, met her eyes again and scowled. "No, I don't. Believe me, if I knew anything I would be onto it, but the first we heard was your lot banging on the door this morning, telling us he was dead, asking us to identify the body . . ."

Dove felt another rush of sympathy for the grieving family. The actual identification of the body had been swift, as often happened when it was considered the death might hold important information relating to a case. But this didn't make it any easier for friends and relatives.

"Do you recognize this woman?" Dove passed a photograph of Tessa Jackson across to the woman.

Jacky studied the unsmiling face with concentration. "I don't. This is the one who's gone missing, isn't it?"

"Yes. We are trying to find out if there is a connection between Tessa Jackson or her family and Charles," Dove explained.

"The name doesn't ring any bells either," the other woman said.

"How about Kevin Hibbs?" Dove tried the other picture, but met with the same response.

"Where are Charles's brothers?" Steve asked, after a quick look at his notes.

"Ben is off doing a few final deals which should take the stock off our hands. He's up in Leeds. After I told him about Charles, I said he shouldn't drive, but he's on his way down anyway. The weather won't stop that lad, either. Mikey is out the back. I can't get him to do anything since we found out. It's all been so fast . . . He and Charles were so close . . ." The man got up and abruptly walked out of the room, scrubbing his face with angry, shaking hands again and again.

"Can we speak to Mikey?" Dove asked the distraught mother. It was always tough getting statements in these early stages, but crucial to the success of the investigation, and essential for a successful CPS prosecution. She popped documents into her bag, along with her iPad, and zipped it up.

Jacky nodded, and waved a hand towards the back of the car yard. "He was working the crusher, last I saw. I doubt if he'll speak to you, though. He doesn't like the police very much, and he went mad after we found out what had happened to Charles." She was crying again, wrapping her arms around her body.

Dove paused on her way out, but the woman waved her away. "Just find out who did this. I'll be all right."

Glad to be out of the cramped, strong-smelling Portakabin, Dove followed her partner across the grit and sand towards towering piles of cars waiting to be crushed. She pulled her gloves on as she walked, wincing as the bitter wind whipped her scarf away from the lower part of her face.

"I suppose he's the guy sitting in the cab," Steve pointed high into the air as a man deftly manoeuvred a winch type vehicle.

They watched for a moment as powerful mechanical pincers plucked a car from the pile, depositing it neatly on the top of another pile. The machine stopped and the man jumped out, landing carefully on the slippery ground.

Dove moved forward. "Mikey Richardson?"

"Yeah." He was bundled up in a thick black Puffa jacket with a sports logo, black work trousers stained with oil tucked into brown leather boots. Like his mother, his eyes were an icy pale blue, and his voice was tight with emotion. "What do you want?"

CHAPTER ELEVEN

As they got closer, Dove could see his eyes were red-rimmed, and although the cold weather or hard work had brought a flush to his cheeks, his face looked sunken and pale. She introduced herself and Steve, and he gave a short bark of laughter and turned away.

"I'm very sorry for your loss, but we need to ask you some questions about your brother's death," Dove persisted.

"You don't, you need to get your arses out on the street and find out who killed him," Mikey said roughly. He moved towards another machine and clambered nimbly up to the controls. "I haven't seen him since October, the night he left. He had dinner with the parents and came out for a beer with me before he went back to the flat." He waved towards a mould-covered mobile home near the back of the yard.

"We need to take a signed statement . . ." Dove began, but her voice was drowned by the noise.

With a massive clanking and grinding, the crusher went to work; two huge rusty metal plates squashing metal as though it was play dough. Dove resisted the temptation to put her hands over her ears as the metal screamed and glass shattered. Within minutes, the pile of cars was reduced to a neat cube, ready to load onto trucks.

Mikey, rather obviously taking his time, jumped down and smirked at them. "You still here?"

"We are trying to find out what happened to your brother, and believe me, there are plenty of officers out on the streets. Anything you can tell us might lead us to the truth," Dove said.

"Fuck off." Mikey turned, and started walking away. "Come back when you have something to tell me. I'm not signing any shit you give out."

They watched him head back towards the crane.

"We'll get uniform to bring him in," Steve said. "If he's going to be uncooperative, he can come down to the station for a statement and stop wasting our time." He pulled out his phone to call it in. "If they can pick him up, we can go straight to Tony Garner's flat and do Ski and Sky before we head back?"

"Agreed," Dove said. It was often tough trying to persuade grieving families to talk about the victims, but an essential part of a murder enquiry was following up on information given by close friends and family, which included last movements and significant witness statements. Sometimes people knew things that gave a whole new slant on the investigation.

Jacky was waiting anxiously at the Portakabin door as they passed it on their way back to the car. Her hands were still twisted round a tissue, shredding it viciously, compulsively. Tiny strips floated unnoticed to the ground. "Told you he wouldn't talk to you. I'm sorry, but he's so angry . . . Ben just called and he's on the M25. He'll be a few hours yet because of the weather and the traffic, but he'll speak to you. He and Charles weren't as close, but if anything helps . . ." Her voice caught in her throat and tears rolled down her cheeks. "Sorry . . ."

"It's okay, we understand, and thank you," Dove told her, pressing her card gently into the cold, shaking hand. "If Ben could give us a call as soon as he gets home, that would be very helpful."

"It wasn't my boys, you know," she said suddenly, blinking at them. "If you're thinking they had something to do with murdering their own brother . . . Just don't, because they wouldn't do something like that . . ."

"We aren't thinking that at all," Steve reassured her with practised calm. "Our job is to eliminate people from the enquiry and collect any information that might be useful. We do respect your loss, but at the same time we have a missing woman still to find."

"I'll talk to Mikey and try and get him to see sense. He's just so angry, you know. I still can't believe it . . . I keep telling myself there must be a mistake and he's going to walk back through the door . . ." Jacky said, tears beginning to fall again.

The FLO, DS Pete Windham, had come over from the family bungalow, and walked out with them to the car. He had his hood up to protect his bald head from the bitter wind, and when he smiled he showed a large set of yellowing teeth. Because of his rather odd, braying laugh, predictably and rather cruelly, his station nickname was 'Donkey', but he didn't seem to mind. "I'll call you if I get anything else. Oh, did you hear Maya and Col have just gone sick, so we're another two down on the first day of the investigation? Hope you two had your flu jabs!"

"Thanks for the concern, Pete, but we're fine. See you later!" Dove said to him, and they walked away, stamping their feet trying to get warm before they reached the car. She hated seeing the grief of families who had lost their loved ones, but it fuelled her desire to achieve justice on their behalf. She couldn't bring someone back from the dead, but she could find the killer.

The car skidded on the icy gravel, losing its back end briefly as Dove drove carefully out of the yard. She corrected easily, and indicated right, back towards the centre of town. At half past four, the winter darkness was already fully closing in, and the car headlights slashed a bright furrow through the slushy tarmac.

Steve was checking his notes. "Tony Garner has apparently been home all day, and SOCO are on their way to check out the flat. They're shorthanded too, so they're running behind. Everyone's down with this bloody flu."

Dove nodded and took a shortcut down the one-way street past the park. Normally, it was busy at any time of the day, but now, just a few dog walkers dressed in thermals braved the icy wind and early gloom. Christmas lights twinkled optimistically from the line of lime trees which grew along the wrought-iron fence line, and a solitary food van was open for business in the car park.

The flat was on the west side, in a rundown area with bins overflowing and bits of car and motorbike decorating the front gardens. A group of hardy teenagers were playing basketball on the court between two tower blocks, hoods pulled up to keep out the bitter cold.

Tony, Charles's flatmate and the man who had reported him missing, was short and athletic, muscles clearly visible under his thin Adidas sports top. He was older than Dove had imagined, too, in his late thirties. Dark shadows around his eyes and a pinched look to his mouth shrivelled his rather chiselled good looks and hollowed his cheeks.

"I got back from my girlfriend's place and found Charles wasn't back. He said he'd be gone six weeks, and it's been over that. He was a bit weird about it all, so when he didn't come back, I tried his phone but it was switched off." Tony had hardly shown them inside when he started talking, muscular arms crossed defensively in front of his barrel chest, chin thrust out. "I called his parents at the yard, and Ben, because he was away too, so I figured maybe they hooked up on a deal? Couldn't get hold of Mikey. His mum and dad hadn't heard from him. I think his mum was worried, but his dad didn't seem bothered. He'd just told them he'd be back when he was back. When I saw the news about the murder and the missing woman I got freaked out, you know?" His words tumbled out, and his eyes darted nervously from one officer to the other.

"You mentioned that he did sometimes go away for work," Dove said, taking quick notes.

"He did, which is why I suppose Jacky and his dad weren't too bothered. Don did say Charles led them to believe he was just getting away from it all and staying with a mate, but that wasn't the impression I got." He sighed. "I'm not some weirdo checking in on every move, but Charles was always on time for everything we did, and we told each other what was going on." Tony wrapped his arms around his torso now, rubbing his arms as though he was cold.

"Did Charles ever do any endurance races?" Dove asked. Tony had intricate tattoos along his arms and a rather beautiful butterfly and rainforest design on his neck. The thin white sports top did nothing to hide the artwork.

"Running, you mean? We both did a few triathlons in the summer, and one year we did Three Peaks, but nothing recently. He would have told me if he was going to do something like that and probably asked me to go too!"

"Okay, that's fine," Dove told him. Her exploratory calls to various clubs and sports event organizers had resulted in the same answers. Nothing was happening. Only the hardcore elites were still in training, and even then in carefully controlled conditions. None of the club members were missing. "Did he belong to any sports clubs?"

"A few. Tennis, swimming and athletics, but he was doing less competing and spending more time at the gym."

"Does the number two mean anything to you or Charles? When Charles's body was found, it was written on his chest," Steve explained.

Tony looked shaken. His eyes opened wider and the big hands clenched on his thighs. "That's fucking weird . . . I . . . I can't think why anyone would do that, but . . ." He picked up his phone and began scrolling through pictures, before turning the screen round and showing the police officers.

It was a photograph from a sports event, showing Tony and Charles halfway through a muddy river. Both men were grinning broadly, and around their foreheads, they had each had a bandana-type scarf. Tony's had the number one in the middle, and Charles's the number two.

CHAPTER TWELVE

"When was this photo taken?" Steve asked, making a quick note, and taking a snap on his phone.

"Earlier this year. We did a Tough Mudder event as a team of two." Tony sounded dazed and passed a hand across his face. "This is so fucked up."

"Anything stand out about that particular race?" Steve was still studying the photograph. "We're not saying it's even connected, just trying to get as much information as we can."

"It could just be a coincidence," Dove told Tony, who was now leaning hunched forward, and silent. "Can we go back to the beginning? When did you last see him?" Dove asked.

"I told you, the evening of the seventh of October. He had dinner at the yard, came back here at about midnight." He paused, thinking. His speech had slowed now, his shoulders dropping, hands relaxed into his lap. "I'm sure he said something about seeing his girlfriend, Anne-Marie. When I spoke to her earlier, she says he did drop in at hers before he came back here."

"Okay, we'll talk to her. How did he seem when he got back to the flat? Was he any different to how he usually was before a work trip?" Steve asked.

Tony shrugged. "He was fine. Excited, maybe . . . He said he would be away for a few weeks, and I just assumed it was something to do with the car yard. It's no secret that times have been hard for them, and the boys have been doing extra work at some of the auction yards up north." He frowned. "Normally, he would have told me, but I suppose I thought it was some kind of um . . . not-quite-legal deal to get rid of the last of the stock. He just told me the date he'd be back, and said he'd buy me a beer and we'd watch the match just like old times . . . That's another thing, he'd never miss a match."

"So he said he was going to be away for longer than you would have said was usual for a trip?" Steve asked. "Was there anything he said about what he might be doing?"

"No, he was a bit weird about it, but he's been pretty down about the yard, so I thought it was just that . . . Normally, a trip to the auctions would be around three weeks, and he might pop back in between if he ran a car down here, just stay the night and head back again." Tony moved towards the kitchen counter and picked up an energy drink. He pushed a couple of bottles towards Dove and Steve. "Charles loved these drinks. We used to live on them when we were in training for an event. Go on, try one . . ."

"Did he tell you where he was going?" Steve took a bottle, cautiously, but Dove shook her head. She had never been keen on the slightly synthetic sugary taste of most sports drinks.

"No. We don't live in each other's pockets, I told you, but we get on well. We're both into sport, and we look out for each other." Tony clocked Steve's hesitation, and smiled reassuringly, "I sell them at the gym sometimes and get them in bulk off the supplier. They're endorsed by an Olympic swimmer." He rattled off a few names of a couple of top athletes, all who apparently used this particular brand of sports drink.

"What about Charles's family and other close friends? How well does he get on with his brothers?" Dove bit her lip to stop herself grinning as Steve took a sip, coughed, and pulled a face.

"Yeah, good." Tony sat opposite them on the edge of the sofa, big shoulders hunched as he cradled his bottle of drink. "Mikey is a grumpy bastard, but he's all right, and Ben's a top bloke. Their dad, he's never been averse to the quick cash payment in exchange for ringing a few cars, but he's mostly sound." He thought for a moment. "Charles is pretty popular. He's a nice bloke, doesn't wind people up, you know? He's been seeing Anne-Marie for a few months now . . . It's lasted quite a long time for him."

"Anne-Marie who?" Steve screwed the top back on his sports drink and placed it carefully on the side table. "If you have a surname, a number — any way we can get in contact with her . . ."

Tony nodded. "Anne-Marie Parsons. She works at the new Hanson's gym, on the industrial estate, but I dunno where she lives. Poor girl. I told her about Charles, and she just didn't say a word for a bit, and then she started crying . . ."

Steve made a few notes. "I know the place. I've been working out there myself, actually."

"Have you? Let me know if you need any personal training, and I can recommend a couple of people. Starting with me, of course," Tony said seriously. "I'm tough, but I get results. Didn't like the restrictions at the gym, so I went freelance. I've got a lot of clients now. I'd suggested to Charles we might go into business together, share the load, but he said he wouldn't until he had enough money to pay his way. Anne-Marie was going to come in with us too, we had it all planned out . . ." Anger was creeping back into his voice, and he suddenly smashed a fist into the coffee table, making both officers jump, and several magazines slide to the floor. "Bastard! Who would have killed him? If I could only get my bloody hands on him right now!"

"We are doing everything we can to find out, and you are being extremely helpful. Do you think it might be possible

Charles went off to earn some money for your new business, nothing to do with the car yard?" Dove queried, deciding a quick subject change was in order after the display of anger. Interestingly, Tony seemed to have a lot of pent-up rage, which jarred with the laid-back persona he had presented so far during the interview. It might be Charles's death, of course. She quite often saw grief expressed as rage, and it appeared they had been very close . . .

"Yeah, I suppose. He was kind of different about this trip, I think, and excited, like I said. I'm worried he got in too deep in some car deal, because he wanted to cut ties with the yard," Tony sighed, his expression still set and angry. "You need to catch the bastard who killed him. He didn't deserve this, whatever he got himself into."

Steve picked up the energy drink, put it down again and asked another question: "Did Charles take any kind of drugs?"

Tony's eyes opened wide with shock. "No chance, mate, he was a sports professional, like me. We don't touch shit like that. Almost as bad as all this diet stuff. Artificial and chemical things we don't need to stay healthy. It messes with your body. The only way to do it is to train hard and eat clean." He stopped, and smiled apologetically, sadly. "Sorry, I get a bit preachy on that subject, but it is my job. Charles was just the same."

"If you could just read through and sign your statement . . ." Steve slid the paperwork over to Tony, who began to scan through.

"Yeah, I'm fine with that. I just . . . I know everyone must say it, but I can't believe this is happening . . ." He sniffed hard and wiped the back of his hand across his eyes like a kid. "Sorry, it chokes me up a bit."

"We understand," Steve said. "Hey, do you have a business card, so I can call you about personal training?"

"Oh . . . I do, yeah." Tony's expression brightened a little, and he opened a drawer in the counter, shoving a couple of cards at Steve. "Take a bottle with you, too . . ."

Steve took the business card in one hand, the brightly labelled energy drink in the other, and shifted uncomfortably. Dove suppressed a grin. "Do you mind if we have a look around Charles's room? We won't touch anything, and someone will be over shortly for a thorough check, if that's okay?"

"Sure. Anything that might help get him justice." He sighed. "Charles was a nice bloke, you know? Not the kind to fall out with people. He just did his thing and got on with life. I keep expecting him to walk through the door with that bloody big smile of his, telling me this was just a shit joke . . ."

* * *

They slipped on gloves before opening the bedroom door, stepping carefully into the dead man's domain. Charles's room overlooked the back garden, and the window was half obscured by dark ivy leaves, which were in turn coated with a sprinkling of frost. The bright day and clean winter sunlight showed up dusty surfaces, but the clothes hanging on the back of the door, and folded into drawers, were well ordered.

"I don't know how many clothes he has but it doesn't look like he took much for a six-week absence," Dove observed. Her gaze lit on a shelf of sports shoes. They were arranged precisely in pairs and there were two rows, so it was easy to see four pairs appeared to be missing.

She noted gaps on the dusty desk where presumably a computer or tablet might have been set up. The bed frame was also coated with a fine layer of dust. No mobile phone, though, so presumably he had taken it with him.

"Hey, look at this." Dove drew Steve's attention to the window ledge. The curtain was half-obscuring it, but a small chess set was set up on the wide ledge. The carved wooden pieces were covered in dust but arranged ready for a game. She snapped a picture on her phone.

"A link to the crime scene?" Steve wondered. "Or maybe he just likes a game of chess. Funny, Tony doesn't strike me as a chess player, so maybe Charles played board games with his girlfriend."

A pile of health and fitness magazines lay next to the double bed, which was neatly made with the navy quilt drawn up to matching pillowcases. A stack of car magazines and car auction lists peeped out from underneath a small table. There were a few toiletries on the chest of drawers and a collection of framed photos above the bed.

Dove leaned over to see better. Family groups — she recognized the parents, brothers, and Tony. A pretty red-haired girl — Anne-Marie? Holidays with his friends — looked like he was into a few daredevil sports, including skydiving and bungee jumping. Lots of happy, laughing party photos . . .

"Nothing else is jumping out at me. Shall we leave it for the SOCOs?" Steve suggested, with a glance at his watch.

"Me neither. A normal twenty-two-year-old with a passion for sports and cars," Dove summarized in disappointment. "We can chase up his girlfriend, Anne-Marie, next. Hanson's isn't far, and we can beat the rush hour if we hurry."

Tony was on the phone when they went back out to the kitchen area, and he waved them towards the front door, mouthing 'call me' to Steve, but they waited until he finished. Dove put in a quick question about the chess set in Charles's room.

"He liked chess, but mostly played online. I hate board games," Tony told them. "Oh, I think he's still got a set in his room that belonged to his mum . . . Thinking about it, I'm sure he said his mum used to be some kind of chess champion when she was a teenager. Kind of cool, I thought . . . Is it important?"

"Probably not, and it's all right, we've seen it. Thanks, Tony." With the statement in the bag, they headed off, Dove making a quick call to update the DI.

"Thanks. I presume you two are going off to find the girlfriend next?" Jon asked briskly.

"We are. She works at Hanson's gym, which is actually opposite Ski and Sky. We'll ring you if we get anything interesting," Dove said, checking her watch. It was past five, and her stomach was grumbling.

"Okay. Just to keep you in the loop as you're doing crossover onto Hibbs, we checked into Tessa's background. Before she left her husband she was a GP, a locum at a couple of surgeries in her area. Before that she worked in A&E at a couple of hospitals. Always up in Manchester."

"But she didn't work as a doctor after she left Hibbs?" Dove queried, unable to imagine why someone would leave such a demanding and lucrative career behind, even if she had struggled with an abusive husband. Perhaps she had been planning to return to medicine when her daughters were older. The picture of Tessa Jackson reformed in her mind.

"No. Her family seems be to supporting her and her bank accounts indicate she has savings. Sorry to add to your to-do list, but with this flu epidemic we're going to be short-handed, and if Hibbs is going to be in the clear, I want him crossed off the list as soon as possible so we don't waste any more time," Jon said.

"No worries, me and Steve are good." She ended the call, pulled into the McDonald's drive-thru and ordered a burger and fries. "Do you want anything?"

Steve shook his head firmly. "Just a coffee. I'll get a sandwich when I get home later. I shouldn't have scoffed that BLT for lunch."

"If you were hungry, you obviously needed it. You'll be starving by the time we get finished tonight," Dove told him. When her order popped out the end window, she chucked him a fruit bag. "Eat something before you keel over on me."

He was laughing. "God, you're so bossy. How does Quinn put up with you?"

She pulled into a layby, and took a massive bite of her burger, speaking with her mouth full. "Simple. He's just as bossy as I am, and we share a love of surfing and junk food. The perfect relationship!"

He ate his fruit without enthusiasm. "Have you set a date for the wedding yet?"

"Next year, probably spring and maybe on a beach somewhere."

"Cornwall? Barbados?"

Dove loved the West Country and she and Quinn liked to sneak down there during any snatched time off to enjoy the sea, the countryside and the quieter pace of life.

"Don't know yet. We were just about to start doing some serious planning when this frozen body popped up." She scrunched her paper bag into a ball and chucked it down onto the floor. "Let's get moving."

With the heater on full blast, Dove drove carefully towards the gym, hoping she would be able to make her date with her sisters Thursday night. They would understand if she blew them off right in the middle of an investigation, but she really wanted to see them. The little piece of sanity that kept her anchored extended from Quinn to her family, and it was lovely to talk about normal things, wedding planning, business plans, gossip . . .

Occasionally, she caught up with her globe-trotting parents too, but they were generally to be found in their commune in California or trekking through jungles and across deserts. Her unusual childhood had fostered independence, but it was only in the last few years she had realized that true independence didn't have to mean cutting yourself off from everything and everyone. It meant giving yourself the choice about who you wanted to be with and enjoying their company.

The roads were beginning to freeze again as the clouds cleared and an early evening chill descended. "Charles's brother is going to have a job driving back down here tonight," she said, peering at the star-speckled skies. It was only just gone 5 p.m., but already looked like midnight. The light afternoon sleet had stopped, leaving piles of tiny ice pellets spread along the roadsides and pavements.

"Hmmm . . . He's probably used to it by now. Seems like from what Tony and the mother said, the yard does a lot of business up and down the motorways. The weather's been crap for the last two months, hasn't it? Anyway, what did you think of Tony?" Steve asked, replying to a text as they turned onto the coast road.

Dove paused before she answered. "Genuine. Got a temper in there but I don't think he was lying about anything he told us. Interesting that Charles should be into his sport."

"Interesting how? Unless Tony poisoned him with that sports drink, which having tasted it, I can confirm would be possible, I don't see anything but two gym buddies sharing a flat," Steve said.

"I mean the numbers on the victim's chests. I can't stop thinking about the sport aspect," Dove explained.

Steve's forehead wrinkled. "You still reckon they were running a *race*? Maybe the killer has a sense of humour and he thinks it's a good gag to mess with us. Certainly bloody twisted, whatever it is."

CHAPTER THIRTEEN

The cold had permeated my soul. I almost felt I had forgotten what it was like to be warm, to savour the heat of a fire, hot water, the sun on my bare shoulders.

My mind wandered constantly over events, past and present, distracting itself to ensure survival.

I knew as soon as they questioned me what was going on, but I needed to make my plans before I gave anything away. It was still possible, then, to keep my life together, but only if I pushed someone to do the unthinkable. A little eye meet, a quick word, and I could tell he was on my side. In another life, there might have been attraction, friendship, but that was impossible.

Did I have that much influence? It shocked me to realize perhaps I did, and a twinge of guilt threatened to derail my mind as the idea twisted and turned like a fish on a line. I was all about trying to come out of my trials with family and honour intact. I had no thoughts, then, of life or death. It simply wasn't an option. How quickly things change from light to dark!

I know some people are evil, and I know some minds work differently. Nobody knows this better than I do. But to see it happen so close to me was still shocking. The truth had been interpreted in such a way that one might even believe the new version. Especially if one was then brought up in that very belief.

It takes a clever manipulator to do that. Someone who can gather followers with care, chooses a moment to strike, and carries that false momentum forward without a second thought. A chancer or a planner? I'm not even sure which, but certainly someone who has the ability to spot an opportunity and run with it.

I realize suddenly I'm not even thinking about the present day anymore. The past is blinding me to the reality of the situation, and the last thing I need is blinkers at the moment. More and more I find my mind drifts freely between past and present. So many memories, and sometimes they are crushing and violent. I want to push them away, bury them deep, but now I have chosen this path, and I will continue. I don't have much time left.

I will do what is right, and I will do it for the ones who didn't make it.

CHAPTER FOURTEEN

Dove pulled into the gym car park, which was crowded with vehicles and bikes. Even the outdoor floodlit courts were in use, with hardy footballers and netballers braving the cold. Everyone else was driven to working out indoors this winter. Even the hardcore runners and beach lovers like Dove were forced into using treadmills, rowing machines and kettle bells to maintain their fitness.

Steve dodged a swarm of yelling kids in karate suits as they entered the main building. The smell of chlorine was so strong Dove felt like she needed to sneeze. No wonder she preferred the peace of the sea, she thought, looking across to the packed swimming pools, set behind huge glass walls.

The receptionist was clearly harassed, already busy dealing with a group of kids wanting swim passes, and man in dripping swim shorts shouting his sauna ticket wasn't working. The queue to the tills was eight deep.

"Anne-Marie is working in the main gym today," the woman said shortly, in response to their query, pointing towards the stairs and turning back to her demanding customers.

The gym was a huge chrome and glass affair, with squash courts, gymnastics halls, an Olympic-size pool and a diving pool. The main gym was on the second floor, and Dove winced at the huge crowds milling around between classes and clubs sessions. "Do you actually enjoy working out here?"

Steve was puffing slightly as they reached the top of the stairs. "Sort of. I'm not really into a routine yet, but the trainers are good and nobody laughs at me when I press the wrong buttons on the machines."

"Plus they do chips in the canteen," Dove pointed out, laughing. "I wouldn't be able to resist those after a workout."

"You know me too well, DC Milson," he agreed. "And don't start on about offering to teach me how to surf again, either."

"Promise. Not until the spring, anyway. Let's get this done."

Anne-Marie Parsons was stacking weights and mats, her custard-yellow name badge clearly visible on her shirt. She was tall and slim, with long red hair tied into a knotted plait.

Dove repeated her introductions and suggested they might go somewhere quiet for a chat. They headed back out the swing doors to a café area and grabbed coffees from the till point.

"I only found out from Tony," the girl said bitterly. "Charles's bloody parents have got my number, and they didn't bother to tell me he was dead."

Her eyes were red and her face pale and pinched. Dove tried to comfort her. "Perhaps his parents are still in shock. We only identified the body earlier today. It may be that they simply haven't considered who they need to contact yet."

Anne-Marie shook her head. "No, it's because they thought I was trying to take Charles away from their stupid business. They hate me."

"How long have you known Charles?" Steve asked, sipping his coffee.

"Eight months. Well, we've been going out eight months, I met him a bit before that." She bit her lip and tears started. "Sorry . . ."

"It's fine, and we are sorry to have to ask you questions, but it might help us find Charles's killer," Dove said. "What

67

did you mean when you said his parents thought you were taking him away from the business?"

She shrugged, all at once very young. "Charles told me the car yard has been practically bankrupt for years, but he didn't want to hurt their feelings by buggering off, when his dad's dream was to hand it down to the three of them."

"Charles, Mikey and Ben?" Steve checked, quickly taking notes as she spoke.

"Yeah. Mikey couldn't do anything else, but Ben is a right slippery bastard. He could sell anything to anyone, so he'll be okay in any industry. I don't know him that well, but that's what Charles always said."

"What did Charles want to do instead?" Dove asked, unwrapping her cake and taking a huge bite.

"Him and Tony were going to start up their own business as PTs, and I encouraged it. Charles loves his sport, all of it. He swims, does weights, runs, boxes . . . and Tony too, although he's more into his weights. I said I could look after the books and marketing to start with, and train as a PT as well, if things took off."

"Does Tony sell sports drinks?" Steve asked.

"He has a franchise for ICEE, yeah. He buys in a load of drinks and bars and sells them to his clients." Anne-Marie leaned forward, enthusiasm overcoming her grief for a split second, "It could work, you know, our idea."

"But Charles was undecided?"

The glow faded abruptly. "When we were together, the three of us, he would say he was going to quit the yard, tell his parents, but the next day he'd ring me with some excuse. Like, his mum had to have some medical tests, or his aunt died, or his dad was struggling with depression . . . Lately, it's been the yard closing. He wanted to get them through the closure and then he was going to leave."

"He wasn't trying to raise money to save the business?"

Anne-Marie smiled wearily. She had very long black lashes, contrasting with hazel eyes. Her make-up was smudged and streaked by her tears, but she was still very pretty. "Hell no, I told you, it's been on the cards for years, the yard closing."

Dove studied her notes. "When was the last time you saw Charles?"

"On the seventh of October. He dropped into mine about 10 p.m. He said he was going to collect his stuff from the flat and he'd see me in six weeks."

"Did he tell you where he was going? Or why?" Dove was finding it hard to believe Charles hadn't told anyone what he was doing for six weeks, and his family and friends seemed to have taken his disappearance for granted.

She fiddled with a gold stud earring, biting her lip. "Okay. He was going to get some money so we could launch the business properly. I don't know how, and I don't think it was legal. I got the impression it was to do with another car dealer."

Similar to Tony's guesswork, Dove thought. "Did you ask?"

"Of course I did! But he shut me down, and if it was stolen cars I decided I didn't want to know. He was desperate to get out, but without the money we couldn't get going. Me and Tony have put a bit in, but my wages here are shit, and Tony pays the rent on the flat they share. Has done for ages since Charles couldn't afford it anymore."

"Did you try to contact Charles in the last six weeks?"

"Yes. He said not to, but I tried ringing and texting a few times. Tony did too. We were worried, but we kept thinking he would just come back like he normally does . . . He . . . he did call back once, and left a voicemail, but the quality was bad, so I deleted it."

"When was this?"

The girl considered, tapping the fingernails of one hand against her thigh, the other hand twisting a strand of hair. "November the second."

So Charles had still been alive then, Dove thought. "Could you make out anything he said?"

"No. It was really crackly, like he had no signal, but I think he said something like *I'll see you soon* and *it's going well.* Oh, and he said something about a cabbie, but I figured I must have misheard. It was like 'I'm staying with a cabbie' or maybe 'I'm in a cab' or something. I rang straight back when I realized I'd missed him, but his phone was switched off, and it stayed switched off after that."

Anne-Marie had nothing more to add to her statement, but when she'd signed, she looked up, frowning. "If he was killed because of some dodgy car deal, Mikey would know about it."

"Why?"

She dithered, but finally loyalty to her dead boyfriend seemed to overcome her reservations. "Charles told me Mikey is part of a group of ringers, took over from his dad. You know, they steal cars, re-spray and change the plates and sell them on at auction. Mikey is dodgy as hell and a grumpy bastard. You ask *him* why Charles is dead!"

CHAPTER FIFTEEN

They exited the gym into the chilly night air, and walked straight over to Ski and Sky, which was on the other side of the industrial estate.

On the way, Steve put in a quick call to his wife, telling her he would be home soon, and Dove left a message for Quinn.

The place was packed with kids and adults, skydiving in a specially constructed wind tunnel, or skiing and snowboarding on two long conveyor belts of artificial snow.

The manager, an athletic thirty-something in a bright logo T-shirt, told them he had bought the southern franchise for Ski and Sky six months ago, and it was one of the largest sports facilities of its kind in the south. "They've got an ice rink in the other two, so I'm hoping to add at least one facility next year. It was a big stretch, but I'm looking at record profits at the end of year one," he added enthusiastically.

Dove pulled up a picture of Tessa's ex-husband, Kevin Hibbs, on her phone. "Do you know this man?"

The manager stared for a moment and then nodded. "Yes, I do. That's . . . wait a minute . . . Hibbs. Can't think of his first name, but he's been down a couple of times from the Manton franchise, just to look around, you know. We're

71

a young business, and the management encourage us to inter-act with the other franchises."

"When was he last down here?" Dove asked, heart beat-ing fast. Any break they could get on this case would give the team a lift and the families hope.

The manager pulled out a logbook and ran a finger down the page. "Last visit was . . . thirteenth of November, and before that, thirty-first of October and seventeenth of October."

Dove snapped a picture of the relevant pages with her phone, running her eyes down multiple entries. "Why did he come so often?"

"I told you, we're thinking of adding an ice rink down here. His team runs that side of things in Manton, and he had to take measurements, check details . . . Is he in trou-ble?" The young man smoothed the pages of his logbook protectively, eyes darting. "Because it has nothing to do with us."

"We are just following up on enquiries," Dove told him soothingly. "To my knowledge Kevin Hibbs isn't currently in any trouble. This is just routine."

Most people didn't believe the spiel, but for peace of mind it seemed the manager chose to accept her banal assur-ances. He nodded briskly. "Well, anything else I can help you with?"

"Not at the moment. Thank you for your time," Dove said. "Oh, there is just one thing . . . I presume you have CCTV?"

"Yes, we do."

"We'll just come and get the CCTV footage from Kevin Hibbs's visits if you don't mind?"

The manager clearly did mind, and was desperate for them to leave, but he took them to the office, downloaded the relevant footage, which showed a pixelated Hibbs arriv-ing and leaving the centre. He presented them with the mem-ory stick with an air of relief.

Dove thanked him and could almost feel the tension dissipate as they walked past him towards the doors, towards the cold evening air.

"I think we made his evening," Dove said, glancing back to see the manager peering after them through the foggy windows.

Crunching across grit and slush as they made their way back across the car park, Steve expressed amazement that the building had been full of people skiing when they could do it outside. "Why would you pay, when you could take a board up to the hills and play in the real snow?"

"Because it's warmer in there?" Dove suggested, banging her gloved hands together and stamping her feet. "Come on, let's crack on and get our reports in before the briefing. I'm dead on my feet, and you must be feeling even worse."

The evening brief was at 8 p.m., short and to the point. DCI Franklin looked exhausted, with his tie askew and coffee stains on one shirt sleeve. But, as usual, he exuded energy and optimism. "Progress report, and then we take a break for the night." He looked at Dove and Steve and nodded. "Charles Richardson, last movements, please . . ."

"He worked for the family firm, a car yard, was well liked, enjoyed his sports, nothing spiked when we talked to the parents. His elder brother was driving back down from Leeds, but has been delayed by traffic, so we are seeing him in the morning. His parents have no idea where he was, ditto his flatmate, Tony Garner," Steve summarized, reading from the notes. "We also checked in with Charles's girlfriend, Anne-Marie Parsons. According to her, Charles was wrapping up the family business and off to start a new one with her and his flatmate. He told her that's what the money was for, and she thinks he was going to earn it by doing some illegal car deals."

"Good," the DCI said crisply. "Jon? What do we have on Tessa Jackson?"

"She has not used bank cards, her mobile phone, made any withdrawals at cash points, or been on any social media sites. The white van on the CCTV is our best possible lead, and we now know it came into Lea Down from the A36 off junction 11 at 2.30 a.m. It was caught on the cameras at traffic lights on Green Lane and again on West Park Road. The plates trace back to a Mr Oliver Grinell, who reported it stolen three weeks ago. He was at a running club meeting, left his van opposite the gym because the car park was full, and when he came back out, it was gone. No CCTV, because it was parked on the opposite side of the road to the Hanson's car park."

Dove considered this, leaning against the wall of the briefing room, biting a thumbnail. "Charles Richardson's girlfriend works at that gym. Tony and Charles both worked out there. Ski and Sky is on the same industrial estate."

"Okay, so we have possible links . . . Make sure you give that lead priority tomorrow. We need to dig further into where the hell Charles was for six weeks while he was 'making money'," the DI said.

"Yes, boss."

"Lindsey?" DCI Franklin said, looking at her with raised eyebrows. His pale blue gaze, almost hidden by pouches of wrinkles, was still sharp and direct. He was an old-school copper, and put his heart and soul into every case. Steve often said it would kill him to retire, because, his life was the job.

"Kevin Hibbs is still being questioned by our colleagues in Greater Manchester. His alibi is looking increasingly shaky, and he does have a motive. He has also been down to the Ski and Sky franchise in Abberley, three times in the last two months, and in contact with his elder daughter." Lindsey checked her notes. "The daughter says her mother had no idea he had found them and was talking to her, but is adamant he wouldn't hurt her mother. She also says the last texts exchanged between them were about whether Hibbs should apply for visitation rights," she added.

"Anything from the family?"

"Tessa's sister mentioned she dates a little, but keeps it casual and hasn't had a steady partner since her marriage to

Kevin Hibbs. She only remembers one of the recent dates, because Tessa seemed a little uneasy about him."

"Uneasy how?"

"She can't quite remember, but she's sure her sister only went out with him a couple of times and then moved on. His name was . . ." Lindsey checked her notes, "Jeremy Masters. She thinks he was a doctor, or maybe a dentist, and says she thought Tessa might have been talking about going back to work after her first date with him."

The DCI picked up his paperwork. "Thank you, Lindsey. Okay, that's it, people. Go home and get some rest, and I'll see you all at eight tomorrow morning. Tech have indicated they should have something for us from the deleted emails by morning, and we should also have the tox report from the lab, which I hope will shed a little more light on Charles Richardson's death."

A skeleton night shift filed in. This included tall, stooping DI George Lincoln, who always volunteered for night shifts and was relentlessly teased about his far-from-ideal home life. He had been divorced for two years and lived alone with a tank of tropical fish. The only time he was seen to smile or show any kind of animation was when he was on the trail of a suspect.

This small group filed off towards the coffee machine, which had, luckily, now been fixed. Someone carried a box of doughnuts for an extra sugar fix. With Tessa still missing, extra bodies had been drafted in, and the night team would provide a sparse cover throughout the hours of darkness, clearing some of the backlog of calls to the crimeline number, checking social media links, and generally working through piles of possible leads to find that nugget of useful information for when the team arrived next morning. It was vital work, and they were lucky to have been allotted the funding for a night shift, albeit a small one.

Checking the time, Dove saw it was gone half nine, and groaned. If the workload continued like this, there was no way she was going to make dinner with her sisters on

Thursday. At least Quinn would probably still be awake, so they could catch up when she got home.

Driving home, the familiar worm of guilt made her clench her hands on the steering wheel in frustration. Checking her voicemail messages she picked up one from her youngest niece, Delta.

No answer from Delta's mobile, so she rang the home phone. "Delta? Is Ren okay?"

"Hi Dove, yeah, fine. Mum's gone to bed with a migraine."

"Oh, poor thing. Do you need any groceries or anything?"

She grinned to herself as she heard the teenager huff crossly down the phone. "Don't fuss, we're sorted, but actually can you call Mum and just have a chat tomorrow? She um . . . She got a message from Dad."

"She what? When?" No wonder her sister had a migraine, Dove thought furiously.

"A letter. He wrote to her. She showed us today. I think that's what triggered her migraine this time." Delta's tone reflected her aunt's fury.

"What did that bastard have to say?" Dove asked, anger boiling up. Ren's husband was in prison, and there he would stay for a very long time. He had betrayed his family in the worst possible way, been involved in sex abuse and trafficking. "I thought he wasn't allowed to contact any of you?"

"I thought he wasn't either. I don't know how the letter got through. It was really short. He just said he was sorry for what he had done and hoped we would be able to rebuild our lives without him." Delta's voice was flat, emotionless.

"Bastard. I'm so sorry, Delta." She was driving with her hands clenched so tight on the wheel her shoulders were rigid. Protective fury burned inside her, but she tried to keep her comments calm. "Are you okay? How did Eden take it?"

"It's all fine, and Eden was shocked, but she knows he can't hurt her now. In fact, it was her idea to burn the letter."

"Good girl. I'll find out how he managed to contact you and stop it from happening again."

"Thanks, Dove."

Dove drove along the coast road, radio on full blast, mind buzzing, exhaustion making her physically drained, but her brain couldn't rest. How dare Alex try to contact Ren and the girls? First thing tomorrow she would put a stop to that. They had all been so brave and strong . . . She was so proud of them for putting the past behind, for getting on with the coffee shop, college, and bringing up baby Elan. No way would Alex interfere with any of the good things that were happening.

She pushed her thoughts away from her family, and back to the case. The sports centre connection was interesting. Was Charles really raising money for his new venture, or trying to save the family business? Uniform would be investigating the possible illegal car dealings, and according to Anne-Marie, there was certainly tension between Charles, his father and the younger brother, Mikey.

And the missing woman? Even though Tessa Jackson's ex had worked several hundred miles away in another franchise, he had been down to this particular town for regular visits, with only his daughter knowing. There was no evidence he had been in contact with Tessa herself . . . But how had Kevin found his family when his ex-wife had clearly gone to such great lengths to hide from him?

As well as a catch-up with Quinn, Dove decided to ring Jess when she got home. Unofficially, just for a chat, and maybe to settle her thoughts on her best friend. Jess was good at slicing through white noise to get to the facts, and once she got the kids to bed, was likely to be found opening a bottle of wine and reaching for her phone and the TV remote. Her husband, Dion, also worked shifts, so she was used to the lifestyle.

Dove stopped at the little shop at the end of her road to pick up some groceries, including her fiancé's favourite breakfast cereal. It was sugar-coated and extremely unhealthy, but according to him, after a night shift it was exactly what he needed.

To her annoyance, the area was busy, and she had to park in at the side of the road just behind the new apartment block. It meant a shortcut down a long alley between the apartments and a rundown row of terraces.

The fence was high and covered in graffiti on one side, and the walls lined at head height with barbed wire on the other. There was one streetlight, right at the end, and she focused on it, walking briskly but taking care not to hurry, not to look scared.

It wasn't a rough end of town, but equally, it wasn't the coastal utopia the apartment developers had promised on their advertising board. The darkness felt claustrophobic, and she flinched at the sound of footsteps behind her, extending her stride, inhaling, gathering more oxygen into her lungs.

This winter, once she discovered the shortcut to the shop, the alley had become another challenge. On her last meet as a source handler she had walked out into an alley just like this one, had headed confidently for the road ahead. Had never made it out the other side.

Now she was trying familiarity to rid herself of the memories. So far it hadn't worked, and tonight was no different. The soft footsteps, the thud as another set of footsteps came over the fence and joined the first. The prickling feeling along her spine and the back of her neck, as though her naked skin was waiting for the knife. 'It's not real,' she told herself, and 'Nearly there.'

Sweat spiking on her forehead, heart racing and hands clamped on her purse, she gave in and sprinted the last few yards, unable to bear it any longer. She burst out onto the busy road, full of lights and bustle and noise, and glanced back into the quiet shadows. No figures pursued her, and the narrow path looked deceptively short from this end.

'I can do it.'

She recovered herself and turned into the shop, returning to normality. Adding fruit and vegetables to her basket, two boxes of Quinn's cereal, and a small sack of cat food for Layla, she turned towards the tills. The queue was long enough for her to dump her basket on the floor and slouch, hands in pockets, idly looking at a noticeboard on the wall.

The usual pinned bits of paper advertising kittens, cleaners and second-hand cars cluttered the corkboard.

But half hidden underneath the clutter was a more formal-looking card. Laminated and typed with a logo.

MEDA is looking for volunteers!

Are you male, aged 18 — 25, healthy with a high level of fitness?

We are looking for YOU to join our elite group of testers.

We pay between £300 — £3000 depending on the time involved.

CHAPTER SIXTEEN

"Shit," Dove said softly, groceries forgotten. She reached over and gently tugged the card until it fell from the board, along with several other notices.

"Come on, hurry up please, or I'll lose my place!" a woman in the queue behind her said crossly.

"Sorry, you carry on and go ahead of me," Dove told her, prodding her grocery basket out of the line of people with the toe of her boot. Several looked at her curiously, but she ignored them, swiftly replacing the fallen notices and rejoining the queue five people further back.

She took out her phone and snapped a picture of the card, sending it to Steve and the DI. The words were ringing in her ears. 'Going away for six weeks . . . Very into his sports and fitness.' What if this was what Charles Richardson had seen? And what the hell was MEDA anyway? Dove thought of Steve's joking remark about the energy drink.

She was about to Google it when the man behind her in the queue gave her a jocular nudge. "Come on love, every-one's moving, and we don't want to be here all night, do we?"

Shaking herself back into action, she hastily marched up to the till, unpacking her shopping from the wire basket. The shop owner was working on the checkout, and Dove had already previously discovered she and her husband knew pretty much everybody in the neighbourhood.

"Do you know who put this card up on your notice-board?" Dove asked, as she handed over a twenty-pound note for her shopping.

The woman peered obliging at the MEDA card, but shook her head. "Can't be sure without my glasses, and I've left them out the back. Come and see me tomorrow when it isn't so busy. Everyone's stocking up like we're going to get snowed in!"

Much to the relief of those waiting in the queue behind her, Dove lugged her bags out the door and turned back down the alley. This time, she was able to control her fears with her new discovery, and made it to the car park without any horrors returning.

Triumphant, she stacked her shopping in the boot, next to a snow shovel, extra blanket and first aid kit, and drove home, eager to check out MEDA for herself.

Quinn was watching a film on Netflix as she dumped her bags in the kitchen, and he walked in to greet her, yawning.

"Evening, babe, you're late. I feel like we haven't seen each other for weeks." He wrapped his arms around her waist, and she took a moment to lean into his solid warmth, before tucking her cold hands down his neck so he yelled in shock.

"Sorry, couldn't resist — and I miss you too, but you know what it's like when I've got a case on and you're on a line of shifts."

He nodded. "Communication by text, my lovely fiancée." He peeked into the grocery bags and started unpacking, heaving a deep sigh when he came to his favourite cereal. "At least I know you do still love me."

She laughed, kissed him and told him about the card in the shop. Quinn listened, frowning slightly, pushing his messy black hair from his eyes. He leaned back against the countertop as she poured them both a glass of wine, and stashed the bottle back in the fridge.

Dove began to relax as she felt the calm assurances of home wrap around her like a warm blanket. The cosy

Victorian end-of-terrace might still be in dire need of decorating, but on a freezing winter's night, Dove looked past the peeling wallpaper and exposed plasterwork. She would have traded any new top-of-the-range brand-new property just for her crackling log fires.

Quinn had already lit one in the lounge, and the pleasant smell of apple logs drifted into the kitchen. There was another fireplace upstairs in their bedroom and she had left it ready to light yesterday evening. It was one of a long list of reasons she had fallen in love with her home.

The large grey cat, Layla, who completed the little family unit, was winding her way around the human feet, purring rustily, her green and gold eyes slanted up at them. Her mouth opened and she uttered a single reproachful *meow* as Dove bent to stroke her.

"Shit, I forgot to feed her!" Quinn said guiltily. "She never asked or anything."

"She'll just store it up for future grievances," Dove told him as she put down her wine glass and picked up the sack of cat food. She tipped a generous measure into Layla's bowl and the cat settled herself to eat, tail curled neatly around her paws.

"I suppose you want to have a look at this MEDA company before you die of curiosity. You have that intense 'detective' look on your face," Quinn said, smiling at her.

"Well, I could do with having a quick look, if you don't mind ordering. Do you fancy fish and chips?"

"We need to start a health drive after this case, and when I next get some leave. All these takeaways, and not enough exercise," Quinn said, patting his stomach. "I'm going to put on weight."

"I think carrying all those patients will keep you fit," she told him fondly. "Steve's on a get-fit jag at the moment. God knows how he's managing to do that with the baby waking them up all night, but he's joined Hanson's gym, and he's suddenly scoffing protein bars and sports drinks."

"I'm not sure they have the right effect if you scoff them," Quinn said, reaching for his phone. "And I might join Steve at the gym at this rate. Cheesy chips or normal?"

"Cheesy, please!"

"You are so disgusting," he told her, but he was laughing.

She was already starting for the little room off the kitchen they called the office. It was more like a large cupboard and the walls still needed decorating, but at least it was private. She slumped in the chair and opened her laptop.

MEDA seemed to be a legitimate enterprise, and there was certainly a link to the fitness theory, which was tugging at the frayed edges of her mind.

According to the official website it was 'One of the UK's biggest private testing facilities . . .' It provided laboratory space and equipment, and specialist medical staff from all fields, who could, it appeared, provide the necessary expertise for just about any clinical trial. Dove recognized several clients listed, including many from the health and fitness arena: supplements, vitamins, diet drinks. Other clients were from the cosmetic industry or the medical field. High profile clients testing vaccines, researching cancer cures . . . This wasn't a backyard business, it was massive.

The contact page showed a business address twenty miles away, just off the A34, and numerous phone numbers and emails. The logo was the same as the graphic on the card she had brought home from the shop, but it seemed odd such an obviously well-respected and established business should be touting in corner shops. She flipped back to the contact page. Yes, there was an email address and a downloadable application form for those who wanted to be part of the clinical trials. None of the phone numbers listed matched the mobile number on the card.

She scanned through the list of directors, before scrolling onto the next page, which went on to the list of medical professionals. There were over a hundred, with their specialities listed underneath photographs. Cardiologists, nutritionists, neurologists, sports science experts, paediatricians . . . This was a well-organized machine.

Dove scrolled down the pages of the medical professionals, clicking occasionally to enlarge biographies, concentrating on those involved in the sports and fitness industries.

One name caught her attention and she frowned, before remembering the evening briefing. Lindsey had added a photograph to Tessa's timeline as she left the room, and Dove had glanced at the board, noting the picture-perfect features and big smile. The photograph had a blurred quality, being an enlargement from a mobile phone snap. Suddenly sure her memory was correct, not bothering to open the case files, she matched the name in her head with the one on the MEDA website. By the time the doorbell went and the fish and chips arrived, she had it all right there in front of her. A biography and profile picture of Dr Jeremy Masters. According to her sister, who had provided the photograph for the timeline, this was the man Tessa had briefly dated earlier that year.

CHAPTER SEVENTEEN

The days were terrifying and at night, through sheer exhaustion, I drifted into a wakeful sleep, like a hunted animal who knows the hunter is watching, waiting . . .

On and on my incarceration continued until I lost count of the days, and nights. Others kept a tally of scratches on the wall or on their own bodies, but for me, the numbness I maintained, the drifting relentless hope that it might all be a nightmare, kept me alive. I functioned, but my soul was far away from my body, untouched and watching helplessly as my physical form went about its daily duties, like a shell with no inside, empty and mechanical.

I kept my head down, avoiding eye contact. Most days I felt barely alive. The smell of blood, terror and sweat, that had filled my nostrils the very first day, became sour and familiar. If you live in a slaughterhouse, such things fill the air and you breathe it because you have to, until it comes to your turn to die, your place in the queue.

I can't remember what it was that kept me going, kept my body functioning while my sanity had fled to a better place, but every morning my eyes opened and I began again.

Certainly it wasn't the thought of rescue. My hopes on that front were crushed early on. I can only think it was sheer determination and a lot of luck. My survival instinct was stronger than I had ever guessed, and it was put to the test time and time again.

Whatever thoughts may have crossed my exhausted mind occasionally, I didn't want to die.

I didn't get to make that decision.

CHAPTER EIGHTEEN

"So now you have a possible link between your victim and your missing woman?" Quinn added salt and vinegar to his chips and took a huge forkful.

"Sort of. I mean, I can't be sure Charles was part of some kind of sports trial for MEDA, but I can easily find out tomorrow," Dove said, licking her fingers as she splashed ketchup onto her plate. "But I can't see how a perfectly legitimate organization would fit with a dead body and a missing woman."

"I agree. Are you sure it's the right Jeremy Masters? Maybe it's just a coincidence . . . Didn't you just say there are hundreds of medical professionals on the list? But then you're the detective." He yawned, rubbing purple-shadowed eyes.

"Did you have a bad day?" Dove asked, suddenly guilty, worried she had made the evening all about her case. She was obsessive and selfish when it came to an investigation, but she was working towards creating a balance.

"No, just the usual." Quinn didn't often want to talk about his work when he got home, claiming he preferred to leave it all outside the front door, locked out in the cold. "Two cases of chronic hypothermia. Both should be okay. An elderly lady living on her own had a fall and it took three days for the neighbours to get worried, and a guy sleeping rough under the pier. He thought a bottle of White Lightning would be a better bet than a hostel for the night. Hopefully, we persuaded him otherwise, and he remembers next time he has to make the choice."

"Have you ever had a patient frozen solid?" Dove queried, finishing her wine.

"Can't say I have." He smiled as she put her glass down and nestled up against his shoulder, inhaling deeply, relaxing for the first time in hours. "Don't want to, either. I prefer to find patients when I have at least a sporting chance of saving their lives."

Before they went to bed, Dove couldn't resist putting in a quick call to the DI. Quinn was in the shower, and she finished locking up the house for the night as she spoke, phone wedged between shoulder and chin.

"I thought you were going home to get some rest, Dove?" Jon had a slight note of amused exasperation in his voice when he answered.

She summarized her discovery and listened to the silence as he digested the new information, while she struggled with the rusty lock on the back door. They really needed to get around to replacing it.

"We don't have a link between the murder victim and MEDA yet," he pointed out. "Sounds more like a perfectly legitimate company has been used as a dupe by someone wanting to pull in a few likely victims."

"Victims plural?"

"I hope not, but possible, as we've said from the start."

"No actual link, you're right, but if Tessa dated one of the doctors it does give us a start from her end of the case. It seems like the kind of thing that might have attracted Charles Richardson. He fulfilled the criteria, and he definitely needed the money. It might be the information we needed to link them together?"

"There's no clue on the website as to what trials MEDA are currently running?" the DI queried.

"Loads. They seem to work with a lot of sports and fitness brands, among others. I want to talk to the girlfriend and Tony Garner again tomorrow."

"Okay, see if you can connect Charles to MEDA. It'll give us better grounds for investigating the tentative link. Good work, Dove. Now for god's sake, get some rest and I'll see you in the morning."

* * *

Dove woke early, stirring when her fiancé slipped out for work, returning his kiss before waking properly two hours later. Her brain was still spinning with possible theories, so she showered quickly and went straight down to her computer, scanning the MEDA site, pulling out strands of information, and saving it to her work files.

Quinn had left a note on the kitchen counter, and she scanned it with interest as she sipped her second latte.

I'm sure Jess thought of this and obvs with no evidence of drowning might not work, but you mentioned about sports — what if he was swimming? Immersion hypothermia would get someone to lose heat very quickly. Not ice cube cold, but enough to trigger unconsciousness if he stayed in too long? Or fell in?

See you later, babe xxx

Dove tapped the piece of paper thoughtfully, rereading several times before she picked it up and shoved it in her pocket. Maybe . . . She would ring Jess as soon as she got to work. Shame she hadn't managed to chat to her friend last night, but the precious moments with Quinn were few and far between at the moment. He worked four early shifts, followed by three nights, before five days off, and when that clashed with an MCT investigation they literally did, as he had said, communicate by text.

Her breath blew clouds into the icy air, and the houses were frosted with sprinkles and spikes. The new apartment block overlooking the beach stretched tall and dark against the grey skies. Ominously dark snow clouds were gathering over the sea, but the roads and pavements were clear. The council gritters had done their work, and for now, at least, traffic was moving slowly around town.

* * *

As they packed into the briefing room, clutching coffees and notes, Dove grabbed Steve and updated him on her late-night find.

"Sounds interesting. I just got the latest from the night shift, and we got some juicy leads. Finally." He coughed and took a sip of his hot drink.

"Thank god for that," Dove said. "Are you okay?"

"Just a cold." He wriggled a packet of painkillers out of his pocket and took two with his coffee. "I might try whisky if these don't work, and bust my healthy diet."

"If you're sick, whatever goes," Dove told him, thinking his cheeks looked flushed and his eyes a little too bright. Glancing round the room, she noticed a few faces had vanished from the line-up, and others coughed into their drinks. Bloody flu was going to take out half the workforce at this rate. From the window, she could see snow starting to fall again in large starry flakes. The sky had darkened to deep grey, clouds edged like bruises with purple and yellow framing a darker centre.

The DI took a swig of his tea and started the briefing. His lean frame seemed more energized today, the fire back in his grey eyes. Dove knew, like her, he thrived on outdoor exercise and wondered if he'd managed to get out for a run before work.

As usual, he quickly summarized the most recent results of the investigation. "Right, so we know Tessa dated a guy called Dr Jeremy Masters earlier this year. Her sister says it was a short-lived romance and she ended it." He glanced at DC Josh Conrad, who nodded.

"We managed to retrieve some deleted emails which show Tessa was in contact with Jeremy Masters from the fifth of August till the twenty-first of September. They appear to have met on a dating app, seen each other a couple of times and then moved on," Josh continued. "According to the sister, Tessa quite often went on a few casual dates, but nothing ever got serious, and Jeremy was no exception." He glanced up from his notes. "She told her sister Jeremy '. . . was a bit clingy and weird. He liked to go out running in the rain, always wanted to go hiking in all weathers.' The sister got the impression Jeremy was just keen on outdoor sports, and Tessa is sporty, but definitely a stay-at-home-with-a-yoga-mat type of girl."

"These are two of our deleted conversations," DI Blackman said, pulling them up on the big screen.

Dear Tessa,
Sorry I missed your call, I was working. I'll give you a ring back over the next couple of days.
X

The next one was slightly different in tone:

Dear Tessa,
I've been trying to call you, and left a couple of messages. Hope you are ok? I need to see you — lots still to talk about.
X

"After Masters sent that one, it appears she blocked him," the DI said. "She didn't respond to either of his emails."

CHAPTER NINETEEN

"It fits with our fitness link back to the victim, if Jeremy Masters liked sport," said Steve. "But it's not so weird he likes hiking in the rain. I have a couple of friends who do Tough Mudder, you know, the obstacle course where you get thrown in baths of ice and electrocuted before you hit the finish line. And Dove likes to swim in the sea in winter."

Dove rolled her eyes. "With my gear on, and not in the snow. Perhaps Jeremy met Charles at the same Tough Mudder race earlier this year?"

The DI grinned briefly, before his expression turned sombre again. "Maybe. We'll check when we talk to Dr Masters. I've done a few races of that kind, and I agree it could seem odd to some people, but I think we need to take this new information seriously. The other news is we now have all the results back from the lab, and I have shared them to the main file. No red markers from the bloods, and the tox screen was negative."

"I wonder if Jeremy and Tessa knew each before they met on the dating app?" Dove wondered. "They both have medical backgrounds, even though Tessa isn't working at the moment. Medical conference? Online forum?"

Josh shook his head. "Nothing that we could find on her old phone or tablet, and we were very thorough. If she did know him and was in touch, it wasn't recent. Since we got the information about Masters, we're running his number through her call records, but it looks like she hasn't used this phone since 2017."

"Tessa's sister didn't mention any other connection," Lindsey put in. "And I get the impression the sisters are generally very close. Tessa seems to have been quite guarded about what she told her parents, though. They had no idea she even dated after she got divorced."

"But we still don't have an actual link between Tessa and Charles," Dove said thoughtfully. "Unless Tessa hasn't been abducted at all and she and Jeremy are somehow responsible for Charles's death? The initial contact between them was in August, wasn't it? Perhaps they set up some kind of fitness trials then, under cover of MEDA, and this is just a way of covering their tracks?"

"She wouldn't leave her kids, though, would she?" Lindsey disagreed. "Not from what I've seen and heard, anyway. Even if they continued their relationship, and faked Tessa's abduction to cover a murder, why leave the body in her front garden to draw our attention to themselves?"

"Let's bring Dr Masters in," DI Blackman said. "Josh and Kerrie, you can do that, please. Do we have anything else on him? Joe?"

"No. He has an impeccable record and works as a consultant; he's been at Abberley General for six years. Not only does he volunteer for the air ambulance every month for a Saturday shift, he also works occasionally for MEDA in various clinical trials. His speciality is emergency medicine, so he has worked on some pretty diverse projects," DS Markam said.

"What about his dating profiles? I want everything on this guy. Any other tie-ins with the medical staff at MEDA? Did Tessa ever work at MEDA when she was practising, maybe?" The DI threw out questions as he paced. "Joe, you get onto that as well, and liaise with Lindsey in case the family can tell us anything else. This woman hasn't just vanished into thin air. Somebody knows something!"

"If Charles signed up for a trial via the MEDA ad I saw in the shop, it was certainly a fake," Dove added. "I spoke to MEDA this morning and got through to one of the directors. They were adamant they don't advertise on postcards and are very keen to preserve their reputation. It sounds genuine. I mean, hell, these people are looking for cures to cancer, not messing with local criminals. Also, Charles Richardson isn't on their database for any clinical trials. I checked and they had no current record of Tessa Jackson, either."

"We need to find out who is impersonating MEDA, then, and why, as first priority. But I still want a team checking out the actual business. If it's that big, there is always a chance for some dodgy dealing at any level, so we won't completely rule it out that one of their employees or freelancers has gone a bit rogue. Jeremy Masters is looking more and more like a tangible suspect," the DI said. "What about the phone number on the card?"

"Burn phone. It's been deactivated, but we were sent the information over to tech in case we can triangulate the calls, or at least narrow down the area it was used in," Steve told him. "And Dove went in to chat to the woman who owns the shop on her way in this morning. She says she doesn't remember who put the card up. They don't charge for adverts on the board, and people just come and do what they want. She has a clear-out every two months when it gets too crowded, takes everything down and puts it in the recycling bin."

"Charles's flatmate, Tony, didn't know about the trial. Neither did Anne-Marie, the girlfriend, but she did think he was going to get enough money to help launch their new business," Dove added. "She said in her statement she was worried it might be a bit dodgy, but also that Charles is pretty streetwise and wouldn't get sucked into anything he hadn't checked out."

Jon narrowed his eyes, frowning. "Okay. You and Steve get started on tracking down this clinical-trial thread from Charles's end. If he signed up for this, I imagine at some point there would have to be an exchange of details, health records or something, or he would have suspected a scam." He paused and called over to Lindsey, who was packing her bag in preparation for a swift exit. "Can you push the medical connection with Tessa's sister and find out why she doesn't practise as a doctor anymore?"

"No problem, boss." Lindsey nodded briskly, gathering up her paperwork. "I've got a meeting with the social worker at 1 p.m. to talk about Allison. She says she has some new information which might be helpful. I'll head back to the house afterwards."

When Dove first joined the team, she had been wary of Lindsey, and the two women had clashed over a few things, but now she enjoyed her abrasive humour and admired her almost obsessive approach to her work — something they had in common.

Dove called Jess as soon as she sat down at her computer.

"Hi love, how's it going?"

Dove told her the latest, before she added, "Jess, could it be possible Charles fell into water? I mean if he was running and slipped into the sea, or even swimming outside somewhere?"

"I suppose so, but there was no evidence of salt water on the body, and certainly no evidence of drowning. His lungs were clear . . . Hmmm . . ." Jess was silent for a moment. "There are dozens of possible scenarios if you are considering this angle. If he had been immersed in cold water, say swimming in the sea, got into difficulty, was hauled out and able to stand upright, that could cause a profound drop in his BP and VF arrest. If he did have hypothermia, either before he was put in the freezer or as a result of being put in there, it has a big impact on the cardiovascular system, causing bradycardia which leads to hypotension . . ."

"If he hadn't been dumped outside Tessa's house, I could see it being an accident. I'm still working on the angle of a sports endurance thing . . . Perhaps he pushed it too far. You know, the race picture I sent you could still be relevant. If someone with him helped him, but then thought he was dead, panicked and popped him in a freezer . . ." Dove suggested.

"I do wonder about you sometimes . . . Popping someone in a freezer is not an accidental death. Bloody hell, girl, where is your mind at?" Jess demanded.

"They might have panicked."

"Nope. But say that did happen, you must have another person taking and displaying the body at Tessa's house and possibly still another abducting her. Tony Garner and friends? The brother, Mikey? You mentioned a bit of dodgy car dealing . . ."

"Okay, you're right, and we're still looking at everyone on the list, but it's getting longer every day." Dove was twisting her hair around her finger, frowning as she tried to imagine Charles's last movements.

"Well, it's up to you to shorten it, love. Gotta go, call on the other line," Jess said hastily, then the line went dead.

Dove sat thoughtfully for a moment, scrolling through Tony's statement. He had seemed genuinely devastated at the loss of his friend. Wouldn't Charles have shared the MEDA ad with him? Maybe even suggested they take part together?

"Right, you lot, Jeremy Masters is downstairs. Keep digging, and I'll see what we can get out of him. At the moment, he's our only link between the missing woman and the murder victim," the DI said, heading for the stairs, a determined look on his face.

* * *

Dove spent an hour talking to various specialists and employees at MEDA, checking out any possible links to Charles, but she drew a blank in all her conversations, growing increasingly frustrated.

"MEDA was a cover. Whoever did this just used the name to snag Charles. I haven't found anything to suggest the testing facilities aren't totally legal and no whisper of lawsuits or dodgy employees . . ." She broke off as her phone rang. "DC Milson."

"It's Anne-Marie . . . You said to call if I thought of anything else."

Dove mentally crossed her fingers and made an encouraging noise as the girl paused.

"I was talking to one of the other trainee PTs down here, and he told me he volunteered for this trial for a new sports drink. There's a card up on the notice board in the main reception . . . He . . . he said he shared the details on his Facebook page because he thought a few people might be interested."

"That's really helpful." Dove was grabbing her coat, energized and hopeful. "Are you at the gym now?"

"Yeah. And Harry, he's the bloke who shared the details, is here too."

"We're on our way," Dove told her, as she ended the call and spoke quickly to her partner. "We've got something from Anne-Marie and we need to get down the gym."

Steve reached for his own jacket, paused to cough and turned red-veined eyes towards Dove. "Let's do it."

She paused, already halfway to the door. "Are you *sure* you're okay?"

He coughed again and dragged a packet of throat sweets from his pocket, shoving two in his mouth. "Fine. Stop fussing and let's get out there."

Outside, it seemed barely light. The sky was dark with snow clouds, and as they reached the car, large flakes began to fall, sprinkling the ground with sparkling ice crystals.

"Great, that's really helpful," Dove said, "I'll drive."

He nodded without speaking and got in, wrapping his coat further around his body, which worried her even more.

The roads were full of vehicles hurrying to escape the weather, and the steady fall of snow was settling on the tarmac. They passed the gritters, but the snow was piling up faster than the teams could clear the way, condensing into a solid mass in the centre lines and pavements.

Shop windows cast soft light into the frozen townscape and brightly coloured Christmas lights had been hung across the main street, flashing a defiant green, red and yellow across the dancing flakes.

Shoppers, huddled in thick coats, struggled from building to building, and the weather forecast predicted another twenty-four hours of near white-out.

The gym was blessedly warm and the canteen served them coffee and cake. Anne-Marie and her friend, Harry, who looked about eighteen, sat opposite the officers, their faces anxious.

Dove introduced herself and Steve, but the boy didn't relax. His fingers were interlaced around his water bottle and his mouth was clenched shut.

Dove stated gently, "Anne-Marie says you might have some information for us?"

He nodded, licked his lips and pointed towards the far wall, opposite the gymnastics hall. "The card was on that notice board. I saw it a couple of months ago. Everyone puts stuff on there, and I was keeping an eye out for some second-hand weights, so I always checked as I came in for work."

Dove looked over to the board and then, hopefully, up into the high ceiling. There were large security cameras pointed in four directions. At least one should have recorded a clear shot of whoever put the card up. "We'll head over for a look in a minute. Can you remember exactly when you saw the card?"

He frowned and Anne-Marie nudged him. "You put a picture of it on your Facebook page, you said. What date was that?"

He started and fumbled for his phone, scrolling through images before he turned the screen towards Dove and Steve.

"The tenth of September," Steve said, making a note.

"And did you tell Charles about the card or did he message you on Facebook or anything?" Dove said, growing slightly impatient.

"He saw me at work and mentioned he'd seen it too. He wanted to know if I'd called the number yet, because he was thinking of giving it a go."

"And had you called the number?"

"Yeah. I spoke to this man and he told me it was for a trial to test a new sports drink. I checked up after I spoke to him, and this MEDA place is real. It all checked out. He said I'd need to be away for six weeks, though, and I had exams coming up. It was pretty tempting, though. He was offering three thousand pounds."

CHAPTER TWENTY

"Did you get his name?"

"Can't remember, sorry . . . I asked him where I'd have to go, and he said they were basing volunteers at a sports centre, and he would be able to give me all the details nearer the trial date. He said there would be a fitness test before we started, and we would have to sign forms stating we were fit and healthy." Harry was staring through the glass walls towards the swimming pool as he spoke, as though hoping to conjure memories from the scene. He picked at the edge of the plastic table. "It sounded real, you know, not a scam or anything."

"Did he say how many volunteers he needed?" Steve asked.

"No . . ." Harry screwed up his forehead, thinking. "Not many, I don't think . . . He might have said five or six? He took my name and number for like, future trials, but never called back or anything."

"Anything else you can tell us about the man? Did he have an accent? Was he okay with you not doing it, or did he seem annoyed, worried?" Dove prodded. "Any background noise during your call?"

"No . . . He was just a normal man. Quite well-spoken, with maybe a London accent, I think, but just normal. He

100

didn't seem fussed when I backed out. I think he might have been in a car on the hands-free, because it always sounds a bit weird, and I think I heard an indicator clicking while we were talking. Oh, he said something about a confidentiality agreement, because this was like a new product, and there was a lot of competition in the sports drink field. He said if I agreed to do it, I shouldn't tell anyone."

Dove thought this might explain why Charles had been so secretive. It had been bugging her that he hadn't told anyone. Perhaps he had signed this agreement, and possibly been told he wouldn't be paid unless he kept quiet, "Did you not think it was bit odd when he asked you not to tell anyone? I mean, how would you explain all that time away to your family, to your friends?"

The boy shook his head. "I already knew I couldn't do the dates, so I didn't give it much thought. If I had wanted to do it, I would have got around the secrecy thing in return for three thousand quid!"

"Did you speak to Charles about it again?" Dove asked.

"No. I went skiing with some mates and I only got back yesterday. I saw Charles was dead on social media but I never thought . . . Do you think this man at MEDA killed him? Anne-Marie told me I should speak to you, or I wouldn't have thought of the card." Harry looked downcast.

The girl rolled her eyes. Her face was still pinched and blotchy with grief, red hair accentuating her pale cheeks and freckles, but determination showed in her expression. "It was so obvious when I spoke to Harry this morning. He said the last conversation he had with Charles was about this MEDA advert. I would have figured it out before, but I don't do Facebook, so I never saw him post it." Her eyes were shining with tears suddenly, her mouth set. "This must be it, mustn't it? He wasn't going off to do a car deal, he went to test this new drink . . ."

"And the drink killed him?" Harry said in horror. "Fuck, I might have spoken to the murderer." He was fidgeting with his phone, now, hands shaking slightly. "I had a few friends comment on that post — I need to get in touch with them!"

"Okay, calm down. We can't make any assumptions at this point. We don't even know if there was an actual energy drink to be tested. You're right, Harry, we need a list of anyone who might have responded to the card. Let's go and check out the CCTV," Dove told them.

The receptionist let them into the back office. Anne-Marie and Harry waited outside, leaning on the desk, staring at narrow window of the office, apparently not in any hurry to get back to work. Dove turned her back on them as the security guard pulled up the CCTV for the past three months, downloaded it and handed it over.

Anne-Marie pounced as soon as they exited the office. "That was quick. Did you find the man who did it?"

Dove admired her fire, but was a bit amused at her assumption the police could do things in record time. "We need to review the footage from the last three months, which will take time. Can you just show us the card on the board before we go? And Harry, I need that list of your friends who may have responded to your social media post?"

"Right here, I've done it already." He handed her a sheet of paper with a dozen names and numbers on.

The notice board was about four feet long and a couple of feet wide, and covered in flyers, cards and even product samples.

"Shit, it's going to be really hard to see who puts what up here," Steve muttered in her ear. "Unless Dr M saunters in, smiles for the camera and pins it up, which I think you'll agree is unlikely . . ."

Dove agreed as Harry pointed to the space between a lurid green dance flyer and an advert for protein powder. "There it is . . ."

The card was exactly the same as the one Dove had snagged from the grocery store, except this one had a large red X across it and underneath the telephone number, someone had written:

MEDA ARE MURDERERS

CHAPTER TWENTY-ONE

Desperate to hear what had happened in the Jeremy Masters interview, Dove and Steve joined their colleagues gathering in the briefing room as soon as they arrived back. As Steve was now struggling with a sore throat and his cough was worsening, Dove had not only rung the DI with an update, but also driven back to the station as fast as she dared in the snowy weather.

Drifts were now piled high in driveways and in the park — where many snowmen stood sentinel, dressed in wonky hats and sporting traditional carrot noses — and still the steady flow of flakes continued, lighting up the darkness when they caught in headlights or streetlights.

In other circumstances, it would have been magical, but even the kids were tired of the cold, restless with staying inside.

"You are calling in sick tomorrow," Dove told Steve, and he didn't argue. He was done in, and even climbing the stairs seemed to be an effort. "Tell me if you need any shopping done, or you need anything from the pharmacy, and I can drop it round."

"Thanks, I hate to admit defeat, but I need to sleep this off. I just hope Zara and Grace don't get it this bad."

"They probably won't, if they rest and keep warm. You've been out in the cold and not had enough sleep," Dove said gently.

Jon called the briefing early, for 7 p.m. "Thank you to those still standing, and for those showing symptoms of this flu, just stay at home until you're better or we'll have the whole team down with it." His eyes picked out a couple of officers including Steve, who hid a cough behind his hand. "The weather forecast is against us, so we're wrapping up early today. If you are right in the middle of something, just take your work home with you. Tomorrow's forecast is better, so if we can still get in after the blizzard forecast tonight, we can crack on."

DCI Franklin joined them, a mug of steaming tea in one large hand. "We have taken a statement from Jeremy Masters, and he has an alibi, which checks out. He confirmed he went on a few dates with Tessa Jackson, but said it was just as friends, and there were no hard feelings when she broke it off." He paused to glance at his notes. "Dr Masters was extremely cooperative, as was his head of department at Abberley General, who confirmed Jeremy was working night shifts covering the night of the murder and abduction. He works an eight-till-eight shift. CCTV and colleagues have confirmed he left the building once during the shift on twelfth, when our victim was discovered, but he went out to his car and returned almost immediately. He claims he left his phone in the car, and was stepping out on his break to retrieve it. The phone shows no recent contact with Tessa Jackson or with Charles Richardson. Background checks show Jeremy Masters got his degree at St Mathew's, and Tessa Jackson at Marlow."

DI Blackman took over again. "Nothing of interest in his flat, but we have his computer and tablet. He has a very smart, very new home security system which he told us he had installed four days ago, and which enabled him to practically give us a print-out of his life since he got it up and running. Regarding our ice sculptures at the scene, we have identified numerous online suppliers, and two local high street outlets, which sell chess set moulds. These are being followed up at the moment. DS Parker?"

Dove, seeing Steve was coughing into his hand and unable to speak, added, "A MEDA card asking for volunteers was also placed at Hanson's gym, and one of the employees, Harry King, shared it on his Facebook page. I have a list of possible responders to chase up. Harry King actually spoke to the person behind the ad, and said he was male, well-spoken, with what Harry thought was a London accent. When we checked to see if the card was still there, it had been graffitied over. I sent a photograph over, and we bagged the card and brought it in, but I've got a feeling from the reaction the extra wording might have been added by Anne-Marie or one of her friends."

"Hopefully, we'll get something from the CCTV from the gym, then, in both instances. MEDA have been exceptionally helpful in sharing files and information with us, and I have been in contact with one of the directors. They are very keen to show they have nothing to do with the case and to prove someone has been impersonating them to draw these young men in." Jon added, "Whether one of their employees is involved or not, this is potentially very embarrassing for a company, so it's in their best interests to be as helpful as possible."

"So we are looking at possibly multiple victims?" Josh queried, "If the whole energy drink trial thing is a smokescreen we could be looking for a serial killer with a thing for young men. Our victim was found naked, so maybe the perpetrator is also part of the fitness industry and has found a weird way of getting his rocks off?"

"It's a possibility, but there was no sign of sexual assault. That doesn't mean the motive *wasn't* sexual, just that there is nothing at this stage to suggest it *was*." DCI Franklin nodded slowly. "So our next problem, apart from where the hell Tessa Jackson is now, is how the hell she fits into this case? If this killer is going for young men, why has he taken a thirty-three-year-old woman?"

CHAPTER TWENTY-TWO

Dove, who kept a stash of everything in her car, gave Steve a couple of painkillers and sent him on his way home, before she drove slowly back along the coast, straining her eyes to see the road through the sideways curtain of snowfall.

She couldn't imagine what kind of energy drink or protein bar would end up killing a healthy young man, so Josh's comment made sense. This possibly wasn't about the fitness industry — it was about trapping young men involved in that industry. A 'type'. The hairs on the back of her neck rose and she shivered at this very serial-killer profile.

Not only a type, but also someone who liked to display his work, and took such care with his victim and scene that evidence was scant. A professional, then . . . Perhaps they were wrong and the body wasn't meant to scare Tessa, it was merely an example of this particular killer's work. If that was it, she really, really didn't want to see what he came up with next. Was the chess left at the scene relevant, or simply adding to the smokescreen?

She had read the follow-up notes on the previous owners of the remote farm where Tessa and her family had found sanctuary, but there was nothing at this point to suggest the location was relevant to the killer. What did Tessa know or

— Dove bit her nails at the sudden thought — what had she *seen* that caused her to be taken? Perhaps while she was dating Jeremy, she had read an email or witnessed a meeting?

Quinn wasn't home yet, but she left him a note, fed Layla and had a quick shower.

Padding back into the bedroom wrapped in a towel, she picked up a voicemail. It was Ren, wondering if she wanted to cancel. She drew the curtain aside and peered out into the whiteness, shivering and biting her lip. But she was desperate to see her family, and the way this case was going, who knew when she would next get the chance? Ren's house was only ten minutes away. In good weather she often walked it, short-cutting across the footpath.

That would be impossible today, but she was sure she could get there. Tiredness washed over her, and she paused uncertainly next to the unlit fire. No, she would go. She yanked on a jumper, jeans, boots and her ski jacket, pulled her woolly hat firmly over her head and headed out.

Dove had been trying very hard, mostly successfully, to see her sisters and nieces on a regular basis. It was a big part of everything which kept her grounded, and Ren needed all the support she could get, after her husband, Alex, had been sent to prison six months ago. It had been a long hot summer, and all three sisters had drawn closer as a result of the horrors exposed by Alex's arrest.

Dove's parents had finally made it to the UK, enjoying time with their family, especially their new great-grandson, Elan, and rejoicing over his mother Eden's return from the dead. Dove blinked as a stray snowflake drifted past her nose, bringing her sharply back to the icy present.

The garden was pretty, even in late November, with holly hedges along the path shrouded in snow and two potted box trees outside the red front door. A beautiful Christmas wreath already graced the shiny brass door knocker.

Dove noted, as she always did, that her brother-in-law's former workshop had been demolished, the area tidied by the three generations of women and turned into a fledgling orchard and herb garden. Next year, it would be full of colour and scent. It was a peaceful place, with no trace of his evil left behind.

"Dove!" Her younger niece opened the door and hugged her. "You're so late, Mum thought you were going to cancel. Shit, this snow is crazy, isn't it? My friends have been off college for a week now because classes were cancelled."

Before she crossed the threshold, Dove said in an undertone, "I got in touch with a contact in the prison service and told him what happened. Just to say you shouldn't have to worry about any more letters turning up, okay? Up to you what you want to say to Ren, and if it would worry her more if she knows he got a friend on the outside to send it."

Delta was a smart girl, and Dove could see her thinking it over. "Might freak her out more to know Dad has a way of getting word to a friend, someone who still communicates with him on the outside. It isn't one of the gang, is it?" Her dark blue eyes were suddenly wide and fearful.

"No! No, of course not," Dove hastened to reassure her.

"I think I won't tell her. She seems fine again now," Delta decided.

Relaxing, Dove found herself swept into the warmth and bustle of Ren's cosy home. "No way would I cancel on you! Work is so busy at the moment, I have no idea when I'll get time off again."

Installed on the sofa, while the girls played with Elan on the rug by the fire, Dove sipped her hot drink and helped herself to a bowl of stew. Ren had a knack for making things cosy and homely, which extended to her cooking. "Is Gaia running late or did she cancel?"

Ren glanced at the clock. "She said she was still coming. Eden, shouldn't Elan be in bed by now?"

The toddler was crowing with laughter as his mother wriggled a toy next to him, showing no signs of tiredness.

"I'm just going to put him down, but you know he hasn't been sleeping well. I thought I'd let him stay up to see Dove and Gaia," Eden said, smiling at her aunt.

The girl had survived her ordeal and was recovering as best she could. At times she would go into a dark place, become obsessive about Elan's health and well-being, and unable to function except to care for her son. She saw a therapist every week and still took medication for her anxiety. Her long thick hair fell to her waist, and her dark blue eyes were fringed with dark lashes. Next to Delta, although they were so alike physically, she could have been ten years older instead of just five.

There was a knock at the door, and again Delta sprang up and went to open it. Gaia's rather harsh voice could be heard apologizing for her lateness. The elder sister was tall, slim and her dark hair was cut short and elfin around her sharp cheekbones. As usual, she was dressed in black, and her high-heeled boots tapped on the flagstone floor as she entered.

Despite her no-bullshit approach to life, Gaia had softened her attitude to her family during the past year, and now, as she grabbed her own bowl of stew and settled gracefully on the sofa, Dove could see nothing but love in her glowing amber eyes.

"So how's the case, Dove? Pretty freaky that someone froze a man, isn't it?" Gaia said. "No sign of the missing woman yet?"

Dove sighed. "It's tough going. The press interest hasn't helped and all sorts of crank theories are coming in. There's a press conference tomorrow. Tessa's family are going to appeal to her abductor to let her go."

Ren put a plate of cookies on the low table in front of them. "I hope you find her soon and that she's safe. Her poor family must be mad with worry . . . and the kids . . ." Her eyes were on her daughters, and Eden looked up quickly and smiled.

"I think I will put Elan to bed now," she said, standing up and passing the toddler between his aunts for goodnight cuddles. "Hopefully he'll settle better tonight."

Gaia watched as she headed up the staircase. "I can't stay long, because I've got to get back when Colin gets off shift.

He's finishing at midnight tonight. Not that we'll have much trade in this weather."

"He still working out as manager?" Ren didn't like Colin, and said he gave her the creeps, despite the fact they had only met a couple of times when she visited Gaia at the club.

"Yes, he's very good." Gaia's tone, as ever when talking about her business, was slightly defensive. "All the girls like him, even that snotty cow Jennifer, and he's great with the client parties. He's a real fitness freak, too, always trying the latest supplements, and trying to get the girls to follow a cardio plan." She snorted with laughter. "You can imagine how that went down."

"I might pop in for a chat tomorrow," said Dove thoughtfully. "My case is swinging towards fitness, and I have a few questions about the industry."

"Colin's your man then," Gaia agreed. "He used to be a personal trainer, and the guy is dedicated. He even got me to quit smoking. Ring him in the morning."

"Jesus, he's brave! No way would I get between you and a packet of ciggies," Delta said, and was immediately reprimanded by her mother.

Gaia winked at her niece. She had a soft spot for feisty Delta and seemed to enjoy their often sarcastic banter.

"How's work going with you, Delta?" Dove hastily changed the subject. Her youngest niece had decided to take a year away from her studies to work in the family coffee shop. Ren had privately said to Dove she wanted the girl to go to university, and hoped she would go back and sit her exams, but for now, she was happy to keep her close.

"Yeah, it's all good. Did Mum tell you I'm doing all her social media now? She's rubbish at it. I've done a new website too. Bollo helped me with a few bits, but it's mostly my own work."

Bollo was Delta's boyfriend, a tech wizard who happened to be a rugby ace as well. The two had got together over the summer, and even Ren, understandably overprotective, admitted he was a nice lad.

"Wasn't he one of the lads running that web vigilante thing?" Gaia fixed her niece with a piercing eye.

"Yes."

Delta got up to make herself a drink, and Gaia looked thoughtfully after her. "I thought you'd given that up."

"I have," Delta assured her, tearing a packet of instant soup, and busily pouring hot water into the cup. Her long dark hair fell forward to hide her face.

"Hmmm . . ." Gaia said, eying the stew Ren had already made, but Ren shook her head, urging her to keep the peace.

Delta's involvement in the online vigilante group, Tough Justice, had been instrumental in bringing her father to justice, but it was both dangerous and illegal. Delta had said she was no longer involved, but at eighteen, she was an adult, hopefully able to make her own choices in life.

"Back to the frozen man," Gaia said, "It's a bit extreme, isn't it? If you want someone dead there are dozens of quick ways to do it, rather than pop them in a chest freezer. Very exhibitionist to leave him outside someone's house too."

Delta giggled, and Dove rolled her eyes. Gaia was known for her often inappropriate gallows humour. It was how she lived her life.

As always when discussing a current case, Dove had to think quickly about what she could tell her family and what had to be kept private as part of the ongoing investigation. She tried hard to follow protocol to the letter, still feeling, even after ten months on the MCT, that she had to prove herself. "The press team put out a statement earlier saying we think the victim was possibly volunteering for clinical trials. Or that was how he was contacted and lured in, anyway."

"He volunteered to be frozen?" Delta's voice was incredulous.

"Natural selection," Gaia put in, wiping a chuck of bread around her bowl and sinking her teeth into it with a sigh of satisfaction.

"No . . . I really don't expect he knew what would happen," Dove said with a sharp look at her sister.

"I do see stuff posted about people wanted for medical trials. You know, like trying new vaccines or for studies into diabetes or whatever," Delta volunteered. "On social media, on forums for students, in chat rooms. Mostly legit — and my friend Abi, she's trying to make some money to go travelling, applied for one of them. It was really strict, and she had to pass a medical, running on a treadmill and taking blood and everything. She says it's for some kind of study into how age affects our muscle tissue and density, and if taking this new supplement will help. Lots of people had already been selected by the time she applied, but they still wanted five men over forty and five girls under nineteen."

CHAPTER TWENTY-THREE

"I suppose one group gets placebos and the other this new supplement. Which company is doing the clinical trials your friend applied for?" Dove asked, making a mental note.

"I'm trying to remember . . ." Delta wrinkled her nose, thinking. "Sorry, don't know. She applied for quite a few and got turned down for one. I can text her and find out the details, if you like? But it's legit, and she gets paid five hundred pounds plus expenses."

"That would be great if you could let me know. I'm not saying it's in any way dodgy. I just want to get as much information as possible," Dove said to her niece. Thanks to the swiftness of social media and online reporting, speculation on Charles's death and Tessa's disappearance had reached an all-time high this afternoon.

The MCT had an excellent media team in place, and they did their best to monitor what went out to the journalists. Despite this, there were always family, friends, or people who had known victims on an occasional basis who were willing to provide a news story. Often these were totally random and threw the general public in a different direction to the one the police wanted them focused on.

It was especially frustrating when this occurred after a press conference or timeline reconstruction. Time and money went into this, and, of course, the victim's family, generally distraught, had put themselves through the ordeal in hope of a result or closure for themselves.

"These clinical trials are bullshit." Gaia finished her drink and glanced at her phone. "You wouldn't catch me putting shit into my body just because some scientist was paying me. That's what lab rats are for . . . Sorry, I've got to head off now. Glad you are all ok. See you both in two weeks — and Dove, if you want to come round tomorrow, make it around five. Colin starts work at four, so you could grab him for chat before we open?"

"I will, thanks, Gaia."

Ren kissed her sister. "Stay safe, love."

Gaia, as usual awkward with any expression of senti-ment, picked up her long leather trench coat and headed for the door. "Say bye to Eden for me. I won't disturb her if she's settling the baby."

"Will do." Ren gathered the dirty plates and mugs and Dove stood up to help her.

Dove stayed half an hour longer, trying to force herself to be present in the moment, but her eyelids were heavy and her mind hamster-wheeled around the case. Where was Tessa? At every text from her phone she expected a call from work, leading them to more bodies.

One, two, three? Was someone experimenting on these young men and then freezing them to hide evidence? Jess had said it was incredibly hard to get anything from a frozen body, so anything ingested or injected might not show up. By why leave him at Tessa's house? She was a doctor, so maybe she'd screwed up somehow, and this was a warning to get back on track, or perhaps she really had stumbled into this by accident, and had been removed by the perpetrator.

Quinn was in the kitchen when she got home, yawning and getting ready to go up to bed. "Good night with the girls?"

She nodded, exhausted herself, but still stuck on the case.

"I checked your phone on the tracker and made you one of these, too," he said, smiling sleepily at her.

Dragging her attention back to her fiancé, she inspected the mug he was offering. "Hot chocolate?"

He whirled the dishcloth with a flourish and leaned back against the countertop. "My special hot chocolate."

She sat at the table, took a cautious sip and nearly spat it back out. "Bloody hell, Quinn, is this neat brandy with a dash of chocolate powder and cream?"

"How did you guess? I was thinking we should have chocolate for our wedding cake. With or without the brandy." He came back to sit next her, his own mug cradled between his hands, hair all messed up and green eyes shadowed with tiredness. "I've the week off from next Thursday, so shall we do some proper wedding planning? Assuming you're over the worst with your Jack Frost case, of course . . ."

It did funny things to her heart that he was so eager to get her down the aisle, so keen to talk about venues and cakes and dresses. She put her mug down and twisted her engagement ring, holding it up to the light, curling her legs under her. "Chocolate cake is good for me. How do you feel about that beach wedding?"

He laughed. "Shall we elope and get married on a tropical island?"

"Suits me fine," Dove replied, kissing him, leaning into his warmth and listening to his heartbeat against hers.

When she crawled into bed later, he was already asleep. She pulled the covers across her legs, careful not to disturb him. He stirred, muttered something and flung an arm around her.

The fire in the bedroom had been lit and the dying flames threw out a gentle red glow, making shadows dance on the walls and curtains. Exhausted, Dove lay for a long time trying to shut down her brain, but the luminous dial of her bedside clock said 2.45 a.m. before she finally felt herself start to sink into oblivion.

Her phone buzzed, and as she blinked back into alertness, peering at the number, Quinn muttered something in his sleep. The number was withheld. Rose. She hastily scooped up her phone and padded downstairs, mindful that her fiancé would have to be up for work in a couple of hours.

"Dove? It's Rose. Can you talk?" Her voice was sharp with fear.

"Sure. What's up?" Dove switched the lights on in the kitchen and gently shut the door, focusing her attention on her friend. "Are you okay?"

"I think so . . . I'm not sure . . . I did cut AJ off. I told him to sort things out his end and come back when he was sure he wasn't in danger, and putting me in danger. Fucking CHIS. Shit, it's 3 a.m., sorry, Dove, I'm not thinking straight . . ."

"It's okay. Tell me what's spooked you. So you sorted things out with AJ, and that's good, right?" Dove forced herself to speak calmly, slowly. Rose was clearly not ringing for a late-night catch-up. "Rose?" she could hear her breathing on the other end of the phone, sharp, shallow breaths.

"I think . . . I'm sure, actually, that I'm being followed. Someone was watching me today in town, when I left work . . ." Rose said. "I had some work to do and I've only just finished and realized what time it is. But I checked out the window and I can see someone watching the house. I've seen him before, but not recently."

"Bloody hell. He followed you home? Did you recognize the man?" Dove asked quickly, phone under her ear as she peered between the blinds out into her own street, mindful of a recent event, so similar to Rose's. "If he's still there, call it in and get someone round!"

"It's one man, I don't catch more than a glimpse of him, because he's always got his hood up, and keeps his face turned away."

"Have you told Chris you're being watched? Bloody hell, Rose, get off the phone with me and get someone over to your place. Why are you even calling me?"

"The thing is . . ."

"What?" Dove was still struggling to understand why Rose was wasting time on the phone to her, and not getting backup.

"This thing that was happening is this weekend with AJ. He got back in touch this evening and gave me some more details about this meet. We could stop this. It's going to be a war, Dove. Loads of stupid kids with knives, not having a bloody clue what kind of trap they're walking into. And I could stop it. If we pick him up in the car tomorrow . . ."

It was exactly the kind of thing that drove the source handlers, kept them faithful to the Unit, but if Rose was in danger . . . "Where are you now?"

"In the bedroom . . . I . . . Shit, Dove, I can see him watching the house. He's coming towards my building. He did the same last night and then I lost sight of him. I . . . I know it sounds crazy, but I haven't called anyone else, because what if I'm just being paranoid?" Her voice rose in panic and confusion.

"I can't believe he's at your bloody house! I'm going to call for backup. Even if you're wrong, at least you'll be safe. Turn the lights off and stay on the line if you can. Can you get out the back door? A fire escape?"

"No, I think I might have done something stupid . . ."

Dove could hear her moving, even as she grabbed Quinn's phone, which he had left on the table, and dialled up her old boss. "Stay with me, Rose, I'm calling for backup now — ROSE!" She could hear a crash and shouting.

"He's coming in!" Her voice rose in panic. "He has a key . . . How the hell does he have a key?"

She dropped the call.

CHAPTER TWENTY-FOUR

She was lying on her side, on the dirty floor. It was very cold that night, and I was so chilled even my bones seemed to ache with the pain of the ice outside. If only I could reach her . . . I stretched out a hand, my fingertips grazing her arm. The flesh was icy and in the darkness, but I could see her stir a little. She was still alive.

The next day he was back. My fears ran deeper as I watched his expression. He studied us intently, watching for a good hour or so as we went about our daily business.

The courtyard was frosted after another winter's night, and the ice had drawn lines across the stones, like a giant chessboard. I was surprised my brain had the energy left to link the images, but just occasionally I would get a flash of something that showed me I was still alive, still me. Despite the trials I was faced with on a daily basis, I wasn't yet completely numbed by the abuse.

Later the same day, there was the hard hand on my shoulder, the harsh voice telling me I had been chosen to help, that both of us were needed. The other woman raised her head, which was always bowed, chin to chest as she scurried around. But this time she looked up, and our eyes met.

"You have been chosen to help."

A tiny sliver of my soul returned to my body and screamed with fear and pain at these words. I knew, we all knew, what happened to those who were chosen.

CHAPTER TWENTY-FIVE

Dove clenched Quinn's phone in her shaking hand, listening to the ringtone.

"Dove?"

"Chris! Rose Greene is in danger. She's got an intruder on the premises. She thinks it's one of her CHISes!"

"Rose? Fuck, I told her to stay away from that prick!" Chris sounded furious. "Okay, I'm on it. Any other details I should know? Is he armed?"

Dove summarized the conversation with Rose as quickly as she could, hearing him grabbing keys, opening the door.

"Thanks, Dove, I'll let you know . . ."

He was gone. Out into the icy winter's night. Dove still held both phones as she pressed her hot cheek against the window. She could imagine the alert going out, Rose's frantic struggles to escape, and tears trickled down her face as she remembered her own terror at the hands of a gang who felt they needed revenge on a two-timing CHIS and had a hatred of police officers.

She was still sitting on the floor, clutching the phones, when Quinn came downstairs, yawning. He looked at her, puzzled. "What you doing? Babe, what's happened?"

The clock said 4.35 a.m. His alarm must have just gone off. Dove told him as quickly as she could, and he pulled her gently over to the sofa. "Sounds like you gave good advice, and we'll just wait to hear what happened. I need to get in the shower and get my clothes on, but shout if you need me."

She was still waiting when he came back downstairs and made coffee.

"Did you even come to bed last night?"

Quinn sipped his hot drink and held her mug up questioningly — *want one?* — but she shook her head, just sat clutching Layla on the sofa.

She was just starting to say she would ring Chris when her phone buzzed.

"Chris?"

"She's okay, Dove, she's all right."

"Thank god for that! What happened? Was it her CHIS?" Dove felt her heart rate finally slow, shoulders drooping as the tension left her body and tiredness returned.

She could hear voices in the background and sirens, fading as he obviously moved away from the scene. "No. It was her ex-boyfriend."

"But she was so sure . . ."

"I know. She'd cut ties with the CHIS, said you told her to, but after she took a call from him last night and what with something happening this weekend . . . Whatever you said really shook her up, Dove, but it wasn't just that, she's been taking on too much, pushing too hard."

"Maybe she just needs a bit of time out," Dove suggested.

"Yeah, maybe. I think her ex-boyfriend didn't take it well when she dumped him, and he's been following her around."

"She didn't ever talk about her personal life," Dove said slowly, adjusting her mental pictures. "And she certainly didn't have a clue it was an ex-boyfriend stalking her, or she would have said. She was totally focused on the job."

There was a brief silence. "Well, you know what it's like when you get wrapped up in the job, nothing else matters, and you can't see past the end of your nose unless it's CHIS-related."

Coming from Chris, who was known for his caustic comments and chauvinistic sense of humour, she realized how rattled he was.

"Anyway, I've got to get on. I'll get Rose to call you when she can, get you up to speed."

"What's the name of Rose's ex?" Dove asked. Quinn was making thumbs-up and 'I've got to go' signals from the door, and she beamed at him and blew him a heartfelt kiss. He laughed and the door closed firmly behind him, a blast of icy air settling in the tiny hallway. "Sorry, Chris, I missed that?"

"I said his name is Tony Garner. He was her PT at the gym before they started seeing each other. He hasn't said much yet, but he's almost falling over drunk, so we won't get much sense out of him until morning, I reckon. No chance of any kind of statement."

"Shit. Seriously? *Tony Garner?* What's his address?"

"Hang on . . ." Chris rattled off the number and road, but Dove knew before he even finished. "Why the interest?"

"Tony Garner is a sig wit in our investigation. He lived with our frozen victim, Charles Richardson."

CHAPTER TWENTY-SIX

"Fuck me. That's weird." He was quiet for a moment and Dove waited, "Do we think it's a coincidence or a connection?"

This quick analysis was so typical of Chris, and having worked with him so closely and for so long, it was easy to slip back into their old relationship. She said cautiously, "Depends what Rose says about the stalking, if he was ever violent towards her, when they split up . . . We don't have any evidence to suggest Tony was involved in either the murder or the abduction on the current case. I'm pretty sure any solicitor will be able to get him sorted with an excuse for tonight. You know, best friend just died and he was unhinged . . ."

"But if he's been stalking her . . . All right, thanks, Dove. I'll get things moving tomorrow morning and let Borough deal with him for now. By the way, I've been seeing human ice cubes all over the news, so I hope Jon Blackman is managing to make some headway."

"One human ice cube, Chris, and we're pursuing new leads," Dove told him primly.

Chris laughed like a loon, as she had known he would, and put the phone down. She was half relieved, half sorry he hadn't done his usual thing of trying to persuade her to go back and work for him. Why was she sorry? It was an uneasy feeling, because she had finished with that part of her life and was happy with the MCT.

After a shower and another cup of coffee, Dove felt awake enough to head out to her car. The radio informed her schools and many local businesses would remain closed today. The morning was crisp and dry, with a brilliant blue sky and a breath of bitter breeze coming inland off the sea. She licked salt and ice off her lips and breathed deeply as she looked down her road towards the path to the sea. Surely the weather would ease soon and she could get back out on the waves.

Insomnia was a sign of her stress levels, and she had learned not to ignore her body's warning signs. Whatever time she got back tonight she would have to do a yoga and meditation class. She groaned inwardly at the thought of taking time away from Quinn, or even from going over case notes on her computer at home. But burnout was real, and she had sworn never to let it happen again. Rose was another example of how reality and fantasy lives could become so entwined you simply couldn't see what was real.

At least the promised blizzards hadn't yet materialized, but despite the clear skies, fresh snowfall from the night was slowing traffic all the way into town.

In the office kitchen, Dove felt oddly lost without Steve to banter with, but she made toast and a mug of tea, carried them to her workspace and settled down, speed-reading her own reports from yesterday to refresh her brain. Rose kept popping into her head, and the Tony Garner connection felt very weird.

She called Steve at home, and he reassured her it was just the flu. "I feel like crap, but at least Grace seems okay now. Maybe she threw it off already, she's a tough little thing."

"Let me know if I can bring you anything," Dove told him. "Or if you need any shopping done. The weather's a bitch, and your wife's got the baby *and* you to take care of."

"She's doing a great job. I feel really guilty about being off."

"Don't be stupid, you're sick."

"Keep me updated on Jeremy, won't you?"

"We don't know it was him," Dove reminded him. "He has a solid alibi for the night of Tessa's abduction. He was working at the hospital, remember?"

"He's our only connection between the victims and MEDA. Don't tell me it's a coincidence."

"All right, I'll let you know, and stay tucked up in bed and get better. I seem to remember that Jon's car heater is crap, so I'm ordering more thermal vests if you're abandoning me. Last time you were off sick and I had to work with him, I wore jumpers, and it was only September."

He laughed, as she had meant him to, but ended in a hacking cough, so Dove told him to get some water, sent her love to Zara and the baby, and rang off.

She kept a watch for the DI but people were slow coming in today, some losing the battle against snow-clogged roads. Josh was in, carrying a huge pile of toast and marmite to his desk, and Lindsey was down to shirtsleeves already but still had a red scarf wrapped around her neck. Her short brown curls bobbed as she simultaneously talked on her phone and typed. Pete, the 'Donkey', FLO for the Richardson family, was slumped over his own desk, hands wrapped round his mug, staring at the computer screen. He was still wearing a black beanie hat on his bald head, and fingerless gloves. Dove switched her gaze back to her case file.

The list of friends who had expressed interest in Harry's MEDA post were currently being contacted, and the post had been taken down. But who else had seen the cards at the shop and gym? How many more did they need? She tapped her pencil against her teeth, squinting as a ray of welcome sunlight hit her screen.

Dr Jeremy Masters was a total saint according to his online profiles, and Jon had noted yesterday in the interview that he couldn't fault him. And yet something tied him to this investigation, she was sure of it. Nobody was perfect, however much they might gloss over their imperfections.

Jon eventually made it through the door, with oil streaks on his trousers and a soaked jacket draped over his arm. He surveyed his depleted team with displeasure, but still exuded the calm confidence of a general going into battle with half an army. "Sorry I'm late, guys, I had a flat tyre on the way in. Dove, we're still waiting on the CCTV results from the gym, but I'd like you to come with me today. Have a look at the Masters file so you're up to date, because we'll be concentrating on him. Lindsey, Pete, anything from the families I should know?"

Pete whipped the woolly hat off his head and consulted his notes. "Uniform have been onto the possible car-ringing business at Richardson Autos. Unfortunately the youngest brother, Mikey, has an alibi, as you know, as does the elder brother, Ben. The latest report from uniform looks like all three brothers, and their dad, have been involved in a string of vehicle thefts and re-sprays in the last six months. None of this appears to be linked to Charles's death at the moment, or to Tessa's disappearance."

"Good. Lindsey?"

"I'm pretty sure Tessa's parents know something more, but god knows what. Might be worth a visit, boss? I think we've finally found out how Tessa's ex-husband managed to contact his family. Tessa's sister let slip she has a few sympathies for Kevin, and she admitted she might have seen him in the summer when she went back up to Manchester in the summer for a hen do."

"And she didn't think to mention this before?" Josh said in disgust.

Lindsey glared at him for the interruption, and he subsided, grinning. Nobody messed with DS Allerton. "She says she ran into him at a club, and they got talking, but so far denies saying anything about Tessa. I've got her phone and told her she is going to need to rethink her witness statement if she has been in contact with him. I'd say that was exactly where Kevin got the address and Allison's phone number.

The sister is the leak. She's sent the kids over to the grand-parents today, so we can sort this out."

"Great, that's our other sig wit also discredited," the DI said in disgust. "What the hell is wrong with everyone? For those who haven't heard, Tony Garner was arrested early this morning. Just what we needed first thing. He broke into his ex-girlfriend's house and attacked her. He is claiming the stress of Charles's death made him crack. We'll keep an eye out to see how the case progresses, but I can thankfully say it's not something added to our list and will be dealt with by our uniform colleagues at Eversham Station." He took off his glasses and smiled thinly. "Right, crack on, people, and let's get this solved and Tessa back safe and well."

Deciding to push ahead with the background, Dove tex-ted Gaia and asked for Colin's number. Her phone pinged with a message minutes later, and she grinned:

Colin's number's 0975 885612. Don't scare him x

Colin had been questioned by the MCT during a case earlier in the year, and she was aware he would be slightly wary of the police. But at this stage, any insight, any piece of information was critical.

She tapped out his number, leaning against her desk, watching her colleagues hard at work.

"Hi, Dove. Gaia was telling me you wanted to know about the fitness industry, but she mentioned clinical trials, and I actually did take part in one a few months ago, if that's any help?" Colin sounded brisk and efficient.

"It might be and I'd be really grateful for anything you can tell me. Who was the trial for?" Dove asked.

"MEDA. They're—"

"I know of them." Dove felt some of her energy return. She glanced at her watch. "I know I said between 4 and 5 p.m. when I spoke to Gaia, but I don't suppose we could meet earlier? Like now, maybe?"

"It's fine. I've got loads of paperwork to do and the stock take, so I'll bill your sister for overtime," he said, amusement colouring his reply.

"Thanks, Colin!"

She drove quickly over to California Dreams, her sister's club, using the time to tick off key points in the case so far. Charles had been involved in illegal activity at the family car yard, but that didn't link to Tessa Jackson or Jeremy Masters.

Which left the little group of people connected to the fitness industry, and did include Jeremy. Tessa was still the anomaly, and Dove was beginning to wonder if the single mother had seen or heard something while she was dating Jeremy. Had he been planning illegal clinical trials back in the summer? And for what purpose? Money perhaps, if he had discovered something revolutionary in the sports field. It would explain why Tessa had suddenly cut off all contact. Maybe she even knew what happened to whoever had number one marked on his chest . . .

The club car park was almost empty, so early in the day. The club didn't officially open until 7 p.m., but Gaia took party bookings during the day in the festive season, and at any time of day or night for her VIP clients.

Dove imagined the weather at the moment was putting the punters off turning out of their warm homes. Her sister was in the office, phone clutched to one ear, but she saw Dove and waved towards the bar.

The club had just opened for a Christmas party. A couple of semi-naked girls entwined themselves sensuously around the poles, eyes bored but painted smiles welcoming, watched by around thirty men and a couple of women. What kind of business decided to come to a strip club for their festive celebrations, Dove wondered, half amused, half disgusted at the scene.

The marble and chrome, the luxurious leather and discreet air of money was Gaia's trademark, and however much Dove might disagree with her business, her sister had clearly found a niche.

Another club had recently been opened in Brighton, with the early indication it was going to be just as profitable as this one. Everything about the club whispered 'exclusive,' and the implication was that in this sanitized, high-class environment it was perfectly acceptable to pay to watch girls dance naked. At least Dove knew the girls were paid extremely well, and Gaia employed a tough door team to protect her staff, but even so . . . It just left a bad taste in her mouth.

"Hi, Dove." Colin, the manager, was stocking the tills behind the bar and arguing with a tall topless woman about her rota. "Won't be a minute." He turned to the woman next to him. "You can't change to Wednesday because Donna has to go early for her babysitter . . ."

Dove waited impatiently as, rota changed to her liking, Colin sent the woman off to get ready for work.

"Sorry about that." Colin sat opposite her, and smiled slightly nervously. His messy mop of blonde hair fell to his shoulders and as he talked, he rotated the leather bracelets on one muscular wrist.

"I won't take up much of your time," Dove said. "Gaia mentioned you would be busy. Can you just walk me through the trial you took part in for MEDA in October?"

"Sure, but it was all legitimate." He was looking questioningly at her, but she nodded at him to go on. Any detail might be important. "Okay, so you sign up online, and then get a call asking a few standard fitness questions. The trial I did was for a new energy shake aimed at the bodybuilding market."

"Did you have to pass a fitness test?" Dove asked, remembering what Delta had said about her friend. Her phone buzzed and she checked, but it was a text from Quinn. "Sorry, carry on, Colin."

"It's okay. So there were twenty of us, and we attended a two-hour session in the main MEDA HQ in their gym." His face glowed at the memory. "That gym is awesome. They've got everything! Anyway, um . . . they just took our blood pressure and stuff before and after, drew some blood, then that was it."

"And they called you to say you had been selected?" Dove asked.

"Two weeks later. I went back in, had a few more tests and then they gave us the shakes to drink." He pulled a face. "They tasted shit, and we had to fill in a questionnaire, so I wrote that down. Afterwards, they put us through a really tough workout, more tests and that was it. Took a full day because they were monitoring us the whole time, but I got paid five hundred pounds."

"Do you remember any of the doctors who were involved?" Dove asked. "Or recognize this man?" She turned her iPad round so he could see the screen.

"I don't know his name, but yeah, he was there with about three others," Colin told her, tapping Jeremy's photograph.

"Thanks, Colin. Oh, did you have to sign a confidentiality agreement?"

"Yeah, I did. I wasn't allowed to say the name of the brand we were testing and all that."

"But could you tell people you were doing the trial?" Dove asked, remembering how Charles's family and friends had been left in the dark by his absence.

"Oh yeah, there was no problem with that," he said, clearly surprised.

So whoever had lured Charles in had simply extended the truth, making it easier for him to sound legitimate. Jeremy Masters, with his MEDA connections, would know exactly how to make that work, Dove thought, bitterly. That poor boy, thinking he was making a bit of cash in an industry he loved, instead winding up dead.

* * *

Pleased with her research, she drove back to the station, snagging a slice of cake and coffee from the machine as she hurried through the corridors to the office.

As soon as she arrived, DI Jon Blackman tapped her on the shoulder. "Anything from your lead?"

"Just background, but Jeremy Masters was present at the trial he took part in. Nothing unusual happened at Colin's trial, but he confirmed the process was similar to what we know about the one Charles signed up for," she said. "No links to Tessa through MEDA?"

"No, but I like the theory she may have seen something she wasn't meant to when she was dating Jeremy. Trouble is, we can't haul him in again so soon without more solid evidence, and he has an alibi."

"He's smart," Dove observed. "We're chasing all over the place trying to find Tessa and if he's got her, all he has to do is sit still and let us hunt."

"He must be hoping we won't find her, especially if he's already killed her," Jon said dryly. "Moving on, then, let's chat with Tessa Jackson's parents. I want to go back to basics and recheck everything. There must be a history here, and we've missed it. Drink your coffee on the way."

"A history?" She shoved the plastic-wrapped cake into her pocket.

"Tessa and Jeremy," he said as she grabbed her coat. "I hate coincidences, and I hate them even more when I'm sure they aren't. What bloody idiot has hung bloody Christmas decorations in the kitchen?"

"No idea, boss." Suppressing a laugh at his obvious disgust, she followed him back downstairs, boots thumping down the corridor, and out into the cold.

Tessa Jackson's parents lived five miles away, on the northern edge of Abberley. Dove sat hunched in the passenger seat, and scanned the file and Jeremy's statement on the way. Her assumption that the car heater hadn't been fixed was correct.

"What do you think?" the DI asked as he drove out of the town and past the new estates.

"About Jeremy? Not much more, I suppose, apart from the 'why would he trash a massively successful career to murder Charles Richardson and abduct Tessa Jackson?'," Dove said. "Unless there is someone else involved? Tessa Jackson's sister was hiding information about her ex-brother-in-law, so maybe she's the weak link here too, somehow."

"I think Jeremy knew Tessa before he contacted her on the dating app," Jon said, turning into a tree-lined road and driving slowly over ice-impacted speed bumps. "We asked several times if he had ever met her previously and said no, but it was just the way he responded. He is very smooth and smart, though, arrived with his solicitor, was so polite I just wanted him to pick his nose or swear or something. You know the type?"

Laughing at his description, Dove considered this. "Okay, but if she knew him from before, why would she have gone out with him? You mean they might have previously had a relationship when they were younger and decided to try again?"

"Possibly. I told Lindsey to ask a lot of questions when the Jackson sister comes in to give a new statement. I don't think she's the brightest out there. It simply doesn't seem to have occurred to her that anything she did has put Tessa in danger."

Dove studied the road ahead, the dirty snow-covered pavements, the white shrouded houses and the ominously grey winter skies. "If she lied about Tessa's ex-husband, what else has she lied about?"

CHAPTER TWENTY-SEVEN

Tessa's parents' bungalow, covered in last night's snowfall, looked like a child's igloo, but the garden path had been cleared and they were able to walk easily up to the front door.

The DI rang the doorbell and a small woman with grey-streaked brown hair pulled back in a plait answered the door. Her eyes were red and her smile strained, but she welcomed them in immediately, hope somewhere at the back of her expression. Beverley Jackson.

"Have you found her?" Her eyes were red and her mouth pinched with worry.

"No, I'm afraid not. I did say on the phone we just needed to ask a few more questions . . ." Jon said kindly.

Her shoulders slumped. "I know you did . . . I just thought . . . I hoped maybe you had some news and you couldn't tell me on the phone."

Tessa's father showed them in and his wife settled the two grandchildren with their iPads in the next room, the door slightly ajar.

"Sorry to disturb you at such short notice," Dove began, one eye on the door. The children were immersed in some game and did not appear to be taking any notice of the adults. But despite appearances, these two were old enough to absorb the severity of their mother's disappearance, and Dove caught a quick anxious glance from Allison, even as she bent over her screen. She murmured something to the younger girl, Cerys, who looked up, staring as she recognized Dove.

"It's fine. Anything we can do to get Tessa back . . ." Frank told her, locking his hands together on the table, his shoulders rigid.

Dove winced at the thought they weren't able to offer even a glimmer of that hope. It sickened her they hadn't been able to find Tessa and the woman seemed to have vanished into thin air.

They started gently, with both police officers accepting tea and biscuits, the DI commenting on the shelf of football trophies in the hallway, and Dove asking about the Allison and Cerys. Sometimes a soft start was all that was needed to get people to open up; Lindsey had been adamant the parents knew something.

After the easy questions — already asked, now repeated by several officers — the DI said, "Can you tell us about Tessa? I mean, her relationships, friends, anything you can think of that might help us to understand her."

"Will it help find her? Do you think her disappearance has something to do with her past? We thought that her ex-husband, Kevin, was behind it, from what DS Allerton said, but now poor Callie has gone off to the police station this morning. She's been so worried about her sister." Her eyes were questioning and her demeanour flustered.

"Why haven't you arrested Kevin yet?" the father, Frank, demanded suddenly. He was short with narrow shoulders and his daughter's green eyes. "It couldn't be anyone else! Nobody would want to hurt Tessa. She's kept herself locked away since she moved down here, we all have, except her sister Callie, and even she's been careful."

Hmmm, thought Dove. *Maybe not quite as careful as you think.* It made her question the information that the sisters had been close. Callie had betrayed Tessa by giving

133

information to her ex-husband. "Did Kevin make specific threats towards his family?" she asked, following the DI's lead, coaxing them towards the harder questions, using ones they already knew the answers to.

"No, he didn't. He just used to hit Tessa whenever he got drunk and felt like kicking off. If she'd told me before she went to the police, I would've given him every single punch right back," Frank retorted.

"We aren't saying this wasn't down to Kevin, but we need to keep exploring other ideas if we are to find Tessa," the DI put in.

"You must have been very proud of Tessa for studying medicine. It's a tough choice," Dove said, admiring a bank of family photos set up along some shelving.

Beverley followed her gaze to a photograph of Tessa collecting her degree, garbed in a black gown and hat. There were other photos too, of Tessa and a few friends standing in front of the university sign, laughing, a young Tessa and her sister in primary school portraits . . . She smiled. "We were. Very proud, but I sometimes think that's . . ." She broke off and looked at her husband.

Dove glanced at the DI and saw he was also looking with interest at the photo gallery. "I saw Tessa got her degree at Marlow . . ." He pointed to a picture right at the back, which showed Tessa in a university sports shirt, arms round her team members, medals clutched in triumphant fists. "So why is she wearing a St Mathew's shirt in that one?"

The lightning exchange of eye talk between the couple was almost audible, but Dove was under the impression it was merely a sharing of memories, rather than an attempt to keep something hidden.

She was aware of the heightened tension in the room, but did her best to subdue the rush of excitement that flowed through her veins, relaxing clenched fists. Jeremy Masters had graduated with honours from St Mathew's in Northingly. He was same age as Tessa, but when the background checks were done, her degree was from Marlow.

Finally Frank shrugged and nodded at his wife, answering her unspoken question. He excused himself, saying he needed to check on the children, and closed the door firmly but gently behind him.

Beverley turned back to the police officers. "Sorry, he is very sensitive about this subject. He feels he should have been able to do more to help Tessa get back on the right path, to protect her, and he doesn't see why we should rake over old ground . . ." Her lashes were spiky and wet, her kind hazel eyes threaded with red.

"I'm afraid that's exactly what we do need to do," the DI said gently. "Often we can solve cases from details in the past. Things you might not think are relevant are, in fact, vital to the investigation." His grey eyes crossed Dove's and she saw her own gleam of hunter's excitement mirrored there. "Just take it slowly."

The mother nodded. "I would say Tessa had no problems in her childhood, or school. She was sociable and clever. Callie was always the wild one, ever since they were babies." She smiled. "Still can be at times. I don't think she'll ever settle. She's a restless spirit."

Dove smiled encouragingly, waiting. The DI sipped his tea as though they had all time in the world, and after a moment, the soft voice continued.

"St Mathew's has an excellent reputation and was her first choice of university. Her tutors predicted excellent results and she was in the swim team, the athletics track team . . . She seemed to have a good circle of friends, and she loved her studies. But one day, in her final year, she called me to say she was coming home. No explanation at all, just that she needed to come home."

"She didn't say why?" DI asked. "Not a hint she was struggling with studies, a break-up, a falling-out with friends?"

"Nothing. We both assumed it was the workload, but she wouldn't say a thing, even when Frank got angry." She met Dove's gaze. "It was weeks before I could get her to tell me. She and a group of friends had been out at a party. It sounded like they were all drunk, and the upshot was Tessa was assaulted."

"Did she report it?" Dove asked, making quick rapid notes on her iPad.

"No. She said she wanted to forget it, but she wouldn't go back, even though she was so close to graduating." Beverley hesitated. "It was a terrible thing to happen, but I always got the impression there was more to it than the attack. I thought for a long time she knew who had done it. I was furious at her for being drunk, for not taking care, and then for not reporting it. He got away with it, and she was left to pick up the pieces."

"People react in different ways to an attack," Dove told her, gently. "Tessa may have blamed herself, wrongly of course, and if she did know her attacker, she may well have been afraid to name him."

"I know. I'm ashamed to say I was angry with her, and Frank was too, but I felt so helpless. I couldn't do anything for her," Beverley said. "So she dropped out. Almost the worst thing for us was that she wouldn't ever tell us who attacked her, she said she was scared of him and she just wanted to forget."

CHAPTER TWENTY-EIGHT

"But she went back to her studies in the end, didn't she?" Dove said, drawing a quick timeline and linking Tessa with Jeremy. Same age, same university, same speciality. Could Jeremy have been the man who attacked her? But surely she would never agree to date him eleven years later?

"Yes, she did. We were able to help her get a place at Marlow, and she finished her course a year later. Her tutor at St Mathew's helped her immensely, and she tried so hard to find out why Tessa wouldn't seek justice." She paused, twisting a thin gold bracelet over and over as she chose her words. "I feel it was a factor in her marrying so quickly and having the girls. She had only known Kevin a month before they became engaged. It was like she was trying to do everything so fast, running away from what happened."

"And Kevin turned out not to be the ideal husband. Presumably you were glad when she came down here for a fresh start?" the DI asked.

"Yes. We had no idea Kevin was violent, of course. They were both always so busy, and when we did see them I never saw him being angry with her or the kids. It just goes to show you can never tell what happens behind closed doors. It almost seemed a repeat of her university trauma." Beverley sighed. "The phone call again to tell us she was leaving . . . running away and moving down south. She had planned it all, rented that remote farmhouse, cut all ties with him. Eventually, the divorce went through and she seems to have been happy enough."

"And you moved with her?"

"Not straight away. We were shocked and Frank wanted to drive over and have it out with Kevin. He turned up at our house before we moved, begging us to forgive him, saying he was getting treatment for alcoholism."

Dove thought of the Ski and Sky job, and the access to vans, to equipment, the freedom to drive between north and south with no questions asked. But also the consideration that Tessa's ex-husband might have worked hard to make amends for his past, to be desperate to make contact with his children again. "Our colleagues have spoken to him, as you will no doubt have been told, and it appears Allison has been in touch with him?"

Beverley pulled a face. "And it's Callie's fault. She told us last night how she met him. But she said he had changed. I told her he might well have done, but he should have gone through the proper channels if he wanted to see the kids, not sneaking around with Callie! She still behaves like a silly child sometimes."

It sounded odd to hear a grown woman described as a silly child, but Dove could see Beverley was torn between her terror for Tessa and her anger that Callie might have unknowingly put her sister in danger.

Tessa had been missing for four days now, and every hour she remained unaccounted for lessened the chance she might be found alive and unharmed. Like a constant ticking clock, a steadily beating heart, the sounds were a backdrop to every part of the investigation. Charles was already dead, and justice would be sought for his family, but Tessa could still be alive . . .

Dove looked back down at her timeline. According to her mother, Tessa's life pattern and personality had completely changed after the university attack. She had married quickly, and, finding herself in another impossible situation, had run away again. Could Jeremy have witnessed the attack? A friend of his at the party, maybe? But again, why would she hook up with him now, if that was the case?

"Did Tessa ever have counselling after the incident at university?" the DI asked.

Beverley shook her head regretfully. "No. I tried so hard, believe me, but she insisted she just needed to deal with it in her own way. And slowly, month by month I could see the life coming back into her eyes, so after a while I stopped nagging. Her tutor tried to persuade her too, talked to her so many times, and kept in touch for a while even after she graduated."

"Sometimes you can put a bandage over a cut, but unless the wound underneath is dealt with, one day, the layers peel away," Dove said, and then bit her lip. "Sorry."

Beverley peered at her. "That's okay. But I never saw any signs of the past coming back to haunt her. She's a brilliant mum, loves her life and her farm. Occasionally she has even mentioned maybe going back to work as a locum when both girls are at secondary school, but she hasn't said anything about that recently. I'm proud of her for pulling her way back from . . . from everything that happened."

"Did Tessa ever mention Jeremy Masters to you?" the DI asked, flipping his iPad round so she could see the photograph.

"No, I don't think so . . ." Beverley studied the smiling profile. "Who is he?"

The father entered the room again. "I just gave them some juice, they're fine," he said in answer to his wife's raised eyebrows.

The DI repeated the name and offered the photograph to him. He leaned in, pulling a pair of reading glasses from his pocket. "Doesn't ring any bells. Is he a suspect?"

"We are just trying to get an idea of Tessa's friends, anyone she might have been in contact with in the months leading up to her disappearance," Dove said.

"I know Tessa is okay, because she's a fighter." His green eyes held Dove's and she recognized the plea for reassurance.

"Klara!" Beverley suddenly exclaimed. "You saying about Tessa's friends made me think of it. She was at St Mathew's with Tessa. In the summer holidays this year, I went over to Tessa's place to pick up the kids. Klara was there, talking to Tessa in the kitchen. Anyway, they both seemed quite shocked to be interrupted, as though Tessa had forgotten I was coming, so of course, I asked what was wrong . . . But they said nothing, and it was obvious they wanted me to go and leave them alone, so I did."

"Did you ask Tessa about Klara's visit?" Dove queried. What could the two women have been discussing?

"Yes of course, but Tessa just said it wasn't anything important and got quite cross with me." Beverley frowned. "I recognized Klara immediately, even after all these years, but I can't remember her second name." She paused and put her fingertips to her forehead as though to draw out her memories. "Sorry, it's gone."

"Is Klara in that photograph?" the DI asked, pointing towards the sports team picture.

"No . . . I can't really put faces to names because Tessa had a constant stream of friends over during the holidays. Klara was regular visitor until Tessa left St Mathew's. She was a very striking girl. Tall and blonde with brown eyes. Unusual-looking rather than pretty, and reserved, not chatty." Her forehead wrinkled and she rubbed her eyes. "Rather intense, but I liked her. Tessa didn't want to see anyone after . . . after the attack."

"Did Tessa give you any indication she had seen Klara recently?" Dove asked. "Had she kept in touch with Klara over the years?"

"No! She was only still in touch with a few friends from school, and one or two in Manchester. She'd cut ties with everyone else. It's part of her anxiety; she likes to be on her own. I got the impression Klara had turned up unannounced the day I saw her, which would have worried Tessa." She glanced at her husband. "She was always worried in case Kevin tried to follow her."

"Did she ever mention Klara again? . . . You say it was in the summer holidays? This year?" the DI asked.

"Yes, twenty-first of August. I only remember because it was Allison's first sports camp the day after. She's very good at swimming, like her mum," Beverley added, with a touch of pride. "I tried to talk about Klara a couple of times after that, but Tessa just shut me down and changed the subject. Her sister didn't know why she had visited either, and didn't remember her from all those years ago. Do you think it's connected?"

"We never assume anything, and please believe me we are doing everything we can to get your daughter back safe and sound. All the information you have given is extremely helpful."

It was the best they could offer, but Dove could tell by the disappointment in the parents' faces it that it wasn't enough, despite the DI's obvious sincerity.

"Can we borrow this photo?" He tapped the St Mathew's picture. "And any others you have from Tessa's time at St Mathew's would be very helpful."

Beverley glanced doubtfully at her husband but he nodded firmly. "Anything that helps find her. Bev, there's an album on the bottom shelf with a few loose ones I found in her room one day after she left."

His wife opened the cupboard door and took out a slim red album. She put the framed photograph on top, sadness evident on her face as she trailed her fingers across her daughter's sweaty, triumphant face. "You will bring them back, won't you? Just in case she . . ." Her face crumpled.

Dove put a gentle hand on her shoulder. She knew exactly what Beverley meant. Just in case they were too late and Tessa was already dead.

CHAPTER TWENTY-NINE

I look back on my early medical misadventures with amusement, and a tiny bit of irony. It seemed to me that my friends were all musical, learning and mastering the piano, the flute, the cello, and I loved to hear them play, but I was focused on a career in the medical world.

My father was convinced my dreams would stay just that, and I would fall into something else. Did he think I wasn't clever enough? I don't think that was the case, I think it was perhaps that he had also been a bright child, from the hints my mother dropped, but had never been allowed to pursue his academic dreams.

His hopes and ambition fell away through lack of care, lack of encouragement, but mostly lack of money. I constantly researched ways I could achieve my goals, and a family inheritance divided equally seemed to point out fate was on my side.

It wasn't. After everything fell apart, I would often comfort myself by disappearing inside my head to hear my childhood friends. Their music all-embracing, the notes floating through my sore head like a balm to the soul.

I also remembered her singing, and in my head, I always rewrote the ending of her song, of all their songs. Eventually it worked and the balm healed my wounds. I was able to function again. Although the money was gone, I was even, in time, able to go back to my studies and rediscover my calling.

But my nightmares will never leave me, my soul is scarred. Often a particular taste or smell will remind me of what happened and the frantic pounding of my heart, my dry mouth and churning stomach take me straight back to my prison.

Unless you know me, you would have no idea of the terrors lying underneath my skin. It's only when you peel back the surface you can see the scars, the rawness imprinted on my soul. Which is ironic in a way, because I used to think, the whole time I was suffering, that my body and soul were separate entities. My soul was untouchable, rising above whatever happened to my physical body. Now I know better. My soul could not survive unblemished, not after what it had seen.

When I look in the mirror, I see an ordinary face, a nice smile, clean shiny hair and someone who is well dressed, clearly has money to spend. It's the part underneath the external polish that is scarred raw and rotten.

My credentials were framed as soon as I earned them, and now hang in my bedroom. The pride I feel whenever my gaze encounters them casts a radiant light across my mind, chasing away the shadows.

The light shows me two girls and their story unravels in my head, like an old-fashioned movie reel at the cinema. The film flickers and fades, but the images are clear enough for me to see their faces.

They ran together through the snow, slipping and sliding, grateful for the occasional tree branch to haul themselves upwards. They gasped for breath, sweat dripping, limbs shaking. They turned often, glancing fearfully over their shoulders without pausing in their frantic flight. I watch them, holding my breath . . .

Soon they will be free. It is the last step of the journey and I wish so much for a happy ending that I always try to leave them there, to step away from the snowy forest.

'Bad things happen in the snow', her voice whispered, her lips so close to my ear that I felt their softness on my skin. It was a singing voice, light and musical in tone, like silver sleigh bells ringing.

CHAPTER THIRTY

They drove through the sleet back to the station, Dove scrunching her toes up inside her boots, trying to warm them and resisting the urge to turn the car heater up to the max. It was a constant joke between her and her fiancé that her feet were never warm. When they first started living together one of his first gifts to her had been a hot water bottle.

She started to flick through the photographs. Lots of smiling faces, but none of them belonging to Jeremy Masters. The album was mostly young Tessa and her sister at school and parties, but there were four loose at the end that showed an older Tessa, with shorter hair, and a more serious expression.

"See anything interesting?" Jon asked.

"Jeremy isn't in any of them, but one of the girls from the sports picture is in another two with Tessa. Looks like a party and a presentation at St Mathew's, because I can see the university crest." She studied the shoulder-length brown hair and freckles, and compared it to the team photo. Definitely the same girl. A close friend perhaps? "I can't see any of Klara as Beverley described her. A few blondes but none with brown eyes and all much younger than university age, I would say."

"Okay, we've got our lead. Let's find Klara and this other girl."

Back at the station, buzzed with the findings, Dove put in a quick call to Steve while she waited for her coffee and bacon roll.

His wife, Zara, answered. "Hey, Dove." She cleared her throat and then coughed.

"How are you all? I just thought I'd check in and see if you need anything. I can shop after work if you like?"

"That's so sweet of you, but I've got an online delivery coming at 3 p.m.," Zara said. "How's the case going? Steve and the baby are asleep at the moment, so I'm putting my feet up for half an hour."

"Half the team is down with the flu, but we're making progress," Dove told her. "I'll leave you to rest, and please don't hesitate to call if you need anything at all."

"Thanks, Dove, I will and I'll tell Steve you rang."

Dove sighed and dived back into her thoughts, twisting the facts around and around, trying to see how everything fitted into place. Had Jeremy and Klara been at the party when Tessa was assaulted? Did they know what happened and who attacked her? An obvious start was St Mathew's. She pulled up the website for the university and picked up her phone.

The admin assistant was very helpful, but couldn't help with anything more than dates of admission and leaving, which tallied with the information they had already gleaned from the investigation. But it was all box-ticking, and solid evidence. Fired up by the recent revelations, Dove went back to her research and eventually found a thread on Facebook. It was a group run by Lizzie Marshall, who seemed to be in charge of updating the alumni social media and annual magazine.

Tapping out the phone number, Dove introduced herself and explained she was looking for information on the former students. "Jeremy Masters, Tessa Jackson, and a girl called Klara, but I don't have a surname for her."

She added the leaving year, but explained Tessa Jackson had left earlier that term. "Any general information, sports teams, study groups and photographs from archives would help immensely."

There was a short silence before Lizzie spoke. "Sorry, DC Milson, I am slightly confused. I spoke to a DI Smith yesterday about these dates."

"I'm sorry?"

"This is about the body in the lake?"

"Apologies, but I think we may have crossed wires. As I said, I work for the Major Crimes Team, and I'm enquiring about three of your former students. I don't have any knowledge of any recent incident at the university." Dove wondered how the hell there could be another murder investigation in the next county that they were unaware of.

"Sorry, it must be local police who are dealing with it," Lizzie said, sounding just as confused as Dove was.

"What happened?" Dove wedged her phone between shoulder and chin and started taking notes. "And did you say DI Smith?"

"Some workman found a body in the lake in July, and I know they've been working to identify who it was. It was a terrible shock to all of us. Nobody has been reported missing and DI Smith told us it had been there for years. It was a skeleton! He said it would be extremely difficult to find out who it was."

"Oh, I see, a cold case." Dove closed her eyes briefly. The world hadn't gone mad after all. "I do appreciate it must have been a shock. I'll talk to DI Smith. Did you say he was asking about the same dates I was?" Dove's heart was still racing.

"Yes . . . well, almost an exact match. You said you wanted information from 2007 — 2011, and DI Smith was looking for information from 2005 — 2011."

"I see. Thank you. Could you possibly send the information over as soon as possible?" Dove finished up the call and went straight back to her computer. Glancing round for DI Blackman, she saw he was in a meeting with the DCI and the office door was shut.

While she waited for the email from Lizzie she went back to the MEDA website, and put Klara into the search. Nothing. She needed a surname. She started scrolling, and was halfway down the third page when the email appeared.

DC Milson,

I've just attached the results of the search on Jeremy Masters and Tessa Jackson. Re Klara, the only times the names are linked are with Klara Payton. They were medical students, as I'm sure you already know, and were in the same tutor group for their final year. The tutor was Professor Claire Renuard. Regarding your request for photographs, I've sent an email to our university archivist, as I only have fairly recent photographs for the newsletter.

Regarding the other girl in your photographs, I'm afraid I have been unable to find a name, but with your permission can pass on the request to our archivist.

If you need anything else please do call me,
Regards,
Lizzie Marshall

Dove did two more searches, grabbed her iPad and went straight over to the DI's office, heart pounding.

"Klara Payton specializes in cardiology, and she was at St Mathew's University with Jeremy and Tessa. She also works at Abberley General, and is on the MEDA list of medical professionals," she told him, adding the information about the cold case at St Mathew's. "We wanted to know why Jeremy got in touch with Tessa . . ."

"Bloody hell," the DI said, slowly swinging round to study the incident board, before turning back to the screen. "So we have Tessa Jackson, Jeremy Masters, and Klara Payton. All doctors, all at university together, and suddenly this summer, Jeremy contacts Tessa, and a month later, Klara also contacts her. When did you say the cold-case body was found?"

"July," Dove told him, her heart hammering. They both stared at the screen in silence, for a moment. High achievers, both Klara and Jeremy, with excellent career paths. And Tessa? The same until she dropped out. "So the body in the lake seems to have made our doctors very worried. Why?"

The DI was studying the photographs. Klara was very attractive, as Beverley had said, with long blonde hair, a fine bone structure and brown eyes. In the photo, her lips were slightly parted in a coldly professional, picture-perfect smile.

The blurb underneath her bio stated she had, in her medical capacity, been involved in many clinical trials for sports brands and medical partnerships, and listed them. Recognizing some of the brands, Dove raised her eyebrows. These were reputable global companies. She switched back to Klara's picture on the hospital website.

"Perhaps Tessa did tell someone who attacked her?"

Dove was there in an instant. "She told her friends and they got revenge?"

CHAPTER THIRTY-ONE

"Perhaps. It would be a good reason not to go to the authorities and report the attack. She may well have been terrified, but the real reason she never reported could be because they dealt with it themselves," Jon said slowly and carefully. "But that doesn't explain why Tessa, who was the victim, has now been abducted, or why Charles was killed, nor the link to the fake clinical trials."

"I was just going to call DI Smith at Northingly and find out more about the body in the lake," Dove said, tapping her phone with a bitten thumbnail.

"At Northingly? That'll be Damien Smith. He's a tosser, but a good copper," the DI said. "You do that, get as much information on the cold case as you can, even if you have to drive down to Northingly, and I'll get Jeremy in for another interview. Klara, we need to talk to, but there's not enough to yank her down here. I don't want her spooked, if she is involved." He was already on the phone. "I'll find out where she is."

"Yes, boss."

As she went back to her computer she could hear Jon updating the DCI, before he delivered a mini brief to those in the room, delegating the updated workload. They were getting closer, she could feel it, almost smell the blood and the fear. A tiny thread of hope for Tessa, too. Dove envisaged her clock-watching, wherever she was, however she was involved, knowing she was being hunted. She refused to picture her dead until she actually saw proof. There was always hope.

She walked through the swing doors into the corridor, where it was quieter, leaned back against the wall and called Northingly. DI Smith answered just as Dove was about to leave an urgent voicemail on his mobile.

"It's DC Milson from the MCT. Are you working on a cold case involving St Mathew's?"

"Afternoon, DC Milson, and yes we are." His voice was hoarse and deep, like a dog barking, and she could hear heavy breathing between his sentences.

"We're investigating three, possibly four, students who were at St Mathew's during the timeframe you have for the death of your cold case, and I think we might have an overlap. Can we meet up?"

He agreed. "I know a café about halfway between us both. I've need to have a chat with someone over your way, so can you be there in half an hour?"

Dove left a message for the DI and drove towards the next county. Luckily the snow had stopped again, but she did get stuck behind a slow-moving gritter lorry, which spattered her windscreen with dirt and slush. She tapped the steering wheel impatiently until the road widened and she could slip past.

DI Damien Smith had cropped sandy hair, a round face and very pale blue eyes. His cheeks were red-veined from the cold, and he was busy on his phone as she walked in. He waved and made a 'tea, please' gesture.

The roadside café was almost empty, so Dove grabbed tea, milk and sugar sachets for them both and sat opposite him in the grubby plastic tub seat. "Thanks for coming to meet me."

His breath smelled of cigarettes as he leaned across the table to take his drink. "Ta. Call me Damien. Dove . . . Great name. You were on the Glass Dolls case, weren't you?"

She nodded warily. The way he said her name, she mentally prepared for an insult. Personally, she loved the very different names she and her sisters had been given, but a lot of people didn't. Ren had continued the tradition with Eden, and Eden herself had admitted she thought long and hard before she called her own son Elan.

"Nice to see you again, Dove. I haven't been out this way long, but I remember responding to that call-out." He grinned at her, showing uneven yellow teeth. "Everyone thought you were going to wind up dead and you walked up the hill butt-naked."

"Thanks for the pleasant memories," she told him, blowing on her hot coffee, wrapping her hands around the warmth of the cup. "Shall we move onto your current case?"

"Fine. Here's the pathologist's report." He pushed some paperwork in her direction. "Essentially, we've got a male, approximately twenty-four years old when he died. Cause of death unknown, but probably drowning."

"Probably?"

"He's been dead around ten to fifteen years, it's a tough case. He wasn't wrapped so well, and the decomposition was pretty far advanced after so long." The blue eyes dropped to his phone again, and he frowned. "Sorry, just need to make a quick call."

She nodded and scanned the report while he paced across the café, talking animatedly and waving an arm in a frustrated gesture. The young man from the lake had not been identified. Unlike Charles Richardson he had plenty of distinguishing features, including fractures to both forearms, broken ribs, the list went on, with the report also noting some of the damage seemed to have come from childhood.

Possibly somebody who had suffered abuse, then? If he had dropped out of the system, been a runaway perhaps, it might explain why he hadn't ever been reported missing. It was tragic to think his death had not been noticed, his life not important enough to be marked by someone.

He had been discovered wrapped in plastic sheeting, and weighted with bricks, so there was no chance this was an accidental drowning.

She raised her eyes to DI Smith, who was still on the phone. He glanced over and mouthed 'sorry' and she shrugged and returned to her thoughts as her own phone rang.

"Hi, boss."

"Okay, what's the update on St Mathew's, and how the fuck did we not know about this?"

She told him, quickly and succinctly.

"Is Damien being helpful? Get what you can and I'll meet you at the university."

"Yes, he's been good, and he's interested in the crossover with our case. St Mathew's? Why?" she asked.

"The DCI's interviewing Jeremy under caution, and Klara Payton is working at the hospital until 8 p.m. I want to see what Jeremy has to say first, and talk to the tutor, Professor Claire Renuard, before we get to Klara, to see if we can get some more background."

"Yes, boss."

DI Smith was back, squeezing his bulk into the plastic seat. "Sorry, crazy busy today. So what's your link to my investigation?"

She told him, adding, "Our first call was the frozen body, Charles Richardson, and . . ."

He held up a large rough hand, "Gotcha, I know everything going on round here, all the gossip, and this is a good one, isn't it? Frozen body, fire, missing mum. All the papers are still dining out on the titbits you tossed them."

Dove, annoyed by his interruption, mentally shrugged, and resumed her fact check. "These three connected to our case are linked by the university. This summer, after you found the body in July, they started contacting each other. Two of them, Klara and Jeremy, stayed in contact after uni. They both work at Abberley General. The other, Tessa Jackson, is missing."

"If they were involved in my vic's death, they might have panicked when his body was finally found," Damien said thoughtfully. "You mentioned Tessa said she was assaulted. Maybe our man in the lake did it, and she and her friends got rid of him."

"We thought so, too. But if they had something to do with his death, why would that panic involve killing another young man?" Dove thought of Tessa again. "There is a small theory that Tessa left voluntarily. Perhaps she was running away?"

"Your frozen body doesn't tie in, mate, does it? Certainly doesn't go with the idea of keeping secrets from their past. It was blatant. God knows what goes on in people's heads. All right, let's keep in touch so we don't get any more cock-ups. Who's the SIO?"

"Jon Blackman."

"Jon! Bloody hell, he's a right wanker." He was laughing. "Top bloke, though. I haven't seen him for years."

They left quickly, driving in opposite directions through the bleak winter's day, Dove picking over the conversation. She turned the new information over and over in her mind. Damien was right: It didn't make sense. The cold-case body had been carefully hidden, in her present-day case, the body had been brazenly displayed. Such different MOs and such tenuous connections. If you had buried a past misdemeanour, a murder even, you would surely want it to stay hidden?

CHAPTER THIRTY-TWO

Dove arrived at St Mathew's first, and stayed in her car with the heater turned to max, putting off the moment she had to venture out into the icy wind.

The university was an imposing set of ancient stone buildings, set among a sprawl of newer architecture. A clock tower rose high among the snow-covered roofs and the hour chimed out as Dove sat waiting for Jon. It was a melodious sound, and curiously festive in this winter weather.

There were few people around, but those students who scurried from lecture to lecture, the university staff who walked briskly with cases heavy of work, were heavily muffled against the cold. It was not somewhere Dove felt entirely at home. Her own education had been unconventional. She and her sisters had not lacked in the formalities of schooling, but this kind of establishment always made her feel like an imposter.

Filling in time, she tapped out a text to Quinn, added heart emojis, and pulled up the case files on her iPad. She kept coming back to Tessa. What if someone connected with the body in the lake had worked out the identity of the dead man, worked out what they had done, and was taking revenge? She yawned and hauled herself back to alertness.

Her eyes felt hot and sore after far too little sleep and too much time staring at a screen. Outside, the sky was a dull grey and despite the pleasant warmth of her car, she opened a window and let a blast of bitterly cold air shock her senses into wakefulness. It worked, and she was able to return to her work, slightly refreshed and certainly wide awake now.

The news item was archived and the page jumped around, popping up random adverts and surveys until she felt like screaming with frustration, but at last she got to the text.

. . . A body was discovered at St. Mathew's University, Northingly, on the George Campus, in a lake. No identity has been released, but police are appealing for any information dating back to fifteen years ago. The body was discovered as wildlife experts drained the lake for rehabilitation purposes and the reintroduction of the university's famed white storks.

She tried to put the pieces together, looking at the class lists Lizzie Marshall had sent over. Jeremy, Klara and Tessa all at uni, all in George Campus studying hard for their finals, which from the website maps was situated next to the lake. Convenient.

But medical students spent a lot of time working in hospitals, gaining experience on the job, so they needn't have been staying at the university much at all. If the body in the lake was connected to their sudden erratic behaviour, he might well have been killed elsewhere . . .

Her mind ran back over her earlier discussion with the DI. If Tessa was assaulted, perhaps she fought back . . . maybe she even killed her assailant and afterwards turned to her friends for help. If they all agreed to dispose of the body, panicking about future careers, horrified by what had happened, it sort of made sense . . . It fitted better than the friends making a cold-blooded revenge killing, but there was still Charles Richardson to consider. He simply didn't fit into any possible scenario.

Fifteen minutes later, she and the DI were walking towards the lodge where Professor Renuard and her husband lived.

"Jeremy is still giving another statement, and as I have no doubt he's involved somehow, let's hope he starts to talk. His solicitor is being a pain. That's part of her job though, isn't it?" Jon updated Dove grimly as they crunched across the gravel.

They passed through the imposing, slightly musty-smelling reception area and were issued with laminate passes. Dove noted the stringent campus security and wondered if it had been the same ten years ago, when perhaps someone else slipped in. Someone who never came out again. A passageway led through the ancient main building, and they passed various students hurrying to lectures or loitering in earnest discussion. Boards with dates and names lined the walls, and she glanced at the dates.

They had nearly reached the end of the passageway when she spotted it.

"Look, boss." She stopped and peered at the board. The names were in alphabetical order, so she was able to pick out those she was looking for.

Awards for Sports Excellence 2009.
Tessa Jackson — Athletics
Jeremy Masters — Swimming
Klara Payton — Swimming

"Not only medical students, but athletes too," the DI commented. He laughed. "The golden gang. Some people were at the front of the queue when it was all doled out! I used to walk into school, go to registration and walk straight out again across the playing fields." He glanced at Dove. "I bet you were a straight-A student."

"Why do you say that?" She was surprised.

"Just the impression I get."

She smiled, remembering her earlier thoughts. "Well, you're right, but my education was pretty unconventional. Look, that must be it, down the driveway."

They walked briskly across a courtyard and the snowy gravel, before turning down a long driveway. The garden was walled, guarded by two stone pillars topped with eagles, and the small stone house was somehow imposing. To their left, the ground sloped down into the frozen river. In the summer months, it must have been idyllic, with a boathouse and small mooring area. In this weather, it looked desolate and forlorn. Out of place among the ice and snow.

"I'm in the wrong job, if she lives here," Jon muttered, eyeing the property.

"She probably doesn't own it, maybe just lives here while she's teaching at St Mathew's," Dove suggested, remembering an acquaintance who taught at a boarding school. "The salary often isn't great, so they give you a house to soften the blow."

As they reached the porch, she paused, taking in neatly stacked recycling in a wooden box, various boots and muddy coats. The porch was a smart oak-framed affair, decorated with a plaque in scrolled writing which read *The Lodge*.

Jon rapped smartly on the brass knocker.

A smart, smiling, middle-aged woman in a thick blue coat welcomed them in, "Claire said to tell you to go through to the living room, just to your left. Sorry, she's just on a call, and I'm heading off now. Go on, you go through!"

The woman ushered them in, then stepped out onto the porch and shut the door behind her. Dove could hear her hurried footsteps on the gravel.

From the doorway in front of them they could hear the murmur of voices. She looked at Jon, who shrugged, and led the way forward. As they approached the door, the voices stopped abruptly. There was a quick exchange of goodbyes and then the professor came out to meet them.

"So sorry, students wanting to catch up on coursework before Christmas. All these Zoom calls, I'm inundated! Put your coats over there . . . I was looking out the window and saw you arrive. I asked Jenny to let you in whilst I extricated myself," she laughed merrily, shutting the laptop and shuffling paperwork.

In the pause, Jon introduced himself and Dove.

The professor motioned for them to sit down at the highly polished table, "Now, you mentioned you were interested in several students: Jeremy, Klara and Tessa were in my tutor group, yes, among many, many others over the years." Professor Claire Renuard was small and grey-haired with bright green eyes, and a pink cardigan wrapped around her body. She picked at the sleeves as she talked. Her small nose turned up at the end and was also tinged with pink.

Which wasn't surprising as the house was freezing cold, Dove thought. Stunning, with oak beams and stone floors, but inhabited by icy draughts and a serious lack of radiators. She had shed her jacket when they were invited to, and was now wishing she hadn't. "Can you tell us about the group? How did they meet?"

"I believe Klara and Jeremy knew each other before they came here, but the others met during Freshers' Week." The professor smiled and smoothed a stray piece of hair back behind her ear. "It's always interesting watching little groups ebb and flow. A study in human nature."

DI Blackman nodded. "Who would you say was the group leader, Professor?"

"Call me Claire. I don't think there was a leader as such. They were all brilliant students. Academically, they were among some of the best I've ever taught. Their various specialist interests gelled in a way that can sometimes happen. Jeremy, I suppose, was the most confident, but the others weren't shy. Klara found it difficult to make friends, as I remember. All that mattered to her was her studies, her research." Claire laughed. "Of course, I encouraged that. I think she dated Jeremy eventually . . ."

"Do you recognize this girl?" Dove proffered the picture of the athlete hugging Klara in the St Mathew's photograph.

"Oh yes, they were all athletes as well. That was . . . Katherine . . . Katherine Weight. Nice girl, and she was very bright too . . . Swimming was the main thing I believe they were all into, but also track athletics, marathon running . . .

Not the road running, but trail events, I believe. I can't remember which of them actually completed the Marathon de Sable one year. Like I say, they were exceptional."

"Did that lead to jealousy from the other students?" DI Blackman asked.

"Yes, but only the usual mutterings. They were well liked on the whole." She paused again, clearly thinking hard, playing with a pencil which was lying next to a notepad full of jottings. "Jeremy and Klara did date, I remember now, and Tessa was with someone for a long time, not sure who . . . I don't recall Katherine dating much. She was quieter than the others, but as I say, extremely intelligent in her own right. She had no family, had had to make her own way, and she was extremely focused." The professor watched them with apparent anticipation, but then smiled as they said nothing. "Would you like some tea?"

"No thanks, we're good. Do you know why Tessa dropped out in her final year?" Jon asked.

The woman pursed her lips, and frowned. "That was dreadful. Eventually, she told me about the assault at a party . . . I remember being extremely shocked, and I encouraged her to report it, to bring the perpetrator to justice, but to no avail." There was definitely anger in her face. "Young women shouldn't have their talent wasted, shouldn't be subjected to such things on campus. We take all complaints extremely seriously, but she wouldn't see that."

"I'm sure you do, and I can see you would have the same problem we do," Dove said. "We can't even attempt to investigate unless the victim comes forward."

"That's right!" Claire nodded vigorously. "With her hard work and talent, she would have easily achieved her predicted grades. I asked the others, Klara, Katherine and Jeremy, but I got the impression she never told them what really happened either." She sighed deeply at past injustices, got up and crossed the room to a large mahogany sideboard.

Dove could hear the stamp of boots, a door banging towards the rear of the house, and a male shout of greeting.

159

Claire came back towards the table, hands full. "Sounds like my husband is back in from walking the dogs," she smiled. "They love the snow and so does he . . . Here, I looked through my archives and found some photographs you might like to see. I remember this group especially, as I have said, because it was one of those clusters of gifted students. Jeremy and Klara have certainly fulfilled their promise academically. Jeremy came back to speak to some of our final-year students during Careers Week earlier this year." There was a warm glow of pride in her voice. She tapped the photo of Klara accepting an award. "They attracted a lot of interest from the other students. Lots of people wanted to be part of their group."

Professor Renuard paused with a handful of albums and files as a man entered the room, and she performed introductions. "My husband, Alain, these are the police officers from the Major Crimes Team."

He was clearly older than his wife, of medium height with a powerful athletic presence and the slate-grey eyes of a wolf. His sharp features did nothing to dispel the image, and Dove couldn't help but liken the two figures before them to Little Red Riding Hood and the Wolf.

Professor Renuard, still standing next to the sideboard, seemed to shrink into her clothing, her little bright eyes darting, once again patting strands of grey hair back behind her ears.

Next moment, the image was shattered as he smiled at the visitors, kissed his wife and offered to fetch coffee and biscuits. "My wife makes wonderful biscuits," he laughed and patted his flat stomach, "I try hard not to eat too many."

His voice was very deep, with a slight accent Dove couldn't place. As they accepted his offer of refreshments, he stripped off his jumper and walked towards the kitchen in a white vest. Like Tony Garner, he had many elaborate tattoos, but while Tony's were quite simple artwork, Alain's seemed heavy and coarse, like someone had smeared black ink in the roughest of illegible lettering, the barest outline of some creature.

As her husband clattered around the kitchen, the professor put down her files, spreading the contents across the table. Dove studied the photographs, full of smiling happy students. Certainly, the little group of four seemed to have been close-knit.

"You were able to help Tessa complete her degree, though, weren't you? That must have been good," the DI commented casually.

"Yes." She tapped another page of photographs. "I was so proud of her for overcoming her fears. Katherine, I remember now, she got her degree, but then went off travelling. I haven't seen any evidence of her practising as a doctor, which is disappointing. I have wondered occasionally over the years if whatever affected Tessa touched her too?" She shrugged, "I always get far too involved, wanting the best for these young people, guiding them through their education and seeing them fly." She smiled ruefully, and turned as her husband brought in a tray. "Thank you, my dear."

He shrugged and smiled at her. "Have I missed anything exciting?"

She tapped his bare arm playfully. "This is not exciting, but it is a murder enquiry."

His face lit up, lips opened, and the Wolf was back. "What can we help you with? Is this about the man in the lake?"

"It might be connected. Did you know any of these students, Mr Renuard?" Jon said. "Jeremy Masters, Klara Payton, Tessa Jackson and Katherine Weight . . ."

"No. My wife told me the administrator passed on a message you were asking about them . . ." He was frowning at a picture of all four students. "Claire remembers everything and everyone." Another indulgent smile for her. "But I am always buried in my computer and tend not to notice the comings and goings. I'm an investor in emerging markets, so I must keep my eyes on the stock market twenty-four hours a day."

The professor had been leafing through her old photographs, but now her nostalgic expression flickered. "A horrible thing to happen. Truly shocking. A dead body in the lake is not going to encourage students or be any good for our sponsors. He wasn't a student we would assume, because none were reported missing, but still, the publicity hasn't been contained well enough."

"Strange. If he wasn't a student here, I wonder what he was doing on the campus?" DI Blackman mused. His tone was mild, inviting comment, but his cool grey eyes remained fixed on the woman's face.

Her husband agreed. "We wondered the same. At first, the gossip was that it was a suicide, but then the police told us the body had been wrapped in a sheet and weighted down." He shook his head. "A shocking business."

CHAPTER THIRTY-THREE

"All the students have always had passes which are checked through the main security gate, but the campus is huge, so you can imagine there is lots of coming and going. We don't run a prison here. These young people are adults, with adult responsibilities," Professor Renuard said, her voice higher and her fingers plucking faster at the cuff of her cardigan. Red spots appeared on both cheeks, and a red flush on her neck was just visible under the collar of her shirt.

Her husband put a gentle, reassuring hand over hers. His large palm covered her small fingers completely.

"Quite," Dove said. "And I suppose all visitors sign in at the gate?"

"They do." She looked hard at both of them. "I can't possibly imagine any of my students would have anything to do with the . . . the death and I've given this a lot of thought, but . . ." She ground to a halt, fussing with her cardigan again before sipping her glass of water. "I'm not stupid, and I can add up. You think this body and your investigation are related, don't you?"

"It's a possibility, as I said," the DI replied.

"Rubbish! It's more than a possibility, or I wouldn't have the Major Crimes Team chatting in my front room."

She moistened her lips. "I knew when you called and asked about these particular students . . ."

"Go on. Anything you can tell us could be helpful. Tessa is still missing, and we are extremely worried for her safety," the DI said.

The professor sat for a moment in silence, anxiety radiating from her sharp, pretty face. "Klara . . . Klara was, and indeed is, amazing, but she worried me sometimes with her intensity, her thirst for knowledge. She seemed to be able to disassociate her research from reality and emotion . . . I found this in my archives, and as I say, I have thought long and hard about this, but after I discovered what was involved in your investigation . . ." She picked some paperwork and passed it over. Her hands were shaking.

It was a pamphlet round-up of various events within her tutor group, and someone had circled a paragraph on the second page:

Jeremy Masters, Klara Payton and Katherine Weight presented a thesis on hypothermia, which was well received by both their peers and tutors. Some, however, commented that some of the data used was ethically unsound, coming from the Nazi Experiments at Dachau in 1943. The students argued that medical data was valid despite its source. Dr Arthurston pointed out that the Nazi data on hypothermia was not only unethical, but also lacked, among other thing, the cardiology to back up the conclusions.

"Bloody hell," DI Blackman muttered under his breath. He looked up at the tutor. "Did you not think it was worth coming forward earlier with this?"

"No!" she snapped, "I didn't make the connection until you called today. How could I? I saw from the news Tessa was missing, but I didn't even remember this piece of research until I started looking through my archives. Then, of course, I made the connection with the frozen body at Tessa's home . . ." Her eyes were bright and her expression angry. "I am only telling you now because I feel sure in my own mind I am doing the right thing."

Alain Renuard was watching, still but alert, his eyes moving from one face to the other. "You are doing the right thing, my dear, I'm sure of it," he said quietly, his hand once more covering hers.

Dove wondered if she imagined the brief flash of fear in the other woman's face. There was something odd and unconnected about the couple, despite their show of loving unity. They could almost have been two strangers forced to play a role. It was a strange impression to leave with, but she couldn't shake it off.

The DI paused in the hallway, seemingly admiring a small Christmas tree, which was already sitting proudly on the stone floor in a festive gold pot. "Nice tree."

Dove, puzzled at his sudden interest in festivities, also looked at the tree. It was decorated with antique-looking silver and glass baubles, and topped with a small silver star. She could see nothing to warrant the boss's interest, and he was already moving away, thanking the couple for their time. "If you think of anything else, we are especially keen to track down Katherine Weight. You mentioned she went travelling after she graduated . . ." This time his gaze lingered not only on the wife, but also her husband.

"Yes, of course, and do keep us updated," the professor said, smiling a little nervously, her husband standing protectively behind her as the officers left the house.

* * *

"I've got a Group meeting tomorrow, and I'll ring Damien Smith on my way back to the station, just to update him and make sure we haven't any crossed wires this time," the DI said, as they walked back to the university reception and signed out. "In view of what the Renuards just let drop, I'm looking forward to seeing what Klara and Jeremy have to say about this little snippet. But hell, it brings up all sorts of potential nightmare scenarios, doesn't it?"

Dove agreed. "Could Jeremy and Klara be recreating their previous hypothermia research, you mean? I get the feeling that's what the professor was hinting at."

Jon nodded. "Perhaps. There is something else I want to look into as well. Just a hunch and it might not come good, but it's bugging me . . ." He shook his head. "Anyway, the information we did get takes us further into discovering the link between Charles Richardson and Klara and Jeremy. But to go as far recreating events from the past . . . I really hope we aren't dealing with a pair of narcissists, who get kicks from doing just that." He paused, apparently thinking hard. "This would put a whole new spin on the case."

Dove caught his thought train at once. "You mean if Klara and Jeremy decided to start their own clinical trials, using faked MEDA adverts, perhaps they tried to recruit Tessa, but she was unwilling?"

* * *

Back at the station, Dove checked up on her messages. One from Steve, who sounded optimistic. Baby Grace seemed to be better already, and it was he and Zara who had suffered the worst of the symptoms. Dove picked up his voicemail as she made the dash from her car to the main building, the hail and sleet bucketing down from an ominously dark sky. It had been so dark on the drive back from St Mathew's she had put her headlights on, and now it seemed night was closing in early, folding away the daylight piece by piece.

Waiting in her inbox was a report from uniform, copied to the MCT, saying Tony Garner had been charged, and the victim had been discharged from hospital and was recovering at home.

Rose had emailed Dove to thank her, and to tell her she had cuts and bruises and a bit of concussion, but would be fine:

But it could have been much worse. I was way out about Tony, but part of it was me not living in the real world. I was so far into my role as CHIS handler I forgot to be careful in my own life.

Dove knew exactly how that felt, exactly how easy it was to walk so far into the darkness you forgot which was fantasy and which was reality. She was lucky, she got out, and Rose . . . Rose might take this as a wake-up call. Or maybe not. Rose would probably plunge headlong back into the darkness. But she got results, and that was what it was all about.

She grabbed a sandwich from the vending machine and was picking unenthusiastically at it and a packet of crisps when the DI beckoned everyone into the briefing room.

"Jeremy Masters gave a statement earlier today. Unfortunately, he has a rock-solid alibi for the night of the abduction, but his name has now also possibly been linked to a cold case in Northingly." The DI swiftly recapped the conversation with the Renuards. "So lots of possible joining the dots, but nothing that warrants us keeping him in, and at this stage, unfortunately, no hard evidence to charge him with anything." The DI's brow wrinkled in frustration, his mouth set in a frown. "He's dancing round the fringes of every single person in this case, but we can't pin a thing on him and he bloody knows it. Josh, I know you and Maya were tracing his movements for the last month?"

"We checked CCTV at the hospital, and his apartment, plus we spoke to a few friends and there are no long, unaccounted-for absences we can find. His sat nav shows he hasn't been anywhere except around this area, mostly trips to work. No visits to within even a couple of miles of Tessa Jackson's place, or Hanson's gym. He does pop into the corner shop on Coast Road, where the first MEDA card was found, but he lives a two-minute walk from the store, in the new apartment block," Josh said.

Just up the road from her house, Dove thought with interest. She was pretty sure she had never run into him before. Like Klara, he was striking enough to stand out from a crowd.

The DI ran through the updates on the St Mathew's cold case from DI Smith, which produced further murmurs of interest. "Klara Payton is next on our list, but she's just had to leave work and drive up to her mother's place. Her grandmother is apparently about to take her last breath, and Klara said she needs to be there."

"Do you think she's lying?" Lindsey asked quickly, eyes narrowing.

"No. I checked it out, and the grandmother, Helena Jacobs, is 105. She shares a house with the mother, Kathleen, and has been receiving end-of-life care for the past month. I spoke to the doctor and nurse in charge of her care."

Dove looked at her watch. "We could drive up there, but if her grandmother really is dying . . . I mean, we don't have anything definite on Klara, do we, except MEDA and St Mathew's?"

"I used to work in that area, so I'll call in a few favours and get a car to watch the house. Our evidence tells me she isn't about to do a runner, but I want to be sure."

"The press would tear us apart if they found out we had gone and harassed someone when she was saying goodbye to her dying grandmother," Dove added dryly.

"Precisely. Can you try and find Katherine Weight? She's the only one missing from our little group, and I want to know where she went after university and, more importantly, where the hell she is now. She might be able to provide valuable insight into the group dynamics," Jon added.

Dove arrived home in the darkness, irritable and exhausted. The idea of getting the team to work from home and the office as much as possible due to the flu and the weather was a good one in theory, but she wanted to be out, battling the elements, physically chasing up leads instead of being stuck behind a screen.

She fed Layla, lit the fire and made herself a mug of tomato soup, before she sat down to work. As usual, the crackling flames in the living room and the purring heaviness of the cat on her lap soothed her a little.

Quinn was stopping off at a mate's house on the way home from work, so probably wouldn't be back till about eleven.

The elusive fourth member of the university group, Katherine Weight, seemed to have dropped off the planet the year after she graduated. Her parents had passed away, and as Professor Renuard had said, she didn't seem to have any other family.

The few pictures of the girl she was able to find in Tessa's mother's albums showed more sports team victories, a few abroad, possibly from a holiday, or perhaps she had sent them to her friend while she was travelling. She flipped two over, and sure enough, there was a date and place. The dates put them at 2011–2012, and she had apparently been travelling around Asia. Yet after July 2012, there was no trace of Katherine Weight. She had not renewed her driving licence, nor did she appear in any official searches.

Dove sighed, shaking out a small, dirty folder which held just three pictures. More smiling travel pictures, but the last photograph had a piece of newspaper attached, stuck to the back and faded to a crisp yellow.

Dove stared at the wide, freckled, smiling face, the frizzy brown hair and hazel eyes. The torn newspaper cutting showed paragraphs in an English-language newspaper from Thailand:

Backpacker Katherine Weight (25) is believed to have drowned after a ferry caught fire on the Koh Samui to Kho Tao route. In total, twelve people are still missing following the tragedy on Thursday 12 February.

The piece was dated the year after she had graduated from St Mathew's, and underneath the report someone, maybe Tessa, had written *AB now* in blue pen. The writing looked fresh against the faded newspaper. A recent addition?

But the fourth member of the group was now ticked off. Katherine Weight was dead.

CHAPTER THIRTY-FOUR

'Three little girls went out to play, but only two came home that day . . .'
I wonder at the pain this memory still causes me. It's like a blow to my
chest, stealing my breath away. Surely the agony should have become
dulled by time, but no, I can see her face so clearly. If I stare hard enough
into the recesses of my mind, she becomes confused with others in the ice.

So many terrified people screaming for me to save them, to get
them warm . . .

The water was always so very bitterly cold, I drew back imme-
diately, my hand pinched and white. When they climbed in, they often
cried out, bodies rigid, an uncontrollable spasm of terror and instinctive
reaction to the ice.

I could almost block out the noises, but not the smell of fear,
the sight of death crouching next to them, pulling them slowly closer
as their bodies shut down, the shaking lessened and their core temper-
ature dropped. Unconsciousness followed, and by then, it was almost
always too late. I came to realize quite soon that all the warmth
from the outside made no difference if you were frozen inside, and
I wondered that I seemed to be the only person in the room who had
figured it out.

It seemed so obvious. If you have a core of ice, warmth must start
from the inside out, or the body will never recover properly. I could have
said this at any time, but I kept quiet. My opinions would never have

been welcome because to the doctors, I wasn't human, merely a subject to be used in the name of medical science.

But as each person died, I felt a little crystal of ice lodge deep within my heart, as though it was a final gift them to me — our skin touching, final breaths intermingling, until at last they were gone.

CHAPTER THIRTY-FIVE

Dove was still hunched over her computer at nine, drawing her own timelines for each person. Jeremy Masters and Klara Payton, both motivated to contact Tessa Jackson after the body was discovered in the lake at St Mathew's. Tessa was now missing . . . Katherine was dead. Finally, the list was narrowing, focusing on just two individuals.

She ran back over the files of university students. Why had Tessa written 'AB now' under the newspaper article. Were they initials? Or was it meant to be 'A Bnow'? No, that didn't even make sense . . .

She jumped as her phone buzzed with a call, and jerked fully alert as she saw the number.

"Professor Renuard?"

"DC Milson." Her voice was low and slightly nervous. "Forgive the intrusion, but I was working late, then reading the newspaper reports and something occurred to me about . . . about Klara. Sorry," she gave a little laugh, "I always forget what time it is . . ."

"It's okay, I was working late too," Dove reassured her, still staring at Katherine Weight's photographs.

"Well, the report mentioned a frozen chess set . . ."

Dove had no idea how that particular detail had made the news, because she didn't think it had been on general release.

"A frozen king and queen. Is that correct?"

"Yes, it is."

"Well, the thing is, I remember it was when they were working so hard on their dissertation, Jeremy used to joke about it . . . he and Klara being the ice king and ice queen. He was always a little vain, and was quite taken with the idea, but Klara hated it. It caused quite a rift, and he used to tease her . . . She was a chess player, too. I don't know if it might be important, such a silly detail to remember but . . ." Her voice trailed nervously away.

Dove considered this, turning it over in her mind. It was interesting, and went some way towards the picture in her mind of Klara and Jeremy's relationship, but she could just imagine the solicitor laughing if it was brought up in an interview. She took a sip of her coffee, forgetting it would be cold now, and pulled a face. "Thank you. That's very interesting. Actually, Professor, while I've got you, do the initials AB mean anything to you? I mean, regarding the case . . . I thought maybe they were initials of another student or something." She trailed off, aware how lame she sounded. "'AB now' was written at the bottom of a newspaper article relating to Katherine Weight's death."

"Oh my goodness! She died? How awful. When was this?" The professor sounded appropriately shocked, but also, what? Afraid, definitely afraid. Another death.

Dove summarized the findings and waited in silence for the professor to speak again.

"Nothing springs immediately to mind. Those four were very close-knit. I mean, there would have been students with those initials, I expect . . . Abi Burns was also in my tutor group, but not especially friendly with Klara . . . or any of them. I can find her details for you. You say the piece was torn from a Thai newspaper? Maybe AB was the person who sent the report to Tessa. Another friend who was travelling?"

Her voice had sharpened with interest now, suggestions tumbling out.

"Yes, that might be a possibility. I'll keep digging, and thank you again for your help," Dove told her.

The professor hesitated for so long before saying goodbye, Dove was convinced she was going to add something else, but in the end she finished the call politely, with a sigh in her voice.

* * *

The phone wrenched Dove from sleep with an urgent buzz, and she reached fumbling fingers for her mobile. Beside her, Quinn opened his eyes briefly, touched her shoulder in a gesture of solidarity and rolled over.

The text alert summoning the Major Crimes Team was often followed by a call with further information. So, unwilling to wake Quinn, Dove slipped stealthily towards the bathroom, hauling on her clothes as she went, her mind spinning at the thought of another victim.

Another frozen body at another remote location, and another missing mother. This time a lighthouse, long disused but now rented to a family. Alice Bentley had made the 999 call at 4.30 a.m. Now, like Tessa Jackson, she had vanished.

The drive took twenty-five minutes, and she nearly missed the turning in the darkness, guided only by the flashing lights as she bumped cautiously up a muddy track.

The track wound up the hill towards the cliff top, stopping abruptly in a gravel car park. Her headlights showed the cliff edge, a wooden footpath sign and a low wall straggling up towards a group of buildings.

"Hi, Dove." DC Josh Conrad was getting out of his own car, and he slipped on the ice, slammed the door. "Bloody hell, it's cold again. Jack Frost has been out tonight, hasn't he?"

"Yeah, my fingers are numb already . . . Another frozen victim? This is just weird." She ducked under the tape, greeting other members of the team as they trudged up the path towards the lighthouse.

Jess and her team hadn't arrived yet, but uniformed first responders were moving quickly and efficiently around the area surrounding the tall, red-and-white-striped building.

DI Blackman nodded as they approached. "One murder victim, frozen solid in the same position as the last one."

"Shit," Dove said.

"And Alice Bentley is another single mum. She was missing when the first responders arrived. Her children are fine, and we've got a friend on the way to take care of them. Twins, a boy and a girl aged five."

Josh frowned, scanning the layout of the property. "Exactly the same as the last one. A fire, an abduction and a victim left behind. This perpetrator is on a roll."

"I sincerely hope not." The DI excused himself as the fire incident commander beckoned. "Have a quick look around, check in with Jess when she arrives."

Dove and Josh headed straight over to the body, marching briskly across the sheep-cropped icy grass, boots occasionally sinking into deeper patches of crisp snow.

There were two vehicles parked nearby, an ambulance and a rapid response car. The paramedic was talking to a uniformed officer.

Dove, immediately recognizing the medic as one of Quinn's best mates, waited until they had finished before she called over to her. "Sarah!"

The woman straightened, and squinted into the floodlights. "Hi, Dove. How are you doing?" Without waiting for an answer, she continued, "Just like the last one, apparently — what the fuck is going on with some people?"

Dove introduced Josh, and agreed. "Yeah. Why are you here, though?"

"The 999 call was a request for us and fire, but he was dead when we pitched up, so we got our stuff back in the truck as quick as we could. We're only hanging around because I was just telling your colleague we saw something weird when we arrived."

"Have you got time to tell us quickly before you go?" Dove enquired.

"Sure, it won't take long, and it isn't much." Sarah leaned back against the vehicle, pulling her green jacket across her chest, yanking the zip up under her chin. "We were first on scene, not by much, but Fire missed the turning to start with." She turned and pointed down to the gravel area where the cars were parked. "As we came out of the lane and turned up here, a van nearly broadsided us. It could only have come from this place, because the lane is a dead end."

"So you must have the plates from the dash cam?" Dove said, buzzed at the thought of getting a lead so quickly.

"Yeah, I've got the footage here." She opened the door and swung inside.

Her partner was studying the footage as well, and he greeted the two police officers with, "I can see the registration, look!"

Dove noted it down and squinted at the cam footage. It was grainy but easy to see the dark-coloured van hurtling out from the turning, scraping paint off the nearside bumper of the emergency vehicle, before correcting wildly and continuing towards the road.

"That's a bit of luck! Hopefully, it might lead you to this freak who likes freezing people," Sarah said. "And find the missing women."

"Thanks. We won't hold you up," Dove said, jumping down from the vehicle. "Sarah, Quinn says we owe you beers anyway, so I'll make it a case for this bit of evidence!"

The crews departed to their next call-outs, leaving the body for Jess and her team, who had arrived and were trekking up the hill. Dove took a minute to call in the registration of the van which had nearly hit the ambulance.

"What is wrong with leaving dead people in a house?" Jess grumbled as she reached Dove and Josh. "A nice warm house." But her eyes were alight with interest, as she focused on the body.

"Nice to see you too," Dove told her, also studying the man on the ground. Same position, as the DI had stated earlier. He was also very similar in height and physique to Charles Richardson. Another young fit healthy victim. But Charles had been dark, and this boy, with his pale frosted lashes, and short blonde hair streaked with ice crystals, could have been playing the part of the ice king in a film Dove had once seen. The similarity was uncanny, and she almost expected him to open his eyes.

She peered closer, shivering and blinking as the icy breeze made her eyes water. "Has he got a tattoo? Look, on his left forearm . . . I can't quite see, because he's frozen in that foetal shape."

Jess glanced at the spot Dove was pointing, "Yeah, that'll help with your ID. Once we get him defrosted, the artwork will be a lot clearer." She called quickly to one of her team, who was carefully photographing the body from every angle, "Get the camera down here, he has writing on his chest. Oh, and I think I can see marks on his wrists, just like our previous victim."

Dove waited until Jess straightened up, her expression sombre. "The victim has what looks like a number three written on his chest. From the clarity, the number was probably written just before the perpetrator left him here, which tallies with the information we discovered last time. Maybe we'll get luckier with fingerprints and fibres with this poor bloke. Again, I'll be able to see more when we move him and warm him up. I want as much information as I can get from this scene while he's posed as the killer left him, so we won't move him yet, but there's your heads up, Detectives," Jess said.

"Shit — really?" Dove felt a rush of nausea, although she had half been expecting the killer to add to his tally. "We really need to get this perpetrator before he has a chance to kill another one. This is sick, and if our perp is freezing these men, what the hell is he doing with our missing mothers?"

Josh, standing next to her snapped his fingers, and made some exclamation under his breath.

Dove looked sharply at him. "What is it? What did I say?"

"Maybe that could be a link. The fact they are both mothers. If he has issues with families, especially single mothers, he may have an unstable background, or be a dad who lost visitation rights on his own children?" Josh suggested excitedly.

Jess, preliminary findings delivered, was absorbed in her work now, her team spreading out, collecting evidence, creating grids, and taking notes from the secured scene around the body. Dove took a last look at the frozen man. The illusion of an actor playing a part was lost in the harsh glare of the floodlights. Now, he could have been carved from marble, the frosting on his hair adding to the impression of an excellent artwork, rather than a human being.

"What about our university connection? Jeremy Masters was supposed to be working tonight, and Klara Payton is supposedly with her dying grandmother in Windsor," Dove said as she turned away. "Catch you later, Jess!"

She was wondering if Klara had been at her grandmother's house all night, but remembered DI Blackman's muttered comment about calling in a favour and having the house and car watched. Dove hoped the favour had worked, because if it turned out Klara was behind this and they let her loose, it would be a bloody protocol nightmare.

Jess waved a vague acknowledgement, and dismissal, without taking her eyes away from her subject, and Josh led the way back towards the lighthouse. "Let's have a quick look inside before we head back. We need to catch the DI with the dash cam footage too."

Outside the front door was cordoned off and Dove could see another little ice scene. "Look, same figures as before, but this time there's a pawn too. Just one at the front by itself, and loads of ice cubes." She thought back to Professor Renuard's call last night. 'The ice king and queen.' Which made the dead boys, what? Human chess pieces? Part of a chilling game or victims of someone's 'research' . . .

"Seriously freaky and twisted. Someone is going to a lot of trouble to set this up, though. No wonder they ended up being short on time and nearly meeting the first responders," Josh replied.

They walked carefully around the back door of the property, and stepped into the warmth and brightness with relief. The lighthouse had been converted into a cosy family home, and the scenes inside were similar to those after Tessa Jackson's abduction. Nothing was out of place, the kitchen was neat and tidy with the usual paraphernalia of family life.

This time, there were more photographs dotted around. Family scenes with Alice and her children, with friends or family. No male presence in the pictures, though, Dove noted.

What was the missing piece that linked Tessa and Alice? Each woman had two young children, lived remotely, and was a single mum. Was Josh right in his initial suggestion that this was about that aspect? Perhaps the perpetrator had issues in their childhood, leading to them targeting mothers?

"She likes her sport," Josh commented, squinting at the pictures on the fridge.

Alice was paddleboarding with some other women, swimming with her babies in little orange floats, running with a buggy, and crossing the finish line at the London Marathon. She was a tall, broad-shouldered woman, with a mane of fiery red curls, and a face full of freckles. In all her photographs she was smiling, or laughing, for the camera.

A cluster of medals hung from the edge of a bookshelf, which was stocked with crime novels and children's classics. Birthday cards were propped along a beam above their heads, and Dove studied them. One had swung open enough to see the message inside:

Darling Alice,
Happy 33rd Birthday! Aren't we all getting old now?
Love Caroline

"Alice is thirty-three, the same age as Tessa, Klara and Jeremy," she told Josh, swinging round and pointing at the cards. "What do you bet she also went to St Mathew's University and studied medicine?" She suddenly swung back to the photos, narrowing her eyes, heart pumping so hard she gasped as though she had been running. "Shit, I'm an idiot! 'AB now'! Do you know who Alice Bentley is?"

CHAPTER THIRTY-SIX

"Er . . . no?" Josh asked, raising an eyebrow.

Dove studied the freckles, the hazel eyes, the shape of the jawline. "I'm almost positive Alice Bentley is Katherine Weight, the fourth member of our little university clique."

"Bloody hell!"

"I know. I can only see it because I spent most of last night staring at her pictures. I should have twigged when I first heard her name, but I was so focused on the fact we have another frozen victim, I missed it! She's changed a lot, and at first I didn't look past the red hair, but I'm sure it's her. Let's find the DI." She told him about Tessa's scribble at the bottom of the newspaper report. "So she supposedly died in an accident in Thailand, and I guess she decided to take on a new identity."

Josh nodded slowly. "Which might mean she was the person in the group who killed the cold-case body in the lake? They all covered it up, but maybe she thought the accident was perfect cover to make doubly sure she could never be traced. You don't just take on a new identity unless you have a pretty good reason."

"Still doesn't explain why she's vanished now, and why we have another frozen body," Dove said in frustration. At every turn this case seemed to lead them deeper down a very twisted rabbit hole. Instead of tying up loose ends, the findings were creating new questions.

They headed back outside, silently absorbing the similarities between Tessa Jackson's disappearance and Alice's, the possible importance of Katherine's new identity. Dove turned at the gate, listening to the urgent voices, the backdrop of the rumbling waves far below the cliffs. Search and Rescue would include the Coastguard this time, to ensure nobody had tumbled down those night-dark cliff tops.

Dove was so absorbed in her thoughts she slipped sideways on the icy path and fell flat into a pile of snow.

Josh hauled her out. "You all right?"

"Bloody soaked through," she said crossly. "I'll have to nip home to change on my way back to the station."

He was grinning at her, and she slapped his arm. "Shut up, Josh! Not funny at all."

"Not at all," he repeated, amusement dying in his face as they continued down the hill past the body.

Jess, busy with her clipboard and iPad, glanced up, taking in Dove's soaked clothing with her sharp blue gaze. "Are you two going to stop playing in the snow and crack on with this case?" she demanded.

"'Playing' isn't the word I'd use to describe it." Dove winced as the soaked fabric of her trousers rubbed icy skin at every step.

Jess pulled on her kit and unloaded equipment from her van. "I'll do my best, but whoever is killing these poor lads isn't making it easy for us."

Jon Blackman was talking to one of the fire crew, and Dove started to walk over, but he waved to indicate he was done and headed their way.

It was so tiny, the ledge that separated life and death, Dove thought, looking down at the pale lifeless form. The body had been carefully rolled now, and the number three scrawled, just as Jess had observed, in black marker pen, still stood out clearly on his chest.

She had seen many dead bodies now, but it never failed to touch her, a finger tap of sorrow to see the vitality, the personality departed, and nothing she could do to bring it back.

But, she reminded herself often, this was one of the reasons she did her job. While she couldn't bring anyone back from the dead, she could certainly prevent further deaths, bring some sort of closure to family and friends, and see justice done.

Just over an hour later, Dove had managed to navigate the traffic, take a quick detour to get changed into dry clothes, and pulled hastily into the one remaining spot next to the entrance to the police station. Annoyed at having set herself on the back foot by falling over, she ran upstairs into the office, and joined the hustle and bustle of the new investigation. New timelines had been set up on the same incident board, adding both of last night's victims to the current tally.

The frozen teenager's name was Elijah Sampson. He was eighteen years old. His identification had been swift as he had been involved in various aspects of petty crime since he was thirteen. His prints were recognized on the system and his father notified of his son's death. As Dove had noted, he had a tattoo of a wild cat on his arm.

In the photograph on the board he was blonde, with a cheeky grin and pale grey eyes. He looked younger than eighteen.

"Any definite leads on his whereabouts before he died?" Dove asked as they hurried into the briefing. Quinn had been gone when she got home to change. His shift started at half past five, and he liked to be in early, sink a couple of coffees, banter with his crewmates, and generally wake himself up. Sarah, the paramedic from last night, would be clocking off, heading home to bed. Sometimes she wondered what it would be like to be a nine-to-fiver.

Josh shrugged. "Not that I've heard yet. At least we know who he was. That's going to save some time. Bet ya he responded to one of the fake MEDA adverts, just like our first victim, Charles Richardson."

"That's two in fairly quick succession," Lindsey remarked, chewing a pen as she considered. "Plus the two missing women. What were you saying, Josh, about single parents?"

He shrugged. "Just that it might be a reason why Tessa and Alice have been taken. Maybe they are being punished or something? Klara and Jeremy both lost parents when they were quite young and neither have kids now . . . I'm just saying it's interesting, not that we're on the wrong path with this ice obsession, but just that maybe there are other grievances within this group we need to explore."

The DI agreed. "Good, Josh. Can you pursue that idea? Now, no word on the whereabouts of Tessa and Alice, but we have thrown all our depleted resources at finding them. Jeremy Masters and Klara Payton both have alibis for last night, but we do have something extra from Jeremy Masters's apartment CCTV."

He looked towards the screen and the footage appeared. A figure wearing so many layers it was impossible to tell if it was male or female moved swiftly around the building from the main entrance to the top of an alleyway.

There were no cameras in the alleyway but the figure reappeared ten minutes later from the opposite side of the building, still empty-handed, and jogged towards the road.

"The security guard on duty says he confirmed with the residents there were no break-ins. He sent the footage across because he made contact when our team went over Jeremy's apartment. He says the only apartments on the west side on the ground floor are Jeremy's and two others. The two other names don't ring any bells in our investigation, so I'm thinking our evening caller was something to do with Dr Masters."

"Didn't he recently have a new alarm system installed?" Josh asked.

"He did, but it only covers his own apartment. The security guard did do a perimeter check of the building after he saw the footage, but there were no signs of forced entry."

A rise of energy in the room at this small step forward gave the team a much-needed boost. After the discovery of a second victim and another missing woman, the press would be going crazy over a possible serial killer they had dubbed 'Jack Frost', and the DI and the DCI would be under massive pressure to solve the case as quickly as possible.

"But he didn't break in? Unless Masters left a window open or something and it was a prearranged drop?" Josh suggested.

"Nothing left outside that the security guard could see, and the windows were shut."

The DCI joined them, gripping a pile of files. "Just confirming we are focusing on the incident at St Mathew's as the possible trigger for our murders and abductions. Northingly just called, and they have identified the body from the lake. It hits bang in the timeframe we are looking at with our former student medics. The deceased was JD Turner, a drifter who was known to the hostel in West Eversham. He was also known to Northingly as a drug addict who received several cautions for possession and dealing. Turner was also banned from the university grounds after he was caught dealing at a Freshers' Week party in 2009."

DCI Franklin's grey hair was spiked in many directions and his face looked crumpled and tired. Dove, passing the glass-fronted offices arranged along both sides of the main desk area earlier on her way to the briefing, had seen the DCI talking angrily on the phone, at the same time as he flipped through a huge pile of paperwork.

She still felt the numbers on the chests of the victims were significant to either the perpetrator or the missing women. What if JD *had* been the original victim? Number one. Three young men who had lost their lives, and a long time span in between number one and number two, yet mere days between number two and number three. Someone was picking up the pace.

As Steve was still sick, Dove was alternating between working with Josh and Jon Blackman, which meant she had to make doubly sure she was up to date with the latest angles on the investigation. Jon was taking Klara and Jeremy, pursuing the university link, and Josh was on the missing women, with emphasis on his single mum theory.

Glancing up from her notes, she saw Jon beckoning. "Bring your stuff, we're going to see Klara Payton, but first up, we've got a video call booked with Jeremy's father. He lives in Switzerland," he added vaguely. "Afterwards, we need to find out more about Alice Bentley, aka Katherine Weight. Better still, Dove, you can find out where the hell she's gone now."

"Jeremy's father?" Dove said, surprised, momentarily ignoring the rest of his information. Jeremy's picture had joined the timeline, and his golden-boy good looks and smile contrasted with Tessa's wary defensiveness and now Alice Bentley's red curls. The two frozen victims had headshots next to them, but it was almost impossible to reconcile the bodies with the grinning social media shots. A bolt of sadness shot through Dove's core every time she looked at the young men.

"Jeremy clammed up completely when we asked about his family. From being really smooth and cooperative, he just stopped talking and sat looking at his solicitor. His father called the crimeline after the press conference yesterday," Jon explained, "I wasn't sure if Jeremy just didn't want his family mentioned, or if there was another reason, but sounds like we could be about to find out."

"What about the vehicle registration from last night?" Dove asked.

"The van was registered to Charles Richardson."

"So they used his own van to transport the bodies," Dove said. "Nice."

"Yes, but at least we can keep an eye out for the vehicle now. By the way, I checked in, and Klara didn't move from her grandmother's place all night. Jeremy was working another night shift. He went home after his interview with us, got changed and went straight off to work. If he's communicating with someone and involved with this case, he's doing it via burn phone, and we haven't been able to find any trace of those. One thing is sure, neither he nor Klara Payton were at Alice Bentley's house last night or early this morning." Jon sounded disgusted.

"So we still have an anonymous Jack Frost to find. Great," Dove said, echoing his frustration.

"Not necessarily. I'd put money on at least Jeremy being involved. He's just not carrying out the end-game abductions and body placing," the DI suggested.

Jon briefed Dove on Jeremy's father as they walked down the stairs. "He lives as a virtual recluse in a chalet in the Swiss mountains. Jeremy's mother passed away when he was eleven, and he has no siblings."

"Did you say he contacted us, though? Did he say why?" Dove asked, dodging a queue at the snack machine.

"Didn't say. He just said he saw the press conference and wanted to speak to someone on MCT about his son."

They settled into the room, checked the screen and placed the call.

The man who appeared on the video link was white-haired, with the same strong bone structure and long nose as his son. His piercing blue eyes were almost hidden under white bushy eyebrows, though, and his hair was the same colour, sprouting in bushy tufts from either side of his head. For the recording, he introduced himself, and nodded as the DI made introductions.

"Mr Masters, can you tell us why you contacted us?" Jon asked, finally.

"Firstly, my son is a good man, a doctor. He rang and told me you had him in for questioning."

"That's correct," Jon confirmed.

"You previously lived in Abberley, didn't you?" Dove said, searching for a way to break the ice. Clearly, the man was having trouble, or even second thoughts, now the moment had come. She hoped she could gently ease him into conversation.

"Yes. My wife died when Jeremy was quite young and I didn't want to move, wasn't ready until a few years ago.

Jeremy stayed in the area, though. He always did. I thought he might want to go right away, but he even went to university at Northingly. St Mathew's."

"Do the names Alice Bentley or Tessa Jackson mean anything to you?" the DI asked.

"I've seen them on the news, and I know they're missing, but no, Jeremy never mentioned either name to me previously, that I recall."

"What about Katherine Weight?"

"No. Is she missing too? What's going on with all these women?" He raised his voice in alarm.

Dove reassured him and added, "Anything you can tell us might help to find Tessa and Alice, whatever information you have . . ."

There was a brief silence, and the man took his glasses off, rubbed them on the back of his sleeve and replaced them. "Jeremy hasn't been himself for a couple of months, and a couple of conversations, including the one last night, have worried me."

"Go on."

"He was worried about Klara, a friend of his, and kept saying he needed to keep an eye out for her, like she might be in trouble or something."

"Klara?"

"Klara Payton. She's a doctor too, but we've known the family from when the kids played together. They were our next-door neighbours. It was her sister who drowned at Fernsham Ponds, wasn't it?"

CHAPTER THIRTY-SEVEN

Another body, this time even further in the past and female. Dove raised her eyebrows at the DI and he shook his head slightly. "Can you tell us about the drowning? What happened?"

"Didn't Jeremy mention it?"

"He didn't."

The old man looked uncomfortable, and fidgeted with his glasses again. "Klara and her sisters lived next door to us when they were kids. It was just the mother and grandmother taking care of them. They all used to mess around together. One night, they drove back from some party half drunk early one morning, ran out of fuel at Fernsham Ponds and abandoned the car."

Dove was taking quick notes, and tapping searches into her iPad as he spoke. All she could think about was, here was a fourth body from Klara and Jeremy's past . . .

Jeremy's father continued, "They were nearly home by then, and you can walk through the field by the ponds and shortcut straight back to where we used to live. Instead, it appears they thought it would be a good idea to walk across the frozen lake. I think from what Jeremy said they were daring each other to walk on the ice to retrieve thrown beer cans or something. Stupid little idiots." He paused to take a sip of water. His hand was shaking as he carefully replaced the glass onto the white lace coaster.

"Please do go on," Jon urged him.

"Klara's younger sister, Isla, was seeing Jeremy at the time. Silly teenage stuff." He sighed deeply. "Isla fell through the ice. They said later it must have been a thinner patch and she got unlucky. Horrible thing to happen, and the stupid kids scared themselves silly. Krystyna, the elder sister, ran off to try and get reception on her phone so she could call for help." He paused. "Jeremy went in after Isla her to try and save her, dropped his phone in the water and got stuck in the lake himself."

"But Jeremy survived?"

"It was January, about five in the morning when they left the car and nine by the time the emergency services found them. Freezing weather too, so it was a miracle Jeremy survived as long as he did. But Klara managed to find him and drag him out on her own. She said she walked around and around the lake shouting, waiting for Krystyna to come back."

"Presumably Krystyna did call for help?" Dove queried.

"Yes, but she had to walk a long way in the dark before she got a mobile signal, and then she hadn't got a clue where she was. It took far longer than it should have done for emergency services to get to the lake and round up the kids." The old man took a large handkerchief from his cardigan pocket and blew his nose with a trumpeting sound.

"Isla was already dead when they arrived?" Jon asked.

"Yes. They assume she got trapped under the ice and couldn't find a way out. Given the temperature of the water, she would have died very quickly even if she hadn't drowned. It was such a cold winter, I remember . . ."

"Klara got Jeremy out by herself?" Jon queried again.

"Yes, I told you, she pulled him out, and started trying to warm him up while they waited for the paramedics . . ." His voice was softer now, more hesitant.

"Was there anything else you wanted to add?" Dove prompted, noticing the change.

"I'd almost forgotten . . . It was an odd thing, but when the ambulance crew got there they found Klara had stripped off her clothes and his and they were both naked underneath a pile of coats the kids had chucked off when they were messing around on the ice. The lake is around half a mile from where they left the car, so she could never have carried or dragged Jeremy back to the vehicle to get him warm." He paused again and took another sip of water. "She said later she remembered body heat can keep people alive when nothing else can. Of course, she was right in a way, and still in shock, but it struck me as odd. Later, they pulled her dead sister from the lake, so who knows what was going through her brain, but I remember it being a bit strange . . ."

"How does this relate to Jeremy and our current investigation?"

The man frowned, his gaze moving from Dove to Jon, fierce and intense. "I know Jeremy and I know something is wrong. He has talked about the case so much since the first murder and abduction. He kept saying how terrible it was . . . I don't for a moment think he's suddenly started putting young men in freezers or abducting single mothers. It's . . . it's hard to explain, but I was glad he hasn't seen Klara for years. I always felt there was something a bit odd about her, too intense, and at university, they were obsessed with each other . . ."

"They dated?" Jon put in, making another note on his pad.

"Yes, right up until their final year. I was surprised given the history, and not really very happy. It was almost as if she chose the same university, the same course, because of him. I can't put a finger on it, but she always seemed to be out of kilter. Incredibly clever to talk to, but a little strange," Jeremy's father said softly.

"And you are worried Klara might be getting Jeremy involved in something?"

"Don't you go after my son; he's a good man and a good doctor," the man warned, his voice rising.

"We simply want to eliminate him from our enquiries," Dove said.

Jon wrapped up the call and they walked back up to the main office.

"Can you check out the drowning, and I'll find out where Klara is?" Jon asked.

"Yes, boss."

Back at her computer Dove looked up the archived reports and found the one for Isla Payton's tragic death. It had been dealt with by Nantich Valley, her old division, and just across the county border. Witness statements and reports showed no red flags. It was a tragic accident. She particularly noted the statement from Jeremy Masters.

Dove also scrolled down the archived newspaper articles, clicking on various possibles until she found the correct one:

Tragic Drowning at Fernsham Ponds

The death of fifteen-year-old Isla Payton has been ruled as accidental by Judge Eric Hamperson today. The teenager was involved in an incident at the beauty spot on the night of 11 December 2005.

The teenagers admitted they had been drinking, and consumed more alcohol after their car ran out of petrol and they decided to walk home across the conservation area. Isla was taking part in a 'silly game' according to her sisters, when she slipped on the frozen lake and fell through the ice. The remaining group called for help, and were later cared for by paramedics before being transferred to hospital.

Search teams later recovered Isla's body. The Natural Wildlife Trust, who own Fernsham Ponds, have warned against attempting to walk on the frozen lake and mill ponds in the area . . .

Dove sat back, not needing to read any more. So it was true. Klara had saved Jeremy's life. Putting him in her debt, perhaps? Had victim number one been an accident?

Klara had had a relationship with her dead sister's boyfriend. Jeremy had installed a new home security system the day after the first victim had been discovered . . .

Her glance fell on the window. "It's snowing again. What if we get stuck in here?"

"Jon'll make us carry on working, and we'll kip on the floor. Don't worry, Dove, you can share my sleeping bag." Josh appeared behind her carrying an armful of paperwork. "You off to get a statement from Klara Payton?"

"I am. See you later!"

"Yeah, it's fine. I'll just stay here in the nice warm office with my admin . . ." Josh pulled a face.

Jon called impatiently over to Dove, "Are you ready? Klara is back home now. Her grandmother passed away last night. Taking into account her recent bereavement and the sensitive nature of the incident, we'll go over to her house to talk."

As Dove sighed at the thought of getting back into the DI's freezing car, but he briskly disregarded her suggestion they take her car. She shoved a load of sports gear onto the back seat as they drove. "Tell me you aren't running in this weather?" she said, noting the muddy trail shoes.

He laughed. "No chance. But I have been going out round the park if it isn't actually snowing or sleeting. I need the fresh air."

"I know what you mean." She stared at the road ahead, brake lights of the vehicle in front reflecting off the wet, gritty tarmac. "I can't wait for this weather to shift."

Klara lived in an older building, one of a pretty row of stone cottages in Lymington-on-Sea. As they pulled up, she was trying to yank a recycling bin over a rut of dirty snow that had collected on the side of the road.

"Klara Payton?" The DI offered to help and she let him position the bin. Her eyes were red-rimmed and her hair tied up in a ponytail. She wore no make-up, but Dove could still see the tall, strikingly featured woman from the photograph.

She led them into her home, offered tea and coffee, and seemed friendly enough, but her brown eyes remained cold and her lips pressed firmly together when she wasn't actually speaking. The aura of grief was dominating the room, like great smoke clouds pulsing from underneath the beams and sneaking up from dark corners.

"We are so sorry for your loss," Dove said gently.

Klara met her eyes with a flash of emotion, which she quickly suppressed. When she spoke she was calm and cool. "Thank you. It wasn't unexpected. My grandmother, as I expect you discovered for yourselves, was 105, and had been sick for some time." A half smile hovered over her pale lips, vanishing swiftly. "She did always say she'd live for ever."

"I'm sorry. Were you very close?"

"Yes, we were. It was always a house full of girls." Her cool stare took in the police officers' sympathetic expressions, and she seemed to draw energy from their empathy. "My grandmother lost her husband just after my mother was born, and we lost my father just after my youngest sister was born."

She didn't elaborate on Isla's story, and now wasn't the right time to push for an answer.

"Can you tell us about Jeremy Masters?" the DI said.

"Jeremy?" Her expression was one of surprise, but it came just a second too late. "We work at the same hospital. Not in the same department, but we also do some research for a company called MEDA." Her voice was smooth and calm again, but her colour rose slightly, eyes brightening as she told them about her work for MEDA. "It's an exceptional opportunity to be able to be part of a global research facility. The different projects are fascinating. Life-changing, some of them."

"I imagine they might be. Do you also know Katherine Weight and Tessa Jackson?" The DI changed the subject, and put two photographs on the polished coffee table.

Klara sat with her hands folded in her lap, absolutely calm. She didn't reach for the pictures of the women, but nodded. "I do. We were all at university together. Jeremy and

I, Tessa and Katherine were in the same classes. I saw Tessa had been abducted recently, and I was horrified."

"Another woman was taken last night," the DI said.

"Really? I haven't been in the mood to check the news today . . . But that's terrible." Her response was mechanical, without obvious discomfort or shock.

"Had you been in touch with Tessa or Katherine since you left university?" Dove was taking notes. The woman was wearing a strong citrusy perfume and it was making her nose itch.

"Only with Jeremy. I had no idea Tessa lived round here." She smiled coldly. "As far as I remember, I heard Tessa got married, and Katherine went travelling after uni. But no, we didn't keep in touch. No reason, just different life paths, I suppose."

"We have reason to believe you visited Tessa Jackson back in August."

"I . . ." She looked down at her hands, which were shaking slightly. "Yes, yes I did. Sorry, my grandmother dying seems to have shaken everything, including my memory. I'd forgotten all about that. I saw her driving along the coast road. We had both stopped at the traffic lights on the new roundabout. I waved, because even after all these years, I was sure it was her."

"And then what happened?"

"I followed her. It seems odd, but I was going the same way so . . . She turned off down a farm track, and I had an hour before an appointment, so I followed her." The sad smile again. "We were good friends at university, and afterwards she vanished, saying she was going travelling, and cut off contact. Much like Katherine did. It isn't uncommon to head off for a year out, but I did my own travelling between college and university. I knew I would want to get to work as soon as I qualified."

Dove handed her the photographs and the newspaper clipping. "Did you know Katherine Weight changed her identity to Alice Bentley?"

Klara flushed again, and sat, lips slightly parted, eyes on the photographs. Finally, she looked up. "She came into the hospital with a friend. He was elderly. I don't know what the relationship was, but he had suffered a cardiac arrest, had a stent fitted and was in for a routine investigation. She . . . Katherine had red hair, but I recognized her immediately."

"Did she recognize you?" the DI asked.

Klara nodded. "I think so, but she pretended not to. In the end, I felt really embarrassed, thinking maybe I had made a mistake. I . . . didn't see her again, and the patient just brushed me off when I asked about her."

"When was this?"

"About six years ago," Klara said. "When I saw Tessa, I asked if she knew Katherine had a new identity. She did know. She said Katherine had reached out to her earlier this year, told her she was Alice now."

"What reason did she give for changing her identity?" The DI was taking notes, leaning forward in his chair.

"Tessa didn't know why, or if she did, she wouldn't tell me." Klara's pearl earrings danced as she shook her head. "My conversation with Tessa was short. She didn't want to speak to me properly, certainly not to catch up."

"I wonder why? Seems strange a group of former university friends wouldn't want to mull over the good times. I know I do with my old set sometimes. Relive the past . . . Tessa didn't finish her final year, did she?" the DI put in.

Klara's fearful gaze flickered between them, and she hesitated before answering. "No. She dropped out. I never knew why. None of us did. We all tried to contact her, and eventually her mum told me she had been attacked at some party." Klara was frowning. "I felt so bad, because she must have thought she couldn't reach out to me."

"Were you at the party when Tessa was attacked?"

"No, I wasn't, and there were so many parties. I mean, we were studying hard, but we also partied hard, and we loved sports. Our group was one of the strongest friendship groups I've ever been in. It was like we were soulmates." Her eyes were shining now, reminiscing. "At times, when we were all together working on a project, it felt like we could do anything."

CHAPTER THIRTY-EIGHT

"You presented a final-year dissertation on hypothermia," Jon said, watching her face.

Her lashes flickered, but she continued to stare at her hands.

"Can you tell us about your hypothermia research?" Dove suggested.

The other woman looked up at last, her brown eyes brilliant. "I wanted to try and develop something that might help warm the body from the inside out. Something that might have helped Isla if Jeremy had got her out of the lake in time . . ."

"Go on."

"You can read my dissertation if you like," a faint smile, "I have it somewhere and I can send it over. I wanted . . . we wanted to create a drug that would work directly on the target area at first, but then I realized the body's metabolism is so reduced by hypothermia, drugs are inefficient, as they simply aren't metabolized."

"And did you come close to finding a drug?" Dove asked, fascinated.

"Yes, we did, but . . ." She frowned. "There is a lot of research into hypothermia, and some of it dates from the

World War Two experiments on prisoners in Dachau. The others were keen to use some of the data, because it supported our findings, but I felt very badly about it. In fact, I almost pulled out of the project." She moistened her lips. "My grandmother was at Dachau, and she was one of the prisoners involved in the hypothermia trials, so you see how wrong it would have been for me to condone using the Nazi data. I felt it was unethical, too, but for me, personally disrespectful."

Dove, having done her own brief research on the hypothermia trials, and been sickened by the graphic horrors involved, couldn't help but agree. It was made even worse by the fact Klara had a family connection to the trials.

"I see," Jon said. "Klara, is it possible that any of your former colleagues could be resurrecting your research project? Could this be why you and Jeremy keep coming up in our investigation, the reason we have two young men frozen to death and left at the houses of two of your former university friends?"

Dove held her breath, as Klara sat, breathing fast, eyes down, her long hair curtaining her face, in a way that reminded Dove of her niece, Delta, when she was in trouble. But eventually the woman raised her head again.

"I'm sorry, but I don't know what you are talking about." Her voice was calm, but her eyes shone, and even as she looked at them a tear slipped out, trembling on her lashes before running down her cheek. "Sorry, talking about my grandmother, you know . . ." She pulled a wad of tissues from her trouser pocket, and wiped her face.

After that brief moment of breakthrough, they couldn't touch her. She wasn't impolite, simply rejecting any suggestions, any offers of help, so they ran quickly through Klara's movements the nights of the abductions. Like Jeremy, she had been working when Tessa vanished and, of course, she had a rock-solid alibi for last night's abduction.

Despite her lapse, and the outward signs of grief and exhaustion, her voice was clear and strong now. She talked in calm, measured tones, pausing before answering, weighing up options.

Dove could easily imagine her talking to her patients, explaining medical complexities with absolute clarity. "You knew Jeremy before university, didn't you? In fact, I believe as a teenager, you saved his life."

Klara studied her, not moving for a several minutes, dark brown eyes expressionless, before she smiled. "Yes, I did. The night Isla died." Her expression changed, and she sighed. "I try not to think about that night. Losing a sister and knowing it could have been avoided is a hard thing to live with. It was my fault we ran out of petrol, my job to fill up the car the day before, and I forgot. But teenagers do stupid things, don't they? Adults too, of course . . ."

"We are sorry to have to bring up difficult memories, but we are just collecting information from everyone who knew Tessa and Alice," the DI said carefully.

"It's okay. It was a long time ago," Klara assured him, before continuing in her smooth, lecturer's voice, apparently recovering her poise. "Jeremy and I were children together, but we never met Tessa and Katherine — Alice — until university, so I honestly don't think Isla's death is relevant to your investigation. It was a tragic accident." She finished the sentence and silence hung in the room.

Klara seemed to feel she had said enough now. She rose from her chair, collected their half-full mugs of tea and turned towards the kitchen. "I'm sorry, but I need to get on now. My mother insisted on staying at the house, and there are things I need to organize . . . My other sister, Krystyna, is flying into Heathrow and I need to arrange a car . . ." She pressed a slim, pale hand to her forehead and her jaw was clenched tight. For a long moment she just stood there, but even as Dove started to say something she recovered, and apologized again for being so 'off balance'.

"There was just one other thing . . ." the DI said. "You may have heard a body was discovered in the lake at St

Mathew's last summer. The deceased has been named as JD Turner. I don't suppose the name rings any bells?"

"Poor man, but no, I'm afraid not. Now I really do need to get on . . ." Klara said.

"Are you sure the name doesn't mean anything to you?"

"I said no. Sorry, I have told you everything I know, and I am completely exhausted. I need to spend time with my mother," Klara said, face tight, jaw rigid with control.

"Thank you for your time. If you could just read through your statement and sign to say you are happy with the contents . . . and if you do remember anything else, don't hesitate to call us . . ." Jon said.

She signed her statement and took the cards they gave her, smiling politely, mechanically as they headed for the door.

The DI turned back just as she was about to close the door. "Just one last thing, Dr Payton. Is that a new alarm system?" He pointed to a bright yellow box above the front door, and a control panel just inside the doorway. The plaster was chipped and the paint damaged where it had been installed.

"I . . ." She seemed at a loss for a moment, clearly unable to see why he had asked. "Yes, it is. Why?"

"I couldn't help but notice Dr Masters had a new alarm system at his flat. The company logo is quite distinctive, with the yellow on black. I just wondered if there was a reason you had one, too?" His voice was casual, and he was still half-turned towards the garden path.

"No reason. I was thinking of updating my system, and when I spoke to Jeremy, it came up in conversation. He was able to recommend the company. Word of mouth. I believe that's how most local business works. There is no mystery there." Her face had tightened again, and her words were touched with something that could have been anger. "I'm afraid I really do have to get on now."

The two officers walked quickly down the path and across the road to the car. When Dove glanced back the blonde woman was still watching them, apparently waiting for them to leave.

"What do you think?" Jon asked as they pulled away, having brushed a dusting of snow off the windscreen.

"She's so calm and cool. The only time she came close to showing any real emotion was when she talked about her grandmother. Oh, and the alarm system. Why would that hit a nerve?"

"Yes, the alarms. And why should she and Jeremy suddenly both install new systems? What could they be afraid of?"

"Perhaps Tessa was blackmailing them about JD's death?" Dove suggested. "It's hard to tell if she's hiding anything or just devastated by her grandmother's death. If the police came round asking me questions the night after I'd lost a family member I think I might be far less polite than she was."

"Hmmm . . . Go and talk to our second victim's father with Josh, then dig up as much as you can on the Nazi hypothermia tests at Dachau. I want to see if we have any other unpleasant surprises in store. Klara said she would email her dissertation. Make sure she does. I was convinced we had her then, and I remain convinced she knows exactly what's going on."

"She's afraid of something or someone," Dove said. "Jeremy?"

"Maybe," Jon said as they arrived back at the station.

He paused as they got out into the icy breeze, breath blowing smoky plumes into the winter air. Dove pulled her hat down over her ears and slammed the car door. "It's a bit odd, isn't it, to go from close friends, to not speaking for years, to suddenly the whole group being back in contact."

The DI didn't seem to feel the cold as much as she did and was heading for the entrance with his jacket unzipped and gloves sticking out of his pocket. "The question is, who initiated this contact?"

They went quickly upstairs into the full force of the centrally heated office, and parted ways. Mentally adding to her to-do list, Dove was thinking about JD Turner again. Had he been at a party? If Tessa had turned to her friends for help, perhaps it had gone wrong when his body was found. She remembered Klara's words, '. . . Soul mates, we felt we could do anything . . .'

Or get away with anything. And if you screwed up, and you had everything to lose, who else would you turn to but your soulmates?

CHAPTER THIRTY-NINE

Klara did send over her dissertation, and Dove opened it slightly hesitantly. She had already reopened her file of research on Dachau and the Nazi medical experiments carried out on prisoners. It made her sick to her core, furious and desperately sad all at the same time.

There was a lot of medical jargon in the dissertation, so Dove decided to ask Jess for help if she needed a translator. The gist seemed to be, as Klara had said, they were trying to develop a drug which could be administered to a patient with severe hypothermia, even peri-arrest, and it would work in conjunction with external warming to, in simple terms, bring the person back from the brink.

It was an extraordinary idea, and Dove could instantly see how the military could benefit, how such a life-saving drug could be used in hospitals, and she could also see how Klara might have felt it was a legacy for both Isla and her grandmother. No wonder she had argued with Jeremy, Tessa and Katherine when they tried to use Nazi data in the project.

At the end of the dissertation was a list of potential hazards from re-warming, including peripheral vasodilatation, caused by venous peripheral pooling. She picked up her phone and called Jess.

"Hi love, how's it going?"

"Have you heard of Nazi medical experiments in World War Two, specifically hypothermia experiments, on prisoners?"

"I'm not sure I like the way this is going, but I am aware of them, yes," Jess said cautiously.

"So could our two frozen victims have been made hypothermic on purpose, and maybe died during the re-warming process?" Dove asked, eyes on the dissertation.

"Yes, but there are so many ways of contracting hypothermia . . . Some patients can appear dead before they even are. They could go into pulseless VT and . . . You mean our killer is actually experimenting with the effects of hypothermia?" Jess was horrified.

Dove summarized the conversation with Klara, and waited, biting her thumbnail.

"Okay, send me the dissertation and I'll go back over the post-mortems and see if anything new jumps out, given we now have an idea why they might have been killed. Bloody hell, Dove, this is insane."

* * *

The father of the second frozen victim, blonde-haired Elijah, lived in one of the new builds on Meadow Green Estate. It was a twenty-minute drive from the station, and Dove pulled over opposite the chemist for Josh to run in for a bag of cough sweets and painkillers. He was slowly succumbing to the flu but, like Steve, refusing to admit it. She supposed it was only a matter of time before she got the bug, although her immune system was normally pretty good, considering her unhealthy diet.

She glanced over the road and smiled to see her sister's café filled with customers, the bright glow of the lights inside casting a flood of warmth across the slushy pavement. The exterior was painted red, adding to the festive impression, and the luscious smells of fresh roasted coffee and pastries floated out into the cold air.

Josh was back, clambering awkwardly into the car, with his blue-and-white pharmacy bag of medicaments.

"You are definitely going to be off sick before the week is up," she told him, putting her window back up, and turning her back on the café.

"I'm absolutely fine," Josh said hoarsely. "Hardcore that's me."

"Just don't give it to me," she told him as they drove carefully through the winding roads of the estate. Neat little brick houses with square patches of soft white snow in their front gardens, cars shrouded by soft white blankets, and all the time the steady fall of new flakes.

Elijah's father was a tall, slightly stooping man. Dove put him to be in his fifties.

"He's never been out of touch for this long, not since we lost my wife five years ago in a car accident." Pain touched his face, furrowing his brow and pinching his mouth.

Shit, Dove thought, *this is going to be bad.*

Josh was coughing again and apologizing, as the man fetched him a glass of water.

"I'm so sorry for your loss," Dove said, when they were seated at the table.

"I can't believe someone would kill him. Why?" The man was bewildered. "Him and the other boy, they were frozen, weren't they? I don't understand . . ."

"Do you have anyone who can come and be with you?" Dove asked gently. She wasn't sure who was acting as FLO, but she hoped they would arrive soon. Hopefully, they weren't also hit by the flu. Organization and communication were all over the place with so many off sick.

The man shook his head, hands pressed against his eyes, scrubbing furiously at the tears leaking down his wrinkled cheeks. "There's just us . . . I suppose I need to let his mates know. And Tommy'll be furious he didn't turn up for work today."

"Where does he work?"

"Ski and Sky," the man said, waving a hand towards the front of his property. "So lucky having good employment opportunities right on our doorstep."

Dove felt her gaze sharpen, and her mind spin back to the industrial estate. Both victims spending time on the estate, working and working out, concentric circles colliding.

But Tessa Jackson's ex-husband was also an employee of Ski and Sky. He had been discounted in the course of the investigation, and so far his involvement was verified as purely related to his desire to reconnect with his daughters. It might be worth double-checking to see if he had been working when Tessa's ex had visited Ski and Sky.

"Can you tell me when you last saw Elijah?" Dove asked. "We just need to get as much information as we can at this stage."

"Yes . . . I . . ." The man took down a black leather diary and flicked through the pages. "He left on the morning of the twentieth. Said he was going on holiday, up to Edinburgh to stay with a friend he hadn't seen for ages. I didn't pry, and like I said, he's good about keeping in touch."

"How long did Elijah say he would be away for?" Dove asked.

"Two weeks," the man said promptly.

Charles had gone for six weeks and Elijah only two? Dove frowned at Josh, who raised an eyebrow. "Have you had any contact with him since he left?"

"I have." Elijah's father was turning pages in his diary. "I write everything down . . . Here. Last Thursday, he sent me a text, and Monday this week, just to say he was okay and would be back on time."

"Can we see the texts, please?" Josh asked.

The man unlocked his phone and slid it across the table. "Here you go."

Are you all right Elijah? Haven't heard from you. Dad

I'm fine. See you soon.

Dove excused herself and called Jon. When he answered, she explained the contact, and he agreed to get back with any updates on Elijah's phone. "We fast-timed the call data this morning, but it's still switched off, to my knowledge." She could hear him tapping on his keyboard. "Last known location was on Monday. I'll send the map over to you . . . Darkwood Lane. But we checked, and there's nothing except forest for a couple of miles in either direction at that particular point. The rest of his call data has been accounted for, apart from three calls to an unknown number in the period of the month prior to his death. Another burn phone, and different number to the one we assume was used to communicate with Charles. This number matches the one used on the ad at Hanson's gym."

He had still been alive on Monday, though. And Charles Richardson had told his girlfriend he was in a cab . . . a cab to where? And he must have left his van somewhere, too. Or perhaps he had willingly let his killer use it?

Dove found she was visualizing Elijah waiting by the side of the road, perhaps becoming doubtful as to the legitimacy of the enterprise, or maybe not. Very few mistakes so far by the perpetrator, so the whole thing must have been well thought out. Was there a bus stop near the south end of Darkwood Lane? The van caught on the ambulance dash cam scrambling to escape could have been used as a pick-up and drop-off.

She felt the familiar buzz of excitement that came with picking up the trail. It was surely not impossible that wherever Elijah had been, Tessa and Alice were, too?

"Was Elijah into sports at all?"

"Yes, loved his sport. Climbing was his thing. He won all sorts of awards for it, and last year he went off with a group to climb Kilimanjaro. For charity, it was . . ." The man put his head in his hands briefly, before looking up with red eyes. "It still hasn't sunk in . . ."

"Did he use Hanson's gym at all?"

"The new place? Yes, it's right opposite his work."

"Do you recognize any of these people?" Dove pulled the photos up on her iPad and tilted the screen towards the man.

He studied the images for a moment, and then tapped a finger on Anne-Marie. "Her . . . Not sure if he might have brought her round one evening, or if he had her in the car . . ."

"Would this have been recently?" Josh asked.

"It would. In the last few months, for sure."

"Did Elijah ever use sports drinks or supplements when he was training?" Dove queried.

The man smiled sadly. "We've got a whole cupboard full of the stuff. You can take a look . . ." He stood up and went into the kitchen, followed by the two officers.

The cupboard was full of samples, boxes and tubs. Dove pulled them out carefully. "Protein powder, gels, energy drinks, bars . . ."

SOCOs had already been through the house, but they were given permission to have a quick look at Elijah's bedroom. Dove felt her heart grow heavier as she looked at the photos stuck on the walls, the posters, the Xbox, the computer, the dirty clothes and clean trainers littering the floor.

There was a box of energy bars, the same brand as the ones Steve was currently addicted to. Her eyes swung to the shelving and she wasn't surprised to see medals and trophies crowding the wide wooden shelves. Another fitness guru. What was it that was making fit, healthy, intelligent young men give themselves up for freezing? Did they know what was going to happen? With no traces of drugs in their bodies, either anything given had already passed through the system when they died, or they had gone into whatever they had gone into completely of their own free will.

Another stash of supplement boxes was stacked untidily under the desk. Josh leaned down and carefully picked up an unopened bottle, with distinctive blue and silver labels, turning it around in his hand.

"That is the same brand Tony Garner was selling, ICEE," Dove said.

CHAPTER FORTY

Freezing cold and still shivering from the icy wind, Dove stripped off and started running a hot shower as soon as she got home. The water took a while to heat up as it ran through the creaking pipes of the old house, meandering its way to the bathroom, so she sat on the bed with her phone.

Quinn would be back soon, and they would have an hour or so to catch up before they went to bed. She sent him a quick text to say she was home and would see him soon.

She was longing to get this case solved, not only to bring the killer to justice and put those missing puzzle pieces into the frame, but to have time with her fiancé. They were supposed to be planning their wedding for next year, but if this workload carried on, they wouldn't be getting married for two years at least.

Jess had sent an email, replying to Dove's queries on hypothermia and the research Klara had possibly resurrected. There was a link to a medical site with an essay on the mammalian diving reflex, and Dove skimmed it with interest, one eye on the shower.

Had Isla's death really been an accident? She could see how maybe the trauma had affected Jeremy and Klara in different ways, but also united them in their determination to find something that would help other patients. How had a desire to help turned rotten? What if JD Turner had been their first human trial case? Perhaps Tessa's assault had nothing to do with Turner's death; he'd just been coerced into taking part.

Although she couldn't imagine how a street-smart dealer would allow himself to get into that situation. Maybe if he had taken something, he may not have been aware what was going on.

But he died, and all the research stopped. After university, the four went their separate ways until Turner's body was discovered . . . But why start researching again now?

Dove ran frustrated hands through her hair, and rubbed her eyes. It was quite ridiculous they had a pool full of suspects and weren't able to pin any hard evidence on a single one of them. It was like trying to catch four bars of soap you had dropped in the bath.

Jess sent a text suggesting they catch up properly when the case was solved, and Dove replied with crossed finger emojis. Her friend also sent over a couple of pictures of her twins. They were gorgeous, chubby-cheeked and round-eyed. As usual, Dove felt a rush of relief that the pain was gone, that she could see baby photos, actual babies out in strollers, and interact with her friends normally. After the incident, after she was told she could never have children, the raw agony — not only of the healing wound, but also at the prediction for the future — had left her broken inside and out.

She stuck a hand in the shower. The water was steaming hot now, and the soothing steady beat of water made her shoulders droop as tension left her body.

Slowly, she had come to terms with her diagnosis after the surgery, had even pondered other options. Adoption was one, and Quinn was on side with whatever she decided. Once again, she felt a warm glow at the thought of his calm confidence in their future together. Her own body might have been cruelly savaged, but she wouldn't let it ruin her life.

She finally switched off the shower and slowly wrapped herself in a towel. The bathroom was a good place to think. A poor substitute for the sea, but at least it was hot, and blasted away the ache in her shoulders.

Sometimes, she would light a scented candle and . . . She froze on that thought, thinking of her favourite scent, which was lemon and rosemary. The strong citrusy perfume Klara had been wearing when they interviewed her had tugged at her memory, but she had been unable to place it.

Now she did. Professor Claire Renuard, the university tutor, had been either wearing the same scent, or Klara had very recently left her house. And yet she had said in her statement she hadn't seen Klara for ages. *Jeremy* had come in for the careers talk . . .

Realizing she was still sat on her bed wrapped in just a towel, Dove brushed out her wet hair, blasted it dry and pulled on comfy sweats and a thick jumper with her purple ski socks.

How the hell could she possibly ring the DI and talk about perfume? And yet . . . She sent a text, just explaining when and why, but even before he answered, she knew they could hardly use her nose as evidence.

We can bring Klara in and talk to her under caution tomorrow. Might be able to rattle her if we imply we knew she has been to see Claire recently. Equally, they might both just like the same perfume.

She wandered downstairs and made a few preparations for dinner, before curling up on the sofa, stroking Layla, who had hopped onto her lap. She checked her phone again, picked up a book, and put it down after five minutes, unable to settle, feeling a twinge of hunger in her belly.

The cat purred, staring up at her with big luminous golden eyes, and Dove wrenched her thoughts from work and fitting those damn puzzle pieces together, back to domestic arrangements. Where was Quinn? They should be ordering pizza by now, to go with the big green salad and garlic bread she had already prepared. Not to mention the bottle of white wine cooling in the fridge.

Worried now, she sent a third quick text, then left another voicemail, and when he didn't reply, she clicked on the phone tracker they both had. The green circle narrowed to somewhere close to the house, and she blinked, puzzled, as the orange dot representing Quinn settled. Why would he be down there?

His phone indicated he was down by the pier, or on the beach. Dove yanked on her thick jacket and snow boots, locked the house and jogged the ten minutes to the pier. Her boots and the icy, treacherous going slowed her down, but at least she got a little warmer, even as the chilly wind whipped her hair across her burning cheeks. She flexed her icy fingers in the wool gloves, whacking them against her thighs in an effort to warm them.

The case was pushed aside, all her senses were on high alert. As she moved, she scanned the darkness, straining her ears above the ebb and flow of the tide on the pebbles.

The pier loomed large and menacing in the darkness. The ice cream stand, the fishing bait shop and the arcades were all shuttered against the winter storms. The funfair, which in the summer months provided so much colour and noise, was dismantled, covers tied tightly over bulky machinery. Like so many closed eyes, the metal barricades prevented entrance to the wooden structure.

The freezing wind screamed in from the sea, numbing her face, tossing her shouts into the darkness. A shape on the edge of the beach, where the shingle met the road, made her pause, heart thumping from exertion and worry.

The figure was still, watching her intently, but even as she moved tentatively towards it, she saw it wasn't a figure, but a tall plastic advertising sign tied to the lamppost. Buffeted by the wind, it gave the illusion of a shadowy figure watching the beach. She fumbled for her torch as she continued to struggle along the stones, sweeping the blaze of light in a wide arc, still calling when she caught her breath.

Then she saw him. A dark shape standing on the tideline, half hidden by the dark wooden struts of the pier, made her falter. "Quinn?"

He turned, clearly surprised to see her. The beach was in darkness, but a faint glow from the security lights on the pier touched his haggard face.

"The phone tracker," she explained, as she slithered across the stones towards him. She gently touched his arm. "What happened?" Dove knew that sometimes cases got to Quinn, in the way her own cases touched her emotions. The last time she had seen him like this, he had been called to an RTC in which a pedestrian had been pushing a pram when a car lost control and hit her. She had gone over the bridge with her twin girls, and into an icy river.

Quinn accepted the pressure of her fingers, closing his cold hand over hers, but still not meeting her eyes. "A light aircraft crashed over at Lea Down . . ."

She could tell there was more, and much as she was keen to get her fiancé home and warm inside, she let him talk.

"Four people on board, a whole family . . ."

"Oh no!" Dove didn't ask, squeezing his arm tighter as though she could absorb some of his pain.

"They all died apart from the mother. Her three sons. Gone. We tried so hard . . ." His voice faltered.

"I know."

"It just got to me. Most of the time I can compartmentalize, but sometimes, especially when we fail, it doesn't work. You know that. I just felt I needed to get out here and freeze for a bit . . ."

"You didn't fail, Quinn . . ."

"You don't know! You weren't there. We did fail. I failed. That poor woman was watching us, screaming, but all the time hoping we could bring her babies back to life. She said she wanted to die, too, when she realized they were gone. Her whole family . . ." he repeated dully.

Dove felt her own tears roll down her cheeks. "Oh, Quinn. I wish I could say something . . . Come home and get warm. Then if you want to talk, I'm here, and if not, I'm still here, okay?"

She held her breath until he nodded and shambled awkwardly up the beach towards his car. He fumbled for the keys, and Dove was silent, treading carefully, her heart torn for him and for the family who had lost their lives.

They reached the house in a few minutes and Quinn parked with exaggerated care. They walked through the door in silence, and as he threw his bag in the corner, he told her he was just going to have a shower and go to bed.

"Whatever you want," Dove said softly, her fingers finding his. But there was no answering pressure this time, and his expression was glazed. He cared so much. Of course he did. It was why he loved his job, but it also left him exposed to heartbreak when he couldn't save a life, or felt he had failed. After the woman and her twins, he had been in a dark place for a long time, finally accepting the counselling offered by the ambulance service.

Dove took the chilled bottle from the fridge and poured herself a glass of wine, realized again she was starving and heated up a can of her favourite tomato soup. She really should learn to cook . . . She settled down at the table, her senses alert to movements upstairs: the bathroom door, the shower, the creak of the floorboards in their bedroom, the heart-rending sigh as her fiancé collapsed into bed.

She began to flick through the case notes in her file, trying to link Charles with Elijah, waiting, biting her lip. Sure enough, a couple of hours later, heavy footsteps told her Quinn was coming down the stairs. She poured him a glass of wine, and as he entered the room, he saw her sitting at the table and half smiled.

Encouraged, she offered the glass. "Hey."

"Hey yourself. Why are you still up?" He picked up the wine but didn't drink it, instead twirling the glass, eyes fixed on the pale liquid.

She shrugged. "I had some notes to go over."

He sat opposite her, and finally met her eyes. "I was thinking . . . I was thinking about the mother and her kids, and it just keeps running over and over in my head. What if we were on scene earlier?"

"You might not have been able to save them even then." Dove took a deep breath and trod carefully, tiptoeing around the subject. "Was there a reason you didn't arrive earlier?"

"No! I mean, just traffic on the Bay Road. It took a while to get through. The helicopter was there, so we had the doctor and the rescue team from Greendown Airfield. That's where they came from . . . It was a family flight because the eldest kid had just got his Private Pilot's Licence. The visibility was good, so they have no idea what happened. Maybe he stalled for some reason. The AAIB will take over now and try to figure it out. Shit! We were too late . . ."

"But when you did get there, did you follow all the protocol and work to the very best of your ability?" Dove's voice grew stronger.

"I . . . Of course I did! What are you suggesting?" His eyes were shocked, his voice rising in anger.

"And your crew? Did they do the same?" She wasn't letting up.

The shock faded from his face and the half smile returned. "Shut the hell up, Dove, I know what you're doing."

"So think about this. Everyone did their job, in fact, I bet everyone went above and beyond to save those boys, and to care for the mother." She paused, weighing up his emotions. He was a little more relaxed. "If you can be honest with yourself and admit that, the second-guessing will fade a little. I'm not trying to be a pain in the arse, but you know that I know as well as anyone."

"Stop bloody counselling me." But there was colour back in his voice and his hand was steady as he reached out to take a sip of wine.

"I bet they've already offered you counselling. This time take it, and let it help you, so you can get back out on the road. You've got two days off, so ring in to the counsellor tomorrow morning. Don't let it fester."

He nodded. "Yeah, they did offer help in the debrief. It's standard, isn't it? I . . . I said I'd think about it." Quinn folded his arms, tucking his hands into the crook of his elbows. "I hate the bloody winter. When I think about it, everything bad happens in the snow. The ice is treacherous, people are freezing under the pier, and in their own homes if they don't have adequate heating, the roads are covered in black ice . . ."

"Don't think about it, do it," she told him. "You know from before the sooner you ask for help, the sooner it will be given. Hell, I know that too, so don't think I'm preaching."

"I know, babe, you're just being a bossy cow as usual." This time he reached for her hand. "It's that instinctive reaction, to punish yourself for failing. I felt like that before, after the RTC with the babies in the river. It's like, they died, so why should I be allowed to get my life back together?"

"So you can get out and save more lives," Dove told him firmly. There was no easy solution to this part of the job for either of them, but they had seen each other broken apart, stripped raw by their own experiences, and built themselves back up.

Together. It hadn't been easy. It would never be easy, but they were finally in a good place. Dove twisted her engagement ring around her finger, touching it like a good luck talisman.

Quinn was silent for a long time and she waited, sipping her wine. Then he smiled, thinly and reluctantly, but it was there. "So are you ordering pizza or are we down to that revolting tomato soup?"

She smiled back in relief. "The usual?"

"Please." His shoulders sagged slightly as the tension was released, and she watched him carefully as she placed the order, but when she put the phone down, he was busy getting the salad out of the fridge, turning the oven on to reheat the garlic bread . . .

They ate on the sofa, balancing their feast on knees and cushions, the television on low in the background. The local pizza restaurant was excellent, and Dove only managed three quarters of her ham and pineapple. Unusually, Quinn claimed he was full without finishing his chicken and chorizo special, and she glanced at him through a last mouthful of garlic bread.

Quinn downed the last of his wine and held out his hand. "If you're done, let's go to bed."

She smiled at him and closed her laptop with a snap. Personal life before professional — and moments like this just reinforced to her that the choices she had made were, more often than not, good ones. She loved Quinn and hated to see him hurt like this, but with their professions, it would happen over and over again. They were good at picking up the pieces.

CHAPTER FORTY-ONE

Dove woke at five and, unable to get back to sleep, creeped downstairs so she didn't wake Quinn. Even in sleep his expression looked sad, and she had to resist the temptation to kiss him.

A mug of coffee next to her plate of toast, she began to pick over her notes from the day before, shoving some paperwork back into her bag, taking a highlighter to other files.

A few months ago she would have been out in the sea with her board as the first glimmers of light hit the water, but now work was taking over again. And then there was the weather . . . Quinn had dropped hints about a yoga class or Pilates on YouTube, but although she enjoyed the yoga, she needed the extra buzz of surfing, the cold sea, salt on her lips and in her hair, to de-stress.

Her research pulled her back towards the computer. In the same year that Katherine Weight supposedly died in the summer, Alice Bentley applied for a driver's licence in September. Alice Bentley looked remarkably similar to Katherine Weight, except her hair was long and blonde.

Fake ID wasn't hard to come by, and presumably she had picked some up on her travels, or she wouldn't have been able to fly home. From then onwards to the present day, the paper trail for Alice Bentley was easy to follow. She had acquired the red curls in her more recent photographs. Like Tessa, she seemed to swerve social media. Alice had no Facebook account. Medical records showed she had given birth to twin girls in Abberley General three years ago.

The birth certificate didn't list the father's name. Dove stopped reading and sipped her coffee. Why had she changed her identity, if it wasn't to do with JD Turner's death? Had something happened during her travels, or was the ferry fire a lucky coincidence? Perhaps she had just seen the chance to disappear, and taken it.

But she had moved back to the area just after her twins were born, after living and working in many different places, never staying more than a year or so. Was she hiding from someone? Tessa had been running from an abusive spouse, so maybe Alice, too, was afraid of something or someone in her own past.

Dove was so engrossed in her files that when her phone buzzed she answered it without thinking.

"Morning."

"Hi, Steve. Are you all right?"

"Coming into work tomorrow. My cough's almost gone and Zara's feeling better too. Grace seems to have shaken it off completely. I think they had it before me, and I don't think it's the flu or we'd all still be knocked out."

"Steve, you've only had three days off. Stay in bed, for god's sake," she said, concerned.

"Don't nag, I'm okay. I saw we have a new victim and another missing woman, so I can't stay away . . . What's up with you? You don't sound your usual wide-awake self," he asked.

Keeping an eye and an ear out for her fiancé, Dove told him about Quinn's light aircraft shout from yesterday.

"I saw it on the news. Bloody horrible thing to happen just before Christmas."

"Bloody horrible thing to happen any time, but you know how these things can get you sometimes," Dove said, speaking quietly as she heard the bed creak upstairs. "Listen,

I've got to go, and if you're sure you're all right, I'll see you at work tomorrow morning."

"Later, Dove."

Glancing at the kitchen clock she realized it was time to get ready for work. She went to the bottom of the stairs and listened. The noise of the shower echoed through the old house, and meant Quinn was definitely up, so at least she didn't have to worry about being quiet.

She went wearily back into the kitchen and flicked the switch for the coffee machine, their one expensive joint purchase so far, and pulled his favourite mug out of the cupboard.

* * *

After the briefing, the DI walked up to Dove. "As Steve is still among the ranks of our sick colleagues, you can work with me again today. We're down to less than half our original team, and we have double the ground to cover now."

She nodded. He was a good boss and she enjoyed working with him. It wasn't like the easy relationships she had with Steve, Lindsey or Josh, but there was mutual respect and understanding. "Actually, Steve rang me this morning and said he'll be back tomorrow."

"Good to hear. And where are we at for today?"

"I think I've dug up all I can on Alice Bentley. She dropped her old identity after the ferry fire, so unless something happened on her trip, I think she could have seen as a perfect way to hide her involvement in JD Turner's death — a gift from the gods, if you will," Dove suggested. "There is also the fact both our frozen victims told their families they were going 'up north' or 'on holiday' when, in fact, it seems from the data we have from Elijah's phone, they stayed pretty close to home."

"I agree. And if the van was used as a pick-up and drop-off, it's likely they were kept somewhere within a fifty-mile radius." He was still studying Alice's file, which included the information Dove had emailed over this morning before she left for work. "I'd like you to see if we can join any more dots between Tessa, Alice, Jeremy and Klara, before we get Klara in."

Dove had just paused to grab another coffee and a packet of jelly sweets when Josh stopped at her desk with a report on the murder victims' phones.

"This has just come in. I wasn't sure if you'd seen it?" Josh said, his eyes gleaming, dimples showing. "Search team finally found Tessa's mobile phone."

"Thanks, Josh, I hadn't seen it. Had my head down on the computer and now I think I'm seeing double," Dove told him, rubbing her eyes.

"Lucky you. Two of me!"

"Idiot. Okay, get on with it. Where was her phone?"" she prompted him, but she was laughing.

"It was two miles on from her farm, heading west for Oxely and Northingly. It was chucked into the woods on the side of the road. Technically, it was a dog-walker who found it and called it in."

"I'm surprised the dog-walker even picked it up," Dove said. "Mobile phones get chucked away all the time."

"It was wrapped in a blue logo T-shirt," his face was serious now, "the one we assume Tessa was wearing when she disappeared. And the phone was half a mile away from the triangulated point on Darkwood Lane, which is where . . ."

"Which is the area where Elijah's phone last pinged a signal," Dove said. "So the killer is in this area, somewhere. Shit, why haven't we found the two missing women!"

Josh ticked off reasons on his fingers, "The weather is great to hide out in if you've got some shelter, and makes it bloody hard for our search teams and the helicopter. Lastly, the countryside around Darkwood Lane is hills, forestry commission pinewoods, and remote farms, all of which have been checked as far as anyone is able."

Dove peered out the window. It was daytime and hardly light, cars had their headlights on, and she could see slow traffic on the main road, crawling along, battling the dirty drifts of snow. "Great weather for a killer with an ice obsession," she remarked with frustration.

CHAPTER FORTY-TWO

Now it was my turn. My footsteps made no sound on the floor. My heart was drumming so fast I felt sick. This change, this added terror had dragged body and soul back together for the past few weeks.

The room was small, and I blinked as he introduced himself, wondering why he bothered. Wondering also at the presence of a large square wooden structure filled with water. As requested, as my first ritual of the day, I dipped my hand in the water, tentatively, always ready to draw back if it burned, was treated with poisons, maybe. But it was icy as usual, so very cold that when I drew back my fingers were pinched and white. This was also normal. A new normal.

One of the figures nodded approvingly and made a note on the clipboard. There were others in white coats and the doctor. Of course he was there, because that's what this was all about — sacrificing in the name of medicine, or science, or to save others. The doctor said firmly, his pale gaze resting somewhere above my head, that if one person died to save ten more, it would be worth it.

I didn't say his estimation of deaths was a long way out, nor did I point out that the sacrificial did not volunteer for this. I wanted to live, so I sat on the bed and waited, still and frozen with horror at what was about to happen, dangling my bare legs above the cold floor. I think once I had lived through it, the horrors were intensified because I knew what

223

would happen. So now I tried to prepare myself, wriggling forward to plant my feet firmly on the floor, bony fingers gripping the thin blanket.

There was a large mirror opposite, reflecting the nightmares which were played out in this room, and I could see myself, but it wasn't the 'me' in my head, in my memories. In the bright light, I was so pale and still I could have been carved like a doll from ice, or a chess piece waiting to be played.

CHAPTER FORTY-THREE

"Have they still got the dogs out?"

"They sent them straight over. Northingly and Eversham have offered extra help, so we may well get some bad news later, but fingers crossed as always!" Josh said.

Dove thought of the naked, frozen bodies of Charles and Elijah, and hoped they wouldn't find Tessa and Alice in a similar state. The spark that drove her often faltered when bodies of missing persons were found. It was a full stop, leaving the search for the killer ongoing but no happy ending for the families.

"In other news, Elijah hadn't applied to any clinical trials that we can find, and had no link to anything like that apart from his involvement in sports. Did you chase up the girlfriend?"

Dove shook herself out of her momentary depressing thoughts. "Anne-Marie? Yes. They did a running race together and got talking, added each other on social media. He is loosely in the same circles as Charles and Tony Garner," Dove said. "Either he saw the MEDA advert at the gym or got it off Harry's Facebook page."

The DI was back. "Dove, let's go. Alice Bentley's ex-boyfriend, Dave, is back. Josh, can you and Lindsey check in on

Klara? We've had eyes on Jeremy since he got home this morning, but I want you to call her, just remind her we're here if she wants to talk. Go carefully, because apart from her involvement as one of the St Mathew's four, we've got nothing on her."

"Yes, boss." Josh looked pleased as he wandered off.

Dove hauled her coat on and knotted her scarf. It was strange, zipping between victim to victim and slotting in and out of various aspects of the case. Normally, the MCT detectives were delegated to follow up on one specific lead and shared information as needed, but this investigation had created a tighter, far smaller team.

"You'll be pleased to know the car heater's now working again," the DI said, as they got into the vehicle. He glanced at his watch. "It's gone half one, do you need to eat?"

"I actually do," Dove said slightly apologetically. She was lucky he'd even asked. Chris, her old boss, hadn't considered his employees needed food or sleep. He was a machine and expected them to be of the same mould. "It's way past lunch and I'm starving. If you stop on West Street, I'll run into the coffee shop and grab hot drinks and sandwiches?" She leaned forward and turned the car heater up to max.

The DI patiently leaned forward and turned it down again. "It's working okay, but it'll burn up if you start with it on max."

"This car is falling apart," she sighed, and tugged her coat collar tighter around her chin, snuggling into the folds. "I feel like we are list-checking. You know, after you've had a bit of a breakthrough, but then you don't feel as though any progress is being made?"

Jon Blackman nodded. "This is part of it, though. It's just a question of being methodical. Hopefully, Tessa's phone will give us some leads. We've got our suspects; we just can't pin them down. It's not unusual, is it? At least we have a generous supply, with our two doctors both firmly in the frame."

"Do you still think Jeremy and Klara are working together?"

"I'll be completely honest and say at this moment in time, my money is on the four of them being involved in some kind of blackmail. It's easy to keep a secret when the murder victim is at the bottom of a lake, but now there's an investigation, someone was bound to get jittery. Friendships have soured, allegiances over the years may have changed. If nothing else, I think the group may have imploded, with Tessa and Alice getting the rough end of the deal." He pulled up outside a neat bungalow, frosted by the weather and hung with sparkly lights. There was a small shed in the front garden, and a tarpaulin covering something that could be a motorbike.

Alice's ex-boyfriend, Dave Squires, showed them into an immaculate, cosy home and offered the usual tea or coffee. "I'm not sure how much help I can be." His brown eyes were earnest, big square face ruddy in the central-heated warmth. "I haven't seen Alice for nearly four years."

Dove picked up a digestive biscuit from the full plate and nibbled. "Can you tell us the last time you saw her?"

He rubbed a hand across his chin. "I've been thinking since you called, and it must be just under four years ago. I saw her in town on a night out with some friends. We um . . . we dated again for a few months, but it was never going to work. It was always on and off, you know? When I met her the first time, she'd just come back from a year out travelling. We were both working in a nursing home in Leicester, sharing an overcrowded rental."

"Can you think of anyone from your shared past who might have worried Alice? Anyone she mentioned, or anything you heard on social media?" Dove suggested, feeling frustrated that this was a waste of time. A huge chunk of police time was spent just eliminating suspects, rather than, as the public imagined, chasing down the bad guys. It was vital to tick those boxes, but often infuriating to be wasting time.

"No. Alice was always a bit of a loner, and she liked her space. Very outdoory girl, and into her running when I knew her."

"And the twins? You don't know who their father might be?" the DI put in casually.

"No idea. I'm surprised she would have got pregnant. It was always a thing with us that she didn't want kids, didn't like them, but I would have been happy to have a few running around." Dove had calculated if he and Alice had broken up when he said they did, give or take a couple of months, there seemed every chance Dave was the father of the twin girls, but it didn't seem to cross his mind.

She looked over at Jon, saw he had drawn the same conclusion, and waited.

But Dave was busy reminiscing, clearly trying to fish up something useful. "Alice's parents are dead, and she was an only child. She never said much about her family, but seemed to like the fact I've got a load of siblings, cousins, aunts and uncles." He gave a short laugh. "Too many, really, and I like to avoid them all when I can!"

"Where did she work when she was with you?"

"We lived all over the place before we came down here. I had no ties and neither did she, so we just moved on whenever she got itchy feet. The most recent place was a nursing home off Glidden Street in Lymington-on-Sea. One of those big old Victorian houses converted into a place for people with dementia. Yeah, she loved her job and she always stayed in the same line of work."

"Any idea what she did previously?"

He frowned and shook his head. "I think she was doing the same thing before she went travelling . . . Maybe at the hospital? They'd have records, I suppose. She wasn't a nurse, though. Said she'd never have got through the training, or afforded to be a student, I do remember that."

The DI stood up. "Thanks for your time, Mr Squires, and if you happen to remember anything else that might help . . ."

He stood up to show them out, rubbing his big hands, worry clear in his face. "Can you let me know when you find her? I know we aren't together anymore, but, well . . . she was a good girl. Everyone loved Alice, and she had a big heart. Makes me sad to think of her baby girls missing their mum."

Dove exchanged looks with Jon as they got back into the car. "What do you think?"

"I can't see anything in his story to pick at, plus the alibi is solid. He was abroad. His boss has already confirmed it. Interesting Alice couldn't stay away from the medical field, even after she changed her identity."

Dove nodded as they drove away, ripping open the packaging on her last sandwich. "It explains why she never used her degree, though. Katherine Weight got the degree, but Alice Bentley didn't go to uni at all."

CHAPTER FORTY-FOUR

The incident board was looking extremely full now, scrawled with green and black marker-pen notes, red arrows and yellow sticky labels. The gates to the station were shut to stop journalists from following officers and shouting questions. Normally, they were pretty respectful of police work, but the Jack Frost Killer was making national headlines. It had caught public imagination at a time when the country was gripped by the Big Freeze.

Trapped indoors, and eager for entertainment, the public found the story of the missing mothers, the frozen young men and the chess figures made of ice to be exciting reading. Unless, of course, Dove thought grimly, you were one of those family and friends grieving for your loved one, hoping each day for news, heart torn into shreds by each snippet on social media, each press presumption and speculative storyline.

Back at the station, Dove went straight back to her desk, checking her watch as she slipped into her seat and tapped in her password. Several emails had come in with information on Katherine Weight/Alice Bentley. She skimmed them, but halted on the work records. Katherine Weight had worked at a nursing home in Oxfordshire a couple of months after she graduated. So she hadn't gone travelling straight away, as she had told Klara.

The nursing home, Victoria House, had employed Katherine as a care assistant. Dove rang the number on the bottom of the email and introduced herself.

"We do have a high turnover of staff, DC Milson, but we keep excellent records," the owner assured her.

"I'm sure you do. You sent me the information on Katherine Weight, who worked for you in 2011. Do you remember her personally?"

"I'm afraid I don't. I have only been the manager since 2018. The records show she was here . . . Oh yes, for three months, from October to December. There is also a note on her file linking her to the deaths of two patients . . ."

"Suspicious deaths?" Dove asked.

Her voice rose. "Oh no. Sorry, no. We ensure our patients have two key workers each, and if a patient passes away, often the family like to speak to, or even stay in touch with, the key worker for a while." She paused. "It's worked very well over the years."

Dove took the names of the two patients who had died under Katherine's care, and ascertained there was nothing on file about a degree, simply a modest set of A Levels and a job caring for an elderly relative. She had just started to investigate the patient deaths when the screen flickered and went blank. The lights did the same and the power cut also set off the fire alarm, which blared a deafening screech across the office space.

"Really?" Lindsey was sitting two desks behind Dove and she grabbed her stuff, ready for an evacuation.

"I know, right? Bloody typical." They walked together, joining the steady queues out of the fire exits.

"How are you getting on with the missing women?" Dove asked. Those who were currently fit to work were taking on a heavy caseload, and as a FLO, Lindsey's time was now divided between a social worker, the emergency foster carer who was minding Alice's young children, and Tessa's family, who were doing the same for her two daughters. "What happened about Tessa's ex-husband in the end?"

Lindsey zipped up her coat as they stepped out into the bleak grey car park. The wind tossed her short curls across her face and put colour in her usually pale cheeks. "Dead end as far as this investigation goes, I think. It seems he did track his family down via the sister, and made contact with the eldest girl, Allison. He changed his statement once our friends up north confronted him with the evidence, but there is no solid evidence to connect him to the murders or abductions other than circumstantial."

"If he has nothing to do with the current investigation, I wish he'd bloody told Manchester when they first took a statement. It would've saved hours of investigation time and paperwork," Dove said impatiently. "Likewise Tessa's sister, the dozy cow."

"Of course it would. But he knew he'd be in the frame if he admitted being down here. Come on, secret meetings with his daughter, right before his ex-wife was abducted, and the history of domestic violence?" Lindsey rolled her eyes.

As soon as the much-depleted team and their colleagues were accounted for, they were given the all-clear and filed back into the building. The lights were back on, courtesy of the backup generator.

"We've stamped all around both women's lives and only found what you've heard in the briefings. Again, it's a dead end. What have you got? And I know you've got something because you've got that smug cow look on your face," Lindsey said, nudging her as they re-entered the office.

"Must just be my usual expression. Apart from the fact we reckon the father of Alice's twins is her ex-boyfriend and he hasn't twigged, we're waiting on Tessa's phone, like everyone else," Dove told her. "Oh, and Katherine Weight went to work at a nursing home after she graduated, as a care assistant, and may or may not have been involved in the deaths of two patients."

"Shit, you get all the good ones. I suppose that would have been a good time for her to disappear. How's Steve?"

"Coming back in tomorrow. Seems like it was just a heavy cold, because he sounded a lot better when he called," Dove said, breathing a long sigh of relief as her computer hummed slowly into life.

She grabbed her phone from her pocket as it buzzed with a call.

"Dove? It's Damien from Northingly. We've got a witness who claims she was JD Turner's girlfriend. She says she thought he was seeing someone else so she followed him to St Mathew's one night. He said he was doing some dealing, but she saw him getting it on with Tessa Jackson. They didn't go through the main entrance because he was banned. There was a way in around by the boathouse on the lake. Tessa was waiting for him, they did their thing in the boathouse, and she watched, presumably furious. A bit kinky, no?"

"If you like that kind of thing. Does she remember when this was?" Dove asked, slightly sceptical.

"Yeah, because it was her birthday, sixteenth of March 2011. According to her she never saw him again. She got scared and had to move away because he owed a lot of money, and his regular customers kept coming for more blow and pills, which she didn't have." He paused. "I think she's sound."

"How does she know it was Tessa?"

"She was a regular customer, apparently. Her and Jeremy Masters. She claims they were all regulars at a certain type of party."

"Her memory seems pretty good, considering how many years we're talking," Dove said. "Maybe she killed JD for two-timing her? Sorry, I'm not throwing shade on your witness, just saying."

"Nah, I thought she was lying to get a bit of attention at first, but she's got photos, customer records, all stashed away. I reckon she thought JD was going to come back one day, just not as a corpse, you know. She's also very small and built

233

like a stick. No way she could have wrapped him up, and dragged or carried him around. He was well over six foot."

"Would she talk to us?"

"She might do. Probably not, though . . . I know her current boyfriend, so she felt she could come to me with the information," he said, dodging slightly.

Dove thought she knew what he meant. But a statement from the girl, backed by the hard evidence she had stashed away might be enough for now. "Did she say she'd been in touch with Tessa or Jeremy recently? Or mentioned Katherine Weight or Klara Payton?"

"No. She only fingered Tessa and Jeremy. I reckon you must have enough to pull him in for questioning for JD's death, at least. Tell Jon I thought about ringing him, but you have better manners and are better looking, so I'm calling you instead."

CHAPTER FORTY-FIVE

Seeing DI Blackman was on a conference call, Dove quickly updated DCI Franklin on their progress. This was part of the process, part of the protocol. Every move they made during an investigation had to be logged, checked and double-checked. It was boring, mundane and slowed things down, but ensured that there was nothing for the prosecution to pick holes in when cases went to court.

With her experience as a source handler, and the recent attempt on her life, Dove always made doubly sure she was following the rules. There was no room on the team for mavericks or wild cards, and it was only now, eight months in, that she felt she had really earned her place on the team. Rose had reinforced the fact she was now on the right track. She wondered how the woman was doing. Apart from a quick text, she hadn't heard anything at all.

The DI approached her desk. "Got the update on Damien's witness. He's a sly bastard, but he's got a good nose. Any updates on Katherine Weight?"

She relayed the information from the nursing home. "The procedure at the care home was a pretty good one, allowing them to see any patterns in deaths, as well as obviously primarily being transparent for the relatives. There are question marks over one of the deaths. The relative of the first patient said she was left in the bath with the window open and she died of hypothermia. They feel she was neglected and the care home was at fault. The legal wranglings are ongoing. The second patient had no family, and his death certificate simply states a cardiac arrest. He was eighty-nine with significant health issues and a DNAR due to these. Katherine was with him when he died."

They were interrupted by Josh. "Klara Payton's had a break-in. Neighbour called it in. Uniform are on scene and asked if we want to take a look."

"Where's Klara?" the DI said, sharply.

"They haven't been able to locate her."

"Okay. Josh, you and Lindsey get out to Klara's house and check it out. Find out if she's actually missing or just gone out for a drive or something."

"Yes, boss." Josh looked pleased at the thought of some action.

"Dove, you and I are going to talk to Dr Masters. If Klara is missing, we now have enough circumstantial to hold him for twenty-four hours until we uncover something solid. We have enough to state he may be a danger, with three women now missing," Jon said grimly.

* * *

Jeremy was taller than Dove had expected. She had to look up to meet his serious, blonde-lashed, blue gaze. He was wearing grey trousers and a pink-striped shirt under a cream cashmere jumper. His blonde hair was cut into a shiny fringe, which in turn was slicked to one side. "Thank you for coming in to talk to us again." She returned his easy smile.

"I wasn't aware I had much option," Jeremy said, with a quick glance at his solicitor. But he spoke without any rancour, and didn't seem nervous. When he smoothed a fleck of dirt from the sleeve of his jumper, his hand was completely steady. "This is the third time I have spoken to you, and I'm starting to feel a little hounded. I do appreciate the case seems to involve people I have known or do currently know, but that doesn't make me in any way guilty for anything they may have done."

DI Blackman started the tape and went through the formalities, before starting the questioning. "As you are aware, we are extremely concerned about the whereabouts of Alice Bentley and Tessa Jackson, and while you are not formally under arrest at this time, as I'm sure your solicitor has explained to you, this interview is under caution."

"I understand. I am, as I mentioned, becoming familiar with the logistics of police procedure." Jeremy exchanged another quick glance with his solicitor. She was a well-groomed brunette with small glasses perched on her upturned nose. Although she kept her expression serious, her pleasant demeanour seemed to have a soothing effect on her client.

"I appreciate we have already covered much of this information, and have your statement to that effect, but we have new information which has led to us re-examining our initial statements."

"I understand, but I have an alibi for both events you are investigating," Jeremy said. He looked slightly less comfortable now, his mouth hardening and the catalogue-model good looks becoming more chiselled, sharper.

The DI spoke pleasantly, but his eyes were sharp and observant. "Thank you, your alibis are not in question."

Dove said, taking her cue from her boss, "Were you aware Katherine Weight changed her name to Alice Bentley?"

"No! How could I be? I admit I did wonder when I saw the news articles on the second incident. Because university and that particular group of friends had been on my mind, her face looked a familiar, but it never occurred to me . . ."

"At university you, Klara, Katherine and Tessa presented a dissertation on hypothermia. You controversially used data from the Nazi medical experiments at Dachau. Why?"

Not a flicker of annoyance or surprise passed over Jeremy's impassive face. A poker face — he was prepared for this one, Dove thought. Surprisingly, the subject seemed to have a calming effect on Jeremy, and he went smoothly through the presentation. "We were studying hypothermia. Klara and I had a particular interest in the subject, mainly due to Isla's death." He glanced at the police officers and they both nodded.

"I regret using that data, it caused trouble, but we were young and stupid, thinking only of the research we were doing, the final-year exams, and future careers . . . What can I say? It was disrespectful and a mistake." His blue eyes were wide and cold. "But it isn't in any way linked to the frozen bodies in your investigation, which I imagine is where you are heading with this?"

"This has all been covered in Dr Masters's last interview. Can we move on, please?" the solicitor prodded. "I think you will soon find there is no cause to hold my client for twenty-four hours."

The DI nodded slowly. "Are you aware a body was found in the lake on George Campus at St Mathew's in August this year, and our colleagues at Northingly are investigating it as a cold case?"

Jeremy's expression remained pleasant, but his jaw was tight now, and he swallowed hard. "I saw a news article, and I was shocked. Awful thing to happen."

"The body has been identified as JD Turner. Does the name mean anything to you?"

"No," Jeremy said quickly, "it doesn't."

"We have a witness who says she has proof you did know JD, and bought drugs from him." Jon spread some photographs across the table. These were the enlargements from Damien's witness, JD's girlfriend.

Jeremy's already pale skin turned white, but he smiled again and shook his head like an indulgent uncle. "Oh yes, Jack, of course. Jack Turner. Another mistake, trying drugs, but again, it was a long time ago." He raised both hands and shook his head. "I'm very embarrassed, but who doesn't do this kind of thing as a student? It's part of university life, isn't it?"

"I'm not sure St Mathew's would agree with you on that one," Jon said dryly.

CHAPTER FORTY-SIX

"You never returned to your original research on hypothermia?" Jon switched back to the main subject.

"It was Klara who dropped the project," Jeremy said. "Her grandmother was in Dachau during World War Two — did she tell you? She told Klara she was never to use anything done by the Nazis for any purpose, medical or otherwise. She was . . . shocked . . . that Klara would do such a thing, bearing in mind the family history. I felt bad, because I pushed for us to use the data. Tessa wasn't keen and Katherine either, I don't think . . . It really was a long time ago."

Lindsey put her head around the door and signalled to the DI, who excused himself briefly.

Dove offered Jeremy and his solicitor another drink and sat waiting for Jon's return. They weren't getting anywhere with Dr Masters. He was on the fringes of everything, admitting to some things, but never part of the bigger picture. Did he know where Tessa and Alice were?

The DI came back into the room, and politely excused both himself and Dove.

Lindsey was still standing outside, holding her iPad. "So Josh just sent these over, and I thought you should see them right away . . ."

Jon and Dove leaned in to study the screen, and the series of photographs from Klara's house. The rooms were neat and tidy apart from the kitchen, where the freezer door had been left open, and a pool of water was spreading across the stone floor.

"And on her back doorstep, they found this . . ." Lindsey indicated with a thumbnail.

The chess set king and queen stood atop a scattering of ice cubes. In front of the artwork, this time, were two ice pawns.

Lindsey added, "Klara Payton is currently still missing. Josh says she didn't turn up for an appointment with a friend earlier this morning, and her mother has no idea where she has gone."

"Damn!" Jon said, rubbing a hand across his shaven head in frustration. "Thanks, Lindsey, I want to know if anything else comes in."

Dove was reflecting on the significance of the chess pieces. "If Jeremy and Klara are the king and queen, maybe the pawns are Tessa and Alice?"

"It might be just a way of throwing something else into the mix, moving us away from the main themes. At least we don't have a frozen body or a fire."

"De-escalation?" Dove suggested.

"Perhaps the perpetrator has now achieved whatever it was they wanted," Jon said, his grey eyes cool and alert. "Let's get back to Dr Masters."

Back in the room, he restarted the tape and continued, "Okay, Dr Masters, so you finished your hypothermia dissertation, and then what happened? Did you ever use the research again?"

Dove was thinking about Klara telling them the group had been so close to developing a breakthrough drug. Ice was the link all the way through. Killing people with the cold and saving people from its effects. Was it really Jeremy who was behind all this?

The doctor sat for a moment, hands linked and neat on the table in front of him, before he spoke carefully. "We were close, you know, close to developing something which actually reversed the effects of hypothermia and warmed the body from the core outwards. Klara is an incredible scientist. It was her response to everything, to try and invent a cure. It's the reason she became a doctor, because she wanted to make breakthroughs, save lives."

He continued, "It has always been a dream of mine to pursue my research, but not purely as an academic. With MEDA, I can raise the funding to work with commercial scientists globally. They offer testing facilities, laboratories, and a wealth of expertise from the medical world."

"Sounds very admirable. Do you play chess, Dr Masters?"

This threw him, but he answered quickly enough. "No, I'm not a fan of board games. Why?"

"This morning someone broke into Klara Payton's house. It appears nothing was taken, but her freezer door was left open, and on her back doorstep we found this . . ." Jon flipped his own iPad round and showed them photographs from the scene. "A chess set king and queen and a scattering of ice cubes. As you can see, in front of the artwork were two ice pawns." He paused before adding, "Klara Payton is currently missing."

Something that might have been panic crossed Jeremy's face. His lips pressed firmly together and his blue eyes were bright. He quickly turned to his solicitor, who opened her mouth to speak when he cut sharply across her. "Oh god, Klara. That must be why she didn't answer my calls this morning . . . Normally, she gets back so quickly. I thought she must be with her mother." His fists had clenched on the table, genuine fear in his face. "You need to find her!"

"And we will, but if you know anything else, Dr Masters, anything at all, now is the time to tell us."

There was a long moment, broken only by the solicitor shuffling her feet under the table.

"I'm sorry, but I can't think of anything else to add," Jeremy said. His eyes were blank now, and clearly he was thinking furiously.

Just as Klara had hesitated, considered and rejected offering more information, Jeremy did the same, Dove thought. Who were they afraid of and what? Was someone else behind this, and killing the friendship group one by one? If so, Jeremy was right to be afraid, as he was the only one left standing. Three down, one to go. So much for soulmates.

"Clearly, my client and his former friends are being targeted for some reason. I need time to talk to Dr Masters," the solicitor said firmly.

CHAPTER FORTY-SEVEN

And so my days now took a different turn, and my soul returned to its lofty position somewhere above my head, somewhere warm and free, populated with family and friends.

My world was reduced to that icy bath. Men, other prisoners, were brought and examined, before being immersed in the icy water. Some prisoners were naked, but some of them were dressed awkwardly in the uniform of the Luftwaffe. Occasionally, the men struggled and shouted, fighting to escape the ice, the almost certain death. After this happened, many were slipped into the water unconscious, anaesthetized by the doctor and his needle.

Most never regained consciousness.

My role was, as the doctor explained, to trial body heat as a means of warming the frozen men. They used four women in rotation, and as the men were dragged from the pool, they ordered two of us to strip naked and lie one either side, pressing our skin to the man's.

Sometimes the time in the bath was short, and when we laid next to the man other orders were given, other horrors carried out. I prefer not to think of these, and my soul rested far away, even as my body was abused.

It never seemed to occur to the doctor that he was using subjects who were malnourished, often tortured, often afflicted by diseases and that this might skew his results. I wanted to ask how he thought his

243

data could be true, when the Luftwaffe pilots had not been subjected to the murderous regime we had. I wanted to scream about the unfairness, but I kept silent, watched and waited.

Because I could see the guards were afraid. Afraid of the doctor, of what they were doing, of what he was doing. In turn, I supposed he might be afraid of his own superiors, and ultimately of Hitler. There were rumours the doctor was close to Hitler himself. I might have believed this, believed he was given no choice but to torture other human beings, but there was something in his eyes, in his expression.

It wasn't enjoyment as such, more a total lack of emotion. If I see his face in my nightmares again, I can see perhaps he wasn't getting pleasure from his experiments, but simply that he didn't see us as human beings. We were test subjects to be used in any way he pleased. The excuse of medical research was, for him, enough, and he pursued his end goal relentlessly as we clung to our lives by tiny threads, as fine and silken fragile as those from a spider's web.

CHAPTER FORTY-EIGHT

"Bloody lying smug bastard," DI Blackman swore as they watched Jeremy and his solicitor disappear back through the swing doors. "How the hell are we going to break him? Everything about him is so squeaky clean he makes me sick, but he's involved up to his neck in this. It's like the lot of them have taken a vow of silence of something!"

Dove considered her answer carefully. "He did seem genuinely freaked when you told him Klara was missing, though — and what happened to Klara's new alarm system?"

"It was disabled, or perhaps not even set," Jon said. "Lindsey said when Josh called, he told her the conservatory doors at the back of the house were wide open, so whoever went in had a key and knew the alarm wasn't on."

"The neighbour said it was a break-in?" Dove said.

"She went round to drop off some flowers for Klara. She said she heard about her grandmother's death and they arranged to have a coffee this morning. Klara didn't answer her phone, and when she walked round the back of the house she saw the doors wide open and the freezer defrosting."

"But with Klara's disappearance we can hold him in custody pending further investigation?" Dove checked.

"Just. It's squeaky and his solicitor isn't happy but I've said with other information coming in shortly, we have further questions," the DI said.

Dove glanced at the incident board. Tessa had been missing for over four days, Alice for two and now Klara had also vanished. And Jeremy Masters had an alibi for every single incident.

* * *

The street lamp next to Dove's house was broken but, laden with a bag of groceries and her work bag, she opted not to bother with her pocket torch. She had walked the garden path so many times, even in pitch blackness and driving wind she knew every bump and missing brick.

Striding towards the front door, her boots coping easily with the ice and slush, she was thinking only of a cosy night by the fire, hoping her fiancé had had a good day. When she slipped, she went sprawling into the thick blanket of snow covering the small front garden. It was like she had walked on a bag of marbles, and she pushed herself upright, confused and sore.

'What the hell?'

She fumbled for her torch, and flicked the powerful beam across the path. Ice cubes. Treacherously covering the path right up to her front door. The yellow glow of the torch traced some small figures set neatly on the front step.

Recovering her belongings and carefully scuffing the cubes out of the way with the toe of her boot, she walked carefully up to the figures.

Miniature ice carvings of the king and queen from a chess set sat looking slightly ominous in the midst of another mound of ice cubes. In front of them sat three pawns. Behind the figures was a little wooden building — a child's toy . . . A stable, maybe? The whole scene had a freaky Nativity slant.

Dove shifted bags to her other hand, took another swift look around, and snapped photographs of the scene on her phone. Weird and familiar. She swung round and cast the torch beam across the garden, down to the road. Snow was falling lightly, covering her footprints. Her own garden path and those of her neighbour were both shovelled clear, with sand put down to keep them safe.

Faintly visible in the street-lamp light, on the horizon was the new apartment block where Jeremy Masters lived. Just because she hadn't ever spotted him, didn't mean he hadn't seen her, but just at the moment Dr Masters was in police custody, so who the hell arranged the little scene outside her front door?

The front door opened and she jumped, catching her breath, then relaxing as Quinn appeared, puzzlement on his face. "I thought I heard someone swearing outside. What are you doing?"

She indicated the ice scene at his feet and he stepped back hastily, peering at the figures. "What the fuck are those?"

"No idea, but let's get inside. I'm freezing and I just nosedived into the lawn, because some bastard has scattered our path with ice cubes."

"Bloody hell. I never heard a thing, and I've been in since half one," Quinn said. In answer to her unspoken query, he nodded, "I went for a walk after my counselling session. You were right, much as I hate to admit it. Are you sure you're okay?"

Having sent her boss the photos, she called the DI before she even took her coat off. Waiting for him to answer, she gratefully took the glass of wine Quinn offered, huddling next to the crackling flames in the fireplace.

"Dove? Are you okay?" The DI sounded confused.

She explained what had happened, and they debated who might have been to the house. "But it doesn't have to be anyone directly related to the case. This Jack Frost thing has been all over the news, and you can buy chess set moulds all over the place, as we already discovered. My neighbours know what I do for a living, not that I'm saying any of them are involved . . ."

"Hmmm . . . Jeremy lives near to you, doesn't he? I remember you saying . . ."

"In the new apartment block. It's feasible he might have seen me in the shop or the takeaway at the end of the road, but he would have had to follow me to see where I lived. The road takes in a big curve three quarters of the way along. But he's safely in custody for the night, isn't he?" Dove said helplessly.

"Yes." He was silent. "And still not talking. All right. I'll get someone over to your chess set and see if we can get anything from it. If anything else happens, let me know. I don't suppose you or any of your neighbours have CCTV?"

"No, they don't, and we don't either." She kept promising herself they would sort that out, but it was another thing that kept getting pushed back to the bottom of the list.

"Well?" He picked up the note of hesitation in her voice.

"If this is the same person they were super careful at the other scenes," Dove told him.

"We'll grab any lead at the moment," Jon told her, and rang off.

She related the conversation to her fiancé, and he nodded. "And your main suspect is at the station?"

"Right."

"So which one of our neighbours have you pissed off?" he enquired.

"Kind of what I was thinking, but who knows?" She was heading for the stairs as Quinn went back into the kitchen.

Dove grabbed a shower, and when she came down, he produced a fish pie with carrots and broccoli.

"God, that smells amazing. Did you actually cook, Quinn?" She eyed him suspiciously.

He grinned. "You had no idea all these years I'm such a multi-talented genius, did you?"

"Where did you get it?"

"Next door. Mary, the new lady who moved in last month. She's very sweet, and I cleared her path for her this morning. She came over with this treat about four."

"How kind of her." Dove stopped with a fragrant steaming forkful halfway to her mouth. "God, she could have slipped on the ice cubes if she was any later."

"True, so that means they were left on the step after four." Quinn topped up the wine glasses. "Because I don't think Mary would have given us an ice scene. I only just met her, and I don't think I managed to offend her in any way."

"What's she like?"

"Very interesting. She's from Brighton, and she's moved over here because her husband died and she wanted a fresh start. Actually, she mentioned her best friend used to be a policewoman, back in the sixties and seventies. Ruby, she was called. Sounds like they had a wild time together."

Dove smiled at him. Quinn was so good at getting people to talk to him. Not only because he was genuinely interested in everyone, but also because nobody felt judged by him. He simply listened and absorbed. Whereas she was very obviously bored, angry, excited in whatever conversation she was having.

"How was counselling, really?" she asked cautiously.

"Good, I think. I felt a bit better today, and I walked along the beach afterwards and thought about our wedding. The counsellor said I should focus on something good in the future, and work towards my goals for the next few years."

"Wow, she sounds tough," Dove observed. "I'm not sure what my goals are for the next hour, let alone years."

"Going to bed?" He raised his glass, and the sparkle was back in his eyes.

Relief made her weak, and it was only then she realized how worried she had been for him, remembering the depths he had sunk to last time. She laid her hand over his and interlaced their fingers. He said nothing, but carried on smiling.

* * *

At the briefing the next morning, Steve was back, and Dove felt her heart lift. It had been good to bounce back and forth, working with other team members, but she and Steve were a solid unit.

The DI called them aside after the briefing. "I just had an email from a mate of mine. Take a look at these photographs."

Puzzled, Dove leaned in at stared at his phone. "Silver ornaments? Shit, is that a swastika? These are what, Nazi memorabilia?"

"Where did you find them?" Steve asked.

"Hanging on Professor Renuard's Christmas tree," the DI confirmed. "I thought I recognized the Imperial Eagle design on several of the antique silver decorations. Among other things, it was used by the Third Reich from 1933 to 1945. An interesting choice for a Christmas tree, don't you think?"

"I wondered why you were suddenly so interested in the tree," Dove told him. "So it might not be just her students who have an interest in Nazi history."

Jon nodded. "Go back and speak to the tutor, Claire Renuard. She's the only person who knew all four of them, and she stayed close to Tessa, helped her graduate," he told them. "And hurry up. Everything we do today has to be focused on getting enough evidence to charge Jeremy Masters with something that will stick, or at the very least get him to spill on what he knows."

"Come Dove, let's get cracking." Steve coughed into his hand and looked guiltily around the office. "As soon as you've finished your breakfast break, we should get going."

"Funny." Everyone knew police officers didn't get breaks. She finished her coffee and chucked the paper cup in the recycling on the way to the door. "Are you sure you're well enough to be at work?"

"I'm fine. Besides, Zara's fed up with me being at home following every news item on the case and trying to work on files at the kitchen table. How's Quinn?"

They walked out of the office and headed down the stairs for the car park. Dove took a breath of icy air. "He seems to be dealing with it. The therapist is a big help, and the fact he's accepting help is good in itself. I can see an improvement after just one session."

"Yeah. Don't take this the wrong way, but sometimes it's harder for blokes." He stuffed the last of his energy bar into his mouth and led the way to the car.

"I know, and it's so wrong," Dove agreed. Quinn was eating properly now, and going for proper exercise along the beach, instead of going out there to brood. She was trying to give him space, but equally, her worry for him made her want to be there all the time. "Anyone should be able to ask for help if they need it, without being judged," she said fiercely, at the same time aware that things were never that simple.

"He'll be all right," Steve said gently. "Give it time. Remind him he's got a bathroom to tile, and a wedding to plan," he suggested.

Dove managed a smile. "I might wait a bit before I write him a list of chores, but you're right, focusing on the present and future will definitely help, when he's ready."

The drive to St Mathew's took forty minutes, by which time Dove had eaten three packets of jelly sweets and Steve had eaten two more protein bars. He still had a cough, but looked a lot better, and told her he was back on his fitness regime.

"Seriously, you need get healthier," Steve told her as they eventually overtook a lorry and accelerated to the speed limit. "Ditch the sugar and get on these protein bars instead."

Dove inspected an empty wrapper he had tossed down onto the floor. "These are good, but you aren't meant to eat loads at once. They're for after a workout. Did you exercise this morning?"

"I nearly went back down to the pool last night," Steve said defensively. "Grace is keeping us awake now because she's teething. It's like one thing after another this winter."

"Okay, I get it. Just get off my case about the healthy stuff. I bet I'm fitter than you are at the moment," Dove told him.

"Bet you aren't. You're a takeaway queen." Steve grinned suddenly. "The DI says he's doing one of those crazy obstacle mud races just before Christmas. It's only a 5k."

"And?" Dove had no wish to get covered in mud, electrocuted and whatever else the organizers might throw at the entrants, but Steve was always up for a wager.

"Bet I can get round faster than you. Twenty quid on it!" He grinned wickedly. "But if you're too chicken . . ."

"Oh for god's sake. You are so immature!" she told him, but she was laughing. "All right I'll beat your arse through a load of mud. Happy?"

"Yup. Think how many protein bars I can get for twenty quid."

"Unbelievable," Dove said, shaking her head at him, as they slowed to inch up the drive between the pillars. To the left were the imposing buildings of the main university, the frozen river curling around, heading west, and to their right, a steep slope up to a cattle barn. A tractor was parked on the slope, its trailer loaded with hay bales.

Instead of turning towards the main visitor car park, they followed the gravel towards the lodge. Steve slowed to a crawl as they approached the gateway. Snow had formed barriers on either side of the driveway, and the car slid as it met impacted snow and ice.

There was some snow-covered scrub either side, and the remains of an older, ruined building, further down the hill. An ancient oak spread bare boughs towards the turbulent winter sky.

Surrounding the lodge, running down to the river, and up towards the farm buildings, a high stone wall had at least six inches of snow covering the top.

"What did you think of the tutor and her husband?" Steve asked.

"She fluctuates between being very helpful and slightly defensive," Dove said. "Alain, her husband, is . . . I don't know. I just felt there was something slightly off about their relationship." She wriggled her gloves out of her pocket. "He also has these tattoos that bugged me. I can't really describe why, but the ink was so thick and the whole sleeves were not really of anything."

"Like they were covering up something?" Steve suggested. "Old girlfriend's initials, embarrassing typo on an old tattoo?"

"Something like that, yes." Dove glanced, preoccupied with the coming interview, glanced at the steep slope to her right suddenly. "Steve! Look out!"

The deafening crash of impact and the whining scream of metal on metal left no chance for defensive manoeuvres. The tractor pushed forward, shoving the car, scraping it further towards the frozen river.

Dove was scrambling frantically to open the door, her heart beating fast and hard. Steve was yelling at the tractor driver to stop, trying to force the car forward and away from the deadly grip of metal jaws. But the walled garden was in front, and the vehicle continued its relentless slide down the hill towards the icy river.

The wall continued almost right down to the river, where the ground levelled out slightly before both vehicles would gather speed for the final plunge into the river.

In the last few yards where the bank in front opened up, and the wall ended, Steve managed to accelerate forward just enough for the tractor to lumber past, continuing its deadly journey, slicing the rear of the car but leaving it skewed on the snowy riverbank.

Dove finally succeeded in getting her door open. "Get out, Steve!" she yelled, throwing herself away from the battered car, and rolling out into the snow. He was right behind her, and they staggered towards the tractor.

CHAPTER FORTY-NINE

The tractor continued onward, huge and menacing, crushing the snowy bushes in its path as they scrambled after it.

"There's nobody driving!" Dove shouted, as the vehicle tumbled onward towards the river, smashing into the ice moments later.

"Shit. They must have started it rolling as soon as they saw us coming, and jumped out of the cab. The slope is so steep just outside the gates," Steve said, still gasping for breath. "I'll call it in. Where are you going?"

"To check out where the tractor came from," Dove said.

"Don't be an idiot. What if the driver is still there, and what if he's armed?" He turned back to his phone and started speaking rapidly, explaining what had happened.

She waited until he finished the call then squinted down the snowy driveway. There were people gathering next to the main car park now, pointing towards the tractor, which was tipped half on its side in the steady snowfall, like some monstrous ice creature. It had smashed through the frozen ice and was trapped, half-sinking, half-floating on a bed of reeds.

"You're right, but we still need to check it out. You call it in, then we can walk back across the driveway and head up the slope towards those farm buildings. If the tractor came from there, we might find something useful."

"You've got a bright red jacket on, and the landscape is white, in case you hadn't noticed," he pointed out, clearly still dubious.

"We can stay shielded by the garden wall, and there's a crowd gathering in the main car park. Chances are good our perp is long gone," she told him breathlessly.

"Okay, let's do it," he agreed, zipping his phone back into his windbreaker pocket.

Keeping the walled garden on their left, they began to climb up the hill, stumbling in the snowy tyre tracks left by both vehicles, keeping a sharp lookout for anyone else. The snow that made it so easy to scan the surrounding area would also make it easy for a hidden watcher to target them.

But somehow Dove didn't think shooting people was the killer's style. Then again, that tractor stunt didn't seem to be in keeping with them, either. "Who do you think was driving?" she asked breathlessly, as they picked their way around the trailer, loaded with bales of hay, and walked towards the small collection of farm buildings.

"Claire Renuard? Alain Renuard? Klara? A whole list of suspects, but it does prove one thing."

She met his eyes, noting the glint, and knew it was reflected in her own eyes. It was the primitive feeling of quarry, prey and the hunters closing in. "We're getting closer and they know it."

A search of the crushed, snowy tyre tracks revealed the tractor had been driven from one of the barns they were now facing. New tracks were evident, but footprints were not.

"Oh hell, they've covered their tracks." Dove pointed at a brush thrown down near the barns, and the scrubbed-out appearance of tracks leading to and fro. The long low brick building looked like a workshop, with rusting doors tightly padlocked. Two barns made a U-shape with a cleared concrete yard in the middle. Sheep were bunched around a feeder near the woods, tearing hay from the bars with short, sharp snatches. Nothing appeared to be disturbing them.

Set on the crest of the hill, with woods to the right and the downland to the left, the buildings afforded a great view of the two crashed vehicles down by the river, the lodge house and, further away, the university.

"I hardly noticed the tractor as we drove down the driveway," Steve admitted.

"Why would you, though? This place is obviously a working farm, so it's not an anomaly to see tractors hanging around," Dove pointed out.

They turned to the smaller barn and found more tyre tracks, and a large patch of oil. The smell cut through the clean snow with a reek and sourness.

"Quad bike?" Steve suggested, squinting at the clear tracks that led into the field and then made a sharp left turn into the woods, far above the sheep. "I bet those just go back to the road. They must have had another vehicle waiting."

They both halted in the yard, hearing shouts from the river as the bystanders made their way down the gravel driveway, distant sirens of the backup Steve had called in. Dove paused next to the padlocked workshop. A small noise made her catch her breath. "Did you hear that?"

Steve was staring at the filthy windows, shoulders tense, face set and alert. "Let's try round the back."

The noise came again, a soft moan and cry for help. Cautiously, mindful of another trap, they walked back across the yard, cut round behind the largest barn, and found the rear entrance to the workshops. A large stable door, bolted but not padlocked.

At a nod from Steve, Dove pushed open the door, revealing a small space filled with tools and farming supplies. On the floor was a young man, bound and bleeding from a jagged head wound.

Steve was back on the phone, staying near the door, his eyes darting around, while Dove went down on her knees next to the man. She tugged away his gag.

"It's okay, we're police. Can you tell us what happened?"

The man, helped by Dove's arm around his shoulders, wriggled into a sitting position. He licked his lips, sweat and blood mixed on his face, despite the cold. He was shaking. "Someone hit me from behind. Knocked me almost right out, and then tied me up. I was standing in here picking up another can of diesel for the quad bike, and came to just now. I heard you talking . . . Shit, my head hurts. What did they steal? The tractor? The quad bike?"

Dove grabbed a wad of tissues from her jacket pocket and pressed it firmly onto his head wound. The cut was deep, and blood was still oozing darkly down through his hair, dripping into a red puddle on the dusty floor. He must have one hell of a headache.

She spotted a shovel thrown down in the shadows, blood darkening its blade. But when she scanned the remote snowy downland, the grey clouds already massing on the horizon, she could see no sign of the attacker.

CHAPTER FIFTY

"What happened with Jeremy?" Dove asked. She and Steve had returned to the station much later, as darkness fell, after both insisting they did not require any medical help. For a full debrief, Dove was sitting opposite the DI, trying not to wince. Now the adrenalin had faded she discovered a few pains and bruises.

DI Blackman shrugged. "He was released without charge twenty minutes ago. Absolutely nothing to keep him here, and you know how hard we were trying. Wasn't even any point applying for an extension just to have it turned down. Damn!" He removed his glasses and rubbed them with his sleeve, frustration in his tired grey eyes.

There were still no leads, and Josh informed them Claire Renuard and her husband had returned from her elderly father's house to discover salvage operations on the tractor. They had both denied any involvement. Claire's father had provided an alibi for his daughter and Alain.

Jon was furious that Jeremy's solicitor informed him her client was considering a harassment claim. Dove winced at this. It had been hard enough dredging up just enough to keep Jeremy in custody, and it looked like the long shot hadn't paid off.

An extensive search of both the tractor and the farmyard didn't produce any new evidence and the assault victim had been stitched up and released from hospital. He was adamant he hadn't seen his attacker and had nothing to add to the investigation.

"At least we know it wasn't Jeremy in the tractor, because he was still at the station when the incident happened," Steve pointed out brightly.

Dove shut her eyes, and leaned back against the window, searching her tired mind for something, anything that she might have missed.

"Right, go home you lot. Better luck tomorrow," the DI said.

The MCT were deflated, running on empty, and now — on her way home, desperate to soak her aches and pains in a hot bath — Dove had taken a call from Gaia insisting they needed to talk. Exhausted and dispirited, going to the club was the last thing she wanted to do, but she recognized the urgency in her sister's tone.

Luckily, traffic was light in the town centre, and although the California Dreams club carpark was fairly full, Dove managed to snag a parking space near the main entrance.

She killed the engine and sat for a moment, eyes closed, head back against her seat rest. Sleep danced dangerously, temptingly, across her mind, but after one long moment she opened her eyes, pulled her long hair loose from its plait and raked all ten fingernails through the shiny dark strands.

The rear-view mirror showed a bruise developing on her forehead, spreading from under her hairline. She prodded it experimentally, and hastily took her hand away as pain shot across her head. Damn.

The icy air revived her a little, and the snowy breeze lifted her hair, tossing it into dark tangles as she stamped carefully through the slush, and into the immaculate chrome and marble lobby area of her sister's club.

She smiled and shook her head at the doll-like dark girl in a short lace dress who greeted her rather uncertainly and offered to take her coat. Another girl, with candy floss pink hair and glossy pink lipstick, watched her with interest. New staff, Dove noted. There was always a high turnover at Gaia's clubs. Gaia told Dove defensively it was the nature of the job, although she did have a few loyal women who had been with her for a couple of years.

The chatter floated across the polished floor behind her and she squeezed behind a group of men in squashy black armchairs. With their beer and bowls of nuts, they looked like they were settling in for the night. Dove recognized a tall, elegant man sipping champagne with a curvy redhead and smiled coolly as their glances crossed. He raised his glass politely at her.

Uri Maquess was a millionaire yacht broker and a significant investor in Gaia's clubs. Dove was fairly sure he had some illegal dealings in his business, but if it didn't interfere with her investigations, that was fine.

Earlier in the year, Uri had been a possible suspect in a murder case, and he had been both helpful and charming when questioned. She reluctantly admired him, even if she wasn't entirely sure what her sister's relationship was with him.

Gaia looked up from her computer as Dove entered the office. Banks of security camera screens sat behind her, and the room was a polished marble sanctuary, with dark wood shelving and a fragrant candle lit on the desk.

"Okay, I'm here in body, but possibly not in spirit. I've just had the shittiest day ever. Is this about Alex?"

"Alex? No. Why would it be about him?"

Dove told her, and her sister scowled at the thought of her brother-in-law. "Okay, what is it then, Gaia?"

Gaia smiled. "What happened to your head?"

"Accident. What's up? I'm dying to crawl into a hot bath and pour a massive alcoholic drink, so spill."

Gaia gave her sister's bruised face another sharp glance, her eyes narrowed. "Come on, then. The party room isn't booked until midnight and Colin can cope until then. We'll grab a drink on the way in."

They sat with their drinks, backs against the luxurious velvet banquettes. "So what's up?" Dove asked, sipping her Diet Coke.

"Delta asked me for a job," Gaia told her.

"What, behind the bar?"

"Nope, as a dancer."

"A dancer? Why the hell would she do that? I thought she was happy working part-time at the café." Dove cringed at the thought of her niece being up on stage at one of Gaia's clubs.

"She says she wants to earn more money and needs two jobs. Her friend Abi is saving up to go travelling, and she's thinking of going, too."

"I hoped she might go back to college," Dove said, biting her lip. "I'm really surprised she'd want to do this after everything that happened."

"Me too. She hasn't said anything to Ren, but there's no way Ren would let her . . ."

"You wouldn't either, though, would you?" Dove asked.

"It's a tough one. No, I would prefer my own family were not up there being stared up by a load of paying customers, but where do you think all my staff come from?" Gaia demanded. "Half of them are students trying to pay the rent, so I sound a bit sanctimonious saying I don't want her dancing."

"Do you think she's still doing the Tough Justice thing with her boyfriend?" Dove suggested. "They were on some very dodgy ground with their vigilante group. Is she trying to infiltrate your club?"

Gaia laughed. "Who knows, but she is eighteen, she can do what she wants. This thing with Alex has been tough for all of them, and I wonder if this is her way of coping . . ."

"By exposing herself to the kind of danger Eden was exposed to?" Dove shot back.

"My clients are not paedophiles, Dove," Gaia said warningly, her amber eyes flashing.

Dove shook her head. "Sorry, I didn't mean that, I'm just shocked, I suppose."

"But if I say no, will she forget it, or will she go to another club and ask?" Gaia said. "We're not short of strip clubs along the coast, but mine is one of the few reputable ones."

Dove finally left the club an hour later, emerging into the darkness and the bitter wind, hunching her shoulders and zipping her coat up to her chin. Exhaustion, the knowledge she had managed to piss off Gaia — who was very touchy about her business anyway — and the lack of progress on the case, made her feel crap. Her body was also making her aware of various new hurts from being in a rolled car. Maybe she should have got herself checked out after all . . .

She joined the queue of traffic out onto the coast road, finally pulling into a vacant spot opposite her house, wearily making her way up the garden path.

Chucking her coat and hat onto a chair, Dove collapsed on the sofa.

"You look wrecked," Quinn observed. His voice sharpened with concern. "What happened to your head?"

She explained about the tractor crashing into the car, insisting she was fine apart from the bruising, but he wasn't convinced, and his forehead wrinkling with worry as he frowned at her.

"You should have got checked over properly. This was an actual attempt on your life! Shit, Dove, this is getting heavy. Don't forget we already had someone here, at our home, dumping a little chess piece display, warning you off. Do you know who did that yet?"

She shook her head, picking at a loose thread on her shirt sleeve.

Quinn persisted, "What did Steve say? Was he okay after your car got hit?"

"I told you, he was fine, and I am too." Dove could hear her voice rising, and stopped her anger from following. "Sorry, I've just had a crap day. It's been one thing after another . . . I need a bath and a drink, and then I'll stop being grumpy. Promise."

He didn't answer, but disappeared into the kitchen. She sighed, feeling like a total cow for snapping at her fiancé when he was only showing concern, and dealing with his own shit. Dove heaved herself up off the sofa, hesitated, and then took herself upstairs to warm up and cool off.

Half an hour later, snug in cosy PJs, thick socks and a hoodie, she apologized to Quinn.

"I'm sorry I never called you after the accident, and sorry I didn't agree to a check-up, but there wasn't time. The pressure is getting to the whole team. Tessa's been missing for four days now, and Alice for two. Whatever the weird set-up between their friendship group, it's more than likely they are both dead now. And we have a list of suspects with nothing but circumstantial evidence."

"I know," he sat beside her, "and I get it." He smiled a little remotely. "You don't have to tell me about pressure of the job. At least people don't deliberately set out to kill me when I piss them off, though."

Dove judged she had said enough. "You'll never guess what Gaia wanted to tell me."

"What?" He allowed himself to be distracted, pouring her a glass of wine.

"Delta wants to work as a dancer in her club."

"Bloody hell, I'm sure Ren's thrilled," he said, raising his eyebrows. "Tell me you're pulling my leg."

"It's true. Delta hasn't told Ren yet."

"Hey, I got a surprise for you," Quinn said, pulling her, groaning, up from the sofa, and leading her upstairs.

He put his hands over her eyes and opened the bathroom door. "Ta-da!"

"You finished tiling!" Dove said in surprise. "It looks great."

The room was neat and tidy, with marble effect tiles running halfway up behind the bath and sink. The floor was grey slate tiles with white grouting.

"It's actually quite therapeutic once you get going, but the grout and sealant are still setting so you'll need to use the old bathroom downstairs until I can finish sealing this lot." His green eyes were gleaming, triumph in his smile, and she kissed him.

After they had eaten, she felt slightly better, the stress and tight feeling in her chest relaxing slightly. She began to think about the case again. How could so many people disappear without being found? Okay, the weather was against any search teams, but there had to be something they had missed . . .

She triangulated the Darkwood Lane area, puzzling over the countryside around it. It was mostly dense woodland, spreading out to the Downs on one side and the coast on the other. It would be easy to vanish in that much green — just like their attacker's disappearing act that afternoon.

Dove yawned, her screen blurring in front of tired eyes. The helicopter had discovered nothing from above. But the many acres of snowbound forest could be holding secrets. She tapped her pen against her teeth, thinking. Could the missing women be held prisoner underground?

Quinn called out he was going to bed and she reluctantly left her files, stumbling with pure exhaustion as she got to the top stair.

CHAPTER FIFTY-ONE

She arrived at the station by seven the next morning, and immediately got to work, downloading property details for all the missing members of the group. Spreading the maps across her desk she tried to be objective. There was something here, she was sure of it. Klara and Jeremy had obviously both separately invested in property, and between them owned three flats and six houses. She discarded the properties abroad and narrowed her search to the local area. Alice and Tessa both rented their properties and owned no others she could find . . . Dove scrolled back through the statements, checking for any scrap of detail that might have been missed, anything she could grab hold of and chase.

Coming to the next file, she frowned at the information, and rang Charles's girlfriend Anne-Marie. "You mentioned Charles's voicemail . . . Did he definitely say 'the cabbie'?"

"Yeah. But I was thinking, like, he might have meant he was in a cab or taking a cab to the station, even?" the girl said promptly. "I've been going over and over it in my head. Have you found something?"

"Not yet." She paused for a second, scanning the property details. A piece of land with space to hide, somewhere deep in the countryside for example . . . "Did Charles take part in any water sports?"

"He used to swim for a club, and he did a sailing course last summer," Anne-Marie said after a pause. "I don't know which club, but he did the sailing course at Slaughter Harbour."

Dove considered this. "Thanks, Anne-Marie. I'll keep you updated when we find out more."

"What are you up to?" Steve asked, finishing his phone call and leaning over her shoulder. "Property? Water sports?"

"Grabbing at straws. I'm going through all the original statements again. I just prodded Anne-Marie, and she says Charles was into water sports too. He did a sailing course last summer."

"Shit. And?"

"Well, Jess sent over that info on cold water immersion, so according to that and the Nazi research document, we're looking at somewhere big enough to hold at least four people, with somewhere to dunk victims in icy water, aren't we? Assuming they are replicating the experiments . . ."

They were silent for a moment, both scanning the maps. Dove pushed her hair back, biting her lip. Where could you keep two or more prisoners in this bitter winter, with access to water? The beach huts were all closed up for the season, and far too conspicuous and cold. All the derelict or empty buildings within the search radius had been checked and double-checked. The properties belonging to MEDA had been thoroughly searched as well, although there was absolutely no evidence the organization had been involved in either the murders or any other wrongdoing.

"The DI's been in a meeting ever since the brief. He did not look happy. Can't blame him with that shit published this morning about useless police not being able to catch the famous Jack Frost serial killer," Steve replied, glancing away from his computer screen, and outside at the sleet. He took his glasses off and rubbed them on his shirt. His eyes were red and sore.

Dove pushed the maps away and closed the tab on her computer. "I was just trying to see if we missed anything . . ."

"And did we?"

"Don't think so," Dove said regretfully. "We don't know who in this little group might be keeping who prisoner, do we, but wherever they are it must be big enough to hold at least four people? We've been assuming Tessa and Alice wouldn't leave their children and voluntarily go, but what if they did? What if this is about blackmail, Jeremy or Klara threatened their kids? It could be their status as mothers that made them extra vulnerable, and the others played on this."

"If Professor Renuard knew, or even her husband, that adds to our list," Steve said. "But logically, there would be no need to start blackmailing, because they all share responsibility. Unless one of them wanted to tell the truth? Perhaps the tutor saw something, and when the body came up, she put it all together. You said she was very smart?"

"Yes, she was . . . Perhaps she got in touch with Tessa, to sound out her theory, but Tessa was taken first, and the body was left as a warning to Alice?"

"But Alice was taken, too, so who was the second body warning?" Steve glanced up at the office door opened and DI Blackman exited with DCI Franklin. Both looking extremely determined. They headed for the exit to the hallway without saying anything to the hard-working team.

"Looks promising. I wouldn't like to get in their way," Pete 'the Donkey' called over from his desk.

Lindsey also looked up. "We need a bloody break. The poor families are going crazy not knowing why we can't just catch the perpetrator. I hate picking up the phone, and that article this morning didn't bloody help."

Dove agreed, swallowed the remains of her cooling coffee, and turned back to Steve, answering his question slowly, thinking over the timeline.

"Go on then, are you saying the second body was a warning to Klara? It's logical I suppose, because she was taken next. Claire Renuard herself? Alice may have worried her new identity would come out. It stands out a mile she must have tried to carry on the research alone but failed, hence the death in the care home and the name change. I'm still waiting for confirmation, but Alice's ex said they moved around whenever Alice got itchy feet, so what do you bet there are a few other deaths in the care homes she's been working in for the past nine years?"

Steve fidgeted with his phone as he considered. "I would say actually Klara and Jeremy have the most to lose, because the university death was the second body-in-a-frozen-lake incident for both of them. Are we sure the first one was an accident?"

Dove nodded. "Sure as we can be from the reports. Case was closed."

"Okay, I like the property idea, so how about I take another look at the maps and land registry?"

She shrugged. "Go for it. I'm working my way down a very short list." Next on her list was Alain Renuard. What was it about the man . . . and those tattoos? Something that made her feel sick, uneasy, but she still couldn't nail exactly what it was.

They sat in silence for a moment, each staring at their computer screens. Her phone buzzed with a message and she grabbed it hopefully, but it was just Rose checking in with a typically brief text.

Back at work next week. Chris can't wait. Catch up soon x

Dove smiled to herself, hoping Rose would be okay . . . Her memory shifted. It was the shape of the artwork on Alain's arms that reminded her of something she had seen before. A CHIS, that was it! Way back she had worked a CHIS called Kes. He had something similar on his back, along with his gang tattoos . . . She remembered faking admiration for his artwork. Quickly, now sure of what she was looking for, she scrolled through the data bank of gang tattoo photos, annoyed she had put this to the back of her mind, or her photographic memory would surely have made the connection earlier.

After numerous pictures, she hit the jackpot. There it was . . . The symbol known as the 'Death's Head' or Totenkopf. It could be mistaken for a pirate's skull and crossbones to an uneducated observer, but it was in fact the symbol of the SS-Totenkopfverbande, whose purpose was to guard concentration camps.

The number 88 also now became clear. The eighth letter of the alphabet is 'H'. Eight two times signified 'HH', shorthand for 'Heil Hitler'.

Coupled with the DI's observation of the Christmas ornaments at the Renuard house, it suggested strongly that either of the couple — but most likely Alain — could be involved in some kind of neo-Nazi group, or at the very least, have a strong interest in the subject.

Steve had taken over the maps, and was typing furiously now, pulling up financial and legal searches, studying land registry maps. Suddenly, he snapped his fingers. "Got something! Professor Renuard. She's getting divorced. Her husband Alain seems to be fairly wealthy in his own right. He has a place in France, a share in a plane, and a flat in Brighton. Might money be a factor for her involvement? If the truth about JD comes out and she is implicated, she'll lose her job and the lodge for sure."

Dove was peering over his shoulder now, still keeping half an eye on the photographs on her screen. "Divorced? They never said anything about that when they were interviewed."

She jabbed at the details on the document, "And look down here, Alain Renuard also has a share in the water sports business at Southview Reservoir."

"What are we waiting for?" Steve asked, catching the energy in her voice, already shoving his chair away.

She beat him to the door, "Let's track down the DI and get this moving."

Josh was in the corridor, pulling packets of crisps out of the vending machine. He grinned as they hurried past, "Got a lead?"

"Let you know!" Dove called, fire and purpose flowing back through her body.

* * *

The reservoir was easy to travel to, along a heavily gritted main road, but when they arrived, the gate was padlocked with a large chain.

"Great." Dove got out of the car and her boots sank in the soft snow. It came to just over her ankles. "I need bloody snow trousers."

"Too dangerous," Steve said. "Leave it to the experts."

The DI swivelled round and checked the other vehicles had arrived.

Behind them were the search and rescue team, who had brought two dogs. The team cut the chain and began to drive in convoy along the snowy track. The four-wheel drive vehicles made nothing of the terrain, thick tyres ploughing slowly but steadily through the ice and snow.

Steve, Jon and Dove stared into the snow, willing the call to come back in with positive news.

The radio crackled. "Nothing here, boss. Place has been shut up for the winter, but we can see through windows into the office. No other buildings, so I suppose they must store their gear somewhere else for the office season. Probably so it doesn't get nicked."

Dove, slumped in the car, felt like a deflated balloon. Somehow, she had convinced herself the double hit on Alain Renuard had been going to smash the jackpot. They drove back in convoy through the thickly falling snow, dispirited and depressed.

"It still needs to fall into place, that's all," the DI said, in an obvious effort to rally his troops. He drove steadily, carefully, occasionally throwing a quick glance at one or other of them in the driving mirror. "We know Alain Renuard has more than a passing interest in the Nazi regime, and possibly even links to a neo-Nazi group, which, given Klara's own family history, is worth exploring further. Let's see if tech can chase up anything else on his computer."

His passengers were silent now. Dove stared out at the falling snow, the grey skies, frustration gripping her insides and twisting them until she wanted to scream.

Dove's phone rang as they finally approached the main road into town.

"Hi, love, I've got a few thoughts on Klara's dissertation, and our modern-day victims," Jess said cheerfully.

"Great. Any good news very welcome," Dove told her glumly.

"One of those days, is it?" her friend answered sympathetically.

"I'll put you on speakerphone. I'm in the car with the DI and Steve."

"Hi to you all," Jess said. "First thoughts are regarding the dissertation. It was good, very advanced. These were extremely bright students with a complex grasp of medicine and science. The part where they used the Nazi experiments as an example is shocking, but they do go on to say the cardiology was almost completely absent from the testing."

"That's what their tutor said, I think," Dove pointed out. "And the fact it was completely horrific and unethical."

"Yes," Jess continued. "But the conclusions they draw from their own totally legitimate, university-regulated tests do suggest they had possibly been drawing on 'other research'. It's just too much and too advanced to have come from the legit stuff."

"JD Turner was the first victim of their testing?" Jon queried.

"Very likely. If they managed to coerce him into it, he may have gone along with them to the point of no return," Jess said.

"Which then scared them all so much they dropped their research, even though they were so close to a breakthrough," Dove pondered, staring unseeingly out of the window. "Tessa may have made up her attack to cover how freaked out she was . . . They disposed of the body and went their separate ways."

"Possibly," Jess said. "The last thing regards your two present-day bodies, or test subjects number two and three, if you follow their thinking. Both young men were coerced into taking part in the same 'trials' JD Turner was subjected to, but both died, whether by accident or by design. If I look at the research, matched with my own test results, it is entirely possible both victims were immersed in freezing water for a length of time, which would induce hypothermia."

"At which point, they became test subjects," Jon said distastefully. "They could have been sedated?"

"Yes. No traces in their blood or in the tox screen, but after being completely frozen for a couple of days, all traces would be undetectable anyway," Jess informed them. "Bearing in mind the latest information, the marks on both their wrists could also have been not from ligature or injury, but from cannulation. It's very hard to be absolutely sure, due to the state the bodies were presented in, but Elijah does have a frozen clot slightly further up the vein in his left wrist . . ."

Dove traced her fingertips across the icy glass, drawing in the condensation . . . She suddenly whipped her fingers away, and swung back from the window. "Cannulation? You mean they may have been hooked up to a drip or something?"

"Possibly. With no traces left in their bodies, it's impossible to say if it was to sedate them or . . ." She paused. "Given the nature of this investigation, they may have been experimenting on the unconscious bodies with different drugs."

CHAPTER FIFTY-TWO

They returned to the station to be met by a uniform colleague, who fell into urgent conversation with the DI.

"Klara's ex-boyfriend says he wants to make a statement. Dr Albert Olsen." Jon caught Steve and Dove up as they climbed the stairs. "He's waiting downstairs now. Dove, you come with me. Steve, get onto digging up more on Alain Renuard, and find out where he and his wife are now."

"Another doctor! She sticks to type, doesn't she? Yes, boss, I'm on it." Steve carried on, and Dove swung back downstairs into the main building with the DI.

The tall, good-looking man waiting for them in an empty interview room was polite and charming, and very similar to Jeremy in looks.

Introductions made, chit-chat was kept to minimum, and the DI invited Dr Olsen to tell them about Klara.

He smiled, showing perfect white teeth. "Klara is very clever. When people talked about some of the companies associated with the MEDA group testing facilities, it was like they were going to do something amazing; find a cure for cancer or invent some new vaccine that would save millions of people."

"I suppose that would be a good end goal for any medical research," Dove said blandly, still thinking about Alain

Renuard. What if he had been involved in some kind of modern-day Nazi group? She knew of such things, but had never dealt with them. He was rich, so was he funding this new research, gathering the golden team back together with an eye to historical glory? Finishing what had been started so long ago . . . The thought made bile rise in her throat.

"What can you tell us about Klara recently, Dr Olsen?" the DI asked. "I assume from what you said earlier you keep in touch on a regular basis?"

"Klara was worried things were getting too commercial. Instead of ethical research being at the forefront, she found some information that research was being sold to other countries, and possibly to a military contact. We haven't seen each other for a couple of months, but I know back in March she told me of her concerns. When I heard she was missing, I wanted to let you know. Not because there is any suggestion of wrongdoing from MEDA, but just because . . ." He seemed to run out of words, less confident than he had appeared at the beginning of the interview. "I'm worried about her."

"How long did you date?" Dove asked.

He shrugged. "Three years, on and off. But we knew each other from earlier on. We had the same interest in cardiology, and we were both posted to the same hospital as junior doctors."

"What else can you tell us about Klara?" Jon asked, glancing at his watch.

He smiled. "Klara loved people to adore her. She needed constant clapping, and she usually got it. I'm sad for her that her grandmother died, and I was happy to help out, because I know how much she adored Helena."

"Was there any particular project Klara was working on? You said she was worried about her research being sold?" Dove put in.

"Just her usual, I think. She's been working on it since uni, on and off. You know her sister died in a frozen lake?"

"Yes."

"Klara's been obsessed with finding a way to reverse the effects of hypothermia. It's like a pet project she never really leaves alone," Dr Olsen said earnestly.

"Klara told us she hadn't worked on the project since university," Dove told him.

"That's strange . . . she has files full of research."

"Do you know of any incidents at university involving Klara?"

"No? Do you mean misconduct? God, no, she sailed through her finals with incredible grades. She really is something special." He glanced down, face flushed. "Sorry, I sound like a right idiot."

"Do you know any of her university friends?" She showed him the photos and he tapped Jeremy's picture.

"I've met him briefly. He and Klara dated at uni. We all met up for a drink, and he was teasing her about being an ice queen." He also tapped Tessa's picture. "I've think I've seen her, but I don't know where. I want to say at MEDA, but I'm not sure."

"What did Jeremy mean about Klara being an ice queen?"

"Oh, nothing really, just that she has that persona, I guess." He shrugged.

The DI raised his eyebrows at this and made another note. "Can you tell us anything else about Klara's hypothermia research? Was she conducting any trials with MEDA?"

"No. She said she used other laboratory facilities, but she didn't say where. I think she's close to a real breakthrough. The last time I spoke to her was two weeks ago, and she said she realized something was missing but she knew what it was."

"This was the drug she had developed?"

"Yes. It was another reason she was worried about research being sold abroad. Imagine how useful this drug would be to the shipping industries, to the mining industry, and finally, to the military," Dr Olsen said seriously.

"And she was close to a breakthrough . . ." the DI murmured to himself. "But I assume there is nothing illegal about selling research abroad? Are you suggesting MEDA *are* involved in something that possibly links to our investigation?"

"No! Not at all. MEDA are an international company, and well respected. I wouldn't dream of suggesting they would do anything that might bring the company into disrepute. It was Klara who objected to research being sold abroad. She wanted to keep control."

Dove studied his face in the little silence that followed. The DI loved to do this in interviews, allowing his interviewee time to digest any comments or questions. More often than not, the person being questioned would break the silence, and equally often, with useful information.

"Klara wouldn't be responsible for the deaths of those two men," Dr Olsen stated, looking uncomfortable. "I know with her history and her research it looks bad, but she wouldn't. She's complex and a little obsessive, but she would never kill anyone."

Dr Olsen had nothing more to add, so they thanked him and headed back to the office. Dove went straight back to her desk and updated Steve. The group of photographs on the incident board stared down at her. Someone had added a picture of the body found in the lake. JD Turner had been the first victim of Klara's own hypothermia experiments. And she had continued to research . . .

She opened her emails and was pleased to see the solicitor in charge of Professor Renuard's divorce had got back with the rest of the information. Dove read through the email quickly, then sat back, surprised. They had given no hint at how bitter things must have become between them. Yet it seemed the professor would be left with nothing. She would certainly have nothing if any evidence of wrongdoing at the university came to light — like, say, an involvement in a murder . . .

Steve was drumming his fingers thoughtfully on his desk, "Sounds like Klara's a tough piece of work, really, and could probably get round anyone. If she manipulated Jeremy

Masters into restarting their clinical experiments, they make a formidable team," Steve said, draining his coffee and pulling out a packet of cough sweets. "I haven't found out anything more about Alain Renuard, but I imagine if we get our hands on his computer, it may yield something. If he is, or was, a modern-day Nazi sympathizer, there are groups on the Dark Web devoted to fantasies like that, underground groups and troublemakers who believe World War Two never actually happened." He made a noise of disgust.

"Perhaps they all have different reasons for reforming the group. We still don't know if the Renuards were aware of JD's death and the original research, or whether they were told, or discovered it recently." Dove felt they were going in circles. Reactive rather than proactive, and the perpetrators were always one step ahead. It was a shit feeling for a police officer.

"Because they were brilliant? They were the A team, everyone said so, predicted brilliant, golden futures, until that night changed the course of their lives. What if her grandmother's illness was the thing that pushed Klara back over the edge? In her mind, it might be perfectly acceptable to force people back into her team. She seems to have been used to coercing her whole life, from what her tutor and ex-boyfriend said."

Dove disagreed. "She didn't come across like that at all. If anything, I'd say Jeremy was the player — he was the manipulator, and she went along with it, and now we have the possibility Alain funded it." She pushed her hair back from her face, thinking. "*He's* the one who makes me uncomfortable."

"What do you mean?"

"It was mainly the way he was when we interviewed his wife — so normal, and yet there was something underneath the surface. He reminds me of some of the CHIS I worked with. They used to keep all their anger and resentment just simmering along, hidden under the surface, until eventually it boiled over." She sighed. "I just don't see Klara as being capable of killing Elijah and Charles. It doesn't fit her profile."

"Yet she's the one who has been pursuing this end goal all along, and she's the ice queen, isn't she?" he said, half joking.

"Do you really think she sees herself like that?" Dove was unconvinced.

The DI called a mini brief to update his team and sent Josh and Lindsey out to talk to the Renuards again. "I'll get things in motion for a warrant, so we can seize his computer. Meanwhile, I want you two to get statements from him and his wife. Take a couple of uniform cars with you as backup." He looked across the office. "Steve and Dove, go to Klara's place and talk to her mother, who's currently staying there waiting for news."

"Why are we taking those maps?" Steve asked Dove as she packed a bundle into her bag.

"After we have spoken to her mother, I want drive to Darkwood Lane from Klara's place," Dove told him. "It's just something I've thought of."

"As long as we don't have to walk around in the snow, I'm good," Steve told her as they walked briskly downstairs and across the car park.

She edged out of town, driving faster as they hit the main road.

"I thought the mother lived in Windsor?" Steve queried.

"She's left the elder daughter up there sorting things out and come down to Klara's place. Understandably, she's devastated to have lost a mother and a daughter in the last week and she's desperate to help find Klara."

A cat padded delicately through the snow along the top of the neighbouring wall as they got out of the car.

Knocking on the door produced no response, so they traipsed round to the back door. Peering through the windows, the house looked as neat and tidy as Dove's last visit, but also very empty. No lights shone, apart from the security light they triggered on their tour of the perimeter.

A car pulled up at the front and a woman started unloading cleaning buckets. She marched straight up to the front door, stopped and stared at the police officers.

Steve introduced them and the woman nodded, her eyes still suspicious. "Got any ID?"

They produced their wallets, and she smiled, showing very white, even teeth. "I'm Sam Raynor, the cleaner. You'd better come in. Mrs Payton said you would be along. She's just gone over to help Arthur Johnson at number fifty-two. He fell and hurt his ankle while I was there earlier, wouldn't let me look at it, but then I heard him calling out when I finished at Martha's place — that's number fifty-four."

"Do you clean all the houses in this road?" Dove asked, when the woman paused for breath.

"No! Just six of them," Sam laughed, flicked on light switches, dumped her buckets and went towards the kitchen. Her grey hair was coiled up in two plaits high over her head and she had a ruby nose stud, which matched her red lipstick. She was certainly the most glamorous cleaner Dove had seen.

"Do you mean Klara's mother, when you say Mrs Payton?" Steve queried.

Sam seemed very at home in her client's house, and made them all cups of tea, an air of pleased anticipation about her. "Of course. Dr Payton is missing, isn't she?" Her cheerful expression faltered. "They said on the news she might be linked to those other missing women?"

"Possibly. Have you worked for Dr Payton for long?"

"A couple of years. Oh, I think I can hear Mrs Payton now," she said, moving towards the door. "I do hope Arthur is all right. It was lucky she was here . . . Did you know she used to be a doctor, too? A surgeon. It must run in the family."

CHAPTER FIFTY-THREE

Mylene Payton, Klara's mother appeared, very pale, with white hair in place of Klara's blonde, but with the same dark brown eyes and slightly aloof bearing. She looked exhausted, and up close her eyes were darkly shadowed, and wrinkles etched around her mouth.

Sam made her a cup of tea and took her mops and cleaning equipment upstairs. Dove had no doubt she was listening avidly.

Mylene apologized for not being in when they arrived.

"It's okay. Mrs Payton, can you tell us anything about Klara that might help us to work out where she might be?" Steve said gently.

The other woman sighed. "I know you're investigating the murders and the missing women. Klara told me you thought she was involved."

"Do you think she is?" Dove asked flatly.

Mylene looked up at that, shock in her face. "Klara would never hurt anyone, but I'm afraid she might be involved, yes. You know about her hypothermia research?"

They nodded.

"When Isla drowned she changed, became so quiet and introverted. Jeremy didn't really change, but he seemed to follow Klara around afterwards. He was just always there, and when they dated at university, I wasn't happy. I could see he was pushing Klara into doing things she normally wouldn't." Mylene pulled a face, distaste and a flash of fear in her eyes.

"Like what?" Dove asked.

"Drugs, parties, and that research on the dissertation. Klara was always a clever child. She could learn things just like that, and when a subject caught her attention she would immerse herself in it. She could go hours just reading and making notes, with no food, no sleep, until she was finished and her concentration broke."

"It sounds like she was an excellent student, though? Did you know Tessa or Alice . . . um, Katherine?"

"No, she didn't mention her friends much. It was always study, and afterwards always work. After university she became more withdrawn, but not depressed now, almost . . . excited, like she was hugging a secret to her heart. Something pleased her, and that thing drove her all the way through medical school and further into her career. She is an excellent doctor."

"There was trouble between you after she used data from World War Two in her dissertation."

The woman pursed her lips, her eyes sad and proud. "My mother was held prisoner in Dachau, as you know. She was selected to help with the medical experiments." She sighed. "As if she had any choice. She was only eighteen, terrified as they all were. Her part was to help with the warming of men who had been immersed in freezing water. She was told she was helping the doctors to gain knowledge which would help their pilots survive if they crashed into the sea. She would repeat that again and again, that she was 'helping'."

Dove bit her lip, her throat constricting at the thought of the horrors she had read, the things that would haunt her nightmares. Klara's grandmother had lived through the nightmares. "Go on."

"The doctors had a list of things they tried to warm the poor men after the immersion . . . one of them was body heat." Mylene met Dove's eyes, her own stony and sad. "The men were naked and Helena was forced to lie next to them, also naked. Those who gradually regained some kind of consciousness were forced to have sexual intercourse with the women who warmed them."

Dove wanted to vomit. The depths of depravity in the name of science and research were shocking. "What happened to Helena after the war?"

The pride was back in the woman's face. "She survived Dachau and finally escaped as the Nazis tried to bury all signs of their depravity, marching the prisoners away from the scene of the crimes as the Allies began to take control. She eventually married a British soldier and became a doctor. They came to live in his home town in Kent. Much later, Helena managed to track down Marta, who she escaped with, after they survived Dachau." Her voice was soft, respectful, and her eyes were full of unshed tears. "The Ice Daughters, that's what she said they were called. Die Eistochter."

"She was a brave woman." Dove felt that was an understatement, but from her research she had been reduced to tears again and again by the sheer bravery and stubbornness with which people in extreme circumstances clung to life.

"The guards who helped with the experiments would tell her again and again they were helping the air crew to survive, that this was important work and she should be proud to serve them."

"They probably truly believed that," Dove said. "And if they had questioned their orders, they would probably have been killed or imprisoned."

"It's true." Mylene bowed her head. "Helena had a great deal of sympathy for everyone, despite her situation." Her head came up. "Except Sigmund Rascher. She hated him, and apart from giving his name in evidence in the trials, she would never talk about him, only the guards."

Dove studied her for a moment. "Jeremy has admitted pushing Klara into using the hypothermia data for their research."

"She said it was the wrong choice, and she was correct. I couldn't believe it after the way she was raised. My mother would tell her, all three girls, about her experiences. She was able to talk about them, and we both agreed it would make the girls stronger, give them a foundation on which to build their lives. Klara, in particular, was a little obsessed with the family history during her teenage years. She had a sort of shrine to Helena and the Ice Daughters in her room. It made me feel . . . uneasy, but I couldn't see any harm in it." She shifted uncomfortably in her chair. "I am proud to have had Helena as my mother."

"And so you should be," Dove assured her. "I can see that Klara was proud of her, too."

"But what are you saying?" her mother asked. "You sound like you know something more, something bad . . ."

Steve answered carefully, avoiding a direct answer. "Can you think of anywhere Klara may have gone, Mrs Payton?"

"No, I thought she might have tried to see Krystyna, my eldest daughter, but Krystyna hasn't heard from her since the night she arrived. She's up at the house in Windsor. They haven't really got on for years. Not since Isla died."

Not since Isla died, Dove thought, and Klara's view of life took on an obsessive angle. Scrabbling for something solid to focus her emotions and ambitions on, the girl had apparently seized on her sister's death and the miracle that had saved Jeremy. In her mind, had that somehow become tangled with the family legacy of the Ice Daughters?

CHAPTER FIFTY-FOUR

They drove in a westerly direction from Klara's house towards Darkwood Lane, passing Jeremy's apartment and Dove's own house. Turning up the road towards Tessa's farm, Dove's phone rang. "DC Milson," Dove said, her heart thumping fast.

"Sorry, I hope you don't mind, but it's Sam Raynor. We met at Dr Payton's house earlier. I'm the cleaner?"

"Yes, of course."

"Well, I was just talking to my sister and she mentioned that Dr Masters bought a small parcel of land from her in the summer. We want to retire and go to Spain, you see. And Karren had this place . . . It's a log cabin, with a bit of land and a fishing lake out at Greendown Forest. Her husband used to love it there, but now he's dead and she doesn't use it . . ."

'A cab, I'm in a cabin?' Was that what Charles Richardson had been saying in his voicemail? she thought suddenly. Not a cab or cabbie, but a cabin? "Go on, that's very helpful."

"Dr Masters was very interested when I told him. He made an offer and paid cash. It never went through the books or anything, but he said he'd change it on the land registry."

"How did you meet Dr Masters?"

"He's Dr Payton's boyfriend, isn't he? They go way back, even though she just laughs when I say it."

Dove pulled over into a layby, and she and Steve bent over his iPad.

Dove was tapping keys, pulling up title deeds for the property. "Is your sister's name Karren Anderson?"

"Yes, and her husband was Bill."

Jeremy had not changed the deeds.

"Karren, can I ask how much he paid for the cabin and land?"

"Of course. He offered Karren twenty thousand, and Karren figured it was a fair offer. Who else was going to want a cabin in the middle of nowhere? It went a good way towards our Spanish retirement too," Sam told her.

"Oh good," Dove said vaguely, her mind still spinning. But more to the point, what exactly was he doing in a remote cabin next to a frozen lake? She ended the call and Steve pulled up another map of the area.

Dove was studying the deeds again. "Look! It's right down here, the cabin, I mean. We could take a quick look and call for backup if we need it. If it's another dead end, like the reservoir, then we haven't wasted any time."

She could feel Steve's hesitation even as she indicated to pull out of the layby. The weather was getting worse. The wind picked up and flung huge fistfuls of snowflakes at the vehicle as they drove slowly down towards the turning in the woods.

"Okay, carry on and I'll call it in," Steve said, putting his phone on speaker.

The DI was sharp and worried. "Have a quick look and get straight back to me. If it looks remotely possible that this might be the place, we'll sort out some backup and send it straight over. Can you send over the exact location? There isn't anything marked on the map."

"Got it, boss. It looks like a track under the trees, but it's passable," Steve said, peering out of the fogged window as Dove edged the car onto the snow-covered track.

"There's a bridleway sign," Dove pointed out, and her partner relayed the information to the DI.

The wind, which had been howling around them, immediately dropped as they entered the sheltered area in the woods. To their right, a steep hill reached above the treetops, further protecting them from the blizzard.

Dove continued slowly and the car bumped over ruts and ice, jolting its occupants. Occasionally a tree branch, laden with snow, brushed the roof and made them both jump.

Suddenly, the path widened out into a rough square area. Dove stopped, but the cabin was nowhere in sight. The space seemed to have been made for machinery and huge piles of logs, which stood to one side. It was partially sheltered by the tree cover, with less snow on the ground.

"Wait here a minute. I think we need to go on foot now. If the cabin is just round that bend, as it appears on the map, we'll be seen in an instant. The land drops steeply, look . . ." Steve was tapping the screen with his fingernail, and Dove also squinted at the thin line on the map.

"Okay, let's do it. It looks like a continuation of the track we followed from the road. If this is their way in and out of the cabin area, it must be passable for vehicles. A quick look and we get back to the car," she said, glancing with anxiety at the already snow-covered windscreen.

Steve called the DI with an update, and he reiterated they were to have a look and then, if the cabin appeared occupied, to wait for backup. Steve rang off and looked at Dove. "Come on then, let's get this over with."

They opened the car doors and received the full force of the snowstorm. Even as they pulled coats tighter around them, beginning the walk across the car park area towards the track down to the cabin, a thunderous noise made them freeze, motionless and bewildered.

"What the hell is going on?" Dove shouted over the rumbling, crashing sound.

"A thunderstorm?" Steve yelled back. "Let's get back to the car!"

They staggered back to the vehicle. Luckily, they had only managed to cover a couple of metres.

Dove paused, her hand on the car door, looking wildly around, up at the sky, squinting painfully against the whirling ice and snow. Her gaze landed on the track they had just driven along, the one leading back to the main road. She blinked hard and dashed snow from her vision with a gloved hand. The roaring noise was dying away, or lost in the soft thickness of the falling snow. "Steve, look! Shit, we're so screwed now."

The track they arrived by wound under the hill, and snow had probably gathered on the very top, weighing heavily on the edge of the sodden chalky grassland and trees. Now, as the wind picked up and more snow fell, adding to the pressure on the ridge, it had collapsed, blocking the way. Nothing could get in or out via that route.

"No fucking way," Steve said, staring at the mass of snow, trees torn from the ground, earth and branches creating a massive roadblock. "This can't be happening. Is that an actual landslide?"

Trees had been torn up by their roots, the jagged white scars of branches were tumbled among the mud and snow, and a huge chunk, like a monster bite, had been taken out of the hillside to the right of the track. The debris was spread far across their escape route.

Dove was blinking, shielding her eyes with her gloved hand. "I think it is. Let's get back in the car. Looks like we're safe enough here at least." She glanced doubtfully up at the steep hillside to the right of the car park. It, too, was packed with conifers, but for the time being, stood strong and unmoving. "We've still got a couple of hours until darkness. Let's call this in and go check out the cabin."

CHAPTER FIFTY-FIVE

At least the car was still warm, and they had brought large thermal cups of coffee with them earlier when they left the station.

Dove waited for the signal to show up on her phone, frowning as the seriousness of the situation hit home. Her phone remained dead. "I don't suppose you've got a signal?"

Steve shook his head. He had pulled his hood down, and his brown hair formed a spikey halo around his worried face. His cheeks were red from the weather, and he put his phone down carefully on the dashboard. "Shit. We are not equipped for this weather."

For a moment, they sat in stunned silence. Without any means of communication, they couldn't warn any team coming in of the landslide, couldn't call for backup if they did find the cabin occupied.

"We've got blankets, extra jackets, a shovel and a first aid kit," Dove said, forcing herself to be positive. Inside the foggy warmth of the vehicle, with the falling flakes muffling all sounds from the outside, it was impossible to believe they had just witnessed a landslide. It was like a dream, a nightmare filled with ice and the deceptively gentle fluff of snow. Dove remembered the phrase 'snow-blind'. It seemed apt.

She rubbed the condensation on the window with the cuff of her jacket, trying to see if the weather was clearing at all, but the snow fell relentlessly.

She checked her phone again, mechanically, without much hope, and then threw it next to Steve's. It landed with a clatter on the dashboard. "We could walk to the top of the track, as we planned, and just look down the hill to see if there are any lights on, or vehicles parked up?" she suggested, putting her wet gloves next to the heater.

"You'll probably cook them if you do that, and they won't get dry, it's too damp in here. I have another idea — instead of going to reconnoitre a cabin which might be possibly full of insane doctors, we could wait safely here in the car with the heater on until we get rescued," Steve suggested, eyeing the blanketed white landscape around them, the whirling clouds of flakes and the increasing depth of the drifts bordering the car park area. "Because even if there are signs of life, what are we going to do? We won't know for sure if it's our suspects or an innocent resident, and at this rate, we might end up going and banging on the door asking for help ourselves," he said pessimistically.

Dove looked at him sternly. "We can't call for backup with no signal, but they know where we were going and our last grid reference, so, weather permitting, we *have* got help coming." She ticked off the points with cold, red fingers. "You can stay here, with your phone, and I'll just walk under the trees to the edge of the track. I'll snap a few pictures, so we know the layout, and can see any occupancy of the cabin, if I can see anything through the snow, and come straight back."

"No way. We'll both go down," Steve told her firmly. "You aren't going anywhere on your own. Equally, we have no idea how unstable that hill is now, so neither of us should stay in the car."

She had a moment of unease, following his gaze towards the hill on the right, imagining for a crazy second that she saw the trees begin to fall, the land begin to slide. "Look, honestly, you stay here, and I'll go and have a quick look down the hill and come back."

"Don't be stupid. First rule of survival in a blizzard is stick together." He tried his mobile hopefully again, and Dove glanced at hers. No reception.

* * *

Leaving the cramped warmth of the car was tough. Dove leaned against the door of the vehicle, yanking the zip on her coat up as far as it would go, tucking her hair in at the back, under her hood. The icy blast of air made her start shaking and gasp a mouth full of snowflakes. But the flakes were smaller, she could see further in front of her. Even though the sky was dark and dull, she could actually now see the clouds. "Steve! It's stopping."

He grunted, pulling his own hood, turtle-like around his head. "My glasses are all fogged up, I need bloody wind-screen wipers. Let's keep under the trees, right on the edge of the track."

They trudged across the carpark towards the track, gasping as the evergreens dumped a load of snow when they brushed past. At last, they reached the point where the track dropped steeply into a little valley, winding towards the large log cabin.

"Look, Steve!" Dove paused, surprised, and pointed down the hill. "It's a big place, almost more like a house than a cabin."

"It was only marked as a cabin on the land registry map, and as nothing on Google. I suppose the planners wouldn't notice if you built an illegal hotel down here — it's so well hidden! They've got lights on and vehicles outside, so some-body is home," he pointed out quickly. "The treeline goes all the way down to the lake. I guess we could get closer without being seen."

"Let's do it," Dove said. Right at the back of her mind was the possibility there might be more victims held in the cabin. Her training told her not to be foolhardy, but her heart told her it couldn't hurt to take a look. As her partner had pointed out, with the treeline and the weather, not to mention fast-approaching darkness, it was extremely unlikely any watcher in the cabin would spot them approaching. And who knew? They might save a life.

They inched down the hill, brushing past the tightly packed conifers, releasing the sharp scents of pine and wood, slipping in the snow, eyes fixed on the wooden building ahead.

The track dropped steeply and opened out into a flat area with the large log cabin perched beside a small frozen lake. As Dove had said, the cabin, although all built on one storey, was certainly far more than a summer sports building. It was a square timber-framed house, clad with the traditional logging. A few ventilation or heating pipes sent thick clouds of steam into the frozen air. A wooden veranda with white-painted railings surrounded the entire cabin, with an additional dock area on the lake side of the building. It looked cosy, festive and entirely unthreatening, with the soft glow of interior lights projecting a homely beacon in the murky daylight.

A parking area under a lone pine tree was clearly salted or gritted and a Land Rover, partially covered in snow, sat waiting. No other vehicles.

"Don't recognize the plates as being connected to any of our suspects, and I'm pretty sure none of them drives a Land Rover. What are we going to do now?" Steve said.

"It might be a while before we get backup." Dove snapped a picture of the vehicle and sent it as a text to the DI. Of course he wouldn't get it now, but if the signal came back and they were incapacitated, her pending messages would be sent. She hoped like hell they wouldn't be incapacitated, and bit her lip, considering. "The snow's easing off a bit, I think. We could stay in the trees if we get a bit closer on the lake side. Looks like there is a path round the lake, or at least some distance between the edge of the trees and the water, so we can keep off that and watch for a bit. We won't risk anything. If it turns out to be some random countryperson seeking solitude, we can at least ask to shelter in the cabin."

Steve took his glasses off, balanced them awkwardly in his gloved fingers and gave them a rub on his scarf. "It might have almost stopped snowing, but I'm not freezing my tits off in a stake-out." He replaced his glasses and glanced at his watch. "Ten minutes, and if we haven't come to any definite conclusions about the identity of the cabin occupants, we go back to the car and wait."

They started trudging slowly, carefully, keeping eyes on the building, scanning the area around the frozen lake, keeping under the pine trees. On this side of the hill, where the snow lay less thickly, it was possible to walk almost normally. There was no sign or sound from the cabin, and it sat pretty and innocent as a Christmas card with the snow swirling around its peaked roof. The wooden porch was decked with the white stuff, and they could see boots and boxes stacked outside the door. The windows cast a warm, welcoming glow across the frozen landscape, and several times a shadowy figure passed inside the cabin, making Dove and Steve pause to watch.

"The lights are on, but only one vehicle. So who is actually here? It's hard to tell if that shadow is one person going back and forth or several. We're too far away," Steve said. He added suddenly, "Can you see up towards the other side of the lake? It looks like another track into the woods. Could be another way out?"

She peered at her phone, rubbing the wet screen with her glove, pocketing it and cursing. Searching the map she had saved, she traced her bare finger along the perimeter. "No, it's not marked as a road or track, but as a bridle path." She traced it across the screen, shielding her phone with her other hand. "It comes out on the main road, crosses it and continues off towards Eversham and the Downs."

Dove brushed snow off her face, clumsily pulled her gloves back on, and pulled her hood more securely around her ears. It was bitingly cold, even in the trees. "I don't suppose you've got any signal yet?"

Steve checked his phone again, but both phones remained obstinately unusable.

"Okay, so we can go back to the car or carry on. Look how closely the trees grow, and our jackets are dark enough to blend in with the trunks," Dove said. She followed the tree line around the lake with her eyes. It wasn't a large body of water, and right in the centre was a kind of tiny island, with snow-covered grasses and the roof of a wildfowl house.

"I don't see how we can get closer without exposing ourselves to danger. We should probably go back and wait it out," Steve said sensibly.

Dove was still looking at the cabin. In the summer months, it was probably idyllic. Her gaze caught something in the woods on the far side of the expanse of frozen water. "Shit. Steve, is that a body? Lying next to that tree?"

He squinted into the icy air. The snowfall had lessened to the odd flurry of ice crystals, and the wind was dropping as suddenly as it had appeared. "Orange jacket, perhaps? It could just be a bag or some kind of equipment dumped there."

"It's not covered in snow, though, so whatever it is was put there recently," Dove said.

They slid and stumbled through the snow to the fringe of the forest, and cautiously skirted the lake, keeping in the trees, eyes returning frequently to check the cabin and its possible occupants. It was impossible to tell if it was a figure slumped beneath the snow-laden pine trees, or some kind of rubbish dumped next to the lake. They struggled on, through knee-deep snow. It was exhausting, and they were soon sweating, muscles screaming a protest at the exertion.

"Even if they're looking out, they won't see us in this weather," Dove said in Steve's ear. The icy air took her breath away. She still felt as though she was caught inside a snow globe, losing her bearings, hands and feet numb from the cold.

"I think it is a body," Steve told her, putting a cautious hand on her arm and they halted, assessing the situation. He pointed silently towards the trees ahead. "There is a direct line of sight from those windows towards where it's lying, though. If we go further into the forest, and approach from the tree side, we'll be less conspicuous — but it brings us very close."

They paused every few metres and peered through the snow, checking for danger. But there was no movement from the cabin and no sound from the person lying in the snow. Edging quickly into the tree cover, walking faster where the snow was thinner, they could now see the slumped figure clearly.

It was a man, tied firmly to one of the pine trunks. He was dressed for the weather, but slumped forward into his bonds and he looked unconscious.

Jeremy. Dove called out, but the man didn't respond, so they inched closer. The door to the cabin remained closed and no one appeared from the woods to stop them.

Dove tugged off a ski glove with her teeth, and, shoving cold fingers into Jeremy's clothing, she felt for a pulse. His head lolled, and his skin was almost blue with cold. "Jeremy!" she almost shouted in his ear.

No response, and her numb fingers couldn't find any pulse. But deep inside his clothing his body appeared to be warm and he seemed to be breathing normally.

She and Steve yanked at the ties that bound him to the tree, but they were plastic and stayed firm. In desperation, Steve grabbed a broken tree branch from above their heads, and yanked with all his strength. It cracked, and he used the wood to lever inside the plastic. Bracing his makeshift tool against the tree trunk, he gave a sharp push downwards, and the ties around Jeremy's waist snapped.

They pulled his body further into the trees and then looked at each other in desperation.

"We'll have to carry him back to the car and try and get him warm," Dove said wearily, trying to force her tired brain to come up with a plan.

Steve agreed, and they pulled the doctor into the shelter of some evergreen scrub, far enough from the path to hopefully be safe. Dove rolled him carefully onto his back, and they tucked his clothes around him as tightly as possible, pulling the zip of his heavy jacket right up to his chin.

"He seems warm enough under his clothing," Steve said. "He clearly hasn't been here very long."

Carrying their burden awkwardly between them, they retraced their steps around the lake and up the hill to the carpark. As the snowfall slowed, darkness seemed to be approaching and the cabin lights threw an eerie glow across the crisp whiteness. No figures emerged from the interior, but they could now see all the windows were barred. The light fell in symmetrical lines, creating prison bars on the pure crisp snow outside.

CHAPTER FIFTY-SIX

Keeping in the trees, they edged slowly back up the hill, aided by the deep drifts of snow that had piled against the trunks. Even if someone was watching from the cabin it would be incredibly hard to spot them now. The snowstorm seemed to have died away completely, leaving just the odd drifting flake dancing on the icy air. Dove's face was numb, her eyes tired and gritty. Even her lashes seemed to have ice on them, although she could feel sweat running down her back inside her heavy thermal clothing.

Finally, they arrived back at the car, and laid Jeremy carefully on the back seat, turning him on his side. Dove grabbed a couple of extra blankets from the boot and tucked them around him. The first aid kit produced a foil blanket, and they added this to his insulation.

Finally closing the doors carefully, the two officers slid into the front seats, and Dove flicked the heating switch hopefully.

Steve raised his eyebrows and she shrugged. "There might be enough residual heat just to keep it warm in here. We haven't been gone that long."

The thermal cups containing coffee were still hot and drinkable. "Thank god for these," Dove said as she felt the caffeine and warmth running through her body. Slowly, her fingers and toes started to defrost.

Every few minutes they checked on Jeremy. His cheeks were pale, lips tinged with blue, but soon he began to stir, to open his eyes. Steve got out of the car and opened the rear door.

"It's okay," Dove said quickly. "You're safe."

He licked his lips, and Steve propped him up, sliding into the seat next to him as Dove held the thermal cup to his mouth. He sipped and his eyes focused properly on her. "DC Milson?"

"Yes, and DS Parker. How are you feeling?"

"Like shit." He was gradually becoming more alert. "You found us. I hoped you would, but I couldn't tell you . . . Where are the other officers? Why are you on your own?"

Dove studied him through narrowed eyes and shot a glance at her partner, seeing her suspicion mirrored in his own expression. "We're just waiting for backup. It won't be long." There was no point in pretending, he would be able to see for himself the track was impassable. "We came ahead, but the blizzard caused a landslide and blocked the way down from the road."

He nodded, and winced as he moved. "I see. Do you . . ." He took another sip of the hot drink. "Do you know what happened down there?"

"Why don't you tell us?" Steve suggested. His movements were slow and measured, but Dove could see he was alert. They had searched Jeremy's clothing when they found him, so could be confident he wasn't armed, at least. Maybe it was a classic falling-out among thieves that had led to him literally being left out in the cold . . .

"In fact, firstly, tell us exactly who is in the cabin down there and if anyone is in any immediate danger," Dove said, slightly more fiercely than she had intended.

He looked alarmed. "Alice, Tessa and Klara are down there. Everyone is fine."

"What about Professor Renuard and her husband? Dove asked.

"I . . . What do you mean?" Jeremy frowned. "Why would they be here?"

Dove narrowed her eyes, watching him closely, but he seemed entirely innocent.

"Why were you tied up under a tree?" Steve demanded.

Confusion crossed his face and one hand went to his head. "I don't know. Something happened . . . I remember arguing with Tessa and being hit from behind . . ."

"Whose Land Rover is parked outside?"

"Mine . . . Well, I drove it up here. I borrowed it from a friend."

"Tell us exactly what's going on," Steve said sharply.

Jeremy nodded, apparently eager to help and relieved at being rescued. "You know about JD. That was what started all this. His death was an accident, but we needed to test the drug we had developed during our research."

"He was number one," Dove stated, remembering the marks on the victim's chests.

"Yes. We . . . we tested the drug on all of us that winter, with limited success, because of course we didn't want to let each other get too cold. Tessa was seeing JD and he found out. He was . . . a junkie, and he threatened to tell on us, so we exaggerated the effects of the drug, made it seem like it might be something for his kind of market, dumbing it down." Jeremy's mouth curved now and his eyes were cold with contempt. "We sat just outside the boathouse in the snow. Tessa and Klara injected themselves, then him. We let him get colder than we should have done."

"You tested it on yourselves?" Steve said, clearly shocked.

"Well, of course." Jeremy looked surprised, blue eyes wide and innocent as a child's. "We had every faith in our abilities, and with JD, well, it seemed too good an opportunity to miss, to push, to wait until he was on the brink . . .

"You killed him," Dove said, glaring at him. She was tense, sensing danger but unsure quite what was going on with Jeremy. The information seemed sound but what was going on in the cabin while they sat out of sight, under the trees in the car. It bothered her.

"He was a parasite, a junkie dealer, for god's sake," Jeremy said impatiently. "Klara and Tessa soon warmed up again, but we left him in snow, half in the lake for a while."

His frank blue eyes held Dove's, and he flashed a charming, slightly hesitant smile. "It was Klara. I tried to stop her but Klara told us it was a perfect opportunity to try it on someone who would never be missed. The whole thing was driven by her, and she made us feel like . . . like we could do anything, like it didn't matter because we were doing important research. She said the drug could save hundreds of lives, so one death was nothing . . ."

"Klara said that?" Steve queried with a trace of disbelief. Dove could tell he was thinking as she was: Why was Jeremy admitting to JD's murder?

"I don't know. I think . . . I think he might have had a heart defect and he couldn't take the cold. We watched his BP dropping lower and lower. Tessa started screaming at us to stop, to get him warmed up, but suddenly he was forty over twenty-five and we tried CPR, the drug, everything — but he was gone."

"So you put him in the lake."

"Yes, we . . ."

Dove flung herself sideways as a massive crack across the windscreen sent splintered shards of glass scattering across the car. Another crack and the iron bar connected with Steve's head. He fell heavily across Jeremy's body as Dove scrambled to escape.

"Stop!" she yelled, launching herself away from the bar, fumbling for the car door handle and falling out into the snow. She leaped up and started to stumble towards their attacker who was moving towards the rear of the car. "Steve, look out!"

The man was tall and muscular, with no hat or gloves. Alain Renuard, with his face twisted in fury. He swung the bar like a baseball bat, smashing into the rear of the car, crunching it like cardboard, before chucking the bar into the snow and turning on Dove.

She dodged, turned to run, hampered by the snow, but strong arms grabbed at her from behind. Bewildered, she directed a blow at her assailant, jerking her elbow back. "Steve!" She could see him crumpled in the back seat. Jeremy had staggered out of the door on the far side and was standing awkwardly at the rear of the car. "Jeremy, run!" Why was he just standing there?

Alain yanked Dove's arms tighter and she swore at him, desperately trying to see Steve.

"That's enough, Alain," Jeremy said sharply to the grey-haired man. "Why did you have to come up?" His voice was heavy with annoyance, but something else too. Fear? "I had everything under control."

"Jeremy?" Dove choked out, still lashing out, cursing her heavy clothing.

"Just stop fighting. We aren't going to hurt anyone. We just need you out of action until we're finished. We saw you arrive. There's a security camera hidden in the trees by the main road, so we planned a diversion for you," Jeremy told her, a little smugly.

Alain, still breathing heavily, holding Dove, swore at him. "Don't tell her anything. I knew we couldn't trust you to sort things out. You're the weak link, Jeremy, and you know it."

"Shut up. You've just created another problem. Hold onto her and I'll check he's okay," Jeremy said, leaning into the rear of the car, avoiding broken glass and bent metal, and bending over an unconscious Steve.

"Leave him alone!" Dove twisted round to watch, trying to ignore the scowl from her captor. She hadn't realized how tall he was, how big his hands were, now clamped firmly round her wrists. "You said you were creating a diversion, so why did you attack us?"

"Shut up, or I'll give you a crack over the head too," Alain told her, in a tone so chilling and full of hatred, she was silent. It wouldn't help Steve if she was also knocked unconscious.

Jeremy wriggled back out of the car and directed another furious look at Alain. "He has a nasty head wound. I need that first aid kit. Not very adequate — he really needs stitches — but I can make him comfortable and safe before we go back to the cabin. Do you want me to do that, or we can just leave him like this, if you prefer?" Jeremy said impatiently.

"Make him comfortable," Dove told him, furious at being outwitted, just as Alain said, "Let him bleed. Why are you fussing over a police officer?"

"Sorry, DC Milson, I really am, and we didn't plan on having to hurt either of you, but we saw you arrive, and it seemed a good idea to divert you for a bit." Jeremy smiled at her. "Your emergency first aid was pretty good. If I really had been suffering from hypothermia, you might even have saved my life. Alain, if I leave him, he might die. He's police — I don't want to be done for murder."

"Bit late for that now." Alain gave a laugh. "You might think you don't have a speck of blood of your hands, Dr Masters, but you're in this as deep as the rest of us. If we need to kill them both, let's get on with it. I hate the bloody police. A few less of these fuckers in the world can only be a good thing."

Dove shivered at the intense, almost blind hatred behind his words, hoping he would listen to Jeremy. She was trying to figure out the best way to play this. Should she bluff they had already called in, that a backup team were on the way? Or would that trigger Alain into more violent rage and cause even Jeremy to cut his losses? They had said they were nearly finished, so it might be better to see what was happening down in the cabin . . . she could see her phone, fallen underneath the driver's seat, but couldn't see Steve's.

Jeremy started to unwrap a bandage with shaking hands, addressing Alain firmly. "Nobody else will condone the murder of police officers, and you'll be out on your own without a share of the profits."

This seemed to keep the bigger man quiet. Dove hardly dared breathe, watching the reassuring rise and fall of Steve's chest, the more worrying cut and bruising on his head. He was lying on his side, and as well as dressing his head, the doctor had draped two blankets over him.

Jeremy said he didn't want him to die, but Jeremy was already proven a liar. Was this some new game? She had done it often enough in her past, switching personalities, switching loyalties . . .

CHAPTER FIFTY-SEVEN

"Is your wife down in the cabin too?" Dove asked Alain, watching as Jeremy finished his work on Steve, and backed out of the car.

"Shut up and start walking," he told her, eyes gleaming with suppressed emotion. "Hurry up, Jeremy, and stop playing doctor."

Jeremy was very pale, his lips set in a thin line, but ignored the jibe, closed the car door and zipped up his coat. "Let's get moving, then."

"I'm not leaving without him." Dove indicated Steve's prone body.

"For god's sake, bloody move," Jeremy snapped. "He'll be fine. We've shut him in the car and he'll be warm enough and in no immediate danger."

Was Jeremy more afraid of killing a police officer or of Alain's temper? Dove took a last quick look at Steve, before the larger man shoved her forward. The clear rift between the two men, the uneasy reliance on each other for an unknown goal, might be something she could exploit to her advantage.

But just now, as the three made their way down the rutted, snow-covered track towards the cabin, the men either side of her, gripping her arms, Dove felt incredibly vulnerable

303

and alone. Worry for her partner niggled away in her chest, and she couldn't help scanning the landslide for any signs of backup arriving. Her face itched and stung from multiple tiny glass cuts. It was almost completely dark now, and the odd flurry of snow, flung sideways by the wind, looked eerie rather than beautiful.

"You saw the track is completely blocked?" Jeremy addressed the other man as they trudged down the hill.

"So? It means no more police officers arriving to screw things up, and we can get out the other way," Alain said shortly.

The lights of the cabin didn't look welcoming anymore, but she held out hope Jeremy didn't mean to hurt her. Whatever was going on down here, she meant to get back to Steve as soon as she could, with as much information as she could . . .

The trio progressed past the Land Rover and stepped up onto the wooden veranda, boots clumping, heavy with ice. They paused on the porch, which, as Steve and Dove had observed from the lakeside, was littered with boxes, boots and a couple of ski jackets.

"Open the door!" Alain demanded.

From the inside someone turned a key and shot a bolt, and Jeremy pushed the door wide. Dove stumbled in, Alain viciously twisting her shoulder as she obediently walked into the cabin. She could almost feel his temptation to hurt her more, the restraint he was clearly having to exert in not doing so, communicated by the strength in his fingers, the venom in his cold eyes. Was his hatred of the police a personal vendetta or was he just furious at having their plans messed up? She was familiar with the former emotion, having dealt with it constantly during her time with the Unit, and the familiarity gave her a tiny spark of hope. She could deal with this; she had dealt with worse.

The door from the porch opened straight onto a main living area. The cabin was as big as it had appeared from the outside, and this large space seemed to have been turned into a sort of field hospital, with screens separating a line of four beds from the area they were currently standing in. Doors leading from the living area were wide open, showing a galley-type kitchen, a door to a makeshift laboratory, and a corridor Dove supposed might lead to sleeping quarters. The sharp chemical smell of disinfectant and warm metal mixed uneasily with the homely scents of wood and cooking.

Medical equipment was everywhere, paperwork and two laptops out on a long table pushed against the far wall. Dove glanced down to see plastic sheeting had been placed over the entire floor, presumably in a further attempt to contain any dirt or possible contamination. Boxes of equipment and other supplies were stacked in a corner, next to a rocking chair, which contrasted unnervingly with the hospital environment.

Jeremy had pushed past and went straight past the screened-off area, but Alain pulled his captive back against the wall, next to the rocking chair. With one hand on her wrist, he pulled a gun from behind the wooden rockers and grinned at her. "I knew this would come in useful."

Dove kept as still as possible, quiet and observing the layout of the cabin, her captor's every move, but most of all, the reactions the other inhabitants in the cabin made to her arrival. The gun worried her even more. Naturally, she had some knowledge of firearms, and it wasn't a modern make . . . A pistol reminiscent of World War Two, with some kind of engraving along the barrel. That made sense, given Alain's apparent interest or obsession.

Professor Claire Renuard was bending over a patient, taking notes on a clipboard, and Klara stood next to her. It was surreal. Lying in one of four narrow beds was Tessa, hooked up to various monitors. Her long dark hair was bundled up into a surgical cap, and a silver foil blanket covered her body. She appeared to be unconscious, and Dove felt her own heart give a lurch of fear.

Both Claire and Klara were staring at the newcomer in horror. Dove was trying to process the information. Of course, Claire was involved. How easy to see with hindsight the little pieces of helpful information she let drop, the way she remembered her golden gang so very well . . . But Claire looked terrified, her eyes going past Dove to her husband. "Alain, what have you done?"

"Why have you brought her down here?" Klara asked, fear in her eyes. There was a bruise on her cheek and her blonde hair was lank and falling across one side of her face. She started towards them, but another woman appeared from the corridor, footsteps echoing briskly on the wooden floorboards, softening as she stepped onto the plastic sheeting.

"For god's sake get a move on, Klara," Alice said, annoyance in her tone. She surveyed Dove coolly. Her red hair was tied up in a knot and she was carrying a tray of equipment. The tension was palpable. Life and death lay in the balance. "Alain, I thought you were leaving the police to Jeremy?"

"We're so close, and Jeremy is . . ." He made a derogatory gesture with his gun hand and Dove held her breath. "It's all good. There are only two police officers, the other one is unconscious in their car, and we can deal with this one. Are you nearly done?"

"There's been a landslide and it's blocked the track to the main road," Jeremy volunteered, still checking Tessa's monitors.

Alice leaned over and tapped a few words into one of the laptops. "We can get out the other way. It doesn't matter. Nothing else matters." She glanced dismissively at Dove. "Shove her downstairs where she can't cause any trouble."

"Or I could just shoot her now?" Alain suggested.

"Alice?" Dove found her voice, although her body was frozen with fear at Alain's words. She was struggling to separate perpetrator from victim, but it was becoming clear Alain was a total loose cannon, and Alice seemed to be giving the orders. Just who was blackmailing who within the group of former friends? She had noted something else as Alice entered the room. Standing so close to Alain she felt his demeanour change, even his voice, still harsh, but now eager to please.

Alice shrugged. "No, don't shoot her. We need to concentrate on getting this done, not murdering police officers. She's not worth it, Alain. Put her downstairs and forget her."

"What's wrong with Tessa?" Dove tried again to establish contact with Alice, but the woman moved away, adding to a list of figures on a clipboard hung on the wall. The constant bleep of monitors was distracting and terrifying, as was Tessa's pale, unconscious face.

It was Jeremy who answered her question. "She's connected to Extracorporeal Life Support."

"Which does what? Is she in a coma?" she asked carefully. She was surprised he had answered so readily, but horrified by Tessa's unconscious state.

Jeremy answered even more readily this time, his eyes already on the monitors, face lit up with excitement and tension. "During hypothermia the body's metabolism is reduced, so drugs tend not to be metabolized. Roughly, for every one degree drop in temperature there is a seven percent drop in metabolism."

"Jeremy, stop lecturing her and get her down there out the way," Alice said, pointing to the corridor. Doubt flickered across her face. "Are you sure the other one can't cause any trouble?"

"Unconscious in the car, I told you," Alain said with satisfaction. His hatred was palpable again, and Dove shivered inside every time she encountered his glare.

Alarm showed once again in both Claire and Klara's faces, but Alice just nodded and made a note on her clipboard. Dove might as well not have been present for the amount of attention she gave her.

"Professor?" Dove looked directly at Claire Renuard, but the older woman dropped her eyes immediately. Her mouth was trembling, and she seemed cowed and afraid. "Professor, what the hell is going on?" They were clearly divided already. She would explore their group loyalties and see if she could push them further apart. But care was needed not to inflame Alain further.

Alain started to pull Dove towards the corridor, but she hung back, aiming her words at Klara now. "Are you testing your drug on Tessa? Klara?"

The tall blonde woman hesitated, and Dove could see the agony in her eyes. "Yes. They . . . she was already hypothermic when I arrived." A spark of anger seemed to override her fear. "They put her in the lake."

"Shut up and get on with the checks," Alice snapped at her. She looked at her watch. "Klara, Tessa will die if you don't crack on." Her tone was sarcastic. "You don't want precious Tessa to die, do you?"

"Is that it?" Dove asked, still talking to Klara, forcing her voice to sound calm and smooth. "Tessa's life in exchange for your professional help?"

Klara had moved back towards Tessa's bed now and was looking at the monitors surrounding her friend. She said nothing, but her tight expression seemed to ease a little as she read from the screens.

"Why? I don't understand why you're helping them when you could have come to us. What about your grandmother?" Dove prodded. "And Alice, what about your kids?"

Alice met her eyes briefly, dispassionately. "Shut up. Alain, for god's sake, get her down there and out the way." Her eyes were cold, emotionless and her expression one of anger. The smiling mother from the photographs was hardly recognizable. She was clearly focused on her objective, but what exactly was that and what would she do with Tessa?

Alain pushed the gun against Dove's side, breaking into her quick thoughts. "Move." He pushed his wife roughly out of the way, but grabbed Alice's arm as she passed. He pulled her towards him, kissed her hard on the mouth. It was a casual display of possession and power, and she smiled at him, before returning to her tasks. Unfortunately, outnumbered as she was, Dove couldn't take advantage of his moment of arrogance.

Alain and Alice? Dove was still struggling to reform her mental pictures of the group as she was hustled out of the room. The corridor was narrow and led to another open-plan area. This one, as she had correctly guessed, had doors opening off to show bunks and bathrooms.

"I suppose you're funding the research, and Alice brought the others back using blackmail and threats?" Dove guessed. Alone with the man and his gun, she was getting warning signals from his body language. He could easily say she resisted as it appeared he was going to lock her in a room, and in the struggle he shot her. Alice wouldn't care, and the others were working to save Tessa. "You're in charge of the whole project, then? The experiments?"

"We're carrying on important work. It was begun and now we are finishing it," he said, leaning past her and unbolting the door next to the bathroom. It swung open smoothly, releasing a smell of damp and mustiness, revealing steep wooden steps leading into darkness. "Go down there."

Panicked now, unable to make any connection with him, she kept outwardly calm, moving slowly through the door, feeling out the steps. He was right behind her, she could feel his bulky body, the cold metal of the pistol barrel on her neck. Why was he following her down? Why not give her a push and bolt the door behind her, returning to his 'important work'?

Nausea churned in her stomach and her heart was pumping so fast her body was shaking. It was the same feeling she had had, alone with the gang member who had tortured her on her last case with the Unit. The warning signs were all there, and again she was alone.

As if he read her thoughts, he whispered, "Keep going. It's dark and cold down here. A nice place for an execution, don't you think?"

She could smell his hatred, feel his hand on her arm, fingers closing harder than he needed to just for the joy of giving pain. Dove had encountered people like him before, so many times. One foot after the other; one breath, slow and controlled, after the other. She would have to fight soon, to go for the gun . . .

"Alain? Alice wants to know if you're done yet?" Jeremy's voice rang out, his footsteps swift on the wooden floor.

Dove gathered herself. Any chance . . . any chance at all.

Jeremy was coming down the steps into what appeared to be a basement storage area. There wasn't complete darkness, as the boards between the ceiling and the upper-level floor allowed fingers of light to illuminate the dust. "Hurry up. You go, and I'll lock the door. Look, give me the gun if you want, but she's not going to cause any trouble. If she does, you can shoot her when she tries to get out."

Dove was holding onto the wooden stair rail, fingers clenching so tight she could feel a slick of blood in her right palm from a splinter. Would it work? Jeremy had taken a chance, surely — perhaps, having seen Alain with Steve, he had an inkling of what the other man might do . . .

Alain stood, undecided, but Alice's voice floated down from the upper rooms. "Alain? I need the password!"

He scowled at Jeremy. "Any trouble, you call me back." And he ran back up the stairs and into the light, feet heavy, large body disappearing back up the corridor.

Dove leaned back against the wall, hand still on the rail, legs feeling weak with relief. "Thank you."

Jeremy shrugged. "I can't let you go, but I guessed he might be going to try something. I need to lock you in now. When we're gone, and it will be soon, I expect you'll manage to get out . . . If I had been able to get his gun off him . . . But he loves it. It's a genuine Walther P38, you know."

That made sense. She recalled the Walther P38 was some kind of service pistol, no doubt taking Alain another step closer to his Nazi dreams. How to keep Jeremy talking, to push her tiny advantage? "So the drug wouldn't work if you just injected it into the patient when they are that cold?" Dove suggested, trying to spark Jeremy's enthusiasm again.

She could see the struggle in his face, but the desire to impart knowledge won. "Yes, with the ECLS the blood can be warmed, the drug infused, and thus the drug is metabolized. It basically re-warms the blood as it circulates. For

Tessa, the test is nearly complete. She'll be able to come off ECLS any time now." He looked at his watch, and she let him take her arm and lead her downstairs to the basement. "You just stay here, now, or Alain will be back and he'll kill you."

"Why is she still unconscious?" Dove couldn't see any way out of this dismal room, apart from the door at the top of the stairs, which led straight into the barrel of Alain's gun.

"She was given a small amount of sedative while her body temperature was taken down." He looked faintly uneasy about this.

"While you put her in the lake? Jeremy, you're a *doctor*!" she prodded.

He said nothing more, but his hands were definitely looser on her arms. If it hadn't been for Tessa, and Alain with his gun, she would have taken him down, but the odds were stacked against a physical retaliation.

They were still standing close together in the half darkness. She said softly and confidentially, "It's not too late. Whatever games you lot are playing, whoever is doing the blackmailing, you could save yourself now. I can tell you don't really want to do this." His expression changed from smug to uncertain, and she pressed home her advantage, laying it on thick, pushing his vanity buttons. "Come on, Jeremy, you're a well-respected medical professional, and from what I've seen, a good one. You're better than this. Better than some arsehole playing at being a Nazi. He doesn't care about ethics or science!"

There was silence, and she kept their gazes locked, could feel his breath on her face. It was a chance. If he repeated her words to Alain, she would probably be dead. Could she turn him? Could she do it?

CHAPTER FIFTY-EIGHT

Jeremy stared silently at Dove. She could almost hear the click of his brain whirring as she waited for his answer. This could be a turning point . . .

Above the basement, in the kitchen, a muffled conversation continued, full of scientific phrases, interspersed with bleeps from the medical equipment. It seemed that Claire was working on a checklist. She read aloud, and Klara answered each question with a set of numbers. Occasionally, Alice intervened with a sharp query.

Jeremy finally spoke, regret in his eyes, "I can't. It's too late and too much has gone on. This was, *is*, an incredible chance for all of us, but we're tied together. Do you understand? It's all gone too far for anyone to pull out now."

He might have said more, but sharp footsteps clacked overhead from the kitchen, heading quickly down the corridor, as Alice called for Jeremy to return.

"Actually, Jeremy, since you seem to be getting on so well with her, I thought you should put these ties on her wrists and ankles, just to make sure she doesn't do anything stupid." Alice clashed furious glances with Dove. "And if you don't fancy tying her up, Alain is just desperate to oblige." Her eyes were bright with malice and cheeks flushed with excitement. "And for fuck's sake, hurry up. We've got thirty minutes left. We've nearly done it!"

Jeremy apologized as he applied what felt like the same plastic ties he had been wearing when they faked his hypothermia. Dove struggled a bit, trying to feel out if Jeremy was going to help her.

Either way, the outcome for her wouldn't be good. She tried one last time. "Jeremy, you don't need to do this!" She stumbled after Alice, who was halfway up the steps leading to the corridor.

Alice turned back, furious, and gave Dove a shove in the chest, knocking her sideways back down the steps and crashing against the banister railing. She caught the edge of her cheekbone on the corner of the railing as she fell. Stars exploded in her eyes and the pain was intense, momentarily knocking her to the ground. While she lay, dazed and fighting through the waves of pain and nausea, Jeremy tied her ankles.

The moment was gone. Alice and Jeremy hurried up the steps, closing the door at the top firmly behind them, boots receding along the corridor. Panting, waiting for the pain to pass, Dove lay for a moment, blinking in the semi-darkness.

She immediately began to explore her prison, dragging herself around within the limited movements the ties permitted. The left-hand side of her face was wet with blood, and the trickle stung and itched as it made its way down her neck to her collarbone. Once again she thought of Steve, hoping he was okay, hoping the weather had cleared enough for backup to be arriving.

She forced her mind back to her immediate surroundings. The basement was a storage area, lined with a few paddleboards and a rack of canoes for the summer months. It was a huge space, stretching underneath most of the building. Big concrete pillars stood in regular lines, supporting the weight of the structure above.

Boxes stacked in a corner were filled with lifejackets and nautical supplies. On the far side, a set of double doors were shut fast, but again allowing some light in around the edges. The place smelled damp and musty. She was covered in dirt from the concrete floor and shivering with cold and fear.

Via the floorboards which made up her ceiling, voices could still be clearly heard from upstairs. "Let her go!" Klara was saying forcefully. "It's nearly finished, so just let her go. You can't kill two police officers! You said the man in the car is still alive, so leave him too. There will be more police here soon anyway, looking for those two."

Dove bit her lip and tried to lick blood from underneath her nose, where it had congealed and was itching. It sounded like Alain was causing trouble again, instead of concentrating on the job.

Alain said something in an indistinct rumble, and Claire answered, "Of course they will! The police aren't stupid. The landslide on the hill won't stop them coming in the other way, and we need to get out by that track!"

"Tessa is regaining consciousness!" Klara said suddenly, her voice coming from further away, presumably the living area, and breaking through the arguments.

Dove bent her knees and managed to inch herself upright, shuffling along, heading for the stairs. A crack of light framed the door at the top, and she sat for a moment on the bottom step, listening.

She could hear Klara protesting at something again. Was she trying to slow things down? Dove wondered what had happened between her and Jeremy, what had gone wrong, turning a friend to a blackmailer. Clearly, the trials were indeed nearly finished. She didn't believe Alice would leave them all here alive . . .

Alice was ordering the two men to start loading the Land Rover now, and Dove could hear a gradual shutdown of some of the equipment. Beeps slowed and stopped, there was a click as plugs were taken out, and lids put on boxes. They were really going.

From her position, she could clearly hear footsteps enter the room above where she now sat — the laboratory room, perhaps? The beep of some kind of test and the hum of machinery. Klara's voice floated down through the ceiling, low and urgent. "We can't let them do this. They'll kill her like they killed the other two."

Claire's reply was muffled but audible. "Try to slow it down again. Someone will come looking for those two, and if they get here before the results are collated, we will be okay, too . . ."

"Tessa still isn't responding quickly enough, and she seems to have developed an arrhythmia," Klara said suddenly and loudly. There was the sound of paper rustling, and the click of machinery.

"She won't leave us alive either, you know that? Alain hates me, and Alice was only too happy to go where the money is," Claire said, fear edging her voice. "She knew exactly how to push his buttons, drag him into bed and talk about his Nazi obsession, his money obsession . . ."

"Can you read these latest results out loud to me?" Klara said loudly, slicing through the other woman's panic. She added in a lower voice, "It will be all right."

"I . . . Okay," Claire said, her voice louder, slightly more confident now.

As Claire began to reel off a load of figures, something was wedged down between the boarding from the upstairs room. A small kitchen knife. It dropped with a small clatter on the concrete floor and Dove hastily left her perch on the steps to hop and roll towards it.

Checklist complete, the two women left the room, footsteps echoing across the wooden floor. The knife was extremely sharp, and it took a few minutes of struggling, her hands now wet with blood, twisting the blade until she had freed her wrists.

Upstairs, there was a warning bleep from the remaining monitors and hurried footsteps. "Tessa? Can you hear me?"

Redoubling her efforts, Dove slashed the ties on her legs in a swift movement. She stood, muscles screaming in pain after being tied so tightly, and gave the double doors a shove.

They moved a little but were clearly bolted from outside. Dove felt like screaming with frustration. She searched the room again but the best weapon available was an oar. She seized it, and went back to the staircase, climbing slowly, carefully.

"You will stay here while we leave now," Alice was saying sharply. "Alain, tie them up and put them in the middle of the room."

Dove, listening on the other side of the door, was confused. Surely they weren't just going to leave all the evidence and run? Exactly who was going and who was staying?

Klara sounded sullen and afraid. "You have what you always wanted. You don't need to tie us up. Just go!"

Alice was talking again. "You have no idea, Miss Perfect. This is owed to me. It was all about you, and now it isn't. If I hadn't had the idea to hide JD's body, you would never have had your careers, and if Alain hadn't helped me and the cause these last couple of years, we would never have made this drug work. You should have been thanking me, not ignoring me and pushing me out!"

Jeremy spoke now. "Alice, we need to go. We've got the data, and we've been lucky the police haven't arrived yet. Let it go, lock them in and we'll disappear."

At that moment, someone's mobile rang, and a gunshot echoed around the lodge. Jeremy yelled something, and Dove could hear other shouts, a fight, the main cabin door banging and running footsteps outside . . . She launched herself at the door again and again, bashing it with the oar. Finally, her heart pounding, she broke through the wood, and emerged into the kitchen.

Klara, Tessa and Claire were tied in a circle in the centre of the floor. Around them, equipment still bleeped, paperwork still spread across the table. Tessa seemed to be barely conscious, propped awkwardly against Klara, head on her shoulder, but at least she was alive.

Outside, Dove could hear the Land Rover starting. She went to the window, watching as the three occupants began to head towards the track and freedom.

Dove grabbed a pair of scissors from the kitchen countertop in the next room and with some difficulty cut the women free.

"Are they gone?" Klara asked. "They really just left us here?" She sounded bewildered.

Dove still felt tense. Something was wrong, but she couldn't yet tell what. Her instinct was to stay in the cabin and wait until help arrived. They were warm and safe now the perpetrators had gone. "Did she get the information she needed?"

Klara nodded slowly, eyes wary, moving from person to person. "I tried to fool her, but she's a good chemist, and that's what it came down to. She was blackmailing us all, you know. This whole thing, it was my fault, my research . . . I wanted to tell you, but by then she had Tessa, had already killed that poor boy. I thought she was just threatening, but she actually did it."

"It was Alice's idea to start human trials back at uni, although Jeremy agreed," Klara said softly. "At first, we were carried away with whole idea of what we had created, the promises of great careers, and the good the drug could do, but after JD's death, I saw Jeremy and Alice were getting greedy, not motivated by anything but money and their careers, so I refused to take part in anything else. I tried to block the whole thing out." Her eyes filled with tears. "My grandmother had already said she was horrified by the data we used for our dissertation, and it came to me that we were on the verge of doing evil in the name of science."

Claire bit her lip, anger crossing her face. "I know we should never have covered up JD's death, and certainly Alain should never have been part of it. He thrives on anger, on hatred. He never used to be so angry all the time . . . Alice came to us with her plan last year, explaining she wanted to resurrect the research, talking mostly to Alain. I found out they had been talking online, that she was part of one of those stupid Nazi groups he plays around with."

"And JD's body being discovered gave them the leverage they needed?" Dove suggested.

"I knew Alain would want to go through with it. Alice was so clever, too, at finding his weakness, feeding his ego. She could see she needed his violence, his strength and his money and all she had to do was provide the sex . . ." The professor was crying again, her grey hair wild, her lip trembling.

"Alice had an affair with Jeremy at university as well, even while we were dating. I could tell she didn't really like me, just pretended to, to get close to him. He was always fascinated by her. She has a way of . . . I can't explain it, but men want her and want to be liked by her, but they can't see she despises them, uses them," Klara said bitterly.

"But . . ." Dove was still looking out the window when the sound of a vehicle disturbed the snow outside. A man emerged from the forest, running, and he was followed by the Land Rover. "Jeremy's coming back on foot!"

"Jeremy?" Tessa said slowly, eyes unfocused, words slurred. She seemed hardly aware of her surroundings.

Jeremy unlocked the door and flung it wide, gesturing frantically to the women inside. "Run! Go now. Get to the woods."

"Why? Why are you back?" Klara asked, fear back in her face.

His own face was wet with sweat and he was inside the cabin now, frantically shoving her towards the door. "The whole cabin is rigged to blow up any minute now. Alain put explosives everywhere. Get the hell out of here!"

Destroying the evidence. Claire was running now and Dove fumbled with a limp Tessa, eventually hauling her across her shoulders in a fireman's lift, half carrying her out of the door. She blinked hard as she stumbled, almost falling off the veranda and down the steps into the snow. The darkness was disorienting, and a wave of icy air took her breath away. Over her shoulder she could see Klara, coming last, casting a fleeting glance back, half hesitating.

"The police are coming! Jeremy!" The Land Rover was back, headlights jagged and bright against the shadowed winter afternoon, and Alice was yelling from the driver's seat.

Alain jumped out of the vehicle and started towards the cabin again, pistol held in his hand as Klara ran back inside.

"Klara!" Dove screamed, muscles giving out as she lowered Tessa to the ground, dragging her across the snow even as she tried to see what the hell Klara was doing.

Dove screamed Klara's name again, and she finally emerged from the cabin, blonde hair streaming out behind her as she ran for the forest. Another gunshot rang out.

Alice and Jeremy were both in the Land Rover now, already heading for the westward track which led to the main road, but Alain was still pursuing the women, pistol held ready. Alice was yelling at him, but he was taking aim. More gunshots shattered the icy darkness as they crawled frantically through the snowy undergrowth.

"Get down!" yelled Dove, as she saw Klara raise her head to look back. As she did so, there was a crack, and Tessa was down in the snow. Dove moved as fast as she dared towards the pair, breath coming in painful gasps, sweat pouring down her back even though her hands were numb with cold. Claire had turned back and was scrabbling back down the hill, shouting something, pointing the way they had come.

Dove paused and turned. Alain had finally jumped into the Land Rover and the vehicle plunged towards the exit. But it was too late. Emergency services were already blocking the way. The Land Rover spun around, Alain firing off shots, causing the lead vehicle to pause.

Alice drove the other way, up towards the blocked track to the road, and Dove gave a cry of frustration. Even though she knew the way was impassable, there was still a chance the four-wheel-drive vehicle could navigate the landslide.

She could see Claire had reached Klara, and between them they were helping Tessa, who was now screaming in pain. The Land Rover had just crested the hill and when another vehicle burst from the car park.

Dove blinked in the darkness, unable to believe it could be possible. Surely that was . . . Yes, it was her own car hurtling down the hill, dealing the Land Rover a glancing blow.

The Land Rover had no chance, spinning sideways and bucketing towards the cabin. It came on, gathering speed down the slope, and hit the cabin full on.

Dove clung to a tree trunk, her cold fingers clenched on the rough bark, nails digging into the roughness. The others were slipping in the snow, grasping at branches, pulling themselves upwards, dragging Tessa. Just as Dove tensed to move from her cover to help, an explosion threw the struggling figures to the ground.

CHAPTER FIFTY-NINE

The noise, the brightness of the flash, and power of the blast left them stunned.

Eventually, Dove lifted her head, blinking, trying to rid her head of the ringing in her ears. There was blood on the snow and she felt her face, her fingers coming away scarlet, her skin starting to sting. She spat ice and dirt, making her head spin. As the initial shock cleared she looked quickly for the other women.

Klara was sitting up, head in hands. A cut at the back of her head made a slash of scarlet against her tangled blonde hair.

Tessa was moaning but sitting up, her hand clutched to her side, and Dove reached out to her first. "Are you okay?"

"Fine. Just a little gunshot wound," she said softly, her face pale and dotted with tiny spots of blood. "What the hell happened? Where did that other car come from?" At least her eyes were focused now, and her words came painfully, but sensibly.

Shadowy figures were beginning to spread out across the area, securing the occupants who were crawling from the wreckage of the Land Rover, avoiding the blaze from the cabin. Floodlights suddenly illuminated the valley, joining the main headlights from the backup vehicles.

Among them, Dove could see the DI starting up the hill, but she was looking for someone else. Someone else she had left unconscious in the car, but who had most definitely not been in the car when it came hurtling down the hill.

The driver's seat had been empty. She could feel tears starting as she finally located the figure starting to trudge slowly, uncertainly down towards them. Steve.

She crawled round to Tessa and Claire, who were holding hands, heads on each other's shoulders.

"Are they dead?" Klara asked in a shaky voice.

The fire in the cabin was already burning itself out: all the evidence of the vile experiments, the deaths in the name of science would be gone, and the icy wind would scatter the ashes across the frozen lake.

Dove tried to stand up and found her legs were shaking. She sat down on the icy ground again and watched as more specialist emergency vehicles gathered.

Tessa sighed, and spoke softly. "They nearly got away with the research. That was the plan, to sell it. Jeremy had already made contacts through a friend of his, and Alain had a place in Spain ready for them . . ." She heaved another sigh and pressed her side tighter.

Klara had been watching them hazily, taking no part in the conversation, but now she spoke, hesitantly. "It wasn't quite finished, anyway. It looked like it was, but I left something out. I . . . I knew they were clever, but right at the end, Alice was getting distracted, flustered, and I knew even if I died I wouldn't be responsible for letting her sell our research. They never quite had the final formula anyway, they just thought they did."

"But you do have it?" Dove asked.

Klara met her eyes, and held out one bloodstained, muddy hand. The fingers were tightly clenched and she slowly opened them, so the others could see something resting on her palm. A memory stick. "Yes. I do. This is why I went back. We did it. Years too late, and I'm not even sure we should have completed it, but I hope Isla and even my grandmother would approve. It will be something that will help people. MEDA will see to that. And yes, it does reverse the effects of hypothermia. But the patient has to be in perfect health for it to work, so it's not magic." Tears began to fall. She looked out towards the icy lake. "She knew, my grandmother, I almost think she knew what was going to happen if we kept working at the research, like a premonition or something. You know what she always said to me? She said, 'Bad things happen in the snow.' And she was right."

"Oh, Klara," Tessa was in tears too, and she leaned over to grasp the other woman's hands, "I'm so sorry."

Klara nodded. "You wanted to do what was right, and so did I, and Claire too."

Claire, who had been silent up until that moment, burst into great noisy sobs, burying her head in her hands, rocking backwards and forwards.

Having been given the all-clear, paramedic vehicles were moving slowly but surely, tyres gripping the snow, drivers peering from windscreens, inching through the tough terrain.

Dove waved to indicate it was safe, and saw they were followed by the fire service, search and rescue teams and paramedics.

Specialist vehicles and equipment were brought to a halt next to the tree line, well away from the burning wreckage of the cabin. The incident commander, followed by the DI, Josh, Lindsey and Pete were all climbing the hill, shadows huge and ragged in the artificial light. Another medical unit had already picked up Steve and was inching back down towards Dove and her little group of bedraggled women.

The vehicle paused and Dove struggled towards it. "Steve!"

He was sitting up on a stretcher, blood on his face and hair sticky with the same. "I definitely have a gift for the dramatic. That was a James Bond trick," he said, smiling at her.

She couldn't speak for a moment, and then laughed through her tears, "You're a bloody idiot, you know, but a bloody genius too!"

She moved away and let the ambulance continue, scrubbing her burning face with frozen hands, only now realizing how much she was shaking.

"We thought we were going to find a lot more bodies," the DI said fiercely. "Bloody idiots going straight in instead of waiting for backup."

Dove cleared her throat. "To be fair, boss, we had no idea what we'd found, and once we realized, we tried to call it in, but the phones had no signal . . ."

He smiled at the four women, grey eyes lightening. "It was a tough call, and you might just have saved three lives."

"How did you know?"

"Jeremy booked tickets on the car ferry from Southampton for tonight," the DI explained. "When you two disappeared into the blizzard and didn't come back, we started after you, but of course the weather slowed us down. We discovered the landslide, but had some of the team coming in by the other track. Halfway up, we heard shots fired and still couldn't get an answer from your phones. Looks like Jeremy was killed outright in the crash, but Alice and Alain are both alive and being treated."

"It was those two against Klara, Tessa and Claire, Jeremy dithering between us all, not certain which way he was going to jump. Ever since JD's body was discovered they've been taking sides, but it was Alice who started the blackmailing. Once she had Alain on side, essential because he had the money for funding, she was finally able to snag Jeremy, who had made the contacts to sell the drug illegally. With that plan in place, she went after the others."

Relief made Dove's legs tremble again, and she accepted a wad of swabbing to press to her own cuts, feeling a foil blanket being draped around her shoulders and hugging it to her for warmth.

She never saw him arrive until a hand round her shoulders brought her round to face Quinn.

"What the hell are you doing, sitting out in the snow?" he asked.

She smiled a bit weakly, but reached for his hand. "What the hell are you doing, back at work?"

"I called in fit this morning. You are my fourth shout of the day." He looked well, strong and confident, with no trace of demons in his green eyes. "Now get inside one of the trucks and get checked over, before I have to tie you into that foil blanket and lift you onto a stretcher." Quinn pulled her to her feet, and hugged her tightly, before they walked slowly towards the ambulances, boots crunching in the snow.

CHAPTER SIXTY

I don't blame the men, they were under orders, and death was the alternative. The guards, too, I feel some element of pity for. They would tell the doctor how proud they were to serve, to be helping with medical research that could save the Luftwaffe pilots when their aeroplanes crashed into the North Sea. But occasionally I would see a flicker behind their eyes, a sudden clenching of fists at the treatment of some prisoner, and I knew.

After a few weeks, one of the guards began to call us 'Die Eistochter' — the Ice Daughters. The doctor never called us anything, but the other guards also began to use the name.

The doctor watched us the whole time we 'warmed' the prisoners, but we could have been cloth dolls for all he cared. He was meticulous in his records, excited only by the figures on the clipboards — the temperatures, the heart rates, the levels of consciousness.

I remember thinking one day, when all this is over, because I have to believe it will end, his clipboards will have recorded the evidence not of medical experiments, but of inhumane tortures.

And one day, I was right. We knew things were changing. There was an undercurrent of restless fear among the guards. Their superiors seemed to be burning things, paperwork. Evidence. The roar of bombers overhead, the distant gunshots.

Just as the chosen ones had been taken for medical experiments and trials, those who defied the rules were shot. No trial, no judge. They died quickly if they were lucky, and if not, their screams of agony echoed across the building, the courtyard, mingling with the smell of the acrid smoke from the crematorium chimney.

Out of the four Ice Daughters, only Marta, Katrine, and I remained. The experiments had long stopped, we were allowed more small freedoms, but equally, many were still dying.

The Death Marches to other camps removed huge numbers, with many sent away just before the Americans arrived. Two dates stick in my mind. The beginning and the end. I was brought to Dachau in 1941, on 13 December, in the snow. The camp was liberated on 29 April 1945, in the snow.

On that date I was marching, with seven thousand other emaciated prisoners, as they moved us from Dachau to Tegernsee.

There was a light covering of last frost on the night we slipped away, as many did, under cover of the forest and the spring under-growth. Gunshots brought down a few, and then a few more, but I kept moving, bare feet crunching on the ice, the darkness carrying me away.

Running feet and more gunshots, and we urged our weak bodies faster, gripping onto tree roots and branches, stumbling and panting. We came to a small river, half covered with ice, and forded it in haste. It was then that Katrine was brought down by a shot, and I felt her hand wrench from mine as she fell face down in the water, her blood blossoming around her head in the half darkness.

Marta was dragging me onwards. "We need to carry on! You can't help her now. Leave her!"

And so we did. The need for survival was great and our chance could not be lost by trying to help those already dead. But it hurts my heart to think how close she was to freedom, how when we finally strug-gled out of the forest in the daylight hours, instead of two faded ghosts who used to be girls, it should have been three . . .

Days later, we were picked up by Allied Forces, and I heard the Americans had liberated those who still survived.

I am old now, but I have passed my stories on to my children, to their children. Sometimes it is hard to speak of the atrocities, the suffering, difficult to comprehend death in that many numbers, but I feel strongly I must pass on my legacy. If they understand, they will never forget. If people never forget, if the memories are passed on, then I hope I am playing a small part in ensuring it will never happen again.

When I think of this legacy, my soul glows with happiness. My body is old and the shell is failing, but my soul, twinned with my body once more, is strong and bright.

I am the last of the Ice Daughters, and I have made my voice heard.

Helena

CHAPTER SIXTY-ONE

She was still standing on the beach when he arrived, jacket zipped up to her chin, long dark hair blowing out from under a woolly hat in the icy wind. She waved and smiled as he jogged round to meet her, boots crunching in the snow.

"I thought you might be down here," Quinn said, his voice gentle. "You okay?"

Dove tilted her head to meet his lips, slipping an arm through his. She sighed. "I still can't help thinking about those boys who lost their lives. How could you use someone like that? I've seen some shit, but using people like lab rats is a new one on me. And Jeremy is dead. He came back to save us, and he was the one who died in the crash."

He put a finger to her chin and she met his eyes. "You can't think like that, DC Milson. You said yourself it was a loyalty split, some on the side of good and others choosing the path that led to Jeremy's death. Those victims, I agree it was inhumane, but you couldn't have saved them either."

She dropped her eyes, scuffing pebbles with the toe of her boot, watching the froth from the waves almost reach them, before receding with a sigh, back towards the turbulent winter waters. "I suppose."

"Ambition and desperation. A powerful combination of emotions. After JD's body was found, suddenly Alice had her chance, and she seized the opportunity to blackmail her former friends," Quinn said.

"Maybe, but she already knew where the body was hidden." Dove started to walk, her arm still in his. The sun shone brightly from a brilliant blue sky, turning the beach and promenade into a winter wonderland. "It's funny, but like Klara, Alice never really wanted to let the research go. She had her own plans, which was why she continued testing, leading to the death after she graduated, and further deaths after that — but for her, it wasn't always about the drug. She had become addicted to her own power of life and death. Not to mention the money they would make from the illegal sale."

"Sick," Quinn commented, and she nodded.

"Alice took Alain away from Claire, but she still stayed on the right side. I mean, they were divorcing and she was going to be left worse off, but she still chose to try and protect Klara and Tessa, refusing to give in to the temptations Alice offered."

"And Alain was going to kill you all," he said with a shiver.

"He and Alice deny that, of course, but he has a history of hating police, a few convictions from way back, not to mention a whole heap of activity on the Dark Web relating to Nazi incitement and illegal weapons dealing. His job as an international investor was the perfect cover for sitting at his computer all night. But it seems he spent more time on the Dark Web in chatrooms than he did moving money around. Hard to say you didn't mean any harm when you were hunting four unarmed women through a forest."

They were passing the pier now, boots back on solid ground, arms linked, her head on his shoulder as they walked.

"And Alice just left her babies?" Quinn said. "Was she intending to come back for them?"

Dove shook her head. "She left a letter with a friend saying they belonged to her ex-boyfriend and he could look after them now. I can't get over how cold and calculating she was, like there was no emotion. Her own kids for god's sake! It was like her entire being was consumed by power and greed in the end."

"Someone who can fake their own death and then fake their abduction is clearly a force to be reckoned with," Quinn agreed.

"She organized her own abduction in a hurry, of course. Professor Renuard told Alain I was probing a bit close with the identity change. Tessa had written the initials on the newspaper article, so I would have got there in the end. They had finished with Elijah's body, and he was in the freezer, so they used him to fake Alice's abduction and put the pressure on Klara, who I understand was threatening to come to us," Dove said. "I wish she had, but for her it became all about saving Tessa and her research."

"And as she would be dead, they must have assumed nobody would ever find out the truth. At least they didn't get away. Jeremy would be pleased, I think, to know their research will be safe, and Klara and the others will take their share of the credit," Dove said.

"It is a scientific breakthrough, but it'll be a long time before it passes through the rigorous testing procedures, and out onto the open market," Quinn said. "Jeremy may have found a black-market buyer, but proper medical development in safe clinical conditions takes years."

They stood silently for a few moments, watching the restless waters. A seabird called, and across the water, a boat was silhouetted against a single beam of sunlight, filtering weakly through the winter clouds. It was beautiful and peaceful, and Dove felt herself relax.

"Come on, let's get out of here," Quinn said, taking her hand, entwining their gloved fingers, pulling her gently away from the beach.

She smiled in spite of herself. "You're right, we should get a move on, we've got the downstairs bathroom to tile still."

He groaned. "Actually, I was thinking more along the lines of planning the wedding."

This time, her smile was heartfelt and happy, doubts and fears pushed to the back of her mind. The weight of the case, the darkness of emotions that pulsed inside her head, started to fall away. "Well, Jess and Steve have already organized most of it. Steve is driving Zara crazy because he's still on sick leave, so he's been suggesting venues for us. Ren and Gaia have apparently picked out my dress, but my parents want us to have the whole wedding on the beach in Malibu and meditate on our future happiness afterwards. It's going to get complicated, love, but I *can* tell you one thing about our wedding . . ." She was laughing now.

He grinned down at her, his green eyes sparkling, dark hair decorated with stray brilliants from the dancing snowflakes which had started to fall again. "What's that, then?"

"It's going to be one hell of a party!"

EPILOGUE

He could see his fingers, but all feeling was gone. They clung to the edge of the tree root, those useless digits. The flesh was pale and pinched, the nail-beds blue.

If he could have forced a sound from his frozen lips, it might equally have been a cry for help, or a sob of regret. He would die with his head in the sunlight, his body wedged awkwardly on a pile of debris. She had died in the blackness of night, beneath the ice, trapped and terrified.

And it was his fault. He remembered Klara laughing, Krystyna shouting at Isla to get on the ice, not to be a wimp, shooting a sidelong look at Jeremy from under her lashes. Krystyna had made it clear at the party she wanted Jeremy for herself, had followed him as he went to the bathroom, waiting outside.

He hardly remembered the conversation, but he knew she had kissed him, knew he had, fuzzy with alcohol, kissed her back. And Isla, coming up the stairs to search for him, had seen his betrayal.

And now she was scared. Isla hadn't wanted to slip and slide across the lake to get a can of beer. He had sent it rolling far into the reeds, had watched her test the ice one cautious step at a time, gaining confidence until she was moving faster.

He'd watched her bend down, pale hair gleaming in the light of the moon and stars, miss her footing and fall. Laughter. Krystyna had been laughing still, but Klara had called out sharply to her sister, her voice anxious. He shouted too, even started out onto the ice himself . . .

The crack and splash came almost immediately, and Isla's frightened cry was cut off by a kind of gasp as she disappeared below the water.

He blinked, aware of the weight of his frosted lashes, the complete numbness of his body, torso still immersed in those same waters that had claimed her life. It felt like hours now since the others had left. Night had turned to day, and this magical snowbound wonderland had woken him from his slumbers. Surely, surely they would have sent help by now . . . A little voice at the back of his clumsy, cold brain, slurred from the inevitable hypothermia, told him they hadn't.

If only he could reach the bridge. So close, and yet unable to escape his icy prison . . . The wooden struts shone with coating of spiky frost, so white and pure. Instinctively, he had scrabbled frantically in his driftwood prison when he realized where he had fetched up, but it was too late.

This was his fault and his punishment. He was drifting again, treacherous waves of fatigue flowing over him, when he heard her voice. It was low and clear, calling his name.

Did he want to live? Through gentle waves engulfing his mind, his body, he thought perhaps it would be better to die now than live with what had happened.

He knew he could have saved a life that night . . .

THE END

ALSO BY D. E. WHITE

DETECTIVE DOVE MILSON MYSTERIES
Book 1: GLASS DOLLS
Book 2: THE ICE DAUGHTERS

RUBY BAKER MYSTERIES
written as Daisy White
Book 1: BEFORE I LEFT
Book 2: BEFORE I FOUND YOU
Book 3: BEFORE I TRUST YOU

Please join our mailing list for free Kindle crime thriller, detective, mystery and romance books, and new releases!

www.joffebooks.com

FREE KINDLE BOOKS

Milton Keynes UK
Ingram Content Group UK Ltd.
UKHW010644041223
433752UK00005B/304